THE CROSSING

Dai Smith was born in the Rhondda in 1945. His writing has encompassed history, biography, essays and criticism. He was Series Editor of the Library of Wales and Chair of the Arts Council Wales from 2006 to 2016, in which year he was made a CBE for services to arts and culture in Wales. He currently edits the Modern Wales Series. With *The Crossing*, Dai Smith has built upon and completed his trilogy of fictional work, *Dream On*, *What I Know I Cannot Say* and *All that Lies Beneath*.

THE CROSSING

Dai Smith

Parthian, Cardigan SA43 1ED www.parthianbooks.com
First published in 2020
© Dai Smith 2020
ISBN 978-1-912681-81-5
Cover design by Marc Jennings
Typeset by Elaine Sharples
Printed and bound by 4edge Limited, UK
Published with the financial support of the Welsh Books Council British
Library Cataloguing in Publication Data
A cataloguing record for this book is available from the British Library.

Before Time

An inquest was held on Monday 6 instant, at the Miners' Arms, before the Deputy Coroner, Thomas Williams, on the body of Thomas Roberts, aged eleven years. Deceased was a doorboy. On Thursday 2 instant, between two and three in the afternoon, while he was at work a journey of trams loaded with coal passed over his legs. He was taken home and attended by doctors but died on Saturday. The verdict was accidental death.

Cardiff and Merthyr Guardian, Friday, 10 July 1863

Richard Thomas, a young fellow twelve years of age was working in a stall with his father on Tuesday when a mass of coal fell on him from the roof and crushed him so seriously that he died an hour afterwards.

Cardiff and Merthyr Guardian, Friday, 14 October, 1864

Fatal accident to a doorboy at Ysguborwen pit. On Tuesday last Ifor Evans of Robertstown was killed when a stone fell from the roof and he was killed instantly. The poor little fellow was only twelve years of age.

Cardiff and Merthyr Guardian, Saturday, 16 June, 1866

Miscellanea. Taliesin Arthur Lloyd Papers. Box16.
National Library of Wales, Aberystwyth.

The lower gorse-covered and stone-strewn flanks of the mountain, bilious yellow in summer and in winter a grey sage hue, almost abutted up against the back of the House where it squatted, square and unseemly, all alone in its hollow, an imitation of a Georgian mansion decked out in Victorian concrete with a whitewashed stucco finish. From its frontage a drive, in truth more a broad cinder path, bisected a tussocky lawn and ran down the slope towards the river and the valley's bottom level. Above the House the mountainside rose steeply to an abrupt peak, a plateau to be crossed on foot along worn narrow tracks and precipitously down its nether side to the adjacent valley, which was then, in the 1860s first heard before it was glimpsed, and, by night as well as day, by the distant clamour and incessant noise of its spawning ironworks and gargantuan foundries, before it was smelled through a rising noxious pall of smoke, a perpetual cloud of sulphur, fire, and falling clinkers drifting over a careless scatter of dwelling houses, shacks, mansions, public houses and shops, large and small, selling goods and all the basic provisions for life. And all of this human settlement, the most populous and the most pungent town ever seen in Wales, dribbled out and along the blackened banks of its river or was etched into terraced rows on the hills, a half-sketched portent of all that was to come.

As a grocer in that spew of a town his father had made enough profit to speculate, with others, in opening up horizontal drift mines for easy coal seams to meet the needs of the ironmasters. If the latter were well-endowed in capital and incomers, these new men were neither. They stretched their pooled resources to limits quickly reached. So, when he, the father, had the House in Ysguborwen built in the further valley he teetered between greater profits yet and looming bankruptcy. The House was not there, in

5

the Aberdare valley, to serve as any kind of rural retreat from the stench and miasmic diseases which hung over every single Merthyr life, whether fabulously rich or sickeningly poor, as a bringer of illness and frequent death. The House was the marker put down by a man intent on success. It was the risky gamble a funded and backed man might take as an earnest of his willingness to engage in more and more speculative ventures. To sink deeper, more costly mine shafts in search of deeper and more lucrative coal seams. If he failed the House would go, and all that went with it.

When the third of the five children who survived within his second marriage was born in 1856, the father, Samuel Thomas, could not be sure his house had any foundations stronger than his own willpower. His recent colliery dealings were unproven. His string of bank-loaned credit was played out. The child, a boy, was born on a March night amidst the shake of high winds shrieking amongst the trees and torrential rain pelting the sullen house, and turning paths into treacherous streams of mud and rocks. Straightaway, after the birth, he had muttered that the boy would likely have no future, that the workhouse might claim them all. And he had left the House, baby, wife and maidservant and gone out into the overwhelming blackness of the storm, the worst anyone could remember, to return to the huddle of men just half a mile away, who had gathered around their braziers for warmth at the site of his latest attempt to sink a wood-lined shaft deeper and deeper to strike into the famed four-foot seam. If they could keep the inrushing water out of the shaft as they drove through layers of mudstone and shale to reach the seam and then secure the shaft to run roadways from it to begin to work the coal, then for the men there would be work to undertake for a foreseeable future and for him, and his partners, financial security from which to move forward. Time was theirs to order if nothing conspired to make them waste it in delays and doubts. So, even as the slanting rain sheeted down from the mountain and made their heavy woollen clothes sodden, he cursed them for stopping in his enforced absence and sent them back to the bucket, clanging from side to side of the shaft. It held steady as four men at a time clambered into it, and the hand-pulled winch was manned to send it down into the shaft even as the water slapped and rose from below and fell without cease from above.

* * * * *

On summer days, in the first ten years of his life at home, his butties would walk from their cottages below the House to come up the short drive to the front door. They would come in small groups, shy at first until made bolder by the constant welcome, to call at the House for him. They did not knock on the door, only stare at the ornate lion's-head iron knocker and look, furtively, into the House's interior through the high multi-paned oblong windows, three on each side of the heavy black-painted door. They waited for their arrival to be noticed inside the house. They glimpsed oak tables and chairs and dressers with gaudy Welsh china and on the walls dark oil paintings of pewter streams and muddy meadows and brown cows, all with gilt frames and hung from rails by brass hooks and chains. The callers were boys about his own age, all coming up from the terraced rows of stone houses in which they lived with mothers and sisters and babies and the fathers who worked for his father as sinkers and hauliers and colliers.

They did not shout out for him directly but, more politely as they thought, when spotted and acknowledged by the opening of the front door they addressed the women of the House, whether maid or cook or mother. He would hear the query and its reply from his first-floor front bedroom where he kept his treasures guarded on shelves, his blown birds' eggs, some fossils from underground brought by his father, sheets of paper holding dried out flowers or grasses, the skeletons of small animals. He would scurry across the passageway and down the stairs to where the door was held ajar by the maid and, this remembered time, there would be his mother, Rebecca, smiling widely, vital and amused, her hands mussing at her uncoiled black hair, a woman vibrantly attractive in her mid-forties, attentive to her inquisitors.

"Missis. Gall Dai ddod mês 'da ni heddi chi'n meddwl, Missis?"

And in a warming sunshine which filtered through the dank air of the hollow and lit up the front wall of that gloomy notion of a gentleman's residence, she would ask her own questions back, mockingly but playfully, in the Welsh they shared as a first tongue.

"Pwy y' chi i gyd 'te, mechgyn i? Ydw i'n nabod eich tylw 'th chi? Ble chi am fynd trwy'r dydd gyda Dai ni?"

They would then, as of practised rote, reel out in turn and one by one, their names.

"Twm Roberts. Harri Roberts. Dic Thomas. Ifor Cardi. Ifor Evans, Sièncyn Williams."

Until she laughed and raised a hand to acknowledge them whilst ushering her son into their company as they all chorused their direction.

"I'r mynydd rhwng Aberdêr a Merthyr."

It was still early in the morning and she knew they would not be back before dusk, so each would have some bread and hard cheese wrapped in a cloth and would carry a tin jack of water to be refilled from a stream. She saw to it that her son would carry the same in the small wickerwork basket hung over one shoulder by a leather strap, but with some apples and freshly baked Welsh cakes to share with them, all to be eaten before he could fill his basket with the treasures he would bring home. She lined them up in front of her with her Dai amongst them, and she waved them on, with the readily understood admonition that he was not Dai to everyone they might meet.

"Cofiwch nawr, mae Mister Thomas yn dweud taw David yw ei enw os gwrddwch chi â'r gŵr ar y ffordd. Dyna fe 'te, boys. Byddwch nol cyn iddi nosi, cofiwch. Cer 'te Dai. Off a chi."

* * * * *

Years before he was born, the mountainside had already been pocked and riddled with drift headings and small mines hacked into and beneath the slopes, and since then pits were constantly being sunk, worked or abandoned, leaving behind narrow, tunnelled entrances of stone and the rusting detritus of failure, or the wooden headgear and iron rails of hope. The boys walked up the mountain past all such marks of endeavour. Where once there had been clusters of deciduous trees, copses of oak and stands of rowan, there were now, as they trudged steadily up and on, mere patches of tree stumps and permanently blackened grasses left from the cutting and hauling and burning which the pits had required. The boys kept to the single file paths, until they were high enough to step to one side of the tracks through the coarse upland summer meadows of stippled grass stalks, finger thick amongst grassy tumps of brown earth. They rested underneath the overhang of a cliff, the limestone scree at its base scoured by the swift pulse of a glassy stream which ran into a broad basin of rock to become a deep, ice-cold pond. They skimmed shards of flat stone across its glaucous green surface. Even in summer the shadow cast by the overhang of rock made for a piebald shade which dappled broken light onto them through the branches of the few scrawny trees which bent sideways out of the loose scree to which their roots clung like claws. It was known that some came up to the pond to drown unwanted dogs and cats, or worse some said. Pieces of torn cloth had been found in the thorny undergrowth beyond the islands of glossy bulrushes at the pond's extremity. So, they never swam in its waters and they only drank, lying face down in its cleft, from where the stream fell directly down from the cliff.

The boys knew the hand-holds and toe-holds they had to use to scale up over the scree and onto the protruding rock slabs higher up on this mountain end-wall. They knew, too, to look where they might find what they all called "Pethau Dai," his treasures. At home, in the House, he had wood-framed glass cases to protect the fragility of the birds' egg shells and cards to fix with the veined tracery of splayed butterfly wings. On the mountain, some bushes that were crowns of purple spiky flowers hosted the tremble of tortoiseshells and peacocks, the displayed quivering of red admirals and painted ladies. He gave his butties thin glass bottles with wide mouths to capture the moths and butterflies. They stoppered the bottles with cork bungs and he placed them in a sack from his basket, along with cuttings of golden saxifrage, red campion and wild columbine and the friable fretwork of tiny, ancient mountainside ferns.

When they had rested and eaten, they would divide into teams of two and separate to hunt out the nests of goldcrests and blackbirds, or of the common willow warblers and darting chiff chaffs, and, with a rarer excitement, of fierce kestrels from the higher niches of the cliff faces below the plateau. Later, in the House, he would carefully pierce and blow out the stolen eggs to add to his collection of the speckled and blue and mottled green and yellows, to whose cases he would affix inked notes of species, time and place. Sometimes on the lawn at Ysgurborwen House he would lay out his cases for the boys to see, the boys who had found them for him, the boys who never entered the House. They looked at his treasures and at the cards on which he wrote in a neat hand with black ink the Latin terms, book-learned, of the things and creatures from the hills which the boys knew and called by different names. They would laugh and sip the lemonade the maid brought out to drink on these hot days, and say "Da iawn, Dai bach. Da iawn, butty."

Through all these long summers of their quickening lives, the boys foraged and scavenged, together, collecting for him. It was lived as if it were a childhood in common. In the higher stretches of the river they fished with bamboo poles and string and attached offal, with scant success, and they swam naked in the swirling eddies of the river and the deeper, pooled water at the bends where the banks were set above the flow. He was not, through all these days of growing together, apart from them, though all understood the difference, the distance. For them there was a rudimentary, fractured schooling but such as it was it was only, as they knew, the prelude for work to come. One by one, in turn, as they grew old enough, with a year here or there to separate out friends or brothers, they would, as if by magic, disappear from the life they had led. They might have as good as fallen, one by one, into the deceptive mountainside crevices, slits covered in bracken through which you could fall to the earth's centre to vanish forever as did boys and girls, despite all family love and warnings, from time to time. Except that these vanished boys re-emerged, by day or by night, aged between ten and twelve, blackened and altered by entering the pits of his father into which they took dim, oil-lit lamps, snap boxes of bread and cheese and tin jacks of water to work in the dark alongside their own fathers.

In the winter, at his bedroom window before dawn, the room crammed with the treasures of summers gone, he would rub a circle into the ice fronded pane to look down the incline of lawn and road towards the black terraced rows of houses to see the small distance-shrunk parade of figures, men and boys, with their hand-held lights before them, clump across the frozen grass of white fields and along the cinder path to the colliery shaft where they would descend. And disappear from his sight.

11

Twm and Harri and Dic and Ifor and Siencyn, and all the others as they grew to be old enough, not yet large, not yet men at all, but workers already, to be lost to him, some even before he himself became ten years old in 1866, and left in the next year to be schooled properly.

When he came back, out of term times, he never looked for them again, not even those who survived their daily disappearance. He knew not all did. His mother would inform him. Never his father. He walked the mountains still, but alone now. In later life he would meet them, his former companions, or their exchangeable equivalents, in the very depths of his own burgeoning collieries, in this valley or the next one over to be opened up for its minerals, and would always greet them with an easy familiarity, born of knowledge and acquaintance, and as if they knew each other yet, because of what they had once been, together. For all that, and he had soon known this, too, such links were quick to break, trifling sentiments, when more profound issues, his own and abstract wider interests, intervened to assert their necessary priority. Not that he was alone in this understanding. They knew it, too, as Dai ceased to be and he became David until he died.

It would be the only story he would wish told of himself. It was not, for all that, the only story. Nor the only one to tell. Nor the only way to tell it at all.

Biography fragment c.1958: Early Days of DA Thomas.

Taliesin Arthur Lloyd Papers. Box 3.

National Library of Wales Aberystwyth.

1987:TIME OUT

I was the Secretary. So, invariably, people believed what I said had occurred, and in the manner in which I made a record of it. That is a straightforward statement, one made in my best secretarial style. Whether it is a statement about the fashion employed in shaping public memory, rather than a statement of unvarnished fact, if there is ever such a thing as you might wish to say, is something I prefer, even now and almost at the very end of life, to avoid. Or, at least, to obscure. And that is because, truly, I have no reassuring answer to give in final settlement of such a question. No matter. It is, in another sense, all the same. To you as well as to me. At least, so far as outcome is concerned. Yet not as to its shaping. The evidence for that which is past, and to be quizzed for the meaning it might tell as history, largely came from such as me, and was filtered through that series of witnessing which, such as I, necessarily perfected, in order for it to seem as if complete, for such as you who came after the event. I was a Secretary. So, I made it up.

Well, not literally so, of course. I did not, how could I, construct the wider agenda of which I was a part. But my role was not insignificant either. Tidying up, guiding, hinting, hiding, giving form and direction to what might otherwise remain in an inchoate state. I formulated the minutes which constitute the public record. I reported it all, or most of it. By which I mean that, in my mind, prior to any sift or sequencing into narrative, I held it all. Thereafter, not everything needs to be verbatim, does it? Or elsewhere on this spinning earth, where would we be? Not everything needs to be out-in-the-open to be known but all requires moulding, assembling out of mess and muddle, if people are to see things one way or the other, and preferably not to understand them another way altogether. That modelling from raw data is what a Secretary does. It became my purpose in life. To be a dissembler in order to be of use to those who wrestled with, or merely submitted to, the place and time we inhabited for our own time. Or so I once told myself. Other times, this one for example, the one I now simply acquiesce in, might tell it differently even in retrospect.

But I cannot do so. I remain the Secretary of that former time and I do not see the account, the record, I once made as any species of lie. It was the way the truth we required needed to be made available as our truth. I was, in this sense, faithful to the story in which I found myself. I did not make up the stories of the lives, public and private, which were being framed. I was not there to invent stories. Put another way, I would not tell of things I did not see, or hear, or had confirmed by a trusted third party. I was thus bland and reliable as a source for enquiry, and I cannot change that now by any pretence of liveliness, of gossip and hearsay. My mode of telling is too ingrained in my sensibility to be either polished for effect or roughed up to seem authentic. As Secretary I was attuned to what was documented and is evidenced, not to speculation or fantasy. I transcribed, and so am myself a transcription.

This has its own sting to be sure. It inevitably makes anything which I may choose to say at this end-point of life, choose to say directly that is, lesser than whatever it once was, although the traces of that are already reduced by the formal telling of it. And there again, any matter-of-fact rigmarole which escaped, or was excused, any casual entrapment of the moment by a contemporary scribe, albeit floating free in its shapeless happenstance in the historical ether of recollection, can only possess the properties of being as a dream of what once might have passed for reality. I baulk at this even as I perforce acknowledge it, for I am no dreamer and, resolutely, long ago decided against such seduction. Yet I was no doer of deeds either. I am, or was the by-stander, the observer, the note-keeper, the diarist, the hoarder, the archivist, the reader, the remembrancer. Never the historian. I was only secretarial to that time, in those years now gone, for those people since disappeared from it all, as I will soon be myself.

I spent my own lifetime paring back, both professionally and so far as I personally was concerned. Cutting back whatever threatened to grow too vigorously, pruning whatever might be overly-luxuriant if allowed to flourish, hedging in any excess. I made it my business to make judicious choices. I sought elegant solutions for all that thrashing about and rambling in word and deed. Sometimes, I now note, from my reading of others, that what I manufactured as verity and left to become forensically verifiable, has become History itself, or apparently so. What I did, in memoranda and notes of advice and in official reports and, yes, by redacted minute-taking, was to remove any shadows which were cast too far and too long, their doubt darkening certainties, or else I blocked out any light which focussed too intensely on aspects better left unseen lest they dazzle and mis-lead.

I had, when young, stumbled, purblind, down that overly illuminated path. I shunned that way in my maturity. I set myself, too, against the deceiving pulse of memory, though it could, at times, beat its way back, involuntary but unstoppable. I silenced it as best I could, as I believe we all must do, if we are to live as if content with our lot. I have lived long enough, far too long, to be able to read, with a certain glum satisfaction, the academics who have been led by my hand to concur with my implicit caveats against the heroic, to embrace my sobriety against the rush of idealism, to indicate, by their revisionism against the sentimentally romantic, my fearfulness of what worse might befall if we do not, did not, settle for what is, assuredly, the lesser but desirable fate of security and compromise when set against risk and aspiration, social and individual. Nemesis stalking Hubris. The world into which I was born, where I was raised to manhood and then

17

withered in through the decades. The twentieth century oscillated absurdly, like no other time has ever done on this earth. And of it and in it, I turned out, against all early hopes and ambitions, to be merely its Secretary.

I accept, of course, the severe limitations which followed making lucid, as accounts, what was, in its ungraspable fullness and fluidity something strictly unaccountable. I mean, that yes, if full-on sensibility was the required thing, then such limited accounting came a poor second. That is if the singer and not the song was the thing. Poetry not paraphrase. Prose not telegraphese. And so on. Poor me, then. But, amidst the blur of life, I still see no reason to apologise for preventing overspills of emotion and expectation. Individuals, as I was to know, cannot live under such pressures. The society we had created, needed, too, a different kind of fostering to bind itself together. Makeshift defences in social care, education, welfare, health were inadequate but essential bulwarks. Pragmatism and limited purposes for the public good and the common weal. It was, then, for that end, the compiling of those statistical measures, that scaffolding of memos and minutes, of official surveys and governmental reports. If I look at these things anew, I see tombstones whose inscriptions were meant to be activators but are now deciphered, long after their time, as if they were proper specimens of life itself. Such is the intellectual taxidermy we mistake for knowing. I do not say it is not knowledge since that category can appear when detail upon detail is crafted into a mosaic, a pattern of insights unattainable at the moment of their happening, one by one. History of a common sort. The problem remains. What is inner and undeniable is vanished in the instant of its becoming, disappeared only to wait and linger elsewhere in memory that scorns recorded history as a river will, until its end, deny the sea which awaits. And so I must choose which truth to tell. I have a final bridge to cross and time yet to find the way. I sit at my desk as I am long accustomed to do, and I pick up my fountain pen in readiness. Later I will type up the notes on the sturdy manual machine which has served me well for years and will do for a while yet. Customary and secretarial. What will follow, however, is not so. For now I wish my collage of memory and data to be personal and bespoke, and to be heard and understood as such in the future I will not have for my own. My unsecretarial reverie is, in my mind and intent, as a prologue to my conjoined Testament and Testimony. I have readied myself. It will take some time, and like time itself will not run along those straight lines with whose perception we conspire to deceive ourselves of destination as we career through the passing years.

* * * * *

I have unpacked my books and placed them in order, authors alphabetically and otherwise thematically, on the wooden shelves I have had made and painted white from floor to ceiling on three sides. Just as well that the room has height enough, with a long, south-facing and multi-paned casement window to let the light in from the garden. When, that is, we have light here amongst the higher hills. Today it is raining, as it has done for a week, that naggingly persistent rain peculiar to these rifted valleys, a rain which seems to drift insidiously down without let from the mountains above, to darken stone and slate to a perpetual darkness with its incessant wetting of them, and to whisper against the clouded glass. It settles me for all that. I can stay, without excuse, indoors and busy myself. I have made the right move at the right time. Certainly it will be my last, and I am content with it.

I have almost a suite of rooms if the smaller attached dressing-room I have had converted into a study-cum-storeroom for my papers can be thought of as such, along with the bedroom and a self-contained, if tiny, bathroom and lavatory they have carved out of the redundant corridor space of the old house. And, of course, my sitting room, formerly his capacious and fire-grated bedroom, where my own few bits of furniture and dusty awards remind me of my solitary days. Anyway, I am content with the few, very few, things I value and have kept around me.

The rooms are straight off the stairs on the first floor of the house. I was lucky to spot its imminent conversion into a Nursing Home, and luckier still to persuade them, with ample cash up-front, to install me as their long term and monthly debited first guest. As a result, I will be allowed to die here. That has been formally agreed as well. When the time comes I will have around the clock nursing care. I have told them I will not socialize with any others who may arrive to stay, and will take all my meals in my room. They think, no doubt, that this is the eccentricity of a well-off old man. That, I grant, would be right on most counts, for I am almost ninety years of age – a strange expression I have always thought – and within a decade, if I last, will be a hundred before this wretched century gets there itself. And, yes, the careful custodianship of a bachelor's life has left me comfortable enough to afford it all, and have sufficient in reserve to do what else I have decided to do.

Which is, first, to collate and organize my records, my notes, my various papers, public and personal, in short my life's detritus of evidence and ephemera, for its ordered dispatch, in due course, to the National Library in Aberystwyth. The boxes will be deposited in my name, for the purpose of utility rather than any vanity, under the rubric of the Taliesin Arthur Lloyd Papers, and will after my days be a partial window onto the world I have seen actually come and actually go. Not many can testify to that, as a witness to the world of coal, its prosperous getting and sending out, its miserable destructiveness and its painful legacies, and all the while the making of a new destiny, sometimes a brilliant and hopeful one, mostly not, for Wales itself in all its being and ways. Now we light the remaining fires with imported, inferior stuff, in this place which once, literally, spun the whole globe with its energy. I can look out of my casement window, through the falling rain, and see across the lower valley to the town of Aberdare and its branching colliery townships and know there is nothing left, other than a dwindling people, of all that once gave force and dynamism to this place. No pits or winding gear or iron rails for drams except what a forlorn heritage industry preserves in hidden corners. No colliery left to give work and purpose other than, to the near north where the waun stretches beyond the valley, the brave co-operative endeavor to salvage something from the wreckage of the defeat of the strike of 1985. One last, ragged hurrah. It will not last.

I look out of the window, the very one I'm sure, through which he gazed at the bustling enterprises of his childhood days, at the hopeful coal sinkings of his father and the comings and goings of men of Capital and men of Labour, and the domestic and civic lives which thereby accrued, and I contemplate again all I now know about him and his ways. And it tells me nothing of his true worth, of how to measure him against what might instead have been achieved. And this is why I have come to live in his once house, his gutted and transformed boyhood home, in Ysguborwen, and why I sit stubbornly at my desk, knowing I will not succeed, trying to trace, or at least reveal, the threaded pattern of the existence he interwove from himself for all the other lives of his own time, and for those that will be lived after all our times have been told.

I have tried before, and I have failed before. I am not alone in this. How do you enter that inner sanctum of his existence to penetrate to the meaning, for him and for the others affected, of such unimaginable power as he once wielded? The images conjured up by such power confound more than they enlighten. There is the Poet's capture of him as a modern-day conquistador astride a Bay

21

gelding, set above his toiling peons as the horse and rider clop imperiously up the unpaved roadway of a nigh perpendicular cwm from the main Rhondda valley bottom to his nest of deep mined pits at the very top end of Clydach Vale. He smashed these concerns into others to make himself a Celtic Croesus. He revelled in the will power and the business acumen of his statistically driven brain which made him more Edwardian Tycoon than Victorian Coalowner. He stood apart. He stood alone. One clue to his singularity was his indifference to all that was communal, and so, to his eye, sentimental. He might stroll with his mine managers through the virtual Company Town he had created in Tonypandy where allegiance was due to him from shopkeepers and colliers alike, and would only take notice of the built paraphernalia all around him—the cavernous emporia, the theatres and music halls, the swaggering confidence of overbearing chapels, the streets teeming from dawn to dusk, the drinkers and shoppers and gawkers—as, all of it, a stage set for himself, a three dimensional tribute to his ability alone to have brought it into being. And nothing and no one beyond all that material creation. After all, there had been nothing of significance in that place, before he had put his hand to it. It is why, I believe, the social upheaval which heralded the year long strike in 1910 of his twelve thousand strong work force did not deeply trouble him. It was a shudder not an earthquake. An inchoate lashing-out not an organized revolt. Growing pains for the world he had conceived and birthed. And, in fact, during the carnivalesque rioting which temporarily turned that world over, he was abroad, sunning himself and nurturing his murmurous heart condition in the warmth of the south of France, far away from the cold and drenching November rains of the coalfield, and keeping astutely silent. In public at least. There can be no real doubt that this former Liberal MP and Party Grandee had not spoken to the Liberal Home Secretary by telephonic communication and had not urged a compliant Churchill to send on to the conflicted district both Metropolitan Police and Troops, who did indeed arrive and stay and effectively police the dispute to its eventual defeat.

It would later be his contention that the native Welsh, God-fearing and respectful colliers with whom he had grown up, had been led astray by incomers, variously labelled as English or uncouth or anarchistic, and all intent on a know nothing ruination. Nonsense, of course, although cited by his heir and daughter in the decades to come as a cause of ruination which, mercifully she said, he did not live to experience after the Great War ended. Yet, if he had lived on it would only have been to abandon those ruins for ventures elsewhere. No one who crossed the Atlantic together with him, as I youthfully did, can gainsay that there was a greater than geographical journey on which his mind was already set. There, that is, in retrospect and simply told, the essence of the story. And so not so at all.

I am, of course, inevitably looking from the wrong end of the historical telescope, at the tail end of a forlorn century, at the fag-end of a life when where else can you look back except back? Is this what is entailed by History? For others, perhaps. For those who live directly through it, for sure. For those who have come after and need to make some deeper sense of it, by all means. Not for me, though. Not any solace from such History for me. I was never an actor in it nor a philosopher about it. I was one who voluntarily came to stand by as, involuntarily, it passed me by, leaving me to merely record its passage. The discretion of a secretary.

Time to be unbuttoned. This will be my legacy. I, who have created no life I can call mine own, yet yearn for life as was and might have been, and might be yet, to continue here, for it and for us to go on, even amongst the ruins, to stay, not to leave, maybe to return. After my time.

2007: TIME WARP

It did not feel like going home. Not even partly so. But it did feel like going back. It was not a comfortable feeling. I drove west into a late afternoon sun that slipped further down the horizon as I let the boxy diesel hatchback I'd hired at the airport scuttle and drone its way down the M4. I fought the mild jet lag of a transatlantic crossing more than I did the lane-switching traffic. Slow lane was fine by me. I needed some contemplation time before the city's lights guided me straight to my hotel bed, and sleep.

You know how it is sometimes, when, because you must, you play a part, but for real I mean, because you don't have any original lines to say or fresh ways to enact them. Too many life scenarios already seen and done, whether originally for real, or not. Journeys. Quests. Homecomings that were nothing of the kind. Umbilical cords that were never quite cut, and so could still strangle. And it's as if you always have the clothes for the part, ready to put on. Where do they come from? You have the words queuing up to be said. How could that be? You even have the end in sight, but it's one stumble at a time to get to it. And what is this ending anyway? Going back was like letting time that was past suck me back in, and I was ready for it. I had the stuff, all of it, that I'd need for the trip. None of it meant that I wanted to make it. After my old man died I had just had everything sold, or destroyed. I wanted no traces of that home left, or of what he had come to mean by that word. Going home was going to a place which was no longer there for me. It was with me all the time, though. Intimacy. That was unavoidable. Knowledge. Now that was a category I truly despised. Something known already. So generally imitative of something else. My old man had never pretended to have knowledge. What he did have was wisdom, and his brand of wisdom was as cold and dark as a gun barrel and as icy and unforgiving as the air through which I had been funnelled home.

It wasn't any kind of wisdom, though, that had brought me home. Worse, it was a lack of knowledge. Of certain knowledge that is, and certain came with two meanings, both of which I had to nail. For what was uncertain I could blame the postcard Gwilym had sent via my publisher around five years before, and for what currently passed muster as certain there was Bran's written reply to my subsequent enquiry. It was "No", as I remembered. I had left no daughter behind, and so I had no daughter now. Her daughter, Haf she called her, was not mine Yet that voice on my phone, in the early hours of the morning in my New York apartment a few days ago, had coupled her own name with mine and mine, it had said, was Daddy. So, yes, I knew what had taken me home, and, wise or foolish, what I needed to do. To find her. To help her as she had asked. But first I'd need to see her mother again. There were things, it seemed, to find out. There were things, unbidden but undeniable, to remember. So, I remembered them. Even if all I had wanted to do for a very long time was to forget.

I slept heavily and woke late. I cleaned myself up, and avoided the hotel breakfast. I'd kept the car overnight. I needed it for a quick burst of re-acquaintance, or rather a fresh acquaintance with the new city and all its novel markers. A proper capital city, I'd been told, at last.

I drove the hired car directly north out of the city centre. It was mid-morning and traffic was stop-start rather than snarling. The day was overcast for late March, but with an opaque white light behind the low cloud. Dishwater grey through the glare. It suited my mood, and my meander past familiar sights which some twenty years plus had done little to change. Not in this part of town anyway. The Edwardian wedding cake civic centre still swelled with early twentieth-century pride. But in the interest of a future promise to be cashed in one day. Natch. And then almost straightaway, because this was a town that had been laid out cheek-to-cheek in its Victorian days of origin, the strings of red-bricked terraces like entrails pulled out and de-kinked. Student lets now, judging from the bicycles piled up in their tiny low-walled fronts and the oblivious helmetless riders weaving in and out of the stuttering line of cars. The dockers, railwaymen and steelworkers, who had once marked these streets with a confident workaday presence and crowded the brassy mahogany pubs, were long gone. I remembered them as men who, amongst themselves, acted as hard men even when they were not, all letting go with an accent, peculiarly their own, which could slice through the thick tobacco blue smoke of saloon bars like wire through cheese. Something else gone from that rich pungency of the old centre was the sweet fug of mashed hops brewed up for the city's own beer, cloying the senses and swaddling early morning streets. Liveners being readied for the thick heads of the previous night and the deep thirsts of overnight workers. Once, and no longer.

It had been too early for a pint when I picked up the car from the hotel's garage. I began to think I'd need a livener myself, and sooner rather than later. Maybe I'd need to find the brewery before I could locate that cream and golden beer which my mouth could still taste. Maybe after two decades away there was no brewery, and none of that beer left as it was.

The thought curdled in the churn of my stomach as I left the centre behind and steered past batteries of traffic lights on every intersection of the four-lane two-way avenue that tramlined me out of the plain. The city had grown outwards, in spreading concentric rings, from its docks and commercial heyday to the commuter and professional housing of the suburbs through which I was now crawling. Tree-lined avenues of brick-and-stucco semis built for the artisan and the salaried, even in the 1930s, a decade which had pissed over most people here with the freewheeling grace of a drunk in a urinal. The interwar houses had weathered better, despite the ceaseless rumble of cars and trucks, than their 1960s counterparts: flat-roofed boxes for domestic living, schools and hospitals. The one style fits-all school of architecture from a decade that had misplaced its brain.

I'd bought a new map. I'd keep for later the grim dual carriageway that I knew from almost twenty years ago as a corridor through the hills and into the valleys I'd once escaped. It looked on the new map as if there were livelier arteries shooting off a pulsing interchange. On the actual ground it was more engineering circuitry than roundabout. I circled it twice before I picked the right lane, and took the slip road signposted for the west and the motorway. I had an appointment at noon back in the city. I took the scenic route. First exit off and flat out down the link road towards the bay.

I was on a highway belt that cinched in the older and flabbier bits as it bypassed them. An ersatz new world to anyone who had seen the real deal of any small American city. Deep cuts isolated the tough council-house estates where I had once roamed, camera at the ready. There were glimpses of skeletal iron frames cranked up out of building-site mud and the apple-green and white cladding of the retail sheds that were the winking outliers of a neon-lit twenty-four-hour world. They didn't convince; more end of the line no choice than any kind of centre.

I slowed down as the road curved upwards on a stilted flyover that was just high enough to offer flashes of the former industrial core of the city to the south. It was gutted, rusty and leaking. Its roadside heralds were apartment blocks whose roofs curved and dipped like skateboard runs. The surfaces were weather-boarded in strips which had already turned from honey to flaked grey in the salt winds blowing in over the mud flats from the sea. Miniscule iron-railed balconies decorated their chunky bulk like bracelets on a bruiser. This was the sense of the place I had guessed from hearsay and the occasional letter but I had not been able to feel for myself: its broken rhythm, its re-drawn boundaries, its pretence of itself. I decided to save the full-blown, street-level version of the bay for when I was more attuned to the whole transformation. Perhaps the woeful tackiness had been avoided there. Perhaps. There would be hope in pretending so. Perhaps not. I followed the signs for the centre.

At least the jail was still stone-stolid and unrelenting in its mid-town location. It greeted me as I re-discovered the city streets and ended the joyride. I returned the car to the parking lot of the hire company and walked back to the hotel – another former office warren now decked out as a travel destination – ideal as neutral ground rather than the location of her doubtless ritzy apartment for a meeting that was as nerve-wracking as a French kiss on a first date. And I had reason to recall that encounter with a shudder of dread pleasure as I waited over a tepid filter coffee for my first sight of Branwen since the winter of 1985.

Even after more than twenty years she didn't disappoint. I'd like to say she never had but I was too old to lie anymore, to myself or anyone else. Still, whatever she was doing to herself, she was doing it well. On the surface at least. There had always been murky depths with Bran even if it had taken me some time to come up for air. I stood up as she scanned the room to see which booth I was in. The smile was tentative but the way she cocked her head slightly to one side was no less coquettish than when she had posed for me with a lot less on than the blue striped seersucker suit, sharp jacket and skirt to the dimpled knee. I had time for the quick once-over before she crossed the coffee-room floor. She imperceptibly slowed down as if she knew it. Of course she knew it. This was Bran after all. Some things wouldn't ever change.

Her eyes held the glint and sheen of anthracite. Her hair, glossy, thick and black, framed the oval of a face which was almost

Mediterranean in complexion. She used to say it was the Iberian heritage of the Celt. I'd countered it was the legacy of randy Spanish sailors shipwrecked from the Armada in west Wales. No make-up, just an *amuse-bouche* of a mouth and, I knew, a personality darker and harder than any mineral. At a modest 5' 10" I seemed to dwarf her compact 5' 2" even with the kitten heels she was wearing. A kiss, for which we both positioned awkwardly, drifted away in unease. She held out her hand. I touched it and the platinum wedding band on it.

"You're looking great," I said.

She shrugged out a thank you. She said that, a few rough edges aside, that at almost fifty I didn't look too bad myself. She grinned. I forced out a smile.

She sat opposite me, ordered a herbal tea, more coffee for me and we stared a necessary while longer. Then, as from long habit, we got down to it.

"Why did you come?"

"I told you on the phone. She ... Haf ... asked me to help her."

"You don't take that seriously, do you?"

"I don't know. I did. Something in her voice. Shouldn't I? Do you know where she is? What she wants?"

Bran fiddled with her granulated sugar packet, shifting the contents around in its unopened paper envelope like a blind fortune teller looking for a lucky grain of truth.

"She can be difficult. She's ... a silly bugger when she wants to be."

"Meaning?"

Her one revelatory weakness, momentary but intense through the translucent skin around her neck, was a flush that wrapped her like a scarf. Or a signal as I recalled and reminded her.

"Oh, you know it means nothing. I just can't help it."

"That's why it says something, isn't it?"

"You're not listening, Billy. I've told you. I really don't know where she went. Honest, as they say. She's been gone for over two months."

"The college?"

"Nothing. She hasn't turned up for lectures. And no messages for any friends."

"The police?"

"Why? She's telephoned me ... you ... other people. You, less than a week ago. She's not lost, Billy.

"She called me daddy, Bran. Why did she do that?"

"For God's sake, she's still a kid."

"She's almost twenty-one, isn't she? I wasn't there, remember."

"Messing about. That's all. I'd have told you, wouldn't I?"

"Would you?"

"She isn't."

"She could be, though, couldn't she?"

"No! It's just a game. Hero worship."

"Hero worship?"

"Of you. Of your work anyway. She's got everything – the books, posters, photographs, clippings. She plastered them over her bedroom walls before she walked out."

"Why? Did you tell her about us?"

"She knows. Not from me. Mal said something one night when he'd had a bit. After that documentary programme about you on television. She cottoned on. Worked it out, that 'friends' was a catch-all word."

"How old was she then?"

"About sixteen. Later she heard us quarrelling. Things were said. Not by me. Look, I've never been close with her, this mother-and-daughter thing and such, and it just got worse after that. She practically moved out then. In spirit if not in body. And this disappearing stuff, that isn't the first time either."

I tried to think it through but all I could see was the deceit by which we had all lived. I didn't know what to believe. It was what had sent me away. It was what had pulled me back. I tried again.

"You were clear she wasn't mine. I asked no more. I'm asking now. Again."

This time the smile was more pitying than playful.

"You're still a fool, Billy, you know that."

She puffed her cheeks. Like an adder, I thought. And blew softly at me a breath that was at once sweet and rank.

"That summer after the strike you got more and more, I dunno, miserable … melancholy. Even before that you were down about everything and everyone. Worrying. Down. And for me it was still what I'd felt, something alive and different, as if that bloody history your old man went on about had come to life, and with me in it. Christ! I was even a star supporter! You and me were coming to an end anyway. You didn't quite see it, did you, but then there were lots of things you didn't see, or didn't want to see."

She paused, and calculated.

"I wasn't wild and I wasn't calculating. Not then. Maybe later. But at the time I just slept with the people I wanted to fuck or who wanted to fuck me. And you were around, too, when you weren't off photographing and documenting and revelling in the whole mess, in your own sad way. So, like I said, I don't know. Take that for a no, from me. And yes, maybe she thinks so."

"Why did you marry Mal?"

"A marriage of convenience."

"That all?"

"We'd been lovers. I was pregnant. Strictly, in case you're still wondering, just after you'd gone, and I told him it was his. A slightly premature birth. No problems. At the time. Later, we just became a partnership. And after that, four, five years ago, we split. Still married."

I could have wondered about a lot. And worried, too, but all I was thinking was whether to tell her now what I knew of that convenient partnership and its convenient continuation and how all that I knew had been in the papers which Haf, in anticipation of my response, had sent and which had arrived without further explanation the day after her telephone call. Instead I gave her my mobile number and asked her to call if Haf did get in touch, that I was going to look around to see if anything of the made-over old patch might stir my professional interest, and that, maybe, we could have dinner before I flew out.

She looked quizzical.

"Seems a long way to come after such a long time for such casual reasons."

"Well, I would like to meet her. Perhaps we'll agree about something or other."

"The only thing you'll have in common with her is a mutual distrust – dislike? – of yours truly."

I didn't demur, just deflected the crack.

"DNA?" I asked.

"For Chrissake! What for?"

"Sentiment."

"Sentimentality is more your bag."

"Do they measure that in DNA?"

"You'd have bucketfuls, you always did," she said.

We seemed depleted, and I was once more, somehow, dispossessed.

* * * * *

I walked out of the foyer minutes after she'd gone, leaving me with her mobile phone number and memories I kept batting away. I held tight to the manila folder I hadn't opened to show her. I turned left

35

and straight on, which were the only directions, my old man had said, that were ever worth taking. The city centre's layout was easily recalled: a pedestrian grid lay on top of its nineteenth-century right angles and a few defiant statues of socialist politicians and Irish boxers had been more recently erected to match up to its capitalist and liberal founding fathers. No role models for women in bronze or marble yet. The girls were missing a trick there. No doubt it'd come. The only female equivalents were in stone, flanking the steps of the Old Library that stood kitty corner from the Victorian indoor market. They were still draped in Grecian finery and clutching books, and they were still called Study and Rhetoric, the monikers by which I fondly remembered them, but they weren't ushering me in to find Power and Knowledge, their more worldly sisters anymore; it was the milk of Lethe, strictly of the alcoholic variety, they had on offer nowadays. The library had become a pub, and not of the kind I favoured. It took a while to find one I did.

If the library was a theme pub, then its satellite hostelries seemed to have become just as thematic. On every other corner there was a piece of Erin that should never have left the fantasy factory or an iron-grilled and Cajun-manufactured homage to New Orleans. The wine bars were like gentlemen's dens with crazed brown leather club chairs and newspaper racks or decked out with splashing fountains, crushed velvet drapes and shameless stone nymphs last seen in a Naples brothel in 1944. Or so I imagined my old man, who'd been there then, might have got around to telling me. At this rate, the breweries would end up making replicas of the old pubs that were actually old, but on the same site. I found one that seemed reluctant to change and sat at its bar in front of its ornate mirror. There was a God after all, and He was still serving up the metallic, brassy and frothy beer I could taste on faraway nights in my close-up dreams.

I found the new replacement library amongst a wall of designer shops and stores. Glass wall fronts soaring high. Berlin, Boston, Basingstoke. The new one had neither the sumptuous wall tiles or echoing terrazzo floors of the old one, and all yesterday's newspapers were no longer preserved intact and bound into a giant's commonplace book, but shrunk onto the pinprick palimpsest of the page-by-page screen. I whizzed as well as the next bozo of my deprived generation, slowly and irritated, blessing my having grown up without all this non-tactile blur of gadgetry. The electronic future had not just arrived, it had hit us on the blindside, uncaring of the way we had once groped with pen or paint or camera to shine some kind of light. What was once unknown or untraceable could be collated now or hyperbolically enhanced to give the impression of holding the water that still inexorably ran on. But my own hard-won vision had been no less fuzzy over time, and had left me sightless, a click or two away from the lies I had stopped peddling.

Haf's papers – copies of letters, of e-mails, of bank statements, of notes on hotel pads, figures and dates on envelopes, on everything except the back of the proverbial cigarette pack only punters and smokers still used – guided me haphazardly to the daily pages of record I needed to see. The story was sometimes half-hidden in an inside paragraph, occasionally hailed as another brilliant success for inward investment and, latterly, brought into the frame of the new government under the rubric of "Regeneration", a concept which had struck me as a cross between the hopeful mythology of resurrection and the hopeless metamorphosis effected by the mortician. Why didn't they just try to generate something instead? The past and its places were never quite the organic thing a notion like *re*-generation so smugly implied. Whatever the case in hand, and there seemed dozens as I read on – from building works to art centres to tip clearances to adult education classes in aromatherapy and IT training – money, large and small packages of subsidy and grant aid, did not seem to be a problem. It was more a question of how did they get it out of the door in sufficient bulk and with the speed that didn't allow bureaucratic windows in Europe to shut. In a de-industrialised region of such classic proportions as this one had been, the fit was perfect even if the outcome was debatable. The longer timescale raised the cynical thought that the actual recipients, if not the potential beneficiaries, would be, one way or the other, long gone before the final reckoning.

I whizzed on for a few hours. My notes grew fuller as I honed in on Haf's direction finder. The penny-ante stuff was all about worthy efforts, statistically measured by lame targets and grandiose objectives, to "up-skill" and "re-train" for the "knowledge economy" that had passed a generation by and was, allegedly, still held back by the low aspirations entrenched in a stubborn work culture, one long dead in practice and suffused, as it resisted the social mortuary, with the undesirable Luddite and gender attributes of a leftover underclass. The jargon fed by sociology to journalism came easy. But my confusion over what was being regenerated by whom for whom for why, grew incrementally. There seemed precious little that had come to fulfilment outside the cities of the plain. It seemed we were still looking to the hills in vain. I began to pucker up for an inner Biblical trumpet of warning. Still, capital projects, with big outlays and vague embracing ambitions, were more realisable, less measurable in their ultimate outcome, and very big bucks indeed. The one thing, it seems, we had going for us, benighted denizens of a blasted past in those hills and valleys, was land. It was filthy, useless, contaminated land, soil and acres where you couldn't grow vegetables or re-create a pre-industrial haven, but it was land that was available, cheap to buy and expensive to purchase even if the purpose was only re-generative, the gain a social one and the project uplifting.

Gradually certain names began to re-appear. A single speech. A stellar proposal. A projected consortium. A political desire. A community need. An educational enterprise. A PR exercise. A feasibility study. A government decision. Names I knew and some faces I recalled. Bran, Gwilym, Ceri and Maldwyn amongst them. I turned off the screen. An escalator took me down to street level. The streets looked greasy in a watery sunlight. People drifted along in a city adrift. I drifted amongst them. A stranger amongst strangers. One of them. Not of them. I began to stare. No kids this time of day, women, alone if young, in twos if not, married couples, yellow-jacketed building labourers in groups of five and six, and all clutching paper bags full of smeared baguettes, and the more than occasional street dweller even more adrift than the rest of us. What I didn't sense, as a taste, or see, in an instant, was the feel of poor people in the way that was all around us a quarter of a century ago. I guessed that it was an advance, but at whose expense I couldn't be sure. Poverty came in all manner of guises, as my old man drummed into his adult classes. Maybe that had been the other problem. The drumming as opposed to the learning. The observing as opposed to the living. I had long felt separated from both. The escaping as opposed to the staying. Coming back was not my idea, I told myself. But I had and now I had to swallow my mistake and leave, or chew it so that I could spit it out and move on.

I headed for the railway station and a train north but first I called ahead to find out when Gwilym could see me. There was no "if" about it. Gwilym, I knew, would want to see me. I might even be an "opportunity", and he would not have ceased his love affair with one of those, animate or inanimate. Late afternoon, lunch unfortunately "not-doable", then wall-to-wall meetings, in his office, say 4.30, chirped a secretary who, if I knew him as I had indeed once known him would have the attributes to go with the breathless little-girl-lost voice.

The approach to the railway station had had a facelift all right. The designer who had worked on it could have made Ava Gardner look like Bela Lugosi. He wouldn't have spotted the reference as an insult. You could still, with a squint, detect the creamy ceramic tiles and wooden 1920s fretwork behind the monumental planed stone with chewing-gummed bench surround which he must have picked out of a Moscow 1950s catalogue of late Stalinist gesturalism. More street people, combining the hippie scruff look with beggarly homelessness, sat or lay in shop doorways wearing their obligatory dogs on leashes as filthy and braided as the owners' hair. I glared back until they looked away. The dogs I mean. The street people kept their own eyes in touch with the infinite.

The platform was crowded. A mix of shoppers, a glitter of mothers who outsmarted their gawky teenagers, older couples in beige and grey and wool, clutching their bags and each other against intrusion, and a swirl of students seemingly intent only on what their touch screens were telling them. I'd been prepared for the rash of bilingual signage in the streets and even for the Welsh-language announcements for "*y trên nesaf*" and, in Welsh, the correctly pronounced valley townships that followed, but what came after a posh and male Welsh accent, even to those whose grasp of Welsh foundered after the first few lines of the national anthem, was more alien yet. The train information given in English was impeccably English, with the syllables of every place name I had ever known or grown up with, separated out into a speak-your-weight tone that managed to locate every wrong inflection and stress possible in the brave new world of desperanto. Most of us on that platform were being addressed in two languages we did not speak. I felt more speechless than I had for two decades. I left the city and let the view between the hills open up. We seemed to stop every five minutes. Then, abruptly, I was there. Destinationville. The town, in a bowl rimmed by a shrug of hills, used to be what I had once called home.

There was a new halt for the Research and Development Park just after the town itself. Gwilym would be at lunch, and allegedly meetings, for a few hours yet, so I got off the train early. The town's river still ran through it. No one seemed to have honed in yet on the one natural asset, apart from the clumpy hills, which might have given it a focus to replace its vanished industries and lost trade. No change there, or in the boarded-up shops of a shopping precinct constructed like a pebbledash concrete box with a flap entrance and a soaked-in stink of urine. It had taken me no more than ten minutes to walk from the station, another architectural glory now lost to boy scout design, past the rash of estate agents, shoe shops, bread shops, junk jewellers and the flashing tumblelights of slot-machine joints spitting the crackle of their noise, endlessly, onto the streets. One or two Italian-owned and run cafés and the cobbled square off the main and winding street whispered urban possibilities. But the indoor market was more shoddy goods and plastic utilities than the piled-high stalls of fruit and vegetables and locally slaughtered meat and home-cooked hams and pies it had once been. People must be eating something, though. There seemed more bulk on the pavements, more waddle in the shop doorways and more roll in the gait. I didn't see any obvious students in the town. They must stay on the train and leave by train for the city when lectures ended. Familiarity was not cheering me up. I needed a drink, and The Lamb was nearby so I went there, and entered the past.

A narrow, low frontage with a door and boxed-in entrance. Two bars to either side, divided by the central run of beer pumps and shelves of bottles, both long and hemmed in like railway carriages from a Western movie. The one to the right was slightly smaller, to accommodate a Ladies at the far end and had an embossed and floral wallpaper pattern to support its claim to be the lounge. No one went there in the day. Some things would stay the same, wouldn't they? I turned left into the bar proper where a rotund, sawn-off and silent, landlord had once patrolled behind his counter. His name was Idris. So he was known as Id. And one night an autodidact from my old man's class had decided that made Id's voluble wife, Mavis, Ego. Both Id and Ego were shades now, as shadowy as the black-and-white poses of half-naked men, some clutching enamel medallioned belts, which were framed and scattered over the spit-yellow, tobacco-stained walls. These were the champions, of the world some of them, from a time even before mine. Their shadow dancing in the ring had been as explosive in the mind as on the canvas. I took them in at a glance. Freddie Welsh, Tom Thomas, the brothers Frank and Glen Moody, Tommy Farr and Jimmy Wilde, Dai Dower and Howard Winstone. All still there. Behind the bar a woman in her late sixties was adjusting a curly black wig in a cracked mirror. She glimpsed me in it and without turning, said "Waddya want, love?" I asked for a bitter. Her fire-engine red lips had been cut out from a pin-up of Marilyn, the effect only spoiled by the paint going up under her nose and almost down to her chin, and the ravines of powder-caked wrinkles that surrounded them. They scarcely moved as she said "Pint or glass, love?"

From a corner at the far end of the bar where the light from the scrolled front window did not reach, a voice which didn't need a bellows to fan fire rumbled.

"He don't drink no glasses, Doreen. Give him a pint of Whoosh."

I moved down the bar towards the voice, and left my tenner on the bar.

"Shwmae, Billo," Tommy said, and stuck out a hand that was no bigger than a shovel.

"Long time no see," said Lionel.

"Siddown, butt," said Tommy, slowly letting my own hand limp free from his calluses and pincer fingers.

I sat at the round wooden-topped table that was held up and steady by buxom iron Brittanias bearing their shields. Either side of me, as in the Town XV's second team front row of my youthful athletic prime, were Tommy "Coch" Harris and his fellow prop, in work and sport and drink, Lionel "Blondie" Pemberton, a surname that hinted less of vanished gentry and more of West Country farm labourers turned late-Victorian colliers. By the time I'd met them, colliers both, in the murk of the Second XV's scrum, they'd already forged a veteran reputation as players who were as dirty as they were slow. Stalwarts by then, protecting a young hooker on rain-lashed nights on muddy fields from opposing sods no rougher or gentler than themselves. Their nicknames were for the ginger crew cut of the one and the tow-haired straw thatch of the other. Their short schooldays had ended with NCB apprenticeships as faceworkers, in the 1950s, and a succession of pits as they followed the few seams that remained stubbornly open as collieries closed as rapidly as flies' eyes in the '60s. Closures and forced redundancies finally drove them out, and into work as labourers and brickies. I had seen no better or tougher sight since I'd been home.

"Aye, long time no see," echoed Tommy.

"Aye, s'right," echoed Lionel back.

"Pints?" I asked.

These boys knew a rhetorical question when it was posed. About drink, anyway. They drained the fullish ones in front of them and Tommy tapped his empty on the table to alert the Marilyn lookalike, who had just pulled one for me, to keep going. Lionel got up to fetch them and set my change and three fresh pints before us.

"Cheers," he said and began drinking as Tommy, without bothering to ask, did what I wanted and gave me a *Whitaker's Almanack* tour of the town in the years I'd been gone. I listened to the lament of decline and deterioration.

"Aye. Same old same-o," agreed Lionel, when Tommy finally drew breath.

Tommy wiped the froth of his grey straggle of a moustache after this reflective and biting bottom-up comment on the panorama of the recent past. Living it had aged them. Neither "Coch" nor "Blondie" quite did it any more as accurate descriptions of the now salt-and-pepper and bare-patched heads nodding and drinking on either side of me. I said as much. "Aye," said Tommy. "That's what a life on the buildings, humping bricks and mixing in the freezing fucking cold will do to you. You should see my bollocks!"

"S'right," Lionel added, and went for three more pints.

Tommy was in full spate by now, a great circular flow of fact and opinion, all revolving around the life and times of artisan builder and bullshitter supreme, T. Harris, Esq. It all came back to buildings. They held us and defined us. So what was wrong was, in his opinion, that what lay behind them had changed. They were cheaper to construct, dearer to buy, quicker to deteriorate. The wood was not seasoned. The foundations were not settled. The exteriors were all cladding and the interiors all slotted together from a kit. So where was the pride in that, he wondered, and offered an answer by widening his viewfinder to people. The town had gone all to hell. Big City incomers, toffee-nosed, hippie, English, Welshy Welsh. The rugby club had gone all to hell, betrayed by Judases of various stripes and flavours. And now there was talk after the demise of Id and Ego of a makeover for The Lamb, to give it a more "authentic feel", with stone-flagged floors and wooden beams and a re-faced bar to replace the truly authentic leatherette, plastic and Formica it had worn in over forty years. All a disaster. Still, in The Lamb maybe, some work out of this for a pair of jobbing builders in semi-retirement, and a few pints on the job thrown in.

"S'right," said Lionel.

"Pints again?" This time from Tommy.

I was tempted. Another and I'd have settled in for the afternoon. That would be no trouble for them, but I had more calls to make before I could slip into forgetfulness with them. I left them swilling away the grime and dust they had absorbed all morning, and across a lifetime every morning since they had left secondary modern entrapment at fifteen with bruised knuckles and a dislike of authority and its preachiness which had sustained them into the righteous anger of their mid-sixties.

I waited at the lights to cross the two lanes of busying traffic and looked up at the platforms and retaining wall of what had once been one of Europe's busiest rail interchanges. A funnel to the world for coal out and people in which filled and emptied day and night for half a century. It had shrunk inside itself like a terminally ill patient in a baggy suit. What was tacked on to the original façade had the unwelcome effect of loose-fitting false teeth set on shrivelled gums. There was nowhere to buy a ticket, and I rode free for the ten minutes or so it took for the diesel to grind its way up an incline beyond the town to the halt.

* * * * *

After the frayed edginess of the town, carelessly spread out beneath the mountain escarpment, there was a surreal feel to the Development Park. At least from a distance. Up close you could still see the railway cutting, now concreted over and the tunnel now bricked up, through which an exodus of coal had once rattled to the sea. Most of the site was a car park. I crossed it, as instructed, until at almost its far end I came to a red-brick wall which sectioned off a lawned area that you entered through open iron gates. The gates were fancy. Their railings were painted silver and had gold spears to top off the effect. You were welcomed in by a slate plaque that was six feet long and four feet high. It was mounted on a granite plinth and stood ten feet up from the lawn. The grass was so green it sparkled. The grass did not quiver even for a synthetic nanosecond. The deeply cut grey lettering on the plaque said: ADEILAD ALFRED WALLACE BUILDING. Another twenty yards down a yellow-brick path took me to the frontage of a very new, low slung two storey building. The oval windows which studded its riveted white cladding were framed in steel and glowed blue. It took me less than a nanosecond to admire it. I went through a series of automatic doors that swished open and closed, into a reception area where I had to state my business at a desk which could have issued airline tickets. I was sent to another series of glass doors, all electronically locked, where I was acknowledged over the intercom and buzzed through to the inner sanctum. I'd been told to ask for The Directorate, and here it was. The last time that one had been up in lights was in the 1790s, just before Napoleon doused them, dissolved the collective and crowned himself, literally I recalled, Emperor. The only thing Gwilym had in common with Bonaparte was an ineffable self-regard and the short-arsed cockiness that often accompanied it.

A door to an outer office opened and Gwilym's PA stood framed in it. I seemed to remember the little guy asked Josephine not to wash until after he'd come home. Maybe Gwil had a different olfactory arousal. This Josephine had definitely washed. And sprayed. And perked and painted. She was to natural fragrance what chemical is to organic. She was to natural blonde what chicory is to espresso. Her jersey silk dress had had its pink and red geometric pattern imprinted big on a size that was a tad too small and too short, and just right. Her voice, when it came, was more doll than baby and excitingly formal, as in "The Director is expecting you, Mr Maddox. Do go right in. Coffee?" And she half-turned on her teeteringly high pink suede stilettos and gave me a smile as sweet as a sucked sherbet lemon as she adjusted her made-for-the-job horn-rimmed glasses. Perhaps she was really efficient, too.

I said, "Yes" and "Please", and did as I was told. Gwilym was sat, head bowed over neatly stacked papers, behind a veneer-inlaid desk that could have done duty as a stage prop for *Il Duce*. It was cleared of any clutter. As pristine as the paperwork looked virginal. Only a mounted and gold-plated rollerball pen broke the gleaming expanse of its surface. *Il Duce* looked up as if he was due for a surprise instead of an announced visitor. He cracked a smile that went all the way from who'd've believed it to whaddya know, well well. He opened up his arms to receive me even before he rose slowly from the desk and advanced around it towards where I stood with Josephine hovering just behind me. She might have seen the move before, because I sensed her sliding out of the room − discretion and all that stuff. I stood my ground as Gwilym thrust his arms up as high as he could reach to pat my shoulders. He was staring lovingly up into my face, a technique Josephine's high heels might have helped him perfect, and saying quietly, but with feeling, "Bill. Bill. Bill. Well. Well. That's just great. Bill."

What could I say back? I thought about a speech, but just said "Gwil. Gwilym. Eh, Gwil!" and wrapped my arms around the back of a dark grey, pure wool suit. We clutched each other a while longer, until he gradually let go with what seemed like the reluctance of Velcro to detach itself. He gestured to a corner of the room where two blue cloth tub chairs squatted either side of a lower splay-legged table. We sat. Josephine returned with a silvery tray on which she'd positioned a white bone china coffee pot with matching cups, except for the gold trim around the lip, a milk jug and a little bowl of white and brown sugar lumps. The spoons rattled as she put it down. Gwilym smiled at her. He called Josephine Morwenna, and thanked her. We poured our own coffee and, as before, she discreetly turned and retreated. I swivelled my wayward head as Gwilym began to speak. It sounded rehearsed. That would be about right for Gwilym who had always been as instantaneous as freeze-dried coffee without the boiling water.

"Fantastic to see you again. All these years. Older," he snickered, "but aren't we all? And looking good, kiddo. Looking good. Are you home for long? Any special reason? Great to see you, whatever."

Kiddo, I thought? Maybe the outmoded slang went with the inquisitional probe. A sort of Welcome Home that was as sincere as a Commercial Christmas. Was there any other kind anymore, kiddo? He slurped a little coffee and sat back, waiting. I studied the dots on his shot-silk tie and the cufflinks in his off-white cotton shirt with its shiny pearly grey buttons, and I contemplated his journey from railway signalman's son to the *Duce* of the Directorate. I didn't feel I was intruding on any secret thought process. He probably contemplated the same route with some satisfaction at least twice a day. He was just a year older than me, and we'd been at university, almost overlapping, in the late 1970s. I'd dropped out. He hadn't. A doctorate had arrived for Gwil via a "comparative sociological study" of the coalfields of Durham, Appalachia and South Wales. He'd met Bran in her undergraduate years after I'd already left to become the next Robert Frank. Another dream. I was surfing on the first waves of published glamour when Gwil had gloatingly introduced me to her. Maybe he thought the fact they were size compatible was sufficient security. Mistake. She dropped him, and we began. I didn't detect resentment at the time. We'd told ourselves it was a freewheeling world and included ourselves in the spin. There seemed less envy of the relationship and more envy of the career, mine, one that was soon worlds apart from graduate fellowships and junior lectureships and monthly pittances. Yet he'd clung onto the educational ladder and occasional letters told me of two marriages, twice divorced, and no kids behind him, and finally a view from almost the top of his particular pole to compensate for all the effort. It worked for him, this viewpoint, gloating being good downwards, envy being pointless upwards. Besides, any other emotion would have taken him too long and too far away from thinking about himself, and his own needs for power and privilege. It was the relative not the absolute nature of these commodities that mattered to him, so I directed the past freight we both carried back to his favourite topic, one so precious he rarely shared it openly with others. Himself. I didn't answer about me, I signalled the comforting topic of Him, and looked around at the framed certificates, at the dusty tomes gathering sightless motes behind glass, and the painting that filled an entire wall with its incongruous rebuke of his inward vision.

"You've done well. I can see. Congratulations."

There was a disconcerting but characteristic giggle in return. He stroked a small razor trimmed beard, one that gave neat, circumscribed length to his small-featured, cutely handsome face. Gwilym had unnaturally round deep brown eyes, almost glassy, beneath his plucked and arched eyebrows. The eyes glistened now in a self-deprecating way that, if you knew him as I did, was anything but. Christ, I thought for a moment he was going to flutter his feathery lashes at me. And then, in a trained instant, almost uncannily quickly, the look tightened and hit-switched to a more attentive, focussed mode. It was as if the whole thing was there, just in that look. The passage from junior lecturer to dean via the journeyman authorship of a couple of convoluted and densely footnoted academic articles, with a bland textbook survey thrown in along the way, to the heights, and salary, of administrative grandeur. And now this, Director of an independent unit for research and development, for business growth and social regeneration. It was the link that was missing which interested me more than the outward show of success and the inner conviction of merit. Gwilym still believed, in his innermost sanctuary, that the latter was a deserved compound of IQ and effort. He never got satire. Not if it was directed against his own deserved needs. Just deserts was a different thing altogether. Not that he would appreciate the distinction.

"It's a terrific opportunity, Bill. Even in these challenging times. Especially in these times. We're bringing together the private and the public. Pulling in the best ideas, and the most go-ahead people. Graduates on short-term contracts. Start-up pods. Peppercorn rents. All the latest kit. Spin offs for commercial ventures. Creative industries. Links into business and government. Able to form partnerships across the piste. Not tied down. Fleet of foot. University connections that do not hamstring us with the caution of academic regulation. Innovative to the core. Mal's idea originally, of course, and he worked his socks off to secure the funding. A dream come true. So when they asked me, the Board, you know, to leave the University, where, did you know? I was the Pro Vice Chancellor, well, I didn't, despite everything, hesitate. What a chance, eh, to put into practice all I'd studied and researched. What else could I do?"

I tried looking impressed. At his bravery. At the opportunity. At the personal sacrifice. And I must have succeeded.

"I can see you're wondering a bit if I've gone mad. Solid career, and all that, thrown away on a, let's be honest, gamble. Now, Bill, I won't lie to you, salary is on a par for a guaranteed five-year contract, so I won't exactly starve, and, as you can see, there are the perks and trappings of power, which are enjoyable, and at my, our, advanced age, why not? Eh, Bill. But the bottom line is, the real thing is, this is a once in a lifetime chance to give a lead. To be, and Christ we need it here don't we, a leader. That's the reward, and that's the responsibility I've taken on."

A smile to dazzle a whole plank of Board members followed the soliloquy.

"So very, satisfyingly, rewarding," he concluded, and folded his hands in case I'd missed the point.

"Rewards, like charity, begin at home," I said as blandly as I could manage. It puzzled him momentarily. I couldn't be that vulgar, could I? Try me, I thought. This time the smile came *sans* teeth.

"It's well paid, as I said. You'd expect it to be. For the responsibility. I don't deny that. Though senior colleagues elsewhere in Academe proper …"

The voice trailed off in a wistful sigh for appointment in faraway universities whose "catchment areas" were not so compromised as those more locally situated, and whose "culture" was more aspirational than needy. The same look came to both our faces. Unbidden and, for him, unwanted. Who'd employ him in such Groves of Academe? He was forgetting his guest and the feel-good factor he liked to create in all possible circumstances. He hurried on:

"Anyway, anyway. What about you, Bill? Really really great to see you, by the way. Great. Exhibitions. Retrospectives. Books. Newspaper articles – I've read them all. And wasn't there a documentary film you made, quite recently? Got shown on BBC4 over here? About Mexican immigrants to Los Angeles who'd made good, as they say? Great title: Wetbacks to Greenbacks?"

I nodded. He changed tack. Opportunities for both of us had just flitted across his radar screen. A better future.

"I just thought," he said thoughtfully. And he probably had. "I just thought … would you consider some, temporary of course, to suit you, part-time, appointment here? A research fellowship perhaps? And we could help, you know, with any, er, archiving, or whatever. A permanent home, perhaps? A depository of your lifetime's achievement under your own name? I don't know about you, but that'd excite *me*. We could get external funding for that, I'm sure. The William Maddox Photographic Centre. Nice ring to it. And, hey, talking of names, what d'you think of ours?"

I smiled. He smiled. I waited. He settled into accustomed pedagogic mode.

"No? Don't blame you. I've had to inform quite a few. Well, he was Welsh of course. And nowadays, things have changed quite a lot in that department, Billy boy, so we have to stress that connection. Born in 1823 was our very own Alfred Wallace. Just as everything in our part of the world was beginning to take off big time. He was from Monmouthshire. Gwent as they say now. Clothes on a poodle but still a dog underneath. Our dog though. And he died in 1913, just as our madcap growth, our boom and bust, iron and coal, and people swarming in, was about to end. Perfect timing. And here's the thing. He was the boy who first came up with the notion of the natural selection of the species, the key concept to understand the evolution of everything. Not Charles Darwin, Bill, but his correspondent and co-worker, our own Alfred Wallace. No one really denies this anymore. Wallace was the originator and the catalyst to Darwin's work. Fantastic, eh? And the thing is, it gets even better. For us to use his name, I mean. Because, you see, Darwin's emphasis was all on competition, between individual units in the same species, so to speak, for there to be any survival of the fittest. But old Alfred, our pal, more in keeping with us, showed that wider environmental pressures were what actually forced adaptation, change, to survive as a whole, in any given local world or environment. So any survival of the fittest, and that phrase incidentally was Herbert Spencer's spin on Darwin's biological theories when applied to economy and society, has to place individual life within the frame of culture and society. Which is, after all, what we need to hear in this benighted part of the globe, isn't it? Moving on together. Sorry about the lecture, you know me, but I thought you'd like the idea."

I dutifully nodded. Gwilym took that as a good sign. He waved his hand in the air. Modest and self-deprecating.

"I'm getting ahead of myself. As usual. You know me. Always the doer! And I still haven't found out why you're home. Bran? Have you seen her?"

I nodded again. I should have been sitting on the back-shelf of a car.

"Yes, I have. That's partly why I'm here."

"Partly?"

"Yes. And for Haf. Why don't you tell me about Haf, Gwil?"

He poured himself another coffee. I waited. He put his cup down, a little too heavily. The coffee spilled from the saucer onto his inlaid and varnished coffee table. He ignored the puddle. He was considering my request. Its innocence. Or not. He began slowly.

"You remember I wrote to you. Perhaps I shouldn't have. Wasn't my place. But, you know, everything had gone – went – so lopsided, for a while, after you left, after you and Bran split. All so uncertain."

He paused and looked up. He switched effortlessly from the academic to the demotic. Just to show he could. Just to show we were still blood brothers. He was wasting his time with that one, and had done years since. I didn't bother to alert him to it. Not yet. He leaned, like a buddy, towards me. Go ahead, kiddo, I thought. And he did, effortlessly.

"Look. I started. We started. That autumn. To see each other again. Just after you'd gone. Casually, of course. Not like you two had been, of course. Then, it ended. Again. Only, as you know now, she was pregnant. Quite soon. The girl, Haf, was born. End of June or July '86, I forget. Bran married Mal after that. Maybe. No, certainly, they'd seen each other around the time I split … she stopped … with me, I mean – around the same time, so I just assumed it was Mal. I didn't, you know, enquire. Well, not for years anyway. Maybe I shouldn't have sent a card. I confess I was out to hurt. Her not you. I'd met her at a party. She wasn't with Mal, and

53

he'd spoken, bitterly, to me, about his bitch of a wife. And, he said, her, from the off he said, lies. I was between marriages myself, and pissed. I tried it on, to be honest. She made it plain, brutally plain, I wasn't a runner, let alone a rider anymore. I certainly wasn't on her radar screen by then and, for Bran, it was all TV reporting and small-screen stardom those days – not PR and networking yet – so, a bit narked, I asked out loud, pissed, who the fucking father was then, and if not me now, then maybe me then, and how she'd be the one to know it. And she just stood. Icy and looking at me, and said "No chance", that I was a tosser then and a shit now and she always knew how to protect herself from any unwanted, 'dribble'."

He swallowed. I think he expected me to feel a twinge of sympathy. I felt a pain elsewhere. Gwilym hadn't noticed. He wanted it all to come out now. He'd stared in the mirror so long that monologue was the sound of sweet reason to him.

"So, naturally, Bill I thought of you. You hadn't come back when your old man died that Christmastime. No one blamed you, I mean. You were away. But, I thought, years later, and, yeah, I was angry, that maybe you needed to know. In case you didn't, I mean. So I just sent the card to the publisher's address. You never replied, so I let it drop. I assumed you'd ask Bran. You know, I mean, if it was yours, or not."

He let his thoughts trail off. I wanted an end to this. I told him I had written to Bran and that she'd sent an even briefer note back, but one that just said, "No." I told him I hadn't known about his dalliance. Or of anyone else. And she had married Mal after all. So QED, and all that. Gwilym seemed to think this made us some kind of blood brothers because his face lit up again. He said that then it must indeed be Mal who was Haf's father but that, for reasons beyond him, neither Mal, nor apparently Haf, now thought so. "Unless ..." he began to say, looking sly and even more conspiratorial. I shook my head and half-turned in the bottom-scrunching bucket that called itself a chair to take in the room again. It was an oval office no less, with high ship-like portals for windows and, as well as the permanently closed books, an array of glass cabinets full of the kitsch and wonky maquettes and shields and framed certificates which academic dignitaries from all over the globe gave each other now, objects as pompous and self-proclaiming as those which former trade union leaders from the self-declared Socialist Republics had once carted over by the suitcase in order to show eternal fraternity and everlasting solidarity. But on the single biggest wall space was an enormous painting in oil and chalk. It would be vivid anywhere. In this room it was positively life-giving. I breathed it in as relief.

"I didn't know you collected art, Gwil," I said.

It was his turn to swivel slightly to take in his exceptional picture.

"Not me. Not really. It's part of the university collection. Hanging in here on loan, for safe keeping, I'm told. Valleys boy. Dead now. I'm told it's good. Is it, do you think?"

It was better than good. It was amazing.

On an overall background of night-falling blue, chalky ribbons of roads, fitfully lit by the groping headlights of cars and the electric fuzz of stalked street lamps, cut their way down the picture, and the outline of a black river curled alongside like an indolent tape worm. It was a map, a flattened-out cartography where hills and stars and the horizon of a sea were boundary markers. At the centre of the painting the artist had placed the open stage set of his house, the stairs, up and down which the same male figure serially, endlessly and repetitiously ran, and doorways in which the figure was framed as in a coffin, and windows to view the figure poised before a miniature representation of the whole. Exploding cones of orange and spurts of red scattered a scintilla of seeds to the horizon, and beyond.

"There seem to be collections of his work, private and public, but I'm told he's not to everyone's taste."

"Not for the palate of those who are without taste," I said.

Gwil let this one lie and returned to the bone I did not wish to pick. Not yet anyway. I told him, but without her equivocation, what Bran had told me that morning in person. I wasn't in the paternity picture. That seemed to satisfy him, but to leave him with other niggling thoughts.

"That really puts Mal right back in the frame, then," he mused.

"Is he around?" I asked.

"Still lives in town. We see each other frequently, of course. Officially, I mean. You know he's my chair. Chairs the board."

I nodded again. My neck was getting used to it. He gave me one of his helpless, not-what-you-think, grins.

"He appointed me, of course. But the thing is, William, we both saw that what this place needed, to take it forward, without losing its mission, its natural constituency if you like, was a leader who … who had the local in his – or her of course, though that was never likely here! – in his inner being, but had risen above, or rather beyond, it. Maldwyn knew my track record in admin and saw my ability to spearhead, well, a new way forward, tying the community and its civic leaders together more."

"Tightening the bonds, so to speak," I supplied.

"Exactly. Well, not exactly like that, but, yes, in a closer intimacy."

I had my moment, like a gap in the field of play. I went for it.

"That's what Haf has been telling me."

"Have you seen her? I don't follow. You're losing me here, Billy boy."

I didn't want to do that, so I passed the folder across the desk. He opened it with the quivering annoyance of a man being told the revenue was making a random check of his self-assessment returns. As he read rapidly through the file, I began to think they should.

56

"Some of this, er, material is private. Confidential. You have no right to this. Not that there's anything amiss, of course, but, what exactly are you doing, going to do, with it? Haf is behind this, isn't she? She's got her own agenda, you know … Green, anarchist, personal. Whatever."

"Whatever you say," was all I said in return, and held my ground.

The Director sighed the sigh of the weary and put-upon for whom all explanations were tasks to perform for the ignorant or unknowing. I interpreted his look for him. "Try me," I said.

"It's quite simple. We are part, or will be part, of a wider consortium putting an entrepreneurial park with equipped office space and conference facilities at the heart of what remains one of Europe's most materially, and socially, deprived areas. We are engaged with our partners to match-fund, mostly in kind – time, salaries, facilities and so on – to secure the European grant, and the private funding, we will therefore attract. These … documents …" he waved an airy arm over them, "are records, open to misinterpretation, of necessary, and frank, private communications to make it all happen for the good in this part of the world in which you no longer live." He snarled the last bit. "Incidentally, I'm the one out of touch, aren't I? What *have* you been doing, Billy boy?"

"Small wars and bigger famines, Gwil. You remember Nye Bevan's late-career crack about sitting on our arses watching the world starve on our television sets? I'm positioned at some useless end of that spectrum. Or I have been. As for private communication as you call it, don't we have a Freedom of Information Act nowadays?"

"Not for all private and corporate issues, you'll find."

"Public interest, Gwil."

There was a different kind of sigh, now, not of resignation but for the reconciliation of understanding he hoped would come. He prefaced it with the interchange of my given name, a trick which he had always considered cute. About as cute as a cat with the chicken roasted and ready on the table.

"Bill, Bill-o. *William!* This is still me. This is you. These are our friends. We, together, all of us are still getting things done. We can't always go around declaring the detail for bureaucrats, can we, or nothing would happen. Again, only good things will come of all this. Believe me."

"Good things?"

"For the people. For our future. For up-skilling and our global profile. For …"

I cut him short.

"Spare me the Rotary speech."

I retrieved the folder. I reassured him.

"This wouldn't convict anyone of anything. Just make a few scribes enquire into the nature of good friends and good things, that's all."

"Then, what d'you want with any of it?"

"I told you. I want to talk to Haf. I want to know why she sent me this stuff."

"Because she's a troublesome little cow, that's why."

"Meaning?"

"Meaning she fucks up her 'A' levels, and just about everything else, and I arranged for her to be admitted to the university and she, I don't know! Spies, is that the word, and steals? Spies on Mal … on her own father? … and me … and her mother and, now even Ceri. God knows how, and makes it seem as if we're a –"

"Conspiracy? Cabal?"

"Oh, fuck off, Billy. That's stupid and you know it. This is all personal with her."

"Is it?"

He suddenly stopped. Polite formalities were to be the order of the day. Back onto safe ground. I felt we were at an end again. He

58

threw me the scraps he felt would take me off his territory. I could be someone else's headache not his. He told me that he had no current address for Haf. She had been living in Mal's house, he thought, in town. He gave me the address. He was sure Mal would explain it all better, and sort out any difficulties I might be misconstruing. He might even know where his daughter was, if she was his daughter. He couldn't resist that one. Meanwhile, he was sure I'd understand, he was very busy and, if I didn't mind, he had to move on. I didn't mind. I'd had my memory of him confirmed. Whoever was hurt, it wouldn't be Gwilym. He played the cards he held in front of him at any one time. Back then they had been those of a political activist with showy zeal in place of any kind of a conscience, and with his upbringing for useful social camouflage even as he distanced himself from it. But the hand he played was always solo. The tricks were all for him. He showed me to the door and asked Josephine to guide me back to the outer world. The look on her face told me she had heard enough to disapprove of me, and seen enough of me to wish me out of her sight quicker than she could flounce. How clever of Gwilym to keep Temptation in his outer office. I didn't let her in on the speculation but I wondered if she was about to enter the inner sanctum as compensation for the bad smell I'd brought into it to spoil her boss's day.

* * * * *

This time, the train took me back to the city centre in under an hour. I kept looking at my watch and not the blurry scenery of my childhood – down the valley, through the market town where rivers met, trading estate, viaduct, castle, weir, human sprawl of back gardens and back lanes in a back catalogue whose pages I had no wish to re-visit. I drifted aimlessly away from the station, moving against the crowds going home. I needed to eat something, but pizza joints with cardboard discs covered in tomato gloop and spaghetti with a thousand meat sauces that all tasted the same held no appeal. A billboard said The Italian Restaurant as if it was the only one possible. I didn't believe, but I walked into the connecting side street to take a closer look. Closer, it was called Casanova's. Perhaps they were serving oysters on the half-shell and Viagra in sweetie wrappings. It was an unassuming shopfront, discreetly shrinking away from the spaceship strut of the nearby rugby stadium that was the nation's new Millennium mecca. It was a human apology in a monumental universe. I'd take priapic Casanova over phallic Mussolini anytime, and its modesty, as to décor and menu at least, sold it to me. I'd take a chance. Again. I could put up with pictures of Naples and coloured maps of The Boot if they really cooked their own food. They did. It wouldn't have been out of place in Brooklyn. I mopped up the juices of a Roman beef stew with bread that tasted of bread, and considered the day that had been and the deeds to be done, and my only sour thought as I drained the bottle of Montepulciano was, if it was this good, how would it survive in this city of food brands and restaurant chains? A crowd came in as I paid the bill. Maybe I'd been given an answer.

It had been a drinking day and a drinking evening. I decided to give the night a chance to join us. I went back to the air-conditioned whirr of my tenth-floor room in the hotel tower block. I hit the button to stop the noise and drew the curtains to cut out the outside sodium-lit night. I located the minibar beneath the TV set. They had Famous Grouse, but Bushmills too. And Welsh water for the Irish I preferred. After that, if I needed it, there was some Welsh whisky to let my palate consider. Penderyn, it said on the tiny bottle. I thought they'd hung Dic, the village's namesake, in 1831 and just two minutes' walk from where I was now. The idea was to end rioting and riots forever. He'd come back though, it seemed, as a spirit. Like me. With that distilled Celtic trio to snuggle up to the beer and wine already inside me I calculated sleep would come when I wanted. I didn't want. Not yet.

Instead I opened the folder. I spread the papers on the bed. Photocopies, faxes, handwritten scrawls, official letters, tables of figures, newspaper articles, photographs, bank statements, and a postcard with a Welsh Dragon on it that said, "Look, please. Then help. Love, Haf." I looked, again. Helping and loving seemed a tall order. And, as Gwilym had told me, there was nothing to startle an old maid in any of it. Not unless she was an old maid who knew a kettle of fish from a posy of flowers. They were traces, indicators, connections, negatives that needed developing, and an investigative journalist to make them stick. I didn't have the time or inclination for any of that. What I did have was a voice on a telephone and a signature on a postcard, both of which worried me in a way I didn't want to think about too closely. That feeling then, and a hunch. I re-shuffled the evidence, some of it keepsakes that had been purloined, and picked up a small white sheet torn from a hotel notepad, somewhere boutique and bijou, by the look of it. Somewhere in London. It looked as if it had been left on the dressing table of a room, waiting for the return and attention of another occupant of the room. It had no date on it, just the message which read: "Ceri love, the Eurocrats' meeting went well. All almost in place. Now Gwil to sort the board next week, with Mal in the Chair! A no brainer then! So, a proposition for you. Light shopping now. Meet me in the bar at 6: will be wearing new purchases but you won't be able to see them … until later. Love, Bran." Oh, and a large X in lipstick in case he was slower on the uptake than a cog-and-ratchet funicular railway on the upward slope. On the downward side, I grimly assumed the proposition had escalated into the position which explained the congregation of partners. My old friends. My dear friends. My friends with faces and parts, real and acted, crowding in on me. I swept all the stuff off the counterpane and reached for the Penderyn that might bring sleep, if not the noose-tightened slumber that had once done for Dic.

This medicine always worked. But in reverse. First you felt better, then oblivious, then distraught. I must have slumbered like a mutt. A drugged one. Curled up and fully clothed. I woke with a growl even before I tried opening my eyes. I tried harder. I blinked to peel the eyelids back. They felt as if they were sellotaped shut, only on the inside of the shutters. I scanned the room until its blur came into focus. There was the untidy mess I'd made and left, and then there was the tidy room-designed and uniform ease of kitsch Cymru, the full spectrum from woollen-covered chairs in a Welsh blanket pattern to artfully placed wooden love spoons as wall décor and miniature miners' lamps as bedside table lights. Any dream would do, except for the one I was in.

The growl turned to a groan as the booze hammered away behind my dilated pupils. But I was master of those pupils and a lifelong student of these pulsating moments. Water. Aspirin. A shower. A sharp shave and vigorous toothbrushing. A naked foray into the corridor to retrieve the local newspaper they delivered daily for free. I guess they had to find readers where they could nowadays. A lingering shit in the company of said newspaper. These two faecal tasks accomplished in one sedentary motion, given the state of my bowels and the standard of the journalism. Another shower followed, and then into my visiting clothes. Old-fashioned jockey Y-fronts. Mismatching socks, but both dark. A button-down Polo shirt, blue-checked in a mix of cotton and poplin. Navy chinos pressed in-house the night before and cinched around my expanding, but still respectable, waist by a broad black leather belt with a rectangular Mexican silver buckle. The boots, bought in Tucson, Arizona after a trip to see the university's photography archive, were squared off in front and slightly heeled, their blackness relieved by a tooled-in climbing vine pattern and a dull metal sheen where they were topped and toed. The jacket was a soft black cashmere, single-breasted and short-lapelled with big patch pockets by Hugo Boss, the burly man's friend. Red capillaries were retreating in fleeing veins from the blue of my eyes, and my sour breath, coming up the airways from a stomach too turbulent for breakfast, was being held off by the mint toothpaste fresh cavern that was my mouth. I looked and smelled as good as I could manage. After all, I was about to call on a millionaire, wasn't I? That, at least, was how Maldwyn Evans was listed. He had got himself into the IT game early on and used that expertise, unusual in this place at that time, to make property deals which tied together entrepreneurial bullshit about the "knowledge economy" with a low level of kitting out. All the buzzwords – regeneration, media, hi-tech, computer literacy, low skills to high skills, Silicon Valley in the Valleys – of the early 1990s, and of course a hotline to public grants. Buildings and land were the more old-fashioned, and more profitable, accompanying attributes. Not bad for the foul-mouthed and resentful Applied Science student we'd all patronised, and put up with and, clearly, underestimated. In the Miners' Strike he had been good for spreadsheets, maps and plans and electronic jiggery-pokery with funds. The things we had all seen as incidental, and maybe he'd already known was the only manageable future in prospect. I checked the mirror. I called down for a taxi. Just hoped the cracks in the veneer wouldn't show.

The taxi driver didn't seem to notice, anyway. He began talking the second I stepped into his rattle-trap and sat on his shiny black, ripped and gaffer-taped seats. At least I blended right in. If I was sick I didn't think anyone would notice the difference. His cab had certainly seen action in the line of fire. By the way he gunned the engine, so had he.

We headed out of the city to the gap in the hills where the city dwellers thought the Valleys began. And he delivered his diatribe about all those beer-swilling, fare-dodging, vomit-flecked, rude and swearing, underdressed Valley girls and their worse, because violent, male paramours. In the end I told him I'd written the script, acted in the play and paid my dues in the audience so why didn't he pull down the curtain and give me a break. I thought he was going to sulk but he just shit-grinned in his rear-view mirror and said "Got you goin' there, mate, didn't I?" And carried on.

There was a time the traffic would have thinned and eased as the road arrowed north of the motorway. Those days seemed to have gone. I clung to the suit strap-handle with my left paw and watched trucks cut in, boom past, get overtaken by midget cars and open-backed council lorries, and road spray kick up and slime windscreens. An unremitting ribbon of rushing vehicles ignored the constant warnings of speed cameras and the electronic boards flashing updates on hazardous conditions. The rain came down more heavily as we entered the driver's fabled Indian territory, and he said, amiably enough, "Always the same up here, mate, innit?"

After thirty sphincter-exercising minutes we pulled off the dual carriageway onto a slip road that entered the southern end of the town, where the green lung of the park wheezed in the damp under a pall of petrol and diesel fumes. It was a smell that brought to mind the once-a-year pungency of the open-air travelling fairgrounds of my youth: leaf mould, crunched gravel, whirring fuel-induced rides, cheap perfume and the tongue-smarting tang of vinegar-sodden chips wrapped in last week's newspaper. All in the mind of course, and about as Proustian a moment as the returning bile in my mouth. I was no more a romantic than my driver, just a tad more resentful. I made him stop at the park's iron gates. The rain had eased. I would walk through the park to Mal's house set above the town. My head told me it wouldn't clear, whatever I did. My heart told my head to shut the fuck up. My guts told them both not to bother.

In the rain the park looked green, almost hopefully so. Hope was relative, neglected and recurring. I heard fat raindrops splatting onto the broken-up concrete at the bottom of the empty swimming pool hidden away behind its faux 1920s hacienda walls, with their red-tiled roofs, terracotta-wet today, and now sheltering only the memory of the echoes of revellers who'd usually been as cold as they were half-naked, and definitely eager to end both states. This was a town of bridges, though only one was worth a second glance. The footbridge crossing the pent-up river which was angrily spitting gobs of white foam over its stone and shopping trolley strewn bed, was decidedly not, but it had its uses. It led straight into the town. I paused at a curve in the High Street and looked up to where bands of terraced housing girdled the town's encircling hills. In the half-light of a grey, cloud-mopped morning they could almost have been designed. Destined anyway, with the colliers' rows in locally hewn stone highest up the ascent, leaching down onto the artisan dwellings of colliery officials and clerks and small shopkeepers, all above the necklace of two grander streets, Victorian chokers of dressed stone villas, embellished with red and yellow brick tracings around confident bay windows. The church below them was a cold mid-Victorian exercise in domination. Inside, I remembered, it was a confection of black tiles with scarlet trim and the penny-lantern dazzle of catalogue-ordered stained glass. It still stuck its spire up like a chiding finger above the surrounding pack of chapels barking at it like irrepressible dachshunds. But all that nonconformity, in religion and behaviour which had once energised the town, meant that such Anglican hauteur could never dominate let alone suppress. Even its symbolic presence had been pushed aside by a glum and tiered car park which out-muscled and overshadowed the once Established

Church as surely as the original workers' terraced houses were now overlooked from the plateau below the mountain by random patterns of housing that had nothing local about them other than their location. Let it go, I thought. A rash is a rash and you shouldn't scratch it. But the splurge made me itch. If no one had thought any of this out, well, no surprise there, any more than the blue-black bruise of a Stasi-type police station. New public symbols, beyond any thoughtful purpose, and the official mind was invariably blank. Blank enough usually for someone else to profit. And no one would have been quicker to do that than Maldwyn, whose house, larger than the rest, turreted and screened by monkey puzzle trees, I thought I could glimpse on the lower slopes.

You entered the house via the back entrance. A few steps down off the street and a solid wood-panelled door. New. With a brass knocker, one that was both shiny and new. It doubled as an electric bell push. I pushed. The sound of the National Anthem – the 'Gwlad! Gwlad!' bit – jangled electronically from my finger. I let go. The straining choristers were choked off from a reprise, and I heard a dog bark in compensation, or maybe better judgement, in their place. Then a loud chesty coughing. Footsteps and chains being released behind the door. It opened. I expected to see Mal Evans, entrepreneur supreme and my replacement at Bran's side. Instead I found myself looking down at a very small man, just five foot tall, around sixty, with a puffy red face set on a body whose dimensions, and solidity, resembled a Tate & Lyle sugar cube. He didn't say a word. From inside the house, past the entrance porch, down a freshly painted passage, a voice reached us.

"Oi! Wheelie, who the fuck is it?"

Wheelie, with me sagely assuming his duties went beyond opening doors to driving the Lexus I had seen parked outside, said nothing. Just looked. I helped out.

"Tell him it's Billy," I said.

"Billy who?"

I pretended alarm, as if after this length of acquaintance I didn't expect speech. Not on our first date. Wheelie wasn't into mockery, whether mine or home-made. He shuffled powerful shoulders and teetered on the balls of his feet. A boxer, then. Certainly a fighter. Wheelie glared. I supplied the cue.

"Just tell him."

Wheelie reluctantly turned his back to me and snarled down the hall in a voice soaked in paraffin rags and squeezed out to dry. "He says to tell you it's just Billy."

There was a moment, a beat, before, on cue too and on time as he would have instinctively felt it, how he always felt it. The voice returned to us.

"Billy, boy. Come on in. Bring him down Wheelie, you daft twat."

The fresh paint smell was like an inappropriate but expensive perfume. The age was originally Victorian. The makeover was garish art deco. Below the dado rail was a deep turquoise shade on original heavy Lincrusta embossed with roses and trellis; above it was a matt black finish on plastered walls hung with three oval and gilt mirrors on one side and three rectangular silver ones on the other. The floor was carpeted in a beige weave with crimson zigzags, which presumably covered the original quarry-floor tiles, too authentic for the glamour in which Mal had invested. Pine doors led off to the right and left, and there was a turned oak staircase at a right angle just before the final and open door at which the faithful Wheelie stopped and shuffled to the side to let me pass. I smiled as unctuously as my hangover allowed. It must have come out as a grimace.

A dog, a hazelnut-brown Boxer with a white mug, worked me over first. The sniff and slobber were harmless; the bared teeth were all show and no delivery. He moved off. I knew Maldwyn Evans, however, for the real thing. He was sitting on a burgundy red leather brass-studded swivel chair in front of a knee-hole desk. He was staring at the glaring square of a laptop. I stood and waited as the screen faded. He didn't turn. He just said to sit down wherever I wanted. I stood and looked at his back, at his pink short-sleeved sweater over a red-striped shirt, at his designer jeans and silver and blue trainers. They all bore names. None of them were his. I guessed that's why he liked them.

Beyond the desk were French windows almost the length of the wall. The other three walls were all tendrilled up in hammered gold and leafy green, with spiky cadmium yellow whorls. There was another mirror, gold leaf on the surround this time, above a black marble fireplace in which plastic fronds of red and green foliage stretched out to their superior wallpaper friends. There was no real friendship between me and Mal. Never had been, even when we'd been friendly. The dislike was more cooperative than mutual. We helped each other out by despising one another. He swivelled his chair around on a dark blue and cream silk Persian rug that filled the room and looked like the only genuine thing in it. "Kosher" would have been Mal's vernacular. Right and wrong simultaneously, as always. He saw me surveying the surrounding, the porcelain knick-knacks, or figurines, the discreetly lit and extravagantly framed oils of fishing smacks, river banks and jagged mountains, the deep blood-red leather wing chairs and the dimpled sofa. Dimpled and studded, to keep up with the matching decor. He waved. I sat. He gestured proprietorially at all his domestic splendour.

"All right, hey?"

I nodded obediently. I'd got into the habit. It beat lying outright. The boxer seemed to approve. The dog sprang up from his spot in front of the fireplace and loped over to an outstretched hand and I caught sight of a shadow fluttering in a pane of the French doors. The driver had not left us entirely alone. I put on my quizzical face.

You could always tell when I did that. It was followed by a question and a thumb jerked over my shoulder.

"You going out for a spin with Wheelie soon, Mal?" I asked.

He frowned back and then laughed like the happy shoulder-clapping best friend he made everyone want to like. At first.

"A spin? You mean him? He's not a driver, Bill, he used to work on the bins, mun. Wheelie bins. Wheelie, see. Hear that, Wheelie? Billy boy, by here, thinks you're fucking Stirling Moss! I wouldn't trust Wheelie in a Robin Reliant, leave alone my Lexus. Mind you, he's quite useful in other ways. Handy, like, aren't you, Wheelie? Oi, go and close that door and fuck off, me and Billy here got some catching up to do."

The old retainer phlegmed a grumble to himself and the door was shut. I began to wonder about a drink. There were bottles and silver-chased ice buckets in a glass-fronted cabinet, and a gin and tonic might have rung a cerebral bell or two. But I mistook Maldwyn yet again. I always had. He just came to the point. "I didn't expect to see you here. Ever, if you know what I mean. Bran told me you'd want to see me and why. About that. But there's nothing I can do for you. Nothing."

I waited.

"And, yeah, Gwilym rang too. Not happy. Not happy at all. So I know all about that too, and the crap you're putting around about papers and deals. Which comes from her, and I don't have to tell you fuck all. But I will. To get it over with, see. And you out of my life. Again. Permanent, and I mean permanent, this time."

"So, tell me," I said.

"Tell you what, exactly, so we're crystal?"

"Tell me how and why a charitable trust, Tir Werin, is acquiring acres and acres of land above the Valleys. Tip spoil, iron and coal tumps, useless until decontaminated, I guess. But expensive, it seems. Twenty million pounds expensive, it seems."

"Gwil already told you. A state-of-the-art facility. For conferences. For research. For regeneration for fuck's sake. And tourism."

"Tourism?"

"Yeah! Get your head round it, right. What else d'you think can happen round here? Industry? Forget it. Have you seen the empty sheds – hangars more like – we got everywhere? And have you seen the buggers walking the streets, the ones that are left now? The smart ones have either gone, or work south of the motorway. Hi-tech here? Californian monkeys would do better. Tourism means using the only thing left once you've got through the streets and the shit to the mountains – a landscape! We can build beyond the valleys and let people come and stay in luxury. And provide jobs for those not too idle to do them."

"As what? To serve your made-over world?"

"Yes. To bloody well serve. As security, as waitresses, as cleaners, as gardeners, as cooks, as … what-the-fuck-ever. What's wrong with that? You tell me."

"Where's the money coming from, Mal?"

"You know, so don't give me that. It's all in the open. European money. Private money. Now or never. And it's got to be now."

"Direct to the trust?"

"Yes."

"Of which Ceri is the leading trustee and public face, and which Gwilym serves as Secretary, when he's not running his research outfit which fronts up, intellectual credibility and all that, for the trust. The same research park whose board you chair with Gwilym as your chief executive, so to speak."

"Yeah. So what?"

"And the money from Europe and elswhere goes to Tir Werin, so that the trust can buy this otherwise useless land. And the seller is Valleyscorp, isn't it Mal?"

"I'm no longer a director."

"I bet you aren't."

"Watch your mouth, Billy."

"Why? There's nothing wrong, is there? Nothing wrong with the bank statements that show you were buying this land, and more, for Valleyscorp over fifteen years ago. For tuppence, or less. That you made it over to Bran and Haf when the IT bubble burst and your holdings crashed and you needed to cash in your nest egg, I'd guess, one way or the other."

He was listening now. The silence was somehow more disruptive than intervention. I was running out of rope, and he knew it.

"You haven't got a clue, have you, pal. Not a fucking clue."

It was time to wait again.

"It's completely set to one side. I have no connections. Not with Valleyscorp, that was doing people a favour anyway, and not with Tir Werin, which is Gwilym and Ceri's vehicle to get some fucking thing done around here. And I don't even live with Bran anymore. As you know. I don't touch no money, see. Get it?"

He knew I didn't. Not yet, anyway. Besides, he didn't get what I really wanted. Maybe because I wasn't too sure about that myself. Not yet anyway. Suddenly, Maldwyn seemed emollient. He stood up. Six feet plus up with the same broad-shouldered, big-chested flat-stomached look and only a hint of a concession to flesh around his clean-shaven chin. Rugged, I think they call it.

"Come and see my garden. You'll like it."

And his eyes, as hazel and flecked as the boxer's, signalled an exit through the French doors. He didn't wait for an answering signal. The handle turned and he stepped out onto a flagstoned patio below which steps led to the garden. The dog was out and down first. Mal beckoned me on.

The rain had stopped, leaving that peculiar hillside tumble of slotted slate roofscape at its best. Its age glistened back to an early

71

promise and the sun was not too weak to hide the wrinkles, and strong enough to promise better. Fat chance, I thought, but then the unexpectedness of the garden swallowed me whole. From the first stone steps down from the patio's platform where the whole town lay before you, you stepped onto a lawn, springy, green and turfy, that cushioned you better than any carpet, and was longer and wider than most of the terraced houses. It was held in on three sides by mature shrubbery which at the far end gave way to a screen of trees, a copse almost, that hid the town and all its ways completely. You could sit on that lawn anytime for over a century and not see the labour that had secured its cultivation or hear, except as a murmur, the friction of any human traffic. You could play croquet on that square.

Mal could tell I was moved. He thought I was impressed.

"Nice, huh." he said.

"Whose was it?"

I knew the identikit ilk of the social group if not the singular identity of any previous owners. Coal mine managers. Town clerks. Solicitors. Publicans even. Provision merchants, wholesale and retail, for sure. Butchers. Bakers. Candlestick makers wouldn't give me a full set, but I had always been a spectator at that particular species of card game.

"Beynons," he said. And it was enough said. Suppliers of bread to a ravenous workaday town and its feeder villages, from handcarts up and down a valley that had burned its Victorian breeches quicker than a liberated Frankenstein, then buttoned them up tight with Edwardian respectability. The bread was moved from carts to vans, and then to shops. The bakehouses were very local and quite profitable before they were sold on to retail moguls who were more profitable than local in every way. The people who had sat on this lawn and smoked Craven A through ivory cigarette holders, with a whisky soda in the other hand, in the tinkling 1920s or the jarring '30s, knew London as Town, and school as somewhere away. They had better taste than Maldwyn, too, or, maybe they just interfered less and let what came naturally just naturally come.

We took a stroll through the copse. Me silent, him talking. This idyllic Eden on a dungheap did not end at the lawn's edge. More terraces of stone and grass, low walls and moss-pocked grey statuary, the usual simpering boys with flutes and attendant dogs, a white-limbed nymph, her marble pudendum discreetly draped. How many wistful adolescent glances had she had, I wondered? The live-in maids, yesteryear teenage girls from the terraced streets, would have been warmer, and dutifully accommodating. The garden fell away in a deceptive arrangement of formal shapes and undulating curves to a high wall, a wooden door and an embankment above the railway cutting. The town below us was back in sight and to the right lay the rugby ground's stand and field on the site of another one of the town's former collieries, a shaft more than a pit where my mother's father had worked. I had played on that field, above the seams in which he had clogged up his lungs with dust. Sentiment didn't even scratch it. I remembered him.

I had to turn Mal away from the trance of his own reverie. Prices. Bargains. Fools. Costs. Where he'd come from. His. Not anyone else's now. Where he was going. But the only dialogue he would understand would have to be confrontational.

"You'll need the transfers to be regular, then. Does she make them out to you, or one of your set-aside accounts?" I asked.

"You what?" he replied.

"As far as I can see the money goes into Tir Werin, then out via Gwilym as Secretary, with Ceri's approval and fixing of the patsies he's corralled, to Valleyscorp, aka Bran, and then, in dribs and drabs, somehow to you. Only Haf would now have to sign the cheques, too, wouldn't she? So why shouldn't she? Or, put in another way, why should Bran pass it on to you if the great divide is as divisive as you suggested?"

"Fuck off" was his not unexpected explanation. I tried another route.

"I've come to meet Haf; she wants to see me. But no one seems to know exactly where she is and she's not on anyone's call list. I only know about all this other stuff because she provided a paper trail. It's no big deal to me to see where that leads. Only her."

"Why?"

I knew he could answer that himself. I waited again.

"You think she may be your fuckin' daughter, don't you? Well, maybe she's mine, eh?"

"Right," I said.

"And wrong, butty. D'you think you and me were the only ones dipping the wick in that honey pot?"

I bridled. He noticed.

"Oh, OK, you were in residence – sort of, as I recall. But there's other possibilities beyond you and me."

"Such as?"

"All I'm saying is that when Bran and I split, or were going to split cos it wasn't getting any better, she told *me* it was you and she told Haf it wasn't me. And you know what, I don't fucking know, or care."

Mal stopped and stood right in my path, right in front of my face. His voice was dry and contemptuous. He said,

"That's why I threw Bran over. Know what I mean? That's why Haf stayed here. See? And what's it to you anyway? You left, remember?"

Mal turned. My time was over it seemed. Again. I put my hand on his shoulder. Heavily. I pulled him back. He made no move to take my hand away. Mal had controlled things, all things in his path, for too long. I took the hand away. Mal said what Mal thought.

"Don't be stupid. You've pissed me off enough."

I said that enough was nowhere near enough and that I would hurt him before I was finished. I said he was one of life's jerry-builders, and a bastard with it, and that I would pull him down. Mal grinned. He said, "A bastard," and, liking the sound of it, repeated it in a whisper to himself. I saw Wheelie at the top of the steps, clutching what may once have been a pit mandrel but was now only a baseball bat.

"I'll see myself out," I said and walked to the bottom garden gate, hoping an unlocked door would save me any grief. Probably very personalised grief. I lifted the iron latch and turned an iron hoop and went out onto the cinder embankment path. I followed it to the railway bridge, then left the path, crossed above the line and headed back into the town. It was time for that drink Mal hadn't given me.

* * * * *

Once upon a time there were more pubs in this town than the buttons on a collier's *coppish*; that's a fly to anyone born before 1960 and a zip to the rest of the world. Me and the dead respected the fashion of fumble. But the buttons had gone from trousers as sure as the pubs from the streets. The Full Moon had waned and The Rising Sun no longer brightened anyone's day. I noticed the council office had abandoned their stand-out 1930s modernity in favour of a re-fit as a cavernous ocean liner's bar-lounge, all shiny tables and chairs and brass-railed mini decks, one which had no doubt sailed into every small town. That was one voyage I would avoid then. But I did need a settling drink.

My head no longer throbbed like a cold diesel engine. My stomach had assumed the role of chief bodily victim. I decided to punish it some more. The rugby ground had once been the pulse, heart and, yes, the strained bowels of the place. I went there. A few cars in front of the clubhouse. The only faces I knew were on the walls, in black and white rows. I was amongst them. So were Tommy and Lionel. The bar had fizzy lager and frothy beer. I had a pint of Guinness and took it outside to the field. A steep concrete stand with plastic flip-up seats on one side, an open-sided shed over the stepped terraces opposite, two posts and a field. A visual cliché, of course. But what turned the truism into its own heart-stopping truth was the setting. From the stand you could take it all in at once, and behind the shed were the street-lined slopes of a town with more guts than sense and more passion in its life than almost anywhere else I'd ever been. Urbane it was not. But it summed up urban as a smack in the mouth to any country boy. Directly to the north the hills opened up to the higher mountains courtesy of a gap so narrow they almost folded over, one into the other. And every few minutes a train measured the distances in-between consecutive townships with that regularity of unstoppable motion which such places had once assumed as their rightful destiny. Only, the motivation to match the punctuality had been mislaid. It was all wound down.

On the field I saw ghosts. On the terraces I glimpsed shadows. My ears boomed with the bass rumble of crowd noise, the smack of boots on ball, the slap or even crack of hands and fists on faces and legs. The stout I was sipping was as black and icy-cold as my soul felt. I didn't have a matching heart anymore. Mal was right: what the hell did I care? What the hell did I want, coming back like this? Or maybe just what the hell? I needed another pint. My stomach stopped complaining so we went together in search of another afternoon of induced quiescence.

I did the damage in a quiet corner of the upstairs bar of a workingmen's club that had somehow survived into the new century. There was no one to bother me as I read the newspapers accumulated on the speckled yellow, blue and red Formica tables.

Formica had been posh, the latest trend when I was growing up. That and green leatherette banquettes. They still had those too, and they still had the Ronettes on the jukebox. Nobody tried to talk to me. I ate a ham roll to see if the bread was still like pap and the meat a slick of piggy plastic. Tasted good to me. I had another to try to fool the alcohol. No fooling. I walked to where the river had once encircled the town's early ironworks and the covered-in canal had once sent the barges to the sea.

At the Old Bridge I took in, as if for the first time, that unity of hills and river which the makers of this town had managed to disassemble with every unplanned decision they had ever taken. The late afternoon light was being pin- pricked by car headlamps. I hoped my last intended watering hole would not have been dried up by the dessication of fashion and youth. I needn't have worried. The squat stone drinking den was intact and, though spotlessly clean and daily swabbed, its interior was as it had looked for half a century. No music. No distractions, and an outside urinal whose basic floor and lime-washed walls would have made a Frenchman blush.

I sat on a wooden chair at a polished wood-and-iron rectangular table which was set beneath a mirror proclaiming Dewar's whisky, and with the insignia VR. I don't think the old girl had ever made it here. It had been a second home to my old man. I stayed as the lights went on against the fading afternoon, and silent drinkers drifted in and out. The rain was spattering against the windows again. It was drumming inside me, too, a persistent beat of melancholy and uncertainty which the booze had only helped dig deeper. When the barmaid began to give me a wondering glance just once too often for me to be misguided enough to consider it as admiration, I decided to move.

I saw them at the pub's corner, idling in the gloom, as I walked past them, but I only sensed their threat an instant before I felt the first blow to the head. Something wooden and weighty had opened up my skull. Baseball bats were far too universal these days. I went down into a loose slurry of small stones and gravel besides a row of empty steel barrels. I reached for the lip of one of them to get to my knees, but I never made it. A steel-capped boot to my arse took me down hard and another pain of sorts drove into my ribs and beat a tattoo on either side with a drum roll follow-up to the head. I was being worked over by boys who knew an established routine, didn't deviate from it and didn't care about leaving a mark and the occasional fracture or broken bone. I vomited the day's pleasure onto a boot and was rewarded for my thoughtfulness with another kicking. The drink had been a temporary anaesthetic but the pain that surged through me was like shards of bone splintering and tearing into flesh. Those were my bones. That was my flesh. My eyes felt as if they were popping inside out and burning up like funeral pyres. Only my ears still seemed attuned to whatever my body was about to leave behind. And they heard a different kind of noise to the rhythm of boots. A shout. A voice. One I knew. Insistent and quiet as it delivered its own message to Maldwyn's messengers:

"That's enough. Leave him be. Fuck off. Go on. Now, I said."

Tommy.

* * * * *

Billy's old man said that "Sweet Dreams" was a lie fed to children. So he was brought up on memories. Sometimes the old man would call them history. Most of it wasn't in any book. Daydreams, he would say, were the narcolepsy of those who drifted through lives too feeble for roots. He taught all this, sourly and as best he could, in and out of classrooms. It was his wisdom, from his experience. Only it didn't connect. And when it did, when a generation appeared to come awake, and finally act, then he was curtly dismissive, in ways that could be both incomprehensible and hurtful.

* * * * *

His old man understood the eager impulse to act. To understand was not to approve. He said it was self-indulgence. He called it social gratification. He thought it was a political wank. He'd say that ignominy was seeking refuge in ignorance. He talked like that. It made it all the harder to pay him any attention any longer. When he was not angry he seemed almost sorry for it all, that it had come to this thrashing about, the lies of rhetoric fuelling the necessary expression of bravery. The way he talked was the way he thought.

* * * * *

His old man would nonetheless turn out of bed with him in the murk of a wintry dawn as the strike's buzzsaw activity lengthened. They would join small nodes of men gathering into guerrilla squads to trudge over mountain roads into other valleys to bypass police blockades, and swoop to picket and push and shove. The old man would begin to argue that to compromise was not to surrender, only to be told to shut the fuck up. Billy would move away from him, using his camera as an excuse, using its viewfinder to find faces, locate gestures, swim amongst the sea of expectation that swirled around platforms of oratory where Arthur Scargill eerily referred to himself in the third person, and to them as if their individual lives had been melded together with his. Perhaps, finally, they had. By his Presidential decree. Images began to define events. But not, ever, for the old man.

* * * * *

His old man cadged a lift from Billy to Paynter's funeral in Golders Green just before the bone chilling cold Christmas of that year. Billy walked with him from the packed car park. At seventy, the old man was stooping a bit now. They walked through a dank late-morning gloom, past incongruous evergreens and dripping shrubbery, towards the crematorium. The old man had nodded to those he knew, acquaintances and former students, comrades he would have said once, all come to acknowledge the deceased eighty-year-old who had once had his teeth smashed out in police cells, couriered Russian gold through Nazi Germany, served as a political commissar in Spain, saw people killed there by decree, maybe even approved of it, and later through various modes of compromise led his union tightly and well. A proper leader, his old man would snarl, not a narcissistic Boy Scout. Billy had seen Will Paynter once, in his retirement, shoulder to shoulder with the old man. Same height, short, and his breadth wide, and his temperament stubborn. Billy had photographed them, never seeing hero-worship in the old man's eyes before. The camera failed to capture it.

* * * * *

His old man had winced and drifted when Billy stood off the path to snap the bareheaded, dark-suited men who walked up in clusters to the crematorium. Some old timers. Current leaders and officials, of a later time and different ilk. Like a family that was cold shouldering itself. Scargill at the centre of a bristling group. Greeted and shunned. Billy clicked. The old man was one of those to be called to speak. The NUM President would have to listen, standing at the back. The old man had been measured about the life, but icy as to its meaning. When the old man mentioned the General Strike and Lockout of 1926 it was not a banner to be waved but a shiver to be suffered. Resilience was always limited, he said. A union was not to be tested to destruction, he said. There was never one last punch to deliver. The President was grim and scornful but the family quarrel was open from then on.

* * * * *

His old man had predicted the way sense would finally be seen. He refused to give Ceri any credit for seeing it. For him that particular recanting had come too late and was as calculated, if self-interest allied to emotion was any kind of forethought, as the earlier embrace of madcap confrontation. For Ceri, he felt, this was yet another tack towards a career of contrariness, of the forthright that was a masquerade, of a transparency that was draped in shrouds of meaninglessness. It was an emptiness, a vacuum, filled only by an estimation of himself in which his own time had betrayed him despite his own best efforts. The old man said this was not, strictly speaking, the opportunism of a careerist; it was more the retreat of an integrity that could not be sustained in individuals when collective aspirations dwindled. There was less and less to be representative about more and more of the time.

* * * * *

His old man was big on generations. Billy's was to be forgiven for its callowness. No choice there. But despised for its parasitical attachment to romanticised others. Utilisation of past experience masked as youthful altruism. The patterns could be seen even then. Gwilym, the railwayman's boy, a PhD underway, one envious eye on Bran, already lecturing, available for blithe comment on TV and radio on "Our People's History". The old man spat at that. Maldwyn, electronics and engineering a genetic inheritance from a colliery electrician father, convinced and convincing that communications technology could democratise everything. Advising Ceri on the logistics of maps, communications and picketing raids. Bran already subbing for newspapers, readily welcomed into inner circles for her evident sympathy as much as her good looks, soon receiving exclusives and scoops and contacts denied others, and parlayed into TV pieces to camera. Billy, with his camera never out of his hand now, exhausted by the pace of things and the unrelenting tirades of his old man.

* * * * *

His old man had never liked cameras. Or so he said. He certainly never owned one, or borrowed one, or used one. He bought one for Billy when the boy was sixteen, out of an act of misplaced generosity, as he wrote on the card. Not so much a card, more a page torn from his sketch pad with a contrite fatherly face drawn in by the same hand which had endlessly drawn Billy's mother. The sketches lay in a drawer, not forgotten but not looked at either. Billy preferred the few snapshots and the couple of studio portraits taken of her as a schoolgirl, looking demure and solemn. She smiled in the curling, fading snaps. At a desk, mussing up her pigtails, in a ruched costume by the sea, a face at the back in a garden, at the front on a protest march. His old man was in that one too. But his old man never took any photographs of the woman who had died giving birth to his son.

* * * * *

His old man said photographs were false prompts. They made the memory stutter out one particular instant which blocked all others. These were the fixed images which surfaced to hint at but not reveal the depth of a life. His son hated him for claiming to know all that. For Billy there were only such images of her, and they were few. They kept no family albums, no shrunken memorials. The old man pointed out that those keepsakes only captured what was meant to be happy or celebratory so, in their want of the ineffable melancholy of life, they betrayed twice over. For being what they were and for only showing the need of the perpetrator. The soul of the captured was never made captive. It only lived on in the mind. In memory.

* * * * *

His old man favoured painting when it probed the relationship of culture to nature. The camera could document and catalogue but its transposition always threatened to be the residual sentiment of nostalgia. When Billy grew old enough to argue he would counter with the works of the great mid-century masters. Magazines and books yielded their fruit to the boy and the old man had to agree that their cut-outs of wars and streets and industrial grind and resistance to it evaded the glib and the condescending. But he still insisted it was the subject that gave the work its substance, not what they had done with it. It was, he'd say, as if only the emotional spasm Bevan had once ridiculed had been revealed, but not the intellectual star-tapping which the Tredegar dreamer had wanted for us.

* * * * *

His old man said that the nouns "artist" and "poseur" were synonyms. Both paradoxically concerned with removing the self in the very act of observation only to show how self-consciously it had been done. For him the vantage and the viewed were inseparable. His riff was that all life was memory even as it was experienced, there and instantly gone, so that we forever lived in the past, even as it left us. We lived on by imagining that past which was the future we yearned to remember. The dream of life was aspiration. Its nightmare was memorialisation. We trapped ourselves in the techno-present by the cloying memento mori that was the falsification that photography bought. Memory, which was History, was a jumble of relationships to be savoured, not a grid of relatives to be connected.

* * * * *

His old man fed the boy scraps about his past as if he was a hungry and insistent dog. Bit by bit. A piece at a time. His mother's grandparents built up the picture of their daughter for him, but it came as coloured shards of a sacred window, so that he glimpsed the child and schoolgirl and trainee teacher only through their blinded eyes. "Good people," his old man would say when Billy came back from visits there, to his own more pared-down home life, set amidst the old man's canvases, brushes, easels and the lingering smell of gooey oils. They had died, young, in their sixties, the one after the other as if arranged. Billy grieved, just like a dog. And asked more about what he didn't know, his teenager feistiness setting up confrontations which the old man diverted with trivia whenever he could.

* * * * *

His old man explained his own being alone in this way. He said his mother had tied him to a high chair when he was barely three years old and fed him, and then walked away. He was in a scullery kitchen. It must have been evening because it was next day that he had been found, his wrists chafed red, tear-streaked and piss-smelly with shit squashed beneath him on the chair seat. He had been given to a relative, his mother's older sister, to bring up and never saw his mother again. His given name was David. Maddox had been her maiden name. She had been a maid, the old man said. In a Big House. It was just after the first Great War. She was unmarried. The old man said he didn't know, for certain, who his father was and that, anyway, at the time of his abandonment the man was dead.

* * * * *

His old man said you could divide life by decades or by smells and tastes. That these vanished along with fashion in clothes or music or speech, but that they were ever loitering, ready to call up a whole time. More than a tired phrase like the "Interwar Years", he said. That was just boxing things for the left luggage room of historical convenience, he said. He said the '20s, for him, smelled of damp and decaying plaster as water seeped through a tiny back bedroom and the sour smell of the lumpy bed he shared with his "Aunty's" three sons. It tasted of cold dripping and sweet, mashed-over tea. The '30s was the acrid smell of cigarettes and the bitter-sweet taste of Fry's Five Boys chocolate bars, and the mingled stink and taste of underground workings in deep collieries where horse manure and fetid air penetrated mouth and nostrils, and his young bones ached day and night, and his muscles tightened and swelled. He had escaped that, and with it the slaughterhouse of South Wales, in factory work elsewhere. The '40s was the taste of fear in the mouth and the smell of burned flesh filtered into human acceptance by the numb of alcohol, and indifference once the killing and the horror was made routine. The '50s, he said, was the last time he knew these things distinctly, and that what he felt for too short a while was newness and happiness, and the taste was of my mother's lips.

* * * * *

His old man was constantly against the grain in all things. He loved to smoke. Usually untipped Players or Capstan Full Strength which came in weirdly effete, mauve-tinted packets. If he had lived beyond the mid-1980s he would have scorned the huddle of fellow conspirators in the fug of a den for their designated dirty habit. For him the addiction, for such it was, was also a ceremony, for such he made it. The old push-up packs with their frisson of silver foil just covering up the plump white paper rolls of tobacco. The spurt and flare from a struck match. The rich field tang of burning leaf. The wispy curlicues of blue metal smoke. And sharing. Billy had been with him once in a crowded bar full of colliers at the start of Miners' fortnight, two weeks of caravans and sand and beer to come, with cigarettes flung the one to the other as individual packets were opened up for all. There were men, the old man told him, who brought the habit home from what was then not a distant war. Then they more often than not shared a match and a fag passed on from one battle-dressed baby-faced veteran to another. If it was the warmth of glamour, no less was it the attitude of bravado.

* * * * *

His old man claimed to have met Burt Lancaster. The actor, he said, was not then either a star or indeed an actor. He was a circus performer enlisted into the US Army to divert and entertain the raw troops, mud-soaked and bombarded to a standstill outside

Monte Cassino in 1944. Everyone "knew" Burt Lancaster by the time the old man asserted his own former friendship. He told his adult students how *The Crimson Pirate*, in 1952, was a deliberate riposte to McCarthyite witch-hunts, with the Red Flag waved in the philistine face of Middle America. And what else was *The Flame and the Arrow* in 1954 if not an assertion of the New Deal which had sustained the young Burton Lancaster in the '30s? The old man met scepticism head-on with an account of getting smashed on rough red vino with the tumbler and hand-springer from East Harlem who'd got a mental and physical education in a settlement home no different from the miners' institutes that had once added intellectual juice and social cohesion to the Valleys. No one quite believed the old man on this.

* * * * *

His old man thought the War might change everything and for a time he thought that it felt as if it had, or would yet. He had returned, on a late demob via Austria after North Africa and the slog up through Italy, to work in the pits again. Nationalised if not socialised, he'd say. It was another front line. Welfare was to be the first step, not the last, welcome public ownership and necessary social care only marking time, but signalling what was to be next. He lived in the front room of an overcrowded house and paid rent to the family. Everything was limited. Beds were shared as readily as scarce pint glasses were fought over, to be filled as they were emptied. For a few, brief years before the 1950s the sense of unfulfilment and possibility irked and sustained them. Underground, men wore army berets instead of the new safety helmets. Nights, if he worked days, were indiscriminately passed between pubs and pictures and political wrangling. If he worked nights he slept days. He grew weary. He was single and coiled with anger. A chance remark made underground took him to a WEA session and to the opening of things up or, at least, an ordering of their otherwise confusion. He was never sure that was progress. But he met the boy's mother, Mona, in Coronation year and she decided self-improvement in order to help others was to be his lot. He could never release his memory of her into any forgiving of himself for her dying.

* * * * *

His old man had been to Spain before package holidays. He said he'd gone as a fellow traveller, and grinned, with the alibi of art-history research as excuse for the stuffed money belt he'd worn for the Party. It was always the only Party, even when he stopped working and voting for it. Mona had fretted but gone with him. Was it there, Billy would wonder, that he was conceived in 1957? Bill Paynter himself, now the president in South Wales, had gripped the old man's hand and asked him to go. The old man said you could never forget Paynter's handshake nor his unrelenting eyes. No forgiveness in them. Not for himself anyway. His own first wife had died in childbirth, in 1940, leaving the young revolutionary with twins to raise.

* * * * *

His old man had thought of Ceri as a son until he considered him to be yet another prodigal. Early on, joining the old man's class he was soon, by calculated choice, attached to an older generation as an acolyte. And so perfectly positioned to link generations, though cannily dismissive of his own contemporaries when it mattered. A potential leader. The working-class hero he would fashion himself into, both for himself and for the needs of others, in the 1970s. By then the leather jacket and rolled Brylceemed quiff had given way to a more class-universal garb, one that was more suburban Rolling Stones than subterranean rock 'n' roll. Either way, whether on his home patch or further afield, Ceri, with his easy, self-assured manner and gentle, yet chiding, malice, offered himself as knowable and serious and exotic and welcoming, open to a future that embraced change, not as tribal as the more common ingrowing political follicle. One like the old man soon seemed to be. Ceri would hug you close and clap you to his confidence. He was difficult to resist. The act was no act, the authenticity was sincere, and not to believe in him was to show a lack of faith in the purpose. And in the old man's weekend schools Ceri gathered others to him like a cultural pilotfish guiding a shoal. In his prime Ceri, now with a craggy face more hewn than sculpted, more planed by intent than moulded by experience, became, in the unofficial guerilla strikes that lit up his special sky, almost the physical embodiment of the Idea others had configured. Men, at this time, admired him and wanted his friendship, and women generally just wanted to fuck him. He generally just obliged.

* * * * *

His old man could hold harsh opinions. He would say that his protégé, Ceri, was a music hall act who came to believe in the propaganda of applause. His old man had been a connoisseur of variety acts and a regular to the variety theatre in its last golden post-war flush. He'd sit through the trick unicyclist, the songbird imitator, the Irish tenor, the check-suited northern comics, the exotic fan dancer, the Hungarian acrobats from Glasgow, the sopranos, crooners and dancers and the dress-suited compères. He claimed to love to read the safety curtain, a kind of commercial Mondrian he'd say, marked out from right to left and top to bottom with squares and rectangles of colour within which haberdashers and hairdressers and animal feed and furnishings and ladies' corsets and liver salts and linoleum and hire purchase and soap and newspapers, all declared their worth and wares. The finale would inevitably be a double act to follow the saccharine warble of Ruby Murray or Joan Regan or the buck-toothed hoofing of Billy Dainty. The old man loved the banter, Socratic dialectic he'd say, between Jewell and Warris or the young Morecambe and Wise. The last two names Billy recognised from television. He doubted the old man had seen them live on stage any more than he'd met Nick Cravat or Burt Lancaster in a mess tent in the drear of an Italian wartime winter. His old man, he thought by the mid-1970s, was full of bullshit.

* * * * *

His old man was not yet sixty when the coal strikes of 1972 and then 1974 derailed any lingering complacency about industrial accommodation. He thought the NUM's own double act of Gormley and Daley had schemed and organised to a tactical perfection and with a moral beatitude that knew its own origins. After those deceiving moments had passed he increasingly railed, and despaired. Nobody heeded. He told Billy, whenever he came home these days, that somehow, somewhere along the line, we'd become a cultural *nomenklatura* parasitic on our own half-dazed working-out of our past or else, like Tommy, just endlessly turned and turned around, with any semblance or aim of self-direction long since lost or repressed. Easy meat for the *nomenklatura*. The old man liked Tommy, so the despair worked in deeper and deeper when Ceri led the charge into 1984, and Billy's generation jumped to offer its support. To be inside, really inside Tommy's head, he'd rage, you'd need a blowtorch, a chisel, a pair of tweezers and an advanced degree in Victim Studies.

* * * * *

His old man told him we'd swallowed our own shit and mistaken it for nutrient. He was good at upsetting people. He told Ceri at Paynter's funeral that the strike had become an orgasmic shudder orchestrated by the pimps of history, himself included. A generation of wannabes actually wanted this release from stasis into an oblivion that would eventually engulf not them but the Tommys and the Lionels who'd tasted the saltiness of being, again, in the collective frame. Except that it was only the glycerine slick of temporary notoriety for them, the stage army. And for Billy, Bran, Maldwyn and Gwilym there was, at last, the longed-for generational credibility and, of course, whatever happened, having for themselves the bonus of not being personally doomed thereafter. On the contrary, his old man said, the dreamers would perish and the doers would profit. And it was clear who he meant and why. He railed but did not convince.

* * * * *

His old man shocked them all – Billy, Bran, Gwilym and Mal – one day by telling them he did not believe in any of it anymore, especially not in their activity in the strike, and even in any struggle that was defined as they defined it. He told them that the moment had passed. He told them, again, of what Bevan had said in 1951, when the moment was still there to seize: that even in the '30s, with three million out of work and ingrained poverty everywhere, they couldn't guarantee majorities for Labour even in the worst hit areas, that building socialism was not about pressing buttons. They argued. The old man was silent. Then he said that, once, when he was eleven years old, in the lockout of 1926, he followed a group of boys down a back lane where, it was said, they would all see something, but only if they had a halfpenny or two farthings or a cigarette butt. At the back garden gate of a terraced house whose steep garden ran up to the steps that led up again to the home itself, there was a queue and an older boy who was taking the coins and dropping them into a tin. The old man said the boy's name was Byron Keys and that his father had been imprisoned for riotous assembly. Stoning blacklegs. That the Keys family were ardent and active members of the Party. That the payees lined up and went in up the garden path, past the wilting rhubarb and the scruffy blackcurrant bushes to the paint-flaked wooden door of an outside lavatory. Each one, in their turn, had to lift the latch and go inside and look and turn and come out. For a halfpenny you could look at Byron's ten-year-old sister, Ginny, sitting on the seat with her knickers round her ankles. His old man said that if they didn't get the point, his own point was well made.

* * * * *

His old man said they acted like participants but were, in reality, avid consumers. He made it worse when he called them parasites. He broadened the definition to include himself, to make the insult seem lighter. It didn't. He tried to explain that he, too, had gone from being inside it all to being – he searched for the correct instance – like Sam Spade in *The Maltese Falcon* when his partner, whose wife he was banging as well, stumbled around in the dark looking, not for clues as he pretended to think, but for excuses for his behaviour, an *Übermensch* of consciousness, with the world he inhabited slipping away without him, which was what, here was the most terrible thing, the very thing he wanted. See? the old man would exclaim. See? More as if it was a statement than a question. All they saw was an old man in delirium and all they heard was a rant against the seriousness which they needed to invest the fun they were having with the ballast of other people's gravity.

* * * * *

His old man didn't live long enough afterwards to witness the successive falls from grace. He had stood on the embankment when the last stand-out colliery workers walked back in behind the thump of a drum and the dirge of a plaintive brass band before dawn on a March day. He watched a more circumspect Billy move in and out and around and from the back of the straggled line, taking pictures. He knew there would be no easy routes mapped out from now on. They'd run off the maps of a known and once cherished world. The dynamics of action had been replaced by the melancholia of that loss. The pits were morphing into mausoleums. Billy looked closer at the assumptions behind his own feverish images and found any traces of the real had gone, or else were just lingering as accusatory, shadowy presences. That last march had been one final act of public exposure before the shades of anonymity closed in.

* * * * *

His old man spent his last autumn and winter in reflection. He wondered how that history which had now left us could be properly remembered. He decided that lists and structured narratives were another species of lie. That the simultaneity of any actual life was what gave it value and so any flattening or compartmentalisation was as much of a subsequent denial of the humanness of living as, in life, was the denial of the interconnectedness of desire. He said that the art of self-perception, in our common life, had been smothered by the perception of ourselves by others, and to which embrace we had too readily succumbed. You would need new forms, fresh categories, a deliberate breaking of the neck of convention wherever it sought to inhibit full expressiveness. Just as the history had been lived. You couldn't do the tragedy bit without it seeping, or even racing headlong, into melodrama. You'd need comedy, black and ironic, to keep it sane, and the surreal to prevent the historic and the epic being registered as romance. Increasingly, he was sure that painting alone, or other types of fine art, provided a field of vision that allowed the otherwise ungraspability of the world to be confronted. At its best, painting was intellect suffused with emotion, working colour and form, beyond the shamanism of music, the pretence of words, the smash and grab in the jewellery window that was the best photography. The old man wrote to Billy to tell him that the adage "show" not "tell" was for adolescents, and that we had all grown up. He said how could you "show" anymore, other than in the gabble of a nursery class seeing everything new for the first time, if what was truly there to be shown now necessarily resided in the act of telling. That the one big thing to hold onto in our ruins was the consciousness of ourselves, not just what had been experienced but how it had been perceived, imagined not only felt. His son had left by then and he was dead when Billy had the last letter.

* * * * *

His old man had once told him that there were no photographs of Crazy Horse. The Oglala Sioux war chief had been assassinated in 1877 one year after the Plains Wars had effectively ended with the pyrrhic victory over Custer at the Little Big Horn. A former ally, the Sioux warrior Little Big Man, had pinned his arms back and a soldier had bayoneted him in a guard house. It was predestined but it was also planned. The other chiefs, the strategic Red Cloud, his enemy, and the indomitable Sitting Bull, his friend, posed for and were captured by the lens, and the names of all of them had been stolen and corrupted into English, even that of Tashunca-Uitco, which properly means His Horse is Crazy. But the face, the body, and therefore mostly the spirit, of course, of Crazy Horse were never taken by whites. Only an Indian pictograph shows us Crazy

Horse. He made sure that what was to tell about him would remain simple, true and ultimately unknowable. His friends wrapped his body in a red blanket and took it with them out onto the prairie, and carried it about with them as they travelled, until they buried the body of Crazy Horse weeks later, in secret and with no traceable marker. They called themselves not Sioux but Lakota, an alliance of comrades.

* * * * *

His old man submitted to one last photograph. It was of his clasped hands. The veins were bunched and somehow pulsing, even in their stillness. There were black, raised blobs of oil paint flecking his knuckles and staining his nails. The fingers were twined, suggesting a prayer. He never said prayers. They were, for all that, the hands of a maker, and of one who had dreamed. Billy would use the photograph as the centrepiece of an exhibition. It came as a shock, since no one had seen the images on which he had begun to concentrate in the dog days of the strike and its sour aftermath. He had no appetite to home in on grief and misery, or even despair and anger. The earlier photographs which had suddenly brought professional recognition and fleeting fame, those faces featuring defiance, rage, bravery, resolution, unity, exultation, the gestures of speaking and listening through all the true joyfulness of what was, in the end, a false and fake scenario, none of those could suffice now, even as negatives. The old man had warned of the vacuous drudgery and drift that was to be the fate of those with no boltholes left to find. Billy surveyed those inhabiting the ruins and instead picked up the bits and pieces left, the segments that told of their fracture. He shot backs. He blew up fists. He took away the support of arms and legs and just left the torsos. He cast down at feet. He pinpointed an eye or two. He showed mouths shut. He closed off the things and cropped the people that had whispered and shouted, and let the ears remain deaf to further entreaty. The photographs he made were a piled-up detritus of humanity. A tangle of hair. A sullen neck. An arthritic knee. A discarded banner. A child's extended arm. An empty seat. A wiped brow. And hands, hands, hands. Fluttering, open-palmed and waiting, held together and praying. Something had fled. Had drained away. Something had been beheaded. Something had been killed. He called the exhibition, and the book of it he made, "No Photographs of Crazy Horse". And when it was finished, he said goodbye to the old man and left. He never saw him again. He carried him inside himself, and would now forever.

* * * * *

Tommy told me I'd slept. On and off. For almost three days. That Lionel had remembered how he'd once been a St John's Ambulanceman – a uniform, a peak cap and International tickets – and had strapped up my ribs. Only thing to do for them, apparently. They'd used Dettol to clean out the cuts. All they had in the house. I'd screamed. And cotton bud tips to swab out my broken nose. They used a lot of those. Tommy didn't like to have wax in his ears. They stayed cleaned. The nose had to stay broken. But that wasn't the first time it had been flattened, they laughed. Then they'd washed me, stuffed me into pyjamas. Old-fashioned wincyette. The jacket had big white buttons and the trousers a drawstring like a small rope. Blue convict stripes all over. Baggy but comfy, said Lionel. They had rammed aspirin down me and later, Tommy said, with a wink, what he called "specials". Painkillers. I told Tommy killers weren't what they used to be. Tommy told me to shut up and be grateful. Then they left for work.

I lay back on an ivory-coloured leather couch with wrinkles as big and rifted as elephant hide. They said that after they found and rescued me they'd carried me here. Tommy's house. They told me it wasn't far and they were strong. So not to worry. It was now mid-morning, according to the alarm clock ticking away with no respect for its surroundings. It sat on a shiny mahogany-laminate mantelpiece above a stone-façade fireplace, all dimpled surface and coloured pastels, baby blue, blusher pink and a woozy pearl grey. The room was a knock-through from front door and white PVC window to artexed walls and ceiling and Goldilocks pine table and chairs, and a scullery that had grown into a kitchenette. It was functionally modernised with dishwasher, humming fridge and ceramic sink in white with chrome mixer taps. The framed pictures on the wall were photographs of rugby players – team photographs season by season, the rows stood behind one another, with the front tier sat on a bench as the club's whole squad assembled pre- or

97

post-season. I was in one or two of those, a sliver between the two behemoths who were my minders. I was duly grateful. Then and now. Above the clock and the mantelpiece was an enlarged portrait, tinted and soft-focussed head and shoulders of a woman with big, frizzy chestnut brown hair, a scatter of freckles, a shy smile made warmer by eyes that looked right at you, and the neckline of a 1970s cheesecloth peasant blouse with teasing drawstring. Norma. Nice Norma. Dead Norma. Tommy's wife.

I swung my feet off the elephant hide onto a wall-to-wall, off-white shagpile that had seen better days. From a sitting position I could see the fronts of houses above their stepped gardens. When I stood up I could see the pavement, road and river. I knew where I was. A few hundred yards down from the car park where I'd been smashed up. If I squinted I could see the humped stone arch of the Old Bridge spanning the river, and the adjacent modern road crossing. Modern being only a century and more away. I sat down again with a necessary suddenness. My head was expanding and contracting like a tango player's bandoneón. A concertina would have been more acceptable. I felt my face, all bristle and grunge. They hadn't bothered to shave me. Understandable. I fingered the broad part of my nose between index and thumb. Yeah, broader than I remembered it. And sorer too. My mouth tasted of fur and bile, clogged up and clingy at the same time. I decided to go back to sleep. It was an easy decision to make.

When I woke next it was to the chimes of 'Ghost Riders in the Sky'. The yippee-ay-yey bit. Only electronic and insistent, so I knew I wasn't dreaming. I could see a small shape on the other side of the frosted glass of the front door. The bell stopped but the image still shimmered through the double-glazed distortion. I was in no mood for apparitions. I stumbled towards the door and fiddled with the lock and catch before wrenching it open into the half-light of a drizzly afternoon. The figure in the doorway tilted her head in a mock-quizzical way. She asked if she could come in. To see how I was. As if she couldn't see that already. I held the door ajar and she stepped inside in front of me. I staggered back to the elephant's graveyard and slumped back down. Bran smiled as I looked up at her.

She had had her hair done so that it framed and softened her face and belled out in a thickly-cut sway above her neck. She didn't sit down so I looked up from her feet, in black and red peep-toe court shoes with a higher heel than you'd expect, to her knees – one bigger than the other I knew – just on show below a short, wheaten-white, belted wool coat.

"D'you still like what you see?"

I tried not to grunt and not to think of the strawberry birthmark on the left cheek of her arse. She loosened the belt and took the coat off, folded it on a chair. Her dress was rust-orange. Linen. Just above the knee. Sleeveless. It fitted and suited. Of course. I shuffled a bit on the Babar couch, partly to ease my pain. I sighed. Not this, I thought. Yes, this, I hoped.

"How'd you know I was here?"

"Chance. Or, sort of chance. I needed some work doing. I rang Tommy. Usually do. He told me you were here. What had happened. I'm sorry."

"Me too."

"You look terrible."

"Feel it."

"Can I do something? Shave? Wash? Toothpaste? Coffee?"

"Can't think of a thing I need," I said.

"Oh?"

I employed the silent trick technique I had perfected in the days when I had once been as intent on pleasuring as on being pleasured. To avoid Rise, Decline, and inevitable Fall, I closed my eyes and Conjugated.

Amo. And meant it.

Amas. And once you did.

Amat. He may still.

Amamus. We were once anyway.

Amatis. Anyone you wanted.

Amant. Our Present. From a Past. Without a Future.

And then the whole imperfect, perfect, and pluperfect knowledge.

Amabam, amabas, amabat, amabamus, amabatis, amabant.

Amavi, amavisti, amavit, amavimus, amavistis and *amaverunt.*

Amaveram, amaveras, amaverat, amaveramus, amaveratis, until *amaverant.*

I opened my eyes. She was still there. I knew she knew no Latin but, as ever, Bran was in no hurry. She decided we needed coffee and she needed a visit to the bathroom while the kettle boiled. She could see the kettle and the coffee in the kitchen and walked in to switch it on, but she didn't need to ask where the bathroom was. She went straight upstairs on the internal wooden staircase to my left. I watched her come back down in a cloud of certainty. I would not be hers to use again. The coffee came in white porcelain mugs covered with the blue of a forget-me-not pattern courtesy of the National Trust. Or so it said on the bottom. That Tommy never failed to surprise.

"Instant OK?" she asked.

Too late now, I thought, as I sipped the scalding hot gravy mix spooned from the industrial size instant coffee tin that was more in keeping with Tommy the builder than the mugs someone had bought for him, but I said:

"Yeah – fine. So, tell me again, what brings you here?"

She gave me a smile so coy she must have employed it last in nursery school. She was perched on the edge of a matching chair. Almost in touching distance. Almost.

"I'd have thought that it was obvious. No?"

"No," I whispered back.

"No" sounded a bit ungrateful, but I was compensating for broken ribs with my new monosyllabic personality. She sucked on her lower lip. That was awful pretty to see. I stirred again but this time, fat chance anyway, refused to be shaken. And my faithless companion was much reduced, and nubby anyway. Age, I guessed.

"What did Tommy tell you?" was my only follow-up now.

"What I told you … that he … and Lionel … found you. Being kicked. Rescued you. Brought you here to get better."

"How'd he know where I'd be?"

"Sorry?"

"No. I am. Tommy's OK. He's just not smart, is he?"

Bran crossed and uncrossed her legs. It wasn't meant to be distracting; it was just a reflex. I tried not to be distracted. My reflexes failed. Old nubby uncoiled a little but I needed to stay coiled. And to remember.

"Bran," I wheedled, uncertain what the dictionary said "to wheedle" meant, but effortlessly capable of it. "Look, whatever mess you're in with Mal, let him bounce, not you. Haf may …"

The name of her daughter altered the rules of engagement. She broke them off, let's say.

"Haf? What's that bitch been telling you? Leave her to her own devices, Billy. Leave her be."

It was my turn to let steel pendulums swing and splice.

"Leave her be? You let her go. Not me. You didn't even tell me about her. When she was born. That she might be mine. Or, yet, how to find her. Why not, Bran? Why the fuck not?"

Bran leaned forward. Her voice was a whiplash.

"You want to know. You want to know. OK, you sappy bastard. You can know. I front, work for, I *am*!, ECA – EuroCymruAssociates – and we, I, lead on institutional bids for Euro initiatives – cash and projects, schemes and funding outcomes. Consultancy. Expertise. Advice. OK? Because the money has to be channelled. From Brussels. They don't just give it away. Well not quite. There's an audit, business plans, bids, and, crucially, match funding. So, that means finessing the time of an organisation's staff – at premium rates – and its established assets, everything from buildings to porters to electricity and IT and onto the notepaper and biros – to ratchet up what can be turned into those particular lines in business plans that say "in kind". Then, if we can, matched in cash from other sources. From government. From business. Keeping up? A trust, one with a worked-out agenda in economic regeneration and social well-being like Tir Werin, and connected to movers and shakers, is not just ideally placed. It *is* the place, the virtual place."

She paused. None of this was exactly news. Check out my legal know-how, I wanted to crow. But this was leading somewhere else so I stayed quiet,but attentive. And continued to ache as her sweetness disappeared and she poured the old Bran vinegar into the wound..

"Yeah, OK. I see you can guess all the moves, but, believe me, the outcome is one to leave alone. The moves … well, you know those; Mal had made a pile, dot com and all that. And he diversified. But not enough, as it happened. So, he took out insurance, buying up land across the heads of the valleys. Cheap. Useless land. No good for local homes or for commuters to travel to work elsewhere, or for factory sheds and inward investors. Good for schemes, though. He persuaded the powers-that-be to establish a Research Park. He invested in it. Of course he made himself the chairman of the board, and had Gwil, dear, sweet, shitty Gwil, appointed as Director. With my contacts and Ceri's profile, we promoted Tir Werin in Europe as a practical vehicle to make real the ideas and schemes dreamed up in the Alfred Wallace Building. Neat name, huh? Mal geared Gwilym up to write the business plan for a major regeneration centre, with social benefits and visitor offshoots. Feasibility studies. Project money. Grant aid and start-up money, to purchase the necessary land. Now, soon, take-off money. Follow?"

I nodded. Bran said nothing. So, I did the follow on myself.

"Only the stuff I've seen kind of suggests the money went round and round, so to speak. From Brussels to the government to Tir Werin, to Valleyscorp, so to you, and Mal? And I'd guess to Ceri. Our old friend and comrade, Sir Ceri Evans."

Bran flicked me a smile. I threw another stick on the fire dying between us.

"Suggest, you say. Doesn't prove anything, does it?" she countered.

"Not yet, no. I'll want to talk to Haf, won't I?" Was that a threat? She seemed to take it as such. She was right to do so. But then she surprised again.

Bran stood. She picked up a soft leather handbag that didn't gleam and was studded with dull bronze metal clasps and non-functional straps. She opened the clasp that was like an antique key and reached inside for a shiny, black fountain pen with a snow cone on top. Nothing cheap for Bran. She unscrewed it, found a scrap of paper and scribbled quickly. She stood directly above me and crumpled it into a ball. She dropped it in my lap. An address, of a kind, for Haf. She said:

"I was hoping you wouldn't go on. I don't like what happened to you, Billy. I wanted to make it up to you. No-go, it seems. Contacting her will do you no good either. But if you insist, go ahead. Maybe you can talk some sense into her after all. Remember she'll lose out, too. Think of that, eh?"

She turned, and then she turned back. I knew it was never going to be that easy.

"You said you wanted to know, didn't you? So, I'll tell you. She thought you were — that you ought to be — her daddy, so when I told her you weren't, she went with Mal. Her stepfather. And ruined our marriage, for what it was worth. Ended it anyway. Since then she's just gone on making trouble and the latest is to have revenge — on him and on me — by spreading these lies. Which will only re-bound on her, the idiot. Or half-lies, if you like. Where the fuck does she think the money for her comes from? It'll do no good. Mal is having her legally removed from Valleyscorp — incompetence, drugs, whatever it takes. Unless you can persuade her not to hold things up, to get in the way of things she doesn't understand. Oh, and one more thing … you're really not the daddy. Honest. Cross my heart. Hope to die."

And she let herself out. I felt, as I always did with Bran, that none of this should have been this way. And that I was not a fool to want it different, only one to think it had ever been possible.

* * * * *

I skipped the shower because of the bandages, and settled for a shave and a shampoo. I cleaned my teeth with my fingers and a pink-striped toothpaste. I found a T-shirt with the least naff print transfer in the quietest colour — army drab — some jeans and deck shoes and a pair of matching white socks and a red and yellow pullover that looked like a dog had revisited his dinner. Apart from my jacket, thoughtfully brushed but still stained with blood and dirt, my own clothes were nowhere to be seen, either torn and useless or washed. I guessed the former. My wallet was on the kitchen table and money and cards were still inside. I expected nothing less. These boys might have been rough, but they weren't muggers. I didn't bother with the thank-you note. I left by the door I assumed I had entered a few days before.

A small rain was falling. Not enough to soak you unless you

walked through it for hours. That wasn't my intention as I winced over some broken paving stones back into the town, but enough for its prickly damp to blur the vista. Moving forward somehow eased the pain in my ribs, though I still had to stop to lean on a garden wall or two. My breathing was all of the outward kind, a desperate wheeze followed by a short hissing intake. I was beginning to sound like my old man. I heaved myself up off a low wall and left the side street. Public transport was fine by me, for all those other people. I needed a taxi. I stopped at a bus shelter to ask where I could find one. Right across the road, they said and pointed.

A waiting driver flipped his lit cigarette out of his window, gently oscillating as he did the "Dim Ysmygu" sign hanging from his rear mirror.

"Where to, butty?"

The name on the scrap of paper which Bran had tossed me said Heritage Centre so I said it, too, and we took off. It took less than ten minutes to navigate out of the circular road system, hit the old road north-east, sweep past the long straggle of what the guidebooks and estate agents so emphatically called "Miners' Cottages", and through the main gates of what had once been a working colliery. I paid. The taxi left, its socially considerate driver only lighting up as he pulled away. I stood in a tarmac-laid car park that was neatly marked out in bays, and looked at the glass front they had erected as a curtain across the dressed quarry stone in order to mark out a modern entrance to the former winding house. Inside was a shop area littered with furry red dragons, giant glitter pencils, and tiny coal maquette sculptures of colliers, their wives and street ragamuffins. The entrance opened up further into a mock-up of shops, a coal-lit kitchen with Mam, her wire hair in a bun, larger than life and even deader than the flanking models of the mufflered collier and the leaping-into-his-arms child. I averted my sensitive eyes. The only thing that was welcoming was the Croeso sign and the silence that truly meant No Visitors. The assistant at the shop's counter hadn't looked up from the receipts she was checking from all the profits the Centre was making in glinting paraphernalia. Everything else appeared to be free.

I walked up the open metal staircase to the first floor. Tables, chairs, coffee, Welsh cakes. And, unexpected by me, a pitch-roofed gallery space. More sentiment I guessed, and so only half-glanced at the walls.

There were five or six canvases and a few drawings from each of the five painters on show. The work was certainly singular in each individual style but it hung together, more like a collective emotion than a group. I felt the need of the old man's guidance for detail but its overall glow washed over me in any case at the fag end of a sodden afternoon, with only the unforgiving glare of the overhead panels of electric light to pick out colour that was insistent but mostly muted. There were no eyeball-teasing globs of colour erupting off board and canvas in great tears of flaking pigment. And though there were entrancing and painterly marriages of acid green and frothy underskirt pink and gritty ochre to quiz comic book blues and reds, this work, as a totality, was not about sensing delight, it was a structure. It was a scaffolding, one erected to climb towards an idea. The work was a counterclaim against what had been stolen, what had been hidden away, or mislaid, or forgotten, or neglected and abused. They had painted the structure of lives. How it felt. How it was. How it should have been understood. How it could be. How, whatever the contrary outcome, it still mattered.

It had been seen, then, transfigured into a vision that was as unmistakeably real as it had once been actual. In all this work there was not a trace of the identikit Valleys, stereotyped and drooled over and caricatured, in words and images. Worth and purpose lost, hollowed out in memorials and monuments, reduced to the heroic they had rightly spurned. In these native hands these places and people had been disassembled, and put back together.

The last section of one wall of work held me longest. It seemed attuned to a future. The painting technique was looser in execution, enormous canvases filled with brushstrokes that owed their liquidity to the reckless arm more than the dab of a controlling hand. The customary framework of a familiar landscape was intact. A look down from the mountain plateau back into the rash of buildings below. Homes slotted in clumps, and rearing public buildings on perpendicularly set street corners. The legacy was there still to view, and to live in, albeit unusually caught, as if in sun traps. But it was the bodies that were so different. They did not stand or sit as if terminally defined. They jumped and raced and swung each other around and somersaulted on trampolines in a riot of upside-down mobility. Arms were muscle taut beneath short-sleeved shirts. Or legs, brown and liquescent, were set running free of flying skirts. The painter moved in and through his mobile subject-matter, refusing the viewer the luxury of seeing anything as settled. If the past was a place that made the present a prison for the mind then this blotchy capture of living was a release. In the light of the exhibition I sensed all my old man's early courage more than his late resignation.

* * * * *

It was dark, a crepuscular enfolding light, when I finally left that gallery. I asked downstairs when Haf would be coming into work since there was no sign of her anywhere. No one had even heard of her. But they were helpful. The senior manager was called. She was young, pert and smiled a lot. I repeated my query. She frowned and asked to see my scrap of paper. Just Haf and Heritage Centre was what it said, scrawled in Bran's near illegible sloping hand in black ink. Mont Blanc ink. And pen to match, I'd noticed. The manager now came all over dismissive. She tapped the paper with a false plum-coloured nail. Maybe, she said, it wasn't the museum and gallery but the hotel just up the road.

The hotel was an unexpected take, in red colonial brick and white stone pediments, on an American cross between a motel-lodge and a small hotel. Its automatic doors slid open to let in the passing, weary commercial traveller, or more likely wedding guests as I sleuthily surmised by the reception rooms and banquetry suites on offer, their insides a glimpse of silver and gilt carved chairs, all set before white-linen-draped tables. I asked for Haf at the main reception desk and was told she was working her shift behind the bar.

The bar room was more wood: upright struts as in a cowboy movie to partition sections, and the black beams of a false plasterboard ceiling as in a Pickwickian tavern. The bar had brass rails at its foot and ran across the entire length of the room. The muzak was an entreatingly twangy Tammy Wynette. The girl behind the bar was pressing a nozzle to deliver flat-topped pints of urine-coloured liquid. Four silent customers sat together, waiting at a centre table which was covered with paperwork and by four mobile phones which the group had placed in front of them in expectation of a call to bring them to life. I stepped a few paces further into the room. I looked across the patterned expanse of swirling brown and orange carpet at the young woman who had called me daddy from across the Atlantic. I stared. It took me a while. She was busy serving and washing glasses. She didn't look up in my direction. From the tables on the outer rim of the room, and a step up behind the railing of uprights, there was the beginning of the buzz of early evening, post-work drinkers. Local government officers, some business people, the newly retired, a collar-and-tie brigade that would have discouraged your Tommys and Lionels from entering as much as the chemical sniff coming off pints of filtered and resurrected lager would have disgusted them. An aftersmell of lunchtime's industrial vinegar combined with the dead pasteurised beer created an atmosphere akin to a formaldehyde gag. I could have done with the devil-may-care rapture of tobacco smoke to remind me that death usually came after life. The cigarette smokers were in the purgatory for exiled puffers outside the main lobby. I chose a table at the back near the door and further from the bar. There was waitress service if you waited long enough. I was happy to wait. I inhaled the forlorn cinema-goer's memory of Jeyes cleaning fluid that came my way every time the toilet door opened and closed. I was beaten-up, tired, emotional, and sober for once. What more could you want? I was beginning to wonder. A wine list, perhaps.

When my turn came I asked for a glass of red wine, anything I said that had never been in contact with Antipodean soil or been inside the staves of an oak barrel. I made myself understood by simplifying it to "Nothing from Australia". Customer service was delivered – to an extent. The wine came in a glass that could have doubled as a small bucket. I tasted more pampas than eucalyptus. A Malbec to put a twist in a gaucho's boleros. I decided sipping would be an effete pastime with this drink, so I just drank. I ordered another, with peanuts on the side. The waitress seemed to approve of this as a gesture to the normality of the local culture. An hour or so passed. The bar was fuller, but still appeared empty as if it was waiting for the Cattlemen's Convention to roll up. I kept the bar and its attendant in my sight. It was early evening when Haf was relieved. She checked out her till. I checked her out as she said her goodbyes and exited via the servants' quarters. At least I presumed that's what the door at the side of the bar was. I followed as discreetly as I could, and into the car park behind the hotel. She walked over to a dented Renault with red trim and the puckered look of a veteran boxer, and the name of a Muse. I moved a hundred yards behind her as she searched in her pocket. The rain was back but softer now. It made water droplets glisten in her black hair. The hair was jagged, off her neck, and spiky on top, fuller on the side, an ugly frame that still couldn't spoil her face, though one that seemed more fatigued than her age deserved. She wore jeans and a shapeless red Puffa jacket and she cursed as she scrabbled for the car keys. I moved closer. She turned the keys in the lock and opened the door and looked up to see me at the passenger side. I was afraid I might startle her but she said "Hello" even before I did, and told me to get in. So I did the same. She ran her fingers briskly through her hair to shake out the drops that had clung to the thick, short strands. She gave me a long enquiring look. I seemed to be attracting a lot of those lately. She saw my bruised face and my puffy eyes, and said nothing But I was not being dismissed. What I saw was how lovely she was. More Bran than me. I stayed silent. Her mouth was turned down at its corners. More me than Bran. I wanted to hold her, to kiss that pursed mouth's hurt away and tell her I was sorry. She could see that anyway, and I was no longer being thoughtfully silent, just struck dumb. She fired up the damp cold car at the third attempt and we jerked out of the car park onto the empty road to the south.

I asked where we were going. She said, "Home", as if she meant it. I was all for that. Besides it wasn't far, a few miles back and on through the town, then a backstreet tour of brick-trimmed homes which were evidently, from the rubbish outside and the old bangers parked up on the kerbs, student accommodation. Owned by Maldwyn no doubt. There was no number on the house. There was a wood-panel partitioned door with peeling varnish and a flaking gold-coloured metal knocker. The curtains of the one ground-floor window were thin and brown and floral, and pulled together like a geriatric's stained lips. The passageway was littered with unopened bills, flyers for takeaways and free newspapers. We walked past the doors to all the downstairs rooms, and up the stairs past a kitchen area which was sending a reek of cooking oil through the house. There was a landing to the right, and at its far end the locked door of what had once been the front bedroom of three-up three-down working-class respectability. There was a Yale lock which Haf snapped open with another key on her car ring. And we were in.

It was not what I had expected. The wood was painted white, the floor-length curtains heavy calico and lined, but somehow light bearing even before she turned on the two yellow floor lamps, and the one on a cubbyhole desk in the left corner. A simple bed, white coverlet and blood-orange scatter cushions in a knobbly silk material, was butted up against the same back wall. She took my coat and draped it on the bed alongside her own. She took a black angora sweater out of a wall cupboard and put it on over her white linen shirt. There was no chair so she waved to a low Scandinavian sofa. I sat and she stood, quizzically in front of me, the third wall behind her. There were no books. No television. No racks of CDs, DVDs or whatever other disc storage system had come to pass. A laptop and printer and all the gubbins was the exception to the rule on the desk. On the wall were photographs. Some copied. Some blown up. Some from magazines and newspapers. Some small and original. All of them mine. She saw me looking at them, taking it all in. Or some of it.

When she finally spoke the voice was low. Quiet. Every Welsh-accented syllable like the ding of an alarm clock's bell. "Well, what did you expect?" she said. "I've been living with you, for years, one way or the other, haven't I? And now you're here. At last. I knew you would be, you know."

I retreated into small talk. How long had she been living here? A year or so. Was the kitchen shared? Yes. Two boys downstairs. Bathroom and lavatory. One up, one down. It was OK. Did I want coffee? She wouldn't be long. I stood up and looked at the pictures.

That one with a Leica. That with a Rolleiflex 2¼ inch that had survived a dunking in a south-east Asian river. That one in a bright sunlight which had made the shadows elongate like dark accusers. This one worked and cropped from years before. These done as quickly as they had had to be. My eyeballing life laid out and reduced to a wall-poster display. I looked away.

The coffee arrived in thick, plain white china mugs. No sugar as requested. We stood, awkwardly, my back turned as hers had been to the wall of memories. I was waiting for her to begin. It was unfair, but whatever had brought me here was her doing and only Haf could make this happen now. So she did.

"You were good," she said.

And I laughed: "Was, is right!"

"Time to be good again, maybe," she said.

"Time has to come with a chance to be good," I said.

"But that's what's brought you here, isn't it?", she said.

"I don't know yet, Haf. I don't know what you think can be done or should be done."

"You said my name," she said.

She sat down. I sat beside her. And Haf told me her story. She already knew mine. Or thought she did. When she finished talking the coffee was cold and my heart was colder. She picked up the two mugs and stood above me as I muttered something that had words about me and sorrow stitched into their hopeless apology. I had learned some things I'd be better off not knowing and some I couldn't forget. She was more stone than flower. It was all over and not finished. Not by any means.

She looked at me as if she meant it and spoke the sentence that I knew I had to hear.

"Do you want to fuck me, too?"

* * * * *

112

The signs to the nearest railway station had encouraged me to walk. A quarter of a mile felt like a marathon. The train encouraged me to sleep. I resisted until I made my way back to the city centre hotel, showered and slept with a Do Not Disturb card attached to a doorknob that the cleaner still insisted on rattling the next day. Twice. At noon and then at one. My deep fellow feelings for those on minimum wage, or less, dwindled, then vanished. I opened the door. I enquired "Yes?" She looked. I was scowling. She smiled. She left. I was sorry. I closed the door. I took my battered and naked body back to bed and slept some more. A lot more.

In dreams, maybe, I had made up my mind.

I made a few calls to old journalist friends, still suppurating away on columns that were always going to be more Wurlitzer than Pulitzer, strictly regional papers whose declining circulation was a constant reproof to their national pretensions. That's what I had to listen to on the phone anyway, from one veteran hack after another until one finally yielded up the extra-directory and private mobile number of Sir Ceri Evans, of whom, once, well more than once, and long ago, my old man had sourly said, "His cock will find him out". He'd been wrong about that, too. So far.

I wasn't exactly surprised to find that Ceri – even after 20 years – wasn't fazed to find me on the other end of a phone. He'd come straight to it after the perfunctory, gushing but patently disinterested, greetings. He said that the others had been a bit put out and were hoping I'd ring so that he could put me straight, clear up any misunderstandings. Relax over a drink. Lunch perhaps, or dinner if I preferred. He mentioned a brasserie on the waterfront. Oysters, ice cold Chablis and a sidelong view of the hot new government building, if you really must, he laughed, or the mercy of nightfall. I opted for dinner and the dark. He was in Brussels, negotiating for Wales he said, but a small plane was bringing the Big Man home the next day. We arranged for dinner around eight o'clock the following night, Wednesday. He told me that on Thursday he had to write and then make the speech which he was to give at a conference on a New Valleys Dawn to be held that same morning. Good, I told him. I'll be there. He thought I meant only at the dinner. Good, I thought. And that gave me the Tuesday to rest, and the time before I met Ceri to be a tidy boy.

The rest of the day passed in a haze of occasional room service and frequent painkillers. When I surfaced from a stupor every now and then I attended to bits of business. I booked an airport hotel room at Heathrow for Friday night and an early Saturday morning flight back to JFK. I read the file Haf had given me one more time, checking dates and facts and figures. Then I slept some more. When the dreamtime ended I got up and showered myself awake. I dressed, ordered coffee, stared out at the usual mixed bag of weather, and then I picked up one of the lined yellow pads which always travelled with me and began to write.

What I wrote was a conventional putting together of quotes from private notes and letters and bank accounts. Conventional and, if read the way I intended it to be read, lethal. And what my friend the hack would make of it was a storyline that had 'A' (or Mal) linked to successive sales of low-grade or contaminated land over a period of years since the mid-1990s. Councillors and council decisions were drawn into this web and innocently so on a separate basis, but more intriguingly not when they and the land parcels were totted up altogether. Then there was the grouping of these heads of the valleys plots under the holding company, Valleyscorp, which had been put in trust in Haf's name but directed by 'B' or Bran until her daughter was eighteen. That date had been reached three years ago. Less formal documentation placed 'C', or Ceri, in the frame as a key player in regeneration policies from Poland to Penrhiwceiber and back. Perhaps they hadn't felt the need for discretion. Why should they? Loans and gifts were not directly connected to any of this, were they? Not until, maybe, the payment details grew more frequent and larger as the scheme unfolded. Which is where 'D', or Gwilym, came into play, as the respected deviser for Tir Werin, adjunct to the Research Park, of an ambitious regeneration project which required both funding – from Europe – and land – available, at a seemingly reasonable price from Valleyscorp. Our 'A' had, by this time, long resigned as a director of Valleyscorp but as chair of the board based in the adapt-or-die Wallace building encouraged, and you might say, led our 'D' to the fruition of his scheme. Or, at least, to parts one and two of it. Money and land. Construction and delivery would be later. With Ceri and Gwilym as principal trustees of Tir Werin, lines of profitable communication would be kept open. What I had was a prospectus for growth that bore all the hallmarks of idealism and was, in its outline, all in the public domain. But I had little doubt that the career of Ceri would be, at the very least, tarnished by the detail of transactions; that the reputation of Gwilym would not be enhanced as he planned for his birthday honours; that Bran could present herself, at best, as a virginal third party with her daughter's interests at heart; and that Maldwyn could be legitimately accused of chicanery, underhand dealings and collusion with others to subvert the use of public funding. Maybe even be convicted. Underneath all this laying of explosives though, was the fuse that had been lit to set it off as dynamite. And the fuse was Haf.

I wrote that story, too. It isn't too pretty but this is how it went.

She'd been born in the summer of 1986. Maldwyn was to be her father figure since Bran and he first lived together then, and married a year later. Both, with the adventure of the strike behind them, had more to do with "getting on" in careers floated by the wider public recognition they had cashed in on, than they did with the daughter who lived with them, and a nanny, until she went to the school from which she could have come home every day but didn't. Haf was a boarder with a home, or changing homes, as property moves took them upmarket, but still just a few miles away from her schooling. Holidays were periods of tension, not release. As she grew older the rifts and the rows between Mal and Bran first upset her as she tried to pull them together in a child's fantasy way, and then they drove her down into herself.

Then, when she was sixteen, she refused to be a boarder any more. Refusal and resistance could not be overturned by an irate Bran. Haf paid lip-service to 'A' level study at a local FE college. Haf tried to shelter from constant recrimination by being closer to Mal. Indifference was her best reward until Mal walked out after a quarrel with his wife that was more explicit and even violent in its threat than before. It was after that splitting up that Bran, cruel or vindictive or just Bran maybe, told Haf that Mal was not her father anyway. That she'd been pregnant before they had come together. Then who? And she said me. Billy Maddox. That I'd left in the winter of '85, and never came back. That my father had died suddenly before the Christmas of that year, when I was on an assignment in the Far East, and uncontactable. There were no other ties for me here after that, and she hadn't told me of the one there was. End of story.

Only, for Haf, it was a beginning. She researched my life, my work, my pictures. Her bedroom filled with the grainy images of photojournalism and the edgy, tricked-out and edited compositions of the dark room. If that was the retreat inside herself, the outer journey was uninhibited by any baggage. She did what the abandoned young do, and on the streets there was booze and pills and sex, and then Mal again. He'd moved by now, and without Bran, back home to his mansion on the hill. Haf moved in with him. To hurt Bran? Not a chance. To infuriate? Every time. She fucked her "father". He seduced his "daughter". Who knows (she certainly didn't) the sequence of these moves? It wasn't a crime, was it? It wasn't, she said, as if they were related.

It was a crime, nonetheless, so far as I was concerned. Mal's crime. For Haf the crime that concerned her was happening elsewhere. When she hit eighteen and Mal talked of university she also found that she was required to be a co-signatory on all kinds of transactions in which there was no common denominator other than Tir Werin. She asked. Bran came into the picture again. She and Mal, it seemed, had interests in common that could elide other divisions. Gwilym spoke to Haf. A career was in prospect for her. He could see to it that she was, despite poor exam results, admitted into a Media Studies course at the university. It was her duty to help the Tir Werin scheme to fruition. She asked what it meant. She was told about Sir Ceri's deep interests in its welfare. What a great man he was. Mal was blunter. If she didn't sign there was no money. What the fuck was wrong with her? What indeed. Bran was less inquisitive. She told it to Haf as directly as Mal, only in language made more personal than maternal by the anger of the self-interested. Mistake. Haf kept signing but she started digging, and enquiring, and collecting, and photocopying. Her silence was interpreted as complaisance at last. It was a cloak for snooping – in drawers, in briefcases, in handbags, in office files. Finally, she stopped signing papers. She moved out.

I spent the next morning re-writing and clarifying before putting it into my laptop. I was a laborious typer. It took me past an in-room sandwich lunch before I was ready. When I finally finished I found a printer and had copies made. I put them into envelopes marked by name for Haf, Ceri, and Maldwyn. I stamped and addressed envelopes to Gwilym and Bran, and a final one to my old friend the hack. I put the first three in the pocket of the navy peacoat I would wear over a pullover and jeans. The others would go into a postbox. The hack would only use his if I didn't have my way another way, and either way it would keep others honest. On my way to the city centre railway station I found a DIY store.

Inside I found a lump hammer, hard and squat and with a comfortable heft to it in my hand, and wrapped it inside a newspaper and dropped it inside a hessian bag. It swung reassuringly to my side as I walked. The rain fell all over the city again, and I used its incessant wetness to wipe clean a face that had seen too much. What I was to do was maybe for Haf, perhaps for me, but mostly for my old man. He would have told me I was another Sam Spade, half a century and more too late. That I was still role-playing and knee-jerk reacting. And I whispered back into the rain that he was right, and that there was nothing else for it in the trap of image and imitation into which we had all long fallen. I didn't wait long for a train. This time the scenery, through the windows, dissolved in the rain.

Haf was waiting for me in the bar. She was bundled up in her Puffa jacket, her jeans tucked into her ankle boots, and only her much too pale face on show. It was a pretty face. I gave her the envelope and drank a bottle of Italian beer whilst she read it. She didn't smile but asked what next. So I told her. Or some of it. I missed out the very next bit, and skipped to where I was going to meet Ceri that night. I told her the plan, and why, and she nodded. I kissed her on the cheek. I looked at my watch. It was time to leave. It was long past the time to make things right. There was time, though, to tidy a few things up before another tomorrow came unwanted upon us. I left her with the promise of a different tomorrow, one still to come.

I got to the heritage centre, five minutes away, about an hour earlier than I'd arranged and just in time for that day's last tour of all somebody else's yesterdays. I took it. They certainly weren't my yesterdays. They were set at a convenient distance, filtered through a haze of nostalgia which blurred any recovery of any real time. The pretend real selves here were bigger than any life-size dummies – cloth-capped colliers, top-hatted coalowners, waistcoated mine managers, moustachioed engineers – all given their lines to say in static cameos with booming stereophonic voiceovers. It took an hour to shuffle from one engine house to another – I skipped the underground simulation – and the only time I felt a twitch of recognition was, irony of ironies of course, when I sat in front of the slide show of old photographs and saw the innocence of all those there captured and exposed, again, for all time. It was because they didn't know, taker or taken, what they were doing that I felt, at last, undone in face of the enormity of it all.

I waited at the tour's end on the wet cobblestoned yard of the former colliery. I was sheltered against the rain by an out-of-time and out-of-service red double-decker bus that was parked side on to the main building. I had left the voice message for Maldwyn to come to meet me in the yard after four. It was now 4.15 and the fine rain was blowing from the hills, overlapping in parabolas against the rain-beaded windows of the bus. I peered through the smearing lines on the glass, back towards the enclosed entrance way and its swishy automatic doors. Two figures stood, not moving, just looking out, not seeing me on the other side of the bus. I put my right hand inside the hessian bag to feel that the short shaft was lying the right way. I called Mal's name out into the rain and then I moved, holding the bag's handles in my left, to the back of the bus. And waited some more.

Through the shadow fall of a rain becoming more and more insistent I saw one of the two move back into the entrance hall where the papier-mâché butcher and baker guarded their heritage shop windows and a collier flung his raggedy son into a flight that would never come down. Then from behind these grotesque mannequins a third man moved and clutched one of the others around the shoulders until he broke abruptly away and moved back to the doors, which whispered open and shut as their sensors invited a response. The glass panels gaped as two men stood on the line, then closed tight as they crossed it and out into the yard. Wheelie was just a step in front and to the left of Lionel. They looked at the bulk of a loaded coal dram to one side of the bus and at the recesses of the engine house wall beyond the bus, and they split, with Wheelie going the longer way around its front and Lionel more directly across the visible side to the back end where I crouched, and waited.

The rain had filled the fissures between the cobbles with small jewelled puddles. The stage props, real enough in the colliery yard, seemed ridiculously familiar. The gold lettering on the bus, the thick rubber tread of tyres that had once jolted paying passengers, the wet cloth smell of the damp moquette seats which I could see inside, their chromium grip bars dulled by the dank. The doors hissed and opened once more, and in their light I saw a third man coming around the front and the side to the back. Lionel was already there, past the conductor's pole and platform. He stopped when he saw me, hesitating while he looked for his back-up support. The bag dropped to the floor of the yard as my right hand appeared with the lump hammer in it. It was a foot away from Lionel when I swung it up, short and heavy, into his balls with all the force I could. His hands fluttered down, useless as butterfly wings and were swatted aside. He grunted and dropped to his knees, from where he felt the hammer, now switched to the horizontal, smash into the bridge of his nose and spit blood, bone and cartilage onto the cobbles. He lay slumped, head down and silent and I turned to threaten Wheelie with more of the same, but his days of dealing with anything that was not already prostrate had gone. He stood stock-still. Then there was the third figure. I swivelled to face him. Of course, Tommy. He pushed me aside to check I hadn't killed his lifetime prop. I hadn't. But I had hurt him bad and the emergency ward would soon see him, a trifle less intact than when he'd woken up in the morning. Like me, he'd live, with a few painkillers, a bandage or two, and a caring friend. The same one.

That friend stood up and said: "You bastard. You fucking bastard." I nodded and held the hammer ready.

"Tommy," I said. It was an acknowledgement, just that.

"He'll fucking kill you," was a reply more than a threat.

"Maybe. He half-tried already, didn't he?" A gambit, but it worked.

"Christ, Billy. That was, you know, business. And in any case I stopped it going too far. Christ, we took care of you, you ungrateful bastard."

An apology? I didn't think so.

Tommy bunched his fists.

"I won't wait for Lionel. I'll do you now. And *I* won't stop. Not this time."

I showed him the easy swing of the hammer as his body tensed to rush me but I really wanted words to stop him. Words to direct him elsewhere.

"D'you know about Haf, Tommy? Really know?"

What I knew was already enough, I gambled, to ease Tommy into the violence that had always mirrored his sentimentality. But I didn't know everything yet. Maybe that was just as well. For all of us.

"What're you fuckin' getting at?"

"You're fond of her, aren't you? Seen her growing up. After Norma died. You with no kids. Maybe Bran even encouraged you to think … well, she's good at that, isn't she? But then she'd have told you 'No', as well, because she wouldn't want you too close, not with Mal and her, making the nest, so to speak. And that's what I want to tell you about your boss, see Tommy."

He wanted to shut me up. I could feel that, like a current whipping back and fro between us. And he could have done it, too. Hammer or no hammer. But he wanted to hear it, too. So much that I was no longer sure I should say it. But then I did, say it outright, because I wanted the dirt to sting and maim. Not him, of course, just Mal.

"You know when Bran and Mal split up. And he'd have told you that, amongst other things, like maybe she was fucking elsewhere when she wanted, maybe even you, for old times' sake, eh Tommy? That she'd told him, her husband of course, that Haf was not his after all and she'd told Haf, her troublesome, meddlesome daughter that it was me all along, her Daddy-in-exile, so there was the row of all rows and Mal left, and later, soon, Haf followed. And you didn't know, did you Tommy, that Mal, your boss, was soon fucking her. His maybe daughter. Haf."

He said I was a fucking liar, but he flinched and whispered when he said it. I told him to ask Bran. Or better still Maldwyn. He looked over my shoulder to where the automatic doors had opened again. Mal was standing where the yard and the rain and the truth began. He shouted – "Tommy, what the fuck's going on?" – and moved further into the rain. I dropped the hammer. Tommy pushed past me and gathered Lionel up.

"Give me a hand," he yelled at Wheelie and he gave me the look that told me even as I walked away that he believed me, and there would be consequences. Because with Tommy there always would be. I dropped the envelope for Mal at Tommy's feet and said, "Read it before you give it to him. Then give it to him."

* * * * *

I walked away from the yard and back out onto the road. I bent into the rain, as naggingly penetrating as ever, and walked up the road. It was a hundred yards or so, but I broke no records getting to the hotel. In the rain, on that road, the hotel looked more incongruous than the first time. Maybe it was me that just wasn't congruent anymore. Out of step. Out of time. Out of place, and yet inside from outside. It was beginning to sound like the soapy wisdom of a moody song. I told it to stop. I had them order me a cab and waited in the dry.

* * * * *

Sir Ceri Evans was running late. There had been no further messages. It was probably the common assumption of what had become an uncommon life. That he could be late with no apology. I was at ease with that. I was even more at ease with the large G & T that was nursing me. The brasserie was at the back of a grooved wooden deck two flights up from the pavement of the washed and scrubbed waterfront. The marble-topped table had been booked and I had been sat at it on a spindly bentwood chair for over half an hour. The view was of a flat viscous lagoon that struggled to reflect back the light of its ambient Venusberg café-bars and restaurants. That, too, was OK by me. I needed a matt finish to soothe the Technicolor of the day. It was more soothing anyway than the signature buildings near to which the taxi had dropped me for my short promenade to the brasserie.

The buildings were new to me. There seemed around the parliamentary one to be a skirt of slate that lapped up the steps and into the building as if to bring to a darker ground the plate glass which promised transparent government. Its pine roof had a funnel of wood which looked like a wheatsheaf ready for harvesting. It felt more sauna than smoke-filled room. I wondered if this county council Cymru had really stripped itself down so soon to such an indecent basic openness. Indecent in comparison with all its past traditions, that is. I was encouraged. And, as a traditionalist, relieved to see that somebody must have commissioned a lot of slate from a grateful constituency. Next door was an architectural Leviathan. A gargantuan sheepfold, in slate again, topped off by a riveted brass-gold biker's helmet with a stencilled message in a bottle about horizons and stones that was in cut-out lettering in English and Welsh. Genius. It glowed in the dark like the jagged mouth and eye-holes of a pumpkin. As quickly as the reverie of despondency allowed I walked through the strip and huddle of eateries, bars and cafés to the restaurant where I sat and waited.

I let my mind, what was left of it to match the battered body where it had found almost fifty years of house room, wander. To Ceri eventually. I had followed his career as it soared from union office to county council eminence and serial chairmanhood as he moved – who didn't? – from left to right and was then rewarded with a knighthood. It had served to transmute him into an elder statesman. Non-executive positions on the boards of public utilities and not-for-profit organisations were added to his portfolio. He was rewarded, appropriately of course, as a consultant on public affairs. Pro-bono, he polished his CV by chairing Task and Finish groups and gave his weighty name to their shelved reports. He graced conferences and sat in on seminars. He became revered, honoured and trusted, the more he grew independent of his, and our, past lives. It was, I suppose, a familiar trajectory. Certainly one which would not have surprised my old man. But would he really have predicted it? Would I have really believed that kind of outcome for that Ceri from that time?

That Ceri. That time. My old man's Ceri had been twenty-five or so when I was first made aware of him. He had, the old man said, just wandered into one of his WEA classes, on Art and Literature in the Industrial Age, or some such stirring title, and sat, apparently transfixed, at the back. He was, in the early 1960s, considerably younger than the dwindling band of educational veterans which my father's grizzled application of social history to culture usually attracted. Ceri was an orphan and an apprentice collier who had married Olwen at eighteen. Lady Olwen now. Ceri never threw anything away that might prove useful, and a lifetime of philandering – early and late – had not broken the utility of his marriage to her, who ran his home and raised his children to be teachers and solicitors, all in his absence. The marriage was no fiction, it was just a side story within the space of his personal, always personal, narrative. He had been recommended to go to the old man's class by the kind of union official who, in those days, acted as recruiting agent for educational uplift. He had been told to broaden his horizons if he was to make a mark in the union. He was already a Young Communist of course. But then that was like saying, for his youth and ardour in that place at that time, that he went to chapel or liked the movies or shagged girls or chainsmoked. But he did believe. And he did see how that helped him to be seen, to be noticed. In the Good Cause, of course.

He became an assiduous attender. Assiduity would become his hallmark. It was funny, how you had to wait to the end, of a life, as of a book, to see how it all turned out. And that it could have been different. Maybe. Choices. Pathways, and all that. Only I didn't go in for "all that" anymore. For some people in some places at some times it was fixed. Our time had been made for Ceri and he always seemed to know it better, quicker, than any of the rest of us. Maldwyn had just seen ways to make money. Bran was a chancer who needed to escape what her good looks had made easy and mundane for her as she looked in the mirrors which were other people's eyes, but for her the exit routes to more satisfying success would never be dependent on the satnav of self-doubt. Gwilym flew high inside cages erected by others, and never understood the difference between fluttering his flashy wings and flying to any purpose. Tommy was collateral damage in a society which had devalued the power that thousands of Tommys together had once shown. Me, I had mistaken my despair for insight and my contempt for courage, and I'd used my small gifts only to direct my retreat. Haf was what was left, hurt and hopeful. If I owed anything to anyone in the ruins of this time and place it was, I thought, to her. It would depend on the price I could exact for damages. It would depend on how bad the damage had been. I was counting on Ceri to tell me.

* * * * *

The voice entered the room first. Greeting the waiter with a "Phillipe!" and a bear hug, and a smile for "Nadine, my lovely," this more quietly said, as a petite blonde bobbed into view and took his coat from his back. A thicker back than I'd remembered but still proportionate to his height, just six feet, and his wide shoulders. His eyes made a quick inventory of the room, three or four couples who clocked him even as he ticked them off on his highly tuned radar screen, and me. He grinned, opening up an abyss of a welcome on his handsome crag of a face. His hair was still shaggy and lustrous on top and greying in all the right places. He was in no hurry to cross the room. This was a piece of theatre for Ceri. He patted the lapels of his well-cut bespoke dark-blue single-breasted suit, fiddled with a black-polka-dot-on-light-grey tie as if he was Oliver Hardy, and let the voice take over again. Out it rumbled from some warm, deep, irresistible cavern. "Well, look at you, after all this time. Little Billy Maddox. How are you, butt? How are you? Bloody well come 'ere."

He was with me before I could even rise from the table. He had made it a lifetime's practice to invite warmth but to make sure he gave it out first. I was grabbed and pulled in towards him, held almost as if I was a child. In anybody else the body cinch, the handshaking wonderment, the brown eyes lit up with an irrepressible delight at being, just the two of us, any old us, together, would have been a giveaway. Politician. Kisses baby. Congratulates Mother. Envies Father. And all that. But Ceri had somehow made natural to himself what in others were lame gestures. What you felt was what you got. Or so it appeared. What you saw was what you truly saw, and what was not to like? Everyone liked Sir Ceri Evans.

He finally let me go, still cracking a smile, and sat down with a thump. As always, he went straight to it.

"Surprised about the knighthood, were you? Can't imagine what your old man would have said. Well. I can, actually! But hey, Lady Olwen loves it, and she bloody well deserves it, doesn't she? More than me, anyway!"

He laughed so all-embracingly that the other diners looked over, happy for him, and so now for themselves. He waved a little self-deprecatingly, as if to say "Enjoy" – me, this hour, your being here, with me. He had lots of ingratiating habits. He deployed the next one. A shy hesitancy, signalled by the repetition of inconsequential words, as if he was readying himself, gearing up for the task, this Ceri, for whom there had never been any hesitation in reaching out and taking what he wanted, the biggest-beaked fledgling in the nest yet with the modesty to tip his head away as he simultaneously swallowed the worm whole. All for him.

"It's, it's … er … a case of recognition," he began. "Recognition, see. Not, uh, not, for me. For what I tried to, we, in the old days, your old man even, represented. See. Oh shit. Fuck the title. That's not important. Though, mind, the Lords was mentioned, too. Aye. But. See. I have to keep active. Working. Mostly in Europe now. For Wales. So, there it is, see."

And he spread his hands on the table and looked imploringly at me. I told him it was OK by me. That I couldn't speak for the old man. But he was dead, after all. Ceri said, "Yes," and looked mournful, as if it was yesterday, not years ago, and he wasn't exactly asking the old man's opinion or permission even in those days. We airbrushed the history we'd filed away. We decided to order. Proper decisions. Ceri was no fine diner. So far as food, his "grub" as he called it out of some further gesture of solidarity with people who had actually eaten it as fuel for work, he liked it large, quick and showy. The blonde waitress drifted to the table like a fish drawn to a hook. He must have tipped well before.

"Shall we have the usual, Billy? My usual, I mean, of course. Sorry, butt. Oysters. Chablis. Fillet steak. Chips, natch. No bloody veg, and a bottle or two of Costières de Nîmes. OK? Rare or medium rare? "À pointe" as I've learned to say, eh, Nadine?"

Nadine hovered, and glowed a little. I'd like to think she was indulging the customer as an old fool. Unfortunately, I could see she was enjoying the exchange. He hadn't missed a beat. Still had the rhythm at his fingertips. The steaks would be rare but not too blue. Wrong colour. Even for an Independent, he said. We agreed, and laughed. That led us to more political banter and reminiscence over the Boys' Own meal we were scoffing. Two bottles of the deep southern red took us into a shared cheese plate. I broached nothing, waiting for him to make a move. He finally came to it over coffee and cognac.

"Anyway, this has been great, Billy. Just great. I'll pay, mind! God! Makes me feel young again, seeing you. D'you fancy that, do you? I think, I think, she's up for it! I know I would be!

"But, anyway, what, what're you bothered about, bothering with, this, er, this regeneration scheme? Bran tells me her daughter, daft kid, is causing, making, waves, trouble 'bout it. Can't see why. It'll do a lot of good, see, for a lot of people up there. Dependent on me, it is, getting all the pieces together, in place. Nothing wrong with that, is there?"

He leaned back. He swirled his spoon in the sugary grit of his double espresso. He made a face of genuine puzzlement. I reached down and opened the folder in which I'd put all the papers Haf had sent me. I scattered them on the table. He scarcely glanced at them beyond a peremptory flick of a few pages.

"Oh that," he said. "Gwilym told me about those. So what, Billy? You don't think we're stupid, do you? Do you? S'all on the level. Derelict land. Deprived communities. *Our* people, Billy. All for *their* aspirations. A portal to the outside world. Valleys on the map again, eh? European money. Welsh welcome. Know-how imported. Knowledge grown and exported."

I rifled through the emails in front of him which confirmed the payments from Bran, or rather from Bran's piddling little PR outfit, into his bank. Thousands that totted up to hundreds of thousands of pounds. I showed him the newspaper cuttings and the committee transcripts that detailed his enthusiasm as he lobbied with all the considerable skill he'd acquired for ear-marked grants. Millions of euros. I read out the letters from the commission in Brussels and the civil service in Cardiff nominating Tir Werin to take a central role in the proposed scheme and to act as recipient of the disbursed money. Then there were more confidential notes about Tir Werin, the plans and drawings of what were, acres and acres of, iron and coal wasted tips and hillocks and plateaux, and what exactly could be cleaned up, and how, and at what cost it could be built upon. Homes as well as the primary project. Retail units as well as research centres. High-end leisure as well as conference facilities. And most of the grant moneys conducted discreetly by Gwilym as secretary into the accounts of the owners of the land. And that was Valleyscorp, the company trust in Haf's name, with Maldwyn nowhere in sight. Valleyscorp was Mal's sleeper. It was a frog which Tir Werin, as princess, would kiss to wake it up into a terrible new kind of beauty.

There was more, of course, but that seemed to me, as it had since I'd first seen it, more than enough for questions to be asked. I asked him to justify how the public good he was espousing worked out as such personal good fortune.

Quite reasonable, I thought. But Ceri, as ever, was not disturbed. He told me that none of it would stand up, that all of it could be explained and indeed justified, and that, besides, the payments to him were fees, registered for consultancy and advice. It would have been impossible to move those mountains of cash without a general political will and inside a common framework of policy far beyond any feeble effort he could individually offer. Also, I should grow up. Also, I should wake up. Also, I had no idea anymore, if I ever had, of how the lives of ordinary people – I loved that ordinary – were settled now, or fucked up, by the dealings of what he airily called envoys to power, committees of notables, and entrepreneurs directed, by such as him whenever and wherever he could, to do social good. Not just to ensure their own gain. Though, of course, and be reasonable, don't be stupid, there was, inevitably, and why not, that too. A little bit of greed, he'd learned, was good. The wheels had to turn. Needed oiling.

He seemed to like the industrial metaphor. His own conversational wheels ran more smoothly from that point, with no grinding of the gears as the Ceri who had only ever used conflict if it served his ultimate, personal purpose came back into view. He'd never gone away of course. It was always, beginning and end, about Ceri. And it wasn't really the incentive of greed that drove his wheels on. It was what he wanted to see in the light of other people's regard for him, and hear in the warm gurgle of his own voice. He leaned across and held my arm down onto the table amongst the relics of our meal.

"Look, I know you're hurt. But you're making it too personal, butt. See, things have changed. You can see that, can't you?"

His thick, strong fingers pressed gently on my forearm. Reassuring. Just like Sir Ceri.

"What I'm saying is, is that, that, there's nothing else, see. To do, mind. What are our natural advantages? What's left? More to the point boy, how can we help? And it is about that, see, Billy, helping, I mean. Because they can't help themselves, see, any more. Perhaps they never could, eh!"

He swallowed. He pressed. He gave me his friendliest shrug that went from smile to body language to actual words.

"Hey, I know your old man would've laughed at all this, eh? You and me having a debate like this, after a bloody bourgeois spread as he'd've put it, eh. But, look, he was great, he was great. Then, see. You have to see that, Billy. It was all then. Only now you can't be romantic like he was. And, you know, he turned from that at the end, too. Too cynical then, he was. You said it yourself at the time. Remember?"

He paused. He took his fingers from my forearm.

"Got to stop beating yourself up, Billy. Difference between me and your old man is that I went and did it, didn't I? And it had to be different. Not saying he didn't teach me a lot, but he couldn't teach me that, could he? And you can only lead what's willing to be led, see. Best thing now is to help. And this, er, scheme, project, is only that. Another way. Look back and you'll see there were always, various, different, ways like this. Find a way to make things happen, is all. Get real, like they say, eh, Billy, go with the flow? You come from a long line of helpers, butt. You could help now."

When I saw he was finished, silent and smiling, I smiled back and gathered up the papers and returned them to their folder. I told him I agreed with him. That that was, indeed, the way it was now. That he had always known how to dance between the cogwheels and neither stop the machinery nor get mangled by the machine. I told him, too, what I still expected him to do, and where the papers would otherwise go. He waved this away like splatting a bothersome fly from a waiting sweetmeat, and snarled, disdainful of my stubborn behaviour, that it'd be a news story for a day, a flash in the pan for a week, a dead duck in a fortnight. I said,

"Sure. And you, Ceri? But you Ceri? Land speculation? Second phase, of course, after the regeneration project is built. But then an infrastructure ready for construction and sale. Well, dirty but OK, I guess. A largely public enterprise expanding, a little too close to some benefactors perhaps, but ultimately benefitting others. Houses and shops and retail outlets and a new road grid. Profits for the prophets. A bit messy. But OK. And then again. A senior public figure. Of some influence. In places of crucial decision-making. Still an idealist. A rebel, even. But one with hundreds of thousands in the bank, directly from a source attached to the whole scheme. You'll be crucified."

I added a "butt" to show there were no hard feelings. Then I told him what I wanted him to do. He looked more amused than bemused. More dismissive than compliant. I reached inside my jacket and took out the envelope marked with his name. I gave it to him. I walked away, leaving Sir Ceri Evans to pick up the bill.

* * * * *

I woke late the next morning, around ten, to the flash and blink of the red light of the bedside table's telephone. I had a message from reception. A Branwen Williams had called at eight thirty-five. She'd meet me in the lobby at eleven fifteen. I blinked back, my eyes as red as the pulsing light. Ceri's booze doing its trick. The one I always fall for. I cleaned up and put on a black T-shirt over black chinos and stuffed my bare feet into a pair of black tasselled loafers. I grimaced into the mirror. Colour co-ordination. Not exactly my game, unless minimalism is to your taste.

I was downstairs at eleven and sat in the far corner of a wannabee atrium. I hid behind a newspaper I wasn't reading. One I couldn't have read even if I'd wanted to try. My eyes wouldn't allow the close attention needed. If there had been a potted fern I'd have hidden myself in its fronds. I could have watered it by crying occasionally. Twenty minutes later, she was late, and at eleven thirty later still. I could feel the blurred newsprint starting to come back into focus. I scrunched my eyes to prevent that. I waited some more. I was good at that. I had long experience, and currently a deeply felt lack of mobility.

I clocked her entrance, in both senses, at eleven forty five. She smiled at the East European behind the desk and gave him my name. She turned at his reply, in the direction where I'd told Pavel I'd be when requested. Bran had definitely dressed down. She had on flat dove-grey suede shoes with an understated silver buckle. The look was not quite casual. Perfectly judged, unlike my own sombre ensemble, from the light grey cotton, flecked and knife-edged creased, trousers to the open-necked pink shirt worn beneath the darker steel-grey of a wraparound cardigan with a loose belt. It left her elegant wrists on display. And on the left one she wore – nice touch this I thought – a silver and turquoise Navajo bangle, late 1940s I'd been told, which I'd once bought for her in Arizona before all the skies of our lives had clouded over. There was no discernible make-up this morning, and her full hair looked tousled. I'd tousled her a few times myself. She was a fine tousler, all right.

And a mind-reader, too. Now she smiled at me. I could see we were going to get along fine. She sat down opposite me in the matching armchair. Its charcoal fabric framed the pretty and complementary picture she made as if it had been designed for it. Somewhere, maybe, it had. She crossed her legs at the ankles. I kept mine straight. She said, "You're all in black," as if colour coordination was her constant and actual game. Maybe it was.

"Thank you for seeing me. Again. You know ...", she said.

I did, and told her that was fine and that we had unfinished business anyway, didn't we? She raised one carefully under-plucked eyebrow, and said nothing. So, I told her I'd seen Ceri the night before and had made him a proposition that might affect all other current propositions, if she knew what I meant. She did. She told me he'd told her. Ah, I thought, with a twinge of discomfort at my all-round slowness, that explains the tousled look and the uncharacteristic lateness then.

I had said nothing about the small suitcase she had been carrying and which sat, shabbily out of place, by the side of her chair. It was clearly not like any overnight bag she might use even if, which I doubted, she'd use one. It wasn't even colour coordinated. Either with her, the atrium or the present day. It was too defiantly retrogressive for the faux retro of the lobby and too rectangular and brown to play off the black-and-white steel-framed pics of Manhattan and Paris and Milan with which this transient space moored its uncertain identity. The last time I'd seen the suitcase was on top of my old man's post-war utility furniture wardrobe. I tuned back in to Bran's insistent murmuring.

"… I understand … I really do, Billy … what you're saying. To Ceri. To me. And maybe, because you know how well I know you, Billy – so much unforgotten between us, isn't there? – I understand your motives. But I still want to get you to see, things have moved on, you know, to see that it would be, well, not sensible, just sentimental if I can say, to let yourself be blinded by them, and you would, really, spoil so much that is good. And necessary even. Good, certainly. We're all convinced of that. If you pursue them."

I pursed my lips. Not in a discouraging way, I hoped. I wanted to give the impression of hidden and unforgettable things. Things that were indeed between us still. Things I could release if I wanted, with the right persuasion. I wanted her to continue, to be persuasive. And I wanted to know what she was doing with my father's suitcase, and what was in it.

The speech I had coming was a good one. Prepared, rehearsed maybe, certainly drafted by Ceri for shape and punch, but clear and committed in its message. It was a speech about bringing hope to the hopeless. How could anyone possibly object? Some things were as undeniable as they were familiar. We'd been too young to appreciate the obstacles to our idealism. We'd imagined a moment when things would be possible because of all that had gone before. We could re-root, re-investigate, fertilise the lives and institutions of ordinary people – like her mentor, Ceri, she fought fashionably shy of that old calling card, the working class – with fresh energy, new ideas and determination. We hadn't been wrong, but we had mistaken what we had really had to play with to make the change possible. OK, maybe we were too excited, even enjoying the world turning upside down but, come on, what was the alternative? And it isn't as if the daily existence of ordinary people was adequate, was it? Even for them. She knew why I'd left. Caught between the icy dismissiveness of my old man and the despair at our generational failure. Which is where, she said, Ceri came in, couldn't I see? It had taken him some time, too, but he had been amongst the first to recognise that the fight was not ended, only re-located. He was our bridge. It wasn't, then, that we had to settle for less, only for something different, because needs and opportunities were no longer the same. The politics had atrophied because the whole way of once being had disappeared or shrivelled beyond use or recognition. Aspiration didn't have to begin at Basingstoke, did it? Community was just a romantic notion. Individuals deserved better, didn't they? What was wrong with that? Wasn't that what we were, really, all about, then and now? You didn't pull the ladder up after you like an Indian rope trick, you helped others up, you encouraged others to climb and you did what you could for those who wouldn't or couldn't.

And I had to see how radically altered people were, hadn't I? They voted unthinkingly in the past and now hardly bothered to vote at all. The past was, OK, often glorious to read about but romanticised like hell and probably shit to live through. Especially if you were a woman. She gave me that from down-under look that told me she knew this instinctively, of course. I nodded her on. Which was why, she confided, they needed not support nor comfort nor flattery but the kind of civic and cultural leadership that could ensure social and structural change. Ceri had given up on the petty squabbling of the remnants of his own political past to embrace the wider vision that a new coalition of interests offered and for which he, and some others with both roots and networks, could serve as a conduit. These channels had to be dug and lubricated by people with the same local knowledge and soaring ambition. But these people – a modest, implicit acknowledgement of herself, Gwilym and Maldwyn this time – were not somehow cheating or conniving to exclude ordinary people. No, they had an extraordinary desire to help people who, in these serially neglected and benighted valleys, could no longer help themselves. As a group, she said. As individuals, she said. It had to change, didn't it?

Bran then led me by the hand through the plans they had devised together to provide an exemplar which would be the envy of regeneration projects across Europe, and wider still. It met all the current needs of its surrounding dependents – economic and social – and, what was wonderfully more, it would bring the sharpest brains and the deepest wallets into a cultural symbiosis. She liked that word. She liked it so much she used it twice. I could see the symbiotic connection she was eager to make. Money and minds, together. Wow. What a sweet combo. When she saw the light bulb was on she gently explained how such deals were always complex, fraught with bureaucracy, be-devilled by rivalry, hamstrung by low expectation and clouded vision. There had to be leaders, big and bold enough to translate their individual ambition into the passion for progressive action that had always inspired them. It still did. That was the point. To create a mini storm by false accusation that would, nonetheless, take time and trouble to refute, with all the collateral, possibly fatal, damage the project would suffer, well, to do that, would be to make the mistake, but in reverse, we'd all made two decades ago. This was now. It was great

I was back but I had to be back, if not for good, then, at least, in the interest of the good. And the people of course. Of course.

Hats off, I thought. She was good. Really good, PR taken to the nth degree, and presented with flair. Reasoned intelligence without too heavy a sell could be a winner every time. Not this time though. What a crock of shit, I thought. We are for them despite themselves. They are finished otherwise. They don't understand anyway. Their usefulness is dependent on how they are used. Their history is cut off from any future they might have. Their remaining purpose is to stand aside or be led to higher ground they don't even glimpse anymore. QED.

I pursed my lips again. She seemed to think this signalled how bowled over I was. Yeah, that and some. I readied myself for the bullet to the brain still to come. She tapped the suitcase with an unvarnished fingernail. Did I recognise it? I said it seemed familiar. She told me the old man had asked her to take it away when he sensed he was dying and to give it to me if I ever came back. That it was full of notes and papers and a few books and magazines he seemed to have researched and culled. Some writing by him and a few letters, she said. She thought, and Ceri had agreed it seems, that it was all revelatory. In an uncanny way, she conjectured, it might be said to connect up me and the old man, and lots of other things which had seemed too large scale to be personal. Yet, here it was, up close and personal. I'd understand.

She stood and formally shook my hand before thinking better of it and leaning down to kiss my cheek.

"I'll leave the case," she said. "It's interesting, I promise. Please look at it. You might say it'll clear your mind. No doubts, eh? Love you, Billy. Really do. Sorry it didn't work out. But life never stays still, does it?"

I watched her leave, smiling at Pavel as she did, making the air around her fragrant by her passage. Funny how deceptive things

137

like that can be. I looked at the case. I sighed for a time long past. I picked it up as I got to my feet, and carried it to the lift and my room. I had some reading to do. It was lucky my eyes were starting to feel up to it.

* * * * *

I placed it bottom-down on the bed and contemplated it for a while. Whatever was inside would do me no good. Bran would not have brought it to do me good. It was what effect it was meant to have which alone concerned her. I went for a walk. Just to the window. I looked out from six floors down through the screen of treeleaf to the wall of the mock castle beneath. That wall was equipped to snarl back. The wall ran alongside the main road which roared past. The wall was topped with stone animals – a whole Victorian menagerie of them – pouncing and crawling and leaping over the battlements that would hold them in still flight forever. A whole city had sprung up around their sculpting, one paid for like them in the same mineral coin that had made it, for a time, the world's Coalopolis.

I crossed the royal-blue carpeted floor back to the foot of the low divan bed and stared at my nemesis. I leaned forward on impulse and released the two rusting metal catches which sprung up and back with an emphatic snap. I paused. I knelt down. I opened the lid of the cheap cardboard and leatherette case as slowly as inevitability would allow. I had no curiosity, only anxiety. If I knew the shallows of Bran all too well, I knew the depths of the old man even better. To be wary of one was to fear the other. A scent of curling brown paper and a whiff of dead days uncurled to meet me.

There were three hardback volumes, dating from the 1920s and '30s. Some magazines, a few maps of the coalfield before 1914, a book of statistics, a red-covered Edwardian railway timetable for coal freight traffic, loosely strewn papers, some typed on old-fashioned 'flimsy' but most scrawled over in my old man's blocky hand. I shuffled through them. Notes, extracts, disconnected paragraphs of continuous prose and his questions, a list of things to do and read, and a typescript biographical essay, or the start of one, which had been sent to him by post. At the very bottom of this pile were twenty or so pen-and-ink drawings on 6" by 4" white paper, bundled together in a folder and each initialled with the old man's D.M. in the left-hand corner. They were of ruins, bombed and blasted, of armoured cars and upturned vehicles, of black-limbed trees and shuffling men. They were of Monte Cassino and 1944. A final buff folder just said *Letters* on its front, and was marked *Personal*. It was obvious, from the books alone, that the material he'd assembled was a foray into the life and times of David Alfred Thomas. The old man had read into the history of the coalfield, and its various makers. But nothing as intensely gathered together as this, so far as I knew. It took me a quick trawl to establish who exactly the object of all this was. The subject had died in 1918 and when he died he did so as Viscount Rhondda. He'd been cremated in Golders Green. The old man must have known that on the day we were there together when Paynter followed Rhondda to the final fire in 1984, because none of the papers seemed to have been worked on, from the few dates he'd added to pages, since 1958. Lord Rhondda's ashes were later buried in Llanwern, his country seat in Monmouthshire, as Gwent was then known.

I resisted pulling everything apart too rapidly for one swift explanation. I wanted to see why this person had caught my old man's attention for this much effort. The cornerstones of the life were no great help. He'd been born in 1856 into the large family of a hustling, bustling mid-Victorian coal speculator, Samuel Thomas, who'd branched out from the Aberdare valley to hit pay dirt with the opening up of rich seams in the mid-Rhondda from the 1870s. Enough to pay for a public school education and then a Cambridge degree for his bookish son who, in turn, inherited what became the Cambrian Combine agglomeration of pits. I could see why that might be of interest to the old man. It was around aggressive managerial demands that the Tonypandy riots of 1910, along with the year-long Cambrian Combine strike, occurred. But this was clearly no historian's quest. No spinning enquiry either into the political detail that festooned the days of a Liberal MP in Imperial Britain until Thomas gave it up to concentrate on a dedicated career as coal capitalist. And more than that, one who longed to control destinies, shape lives, fulfil them through his own power and will. He had spelled it all out in chilling detail in essays and speeches of overweening ambition.

I skimmed a book of memorial essays by his devoted daughter and other contemporaries, along with a hagiographic biography, picking out the salient factual points: that he had been a fortunate survivor when the Germans torpedoed the Lusitania, with the loss of twelve hundred lives, on its return transatlantic voyage from New York in May 1915, and that his chief contemporary and one-time political rival, Lloyd George, Minister of Munitions in that year and made the Prime Minister of the British Empire in December 1916, had been quick to use Thomas's negotiating skills in America to ensure consistency of supply in the wartime crisis over munitions, and then placed him in his wartime cabinet, from 1917 as Food Controller, from where supreme administrative and imaginative genius allowed besieged Britain to live on rations rather than borrowed time. That won Thomas his Viscountcy, and probably hastened his early death at sixty-two. How large their lives were. How central was their Wales. How significant was coal itself. How it all still lingered.

* * * * *

It was late afternoon by the time I read, and re-read, everything. I had been hungry for nothing else through these hours. I put the overhead light on as rush-hour traffic began to back up alongside the city's castle walls. I had saved the "Personal" folder to the last. It was the least of all the papers in bulk. I had already read the four letters inside, however, several times over. Two of them copies made out in my father's handwriting. One more time, then. I fetched a cold bottle of Mexican beer from the room's fridge, uncapped it and drank from the bottle without the benefit of a salt rim, a glass or a segment of lime. The letters were zest enough, and my blood pressure had every reason to avoid a saline solution. I had more problems than solutions. But I did have questions, and maybe as echoes, a few answers. The first copied-out letter was as if from Llanwern Park, and its date written down as 16 December 1915.

"My darling Gwennie,

I send this with Blackmore to deliver to you by hand. He will bring me your reply if you will. Do not be afraid, for I will not abandon you. I know your time is near and when it has come you will return here, with the infant, and there will be no questioning of you, or of his presence, in my house.

What you have given me is not forgotten either and my joy in that gift of love and ecstacy sustains me in my labours. These, as you know, will increasingly confine me to London and Whitehall but, when you are ready, we will find time to be together again, and, I hope, find happiness in our meetings, so unexpected and vital for me, again.

Your David

Or, as you call me in memory of my place of youth,

Your Dai"

The second copied letter had the same date inscribed. It was just marked as from "Cheltenham". It read:

"My Dai,

For that is how I do always think of you now even if it is not the right and proper way to call you, and I will use David if you do prefer, though you do not, do you, as I know all too well. Well, I am near to the time now and they all take good care of me here, with no questions or evil looks which some can give you. I long to see you again and to meet like you say and am so happy you came back safe from America this time. What a fright we had in May and I will never forget it nor the way you saved my life, or I could say now, can't I, both of our lives. What I will do or say when I come back to Llanwern I worry, but I will be discreet and with your help pass it off, though I do think Miss Margaret, Lady Mackworth I should say, has her own thoughts which, what can I say, are true as you know my dear Dai.

Until we "meet"

Your very own Gwennie

The third letter was dated 3 July 1958 and the address was in Piccadilly. It was more formal.

"My dear Mr Maddox,

You will wonder, perhaps, that I only write now to acknowledge your note, of the 24th of September, 1953. Please be assured no discourtesy was intended and I had my reasons for not replying then, which are, indeed, different now.

I would be glad to see you if you care to come to the above address in the afternoon of the 3rd of July after two o'clock, when I will be pleased to explain to you what I can of the

142

circumstances of my family's connections to you and to which your earlier note, and its enclosures which I have kept safe to return to you, alluded.

Yours sincerely,

Margaret, Rhondda."

The final, and fourth, letter was not dated. It was from my old man to me. I'm not sure it explained what he thought he was explaining at the time of writing, probably the mid-1960s, but it would have to serve me half a century later as a settlement and a legacy. It did.

"Dear Billy,

I've often toyed with the idea of writing you a letter when you're too young – not quite ten yet – to understand it and yet when, with a life to come, I can speak more openly and fully to you here than, perhaps, when you are older and, believe me, face to face is often less than transparent.

But then it seems so artificial and I would not wish to write like some latter-day on-high purveyor of advice. So this is not, wherever this finds you and whatever you will have done by this time of reading, any advice at all. We will, no doubt, exhaust that, wastefully I suspect, as you grow up and away from me. No, this is information. Of a sort. Information I include here with the notes and for a work of research I began and will not now finish.

That I started at all is down to your mother. Shortly after we married in 1953 – amidst the ballyhoo of a Coronation year and the stupid bastards with their flag-bedecked street parties. Here, of all places, but I do go on, don't I, so I'll stop Here! – I showed the two love letters to her. Gwennie was my mother. I had had nothing to do with her and no contact with her until the letters came through the post in late 1952. They'd been sent to the address of my cousin Jimmy's mother, her sister, long deceased, and so then passed onto me by him. It seems I had a half-brother and he wrote, at her "dying request" he said, from Birmingham to give me the correspondence. Nothing else. No message. No explanation. Frankly, I did nothing. Not even a reply.

Your own mother's curiosity was something else. She worked out Llanwern to be, possibly, the country house, ironically enough demolished in 1952, and "David" or "Dai" to be D.A. Thomas, the coalowner of ill repute, so far as I'm concerned, who became Lord Rhondda. Well, well, I hear you say. If true, the capitalist bastard was shagging my proletarian mam. Joke here, eh Billy? And, bigger joke yet, I was the bastard she was carrying, to be born on 28 December, Holy Innocents' Day, 1915. Or not so wholly innocent, as it turned out.

Margaret, his daughter, was still alive. I sent her a polite note, asking for information and hopefully a meeting. I'd copied the letters and – foolishly, maybe – sent her the originals. I heard nothing back. But, egged on by your mother, I did some research, became hooked and even after she died, leaving you bereft and me a mess, and both of us alone, I tinkered with stuff, some of it sent to me unasked, then just stopped. You have the fragments in the suitcase. So you'll see I got so far and trailed away. With no regrets, I must say. I'd seen what I needed to see.

There's just one more capstone. The letter inviting me to meet Margaret came after your mother had died. I hesitated to go and, truthfully, in the end did it because I could feel Mona, your lovely and wonderful mother, urging me to square the circle. Well, I guess I did and I didn't.

Oh, Lady Rhondda was pleasant enough. And very grand, her flat more intimidating, with knick-knacks and occasional tables and paintings, than any home I'd ever been in. Also there were photographs of him, and her, separately and together in chased-silver frames. I'd seen photos of him in the books. No resemblance there I could see. Can you?

Anyway, she told me that my mother had been "rather a forward young woman." "Pretty", she'd grant, "but decidedly forward." It was possible, "likely but regrettably" she said, that her father, under some strain and relaxed by the sun he sought, "took advantage" or "was possibly seduced" by the dark-haired eighteen-year-old from Pontypool who'd been in service with them for over a year. Margaret added that she thought it "most unlikely" that my mother, at that age and coming from where she came, was "altogether innocent in such things".

That much was conceded but no more. In her opinion my mother was as likely to be pregnant with the child of the chauffeur, Blackmore, or maybe someone from the village, as she was with the offspring of a man nearing sixty, one afflicted with rheumatic fever and a heart condition. As for his letter, it was a recognition of their tryst and of her condition, and of his generosity and nothing more. My mother did indeed return, with her son, to Llanwern, in the spring of 1916.

By December that year D.A. Thomas was President of the Local Government Board and in Lloyd George's cabinet, and absent, by and large, from Llanwern thereafter until his final ill health and lingering death in the summer of 1918. She said that she believed relations between her father and the parlourmaid had ceased long before. Margaret, for so I will insist on calling my half-sister, said she "vaguely" remembered me and "vividly" recalled my being discovered in a high chair, "in an almighty mess", the day after my mother absconded, at the age of twenty, without "so much as a by your leave" and only a note to the effect that, if required, her married sister could be

145

contacted to come to fetch me. As she soon did. But that's another story, for another time as they say and never tell.

I could have argued with her. I did demur. I said the letters seemed proof enough. That I had only wanted to meet her. I was ready to leave, when she softly, very softly, said she was indeed sorry. Perhaps there was more to it than she had wanted to know or believe. She had found it so difficult when her father, stricken with angina, sat in the semi-wild garden at Llanwern, amongst the spring flowers with his gramophone playing his favourite tunes from musical shows, my mother sat at his feet or dancing in front of him, whilst I tottered across the lawn. On the morning he died, Margaret forbade my mother directly from going to his cremation in Golders Green and to the subsequent burial of his ashes, which she planned to place beneath the ancient yew tree in the churchyard at Llanwern. My mother did not wait for any change of heart. She left the house forever, and me of course, on 4th July, the day after he died. Did she know it was Independence Day? Margaret said – and these were her very last words as I stood to go – "I do not expect you to forgive me. I do not even expect you to understand. But I loved him. And him alone. And I wanted you, of all people perhaps, to know that before I, too, die." You know me well enough, Billy, to know I neither wanted nor asked for nor received anything else. Besides she had shown no interest in my life, not Cassino or the pits or anything, not in Mona or in you. Why didn't that surprise me, I wonder. So, sod her, I thought. And all that the foul air around her brought with her. We had no need of it. Then or now. I left all the letters with her. Her worry, not mine I thought. My half-sister died in Westminster Hospital just a few weeks after we had met for the first and only time.

There was a postscript, of a kind, to these matters. After her death I was sent a package addressed to me, with a short note from a T.A. Lloyd, saying he would be happy to talk further with me if I so wished, and that he had known Margaret Rhondda, had worked when very young for her father, then plain Mr.D.A.Thomas, in a slight secretarial capacity, and had known others in his immediate entourage. He said he had begun to write a biographical essay, as yet unfinished, a portion of which he enclosed for my interest. That is with the other related papers I gathered together if you want to read it. I did not write back.

I have mulled it over, and over, of course, again and again the past few years since your mother died, and I met my half-sister. And I decided to let it all go, for me at least. But I determined that one day you should, if the occasion arises, know the connections for yourself. That they are significant I do not doubt. What it means as we go on, I don't know. Will you? I suppose that he was ours as much as we are his, but I certainly do not think, so far as I am concerned, by any meaningful ties. Only the unbreakable, inexorable, irredeemable bonds of a society which has been as little as it has been so much and as hopeful as it has been wretched continue to have human meaning for me.

Love (of course)
From Dad

* * * * *

The American Prince of Wales
By
T.A. Lloyd

His was a concept as much as it was a reality. He ached to make of the reality he had been given something inconceivably greater than its material form. But it was, he knew, that which was merely material which was the matter he must dynamite – but how? – into the future that lay still and inert in deep fissures. Of coal. Of that mineral which, alone, vitalised the blood and iron of conflicting Empires and for which he had more beneficent dreams.

It was said of him that he knew Jevons' 1865 tome, *The Coal Question: an Inquiry concerning the Progress of the Nation and the Probable Exhaustion of our Coal-Mines,* nearly by heart and could and would cite chunks of it out loud, as if it was an amusing party piece. For him it was Nirvana and Apocalypse both. In drawing room and office, at the dinner table or the theatre, he would bore and impress, rant and reason, to the effect that to be born into a coalfield such as South Wales, more, to be charged with its destiny, was to bear a gift incomparable to birth by lineage or politics by choice. The world itself, he would say, could thereby, by this vast reserve of coal, be secured, for a time, for ourselves. Time bought to grow and develop. Elsewhere if need be. He was, this Welshman, in the phrasing of the day, no "little Englander"; but nor was he, this modern Prince, to be defined by the happenstance of being Welsh.

In spate, his clipped conversation raced into speech, and his speech roared into exhortatory impatience. In 1896, when Lloyd George, his Liberal parliamentary colleague, and fellow radical, sought a different future, the notion of Cymru Fydd, a version of Home Rule tailored around the confident sense of a distinctive and prosperous Liberal Wales from north to south, it was D.A. Thomas who stymied the politics of geographical unity and urged wider horizons beyond this, as he saw it, cultural myopia. That year, in counterblast, he wrote a paean to his dream, a world spinning on the axis of his locus:

"… there is no part in the United Kingdom which has so many national and artificial advantages as Cardiff; and these must tell in the near future. In a geographic sense the Welsh capital is admirably situated for the North and South American, West Indian, African, Pacific, East Indian, Australian, Mediterranean, Black Sea, and South and West Continental trades. As a loading port she is unrivalled; numerous vessels having to come to her from London, Liverpool, and Continental ports for outward cargo. Coal is the heaviest of all our exports, and the coalfield of South Wales is the most valuable in the Kingdom for export of cargo and for bunkering steamers.

"… The time has fully arrived when Cardiff should seek to form a large Atlantic trade, both in goods and passengers … Cardiff is first for minimum distance New York to Birmingham, and second to London … In all these phases of trade and convenience for commerce there is a distinct advantage on the side of Cardiff … It is true the principal item [of deadweight tonnage] is that of coal. But it must be borne in mind that coal forms the staple at present for the outward cargoes of all outward bound ships. It is something like three fourths of the whole deadweight of cargoes in our overseas trade. Cardiff has an unlimited supply of the best bunker coal in the world behind her. The coal of the South Welsh basin, as yet unworked, is estimated by the Royal Coal Commission at about 34,000 million tons. Just conceive it!"

His ambition was not to be confined. Neither by the conventional limits of a commercial life set by others nor by the root of the place where he was born. He intended, on the contrary, to use that rooted vigour to reach out beyond the circumstances of birth and upbringing, and to use his own given time and allotted space to make a great social experiment. In essence this is what America meant for him. And in this was he so very different from those who opposed him?

He made it plain that, although he made a great deal of it through his extensive business dealings, he was not ever merely seeking to make money. It was more that wealth and an assured fortune were his means to make the success he desired follow on. His definition of success was not a narrow one: it would be broad enough to encompass all manner of social and cultural growth. Seeded, tended and controlled by him. His people, as he never ceased to think of those amongst whom he'd lived and who now toiled for him, were, in literal fact, his end. The end purpose of his means. They, he often explained to those who asked, whether in the Press or in Parliament, thrashed about, in a welter of strikes and riots and grumbling, because they, by the nature of things, did not, and could not, possess the means to attain the impossible Nirvana held up before them by Social Idealists who, in every other sense than for their foolishness, earned his respect. Indeed, he was, he averred, one such himself. The difference was that he had both a finite goal and the practical means to achieve it. He was with his people in this, neither for impractical Socialism nor for the sticking-plaster Welfarism of Lloyd George. He had imagined how a novel collectivity, educated and disciplined and led, could come to a similar understanding of both the benevolence of such a system on this earth and the absolute necessity of the kind of leadership he could ensure in and beyond his time. And the key to this was the happenstance of Coal, its supreme importance. He would invoke his admired Jevons to the effect that coal "is the mainspring of modern material civilisation ... not beside but entirely above all other commodities ... the material source of the energy of the country, the universal aid, the factor in everything we do, without which we are thrown back into the laborious poverty of early times." Given this faith, this responsibility, he knew how to conceive of his duty. Being humble was not part of it.

His was a Faustian impulse, to build in despite of the frailty of Humanity and the febrile vitality of the Valleys. He recognised both these tendencies in the pre-War fever for Syndicalism, or workers' control, where all leadership, of owners or by union bosses, would be eschewed in favour of direct democracy and decision-making. Again made feasible in this place as in no other by the concentration here of power and people through coal.

'Welsh syndicalism' echoed the advance nature of coal capitalism, expressed here in the words of its foremost theorist, the miners' leader, Noah Ablett: "where the tendency to place the whole industry into the hands of one firm is proceeding at a phenomenal rate, scarcely a month passes [in 1917], but that there is news of two large companies amalgamating, or steps taken to form a large combine." So, the answer for Ablett and his followers was to be "an industrial union – on a revolutionary basis for the abolition of capitalism", since "we shall never attain freedom by looking backward. We must go on with the times." But that was where D.A. Thomas already felt himself to be and he understood Ablett's insight into the fearful plasticity of their world because he shared it. In their self-created landscape the spirit abroad was that of an absolute social being – Capitalist or Socialist – which haunted the mind.

Ablett's ideas would resound for a short time, then dwindle to survivalism and welfarism in the devastated industrial backwater of the 1920s. D.A. Thomas would not live to see this, and by the end of his own days in 1918 had come to personify the mining valleys as a cutting edge for the entire modern world. He died before his realm crumbled. But it was never, for him, a mere industrial concern and therein lies his fascination for those of us who have indeed come after him.

All of the missionary zeal that fired him – "The wise thing for democracy to do is to give every child in the land an equal opportunity for making the best use of its talents, so that where there are now hundreds of industrial organisers there may one day be thousands" – as he saw it, to create wealth to increase happiness was founded on the inheritance in coal he had received from his father in the Glamorgan hills. Did he think of this inheritance, as such, as an "equal opportunity?" Talent as an industrial organiser was nonetheless certainly his. He turned the Cambrian Combine in mid-Rhondda into one of the largest integrated coal concerns in the world. Nor did he stop there: agencies in the sale of coal, companies to import pitwood from France, distributive organisations in ship-owning, companies to establish coal depots, insurance, stocks and shares, and ever more collieries, all were engrossed in his maw. He operated in France, Spain, North Africa, and North America – and all on the basis of steam coal from the Valleys. How his world was to be perceived was also within his remit, for he had financial control of numerous journals and newspapers in Wales, and planned for an influential journal of opinion in London.

He stepped aboard the *Lusitania* in March 1915 to further his growing North American business interests. Even after the *Lusitania* had been sunk with him aboard ship on a return transatlantic crossing in May, his American connection was not over. He had almost immediately returned, now with a formal remit from Lloyd George, to establish the means to finance through extensive borrowing the purchase of munitions Were the two voyages linked somehow? Why else would he have told a close confidante, at the end of the war that "the experience of the *Lusitania*" had, after all, been worthwhile? He was, he knew, a colossus beyond all mere politicking, and one centrally placed at the core point of his age. If he and his entourage, his daughter Margaret, his Secretary, an assistant secretary and the maidservant, had perished on their return journey the story, remarkable enough for its Tycoon lineaments in the age of the Industrial Titan, would still hold interest. But there is, of course, more: the emergence in wartime of a dedicated Public Servant of enormous capability and, at the Ministry for Food, the boss of Sir William Beveridge, whose later imprint on Welfare Britain would be so immense. As a Minister D.A. Thomas was confronted officially for the first time – since he must surely have known the average rate in his own Rhondda of almost 200 deaths per thousand live births in the decade to 1910 – by the appalling nationwide statistics for infant mortality. He now dreamed, as his legacy, of a nationwide Department of Health, one whose creation he demanded immediately. What emotion had ignited this principled ambition? What lives crossed and ended and led out from here to the world he would never see? Why did Lloyd George exclaim that an "interest in the health of infants is rather an unexpected passion for Rhondda."

* * * * *

I lay back on the bed amongst the rubble of my old man's literary excavations. I had been spun back to a beginning I had not suspected. In the early years of this new century I was being told that the false dawns had all come and gone, and the one that might have been different was the only one from the early years of the last century which had offered a glimpse of the something else as actually possible. A final wake-up call. I was not remote from that. I was a living part of it. But all circumstances had changed, maybe beyond redemption. It was, it seemed, pure sentiment to dream of

153

any way out other than through the order and the social gradation and the acceptance of discipline which leadership and vision offered to those who had forsaken the one and lost the other. What doubt of that could be left? Ceri had discovered the hard truth of this for himself, and acted upon it, filling the void with his engorgement of it. My old man had moved over a hard lifetime from gritty indifference to trust and hope and back again to a railing anger when what was in reach, for control, had been let slip, and politics proved inadequate when its hinterland of support shrivelled. His own lost and found father had scorned airy idealism and secured the future for himself, anchoring it in the management of the affairs of men and women whose lot was indeed to labour, but not, he would say, in vain. All this I weighed up and now understood in a detail and with a specificity I had not possessed before. Ceri would have his answer. I'd phone him in the morning. He could do what he liked after that.

Haf picked me up, as arranged, at nine in the morning outside the hotel. She was leaning against her car. The rain had stopped. She raised her right hand in a wave and dropped the cigarette in her left. There were no half measures about the smile. I liked that smile. I could grow to like someone who could smile like that at nine in the morning. She looked as if she'd just stepped out of the shower, shaken her hair, tied together a cardigan, dark green, over a T-shirt, a white one, pulled on jeans, blue, and boots, black, and was ready to go. She was an energy burst to cancel my sombre mood and grey suit. I gave her a paternal hug and a kiss on her cheek. I had told her what I had done and what I intended to do if other things did not happen that morning. She smiled.

She drove carefully and skilfully out of the traffic dodgem-ride that was the city centre. We were going east through avenues full of lofty semi-detached villas that gave way to retail warehouses and elongated superstores, until we finally made it to the motorway. She pushed the Clio as much as was possible and the needle flickered gallantly around seventy in the slow lane. We exited to the north, through the overspill estates that marked the city's boundaries, and up into a switchback succession of interlocking valleys, seeking out the new bypass roads that kept the narrow, terraced streets well away from us.

The roads cut across the slopes instead of following contours. They seemed the latest way to ignore all these settled places. In Haf's car, window-gazing was easy. She couldn't go quickly enough to cause any blurred vision. So I caught the salute of a thousand satellite dishes above or below, whichever way the road swooped or rose, and felt the sinister ranks of sitka pines – the biggest forestry plantation in an industrial area of Europe, Haf had told me – bristle above the topmost terraces like a buzz of crew-cut hair. I wondered if anyone could now recall these valleys as once properly industrial. They certainly weren't really post-industrial. More like shagged-out-and-thrown-back formerly industrial. Her own politics were young politics, green shoots and all that, but not cosily environmental, more angrily mental. She said she worked with groups who were out to occupy the husks of former workmens' institutes to create and diffuse a virtual and alternative culture based around community time-sharing. I must have looked blank. It was people, she said, who mattered for her, who "made" a place. I let that one pass. It was why she'd told me she'd been so bothered by the book of my *Crazy Horse* exhibition. I had, she'd felt, blotted out the people, the good with the bad. I told her I didn't do those categories, even then. But Haf was too intense to let that pass. Removing their faces was denying them their humanity. I had disassembled them into machine-like pieces. I was not seeing anything beyond fragments. I had to put them together again. I said I'd hoped I was acknowledging a spirit that could not be seen or captured, only remembered. She said that now it was she who didn't understand. That there was no sense in having memories that did not serve life.

We left it there for a while, though we weren't seeing much life ourselves as we climbed higher and further until we came on the eastern rim of the former coalfield to one of the old iron and coal townships almost at a valley's end, and even then we didn't stop but left behind its great clefts of re-planted landscape and the concrete silos and sheds of the dead steelworks, on whose re-claimed acreage the windows in clusters of executive houses now winked hopefully in the fitful sunlight. We followed the signs that proclaimed, in stylish blue-and-gold Euroscript, *Canolfan Cymoedd y Dyfodol* : Future Valleys Centre. The road took us through a gothic arch, a stone gateway, down a drive through a thickly wooded deciduous copse with ornamental ponds and lichened statuary hidden behind glossy evergreen shrubbery bushes. The square coal owner's house that had long ago become council offices waited at the end of a rutted and potholed drive, but to its right a newer strip of road led us on to a glass and chrome cube, the *Canolfan*. The car park was to the side and the back and already full of cars more recent and gleaming than Haf's French banger. She lined it up between a black Saab convertible and a steel-grey Golf.

The short walk back to the *Canolfan* gave us the 360° perspective on the higher hills of an escarpment above us and the wooded slopes, screening any unsightly human habitation, below us. At the entrance to the *Canolfan* I waved an embossed press card and steered Haf, with a knowing smile at the doorkeepers, into the downstairs atrium. A couple of hundred people were either queuing up for coffee at long linen-covered tables or clutching their cups and moving thoughtfully in the very centre of the space around a glass-covered dome which contained a model of the proposed development. Haf and I skipped the coffee and went straight for a gawk. The modelled development ascended in pentagon-like building pods from the lower wooded slopes above the valley townships until they scattered, seed-like, around the *Canolfan* on this flatter ground and then climbed again, built into the walls of the escarpment, nestling in abandoned quarries, colonising mountain pools and rivulets as in the trajectory of a waterfall going in reverse. The model's landscape had been sculpted with an eye for the detail of the terrain, down to tinted pathways and the painted-in re-planting, a colour scheme of sage green and eggshell blue hinting at an outdoor/indoor Georgian idyll. But the pods, the capsules, were the thing. They were individual pentagons of glass-fronted rooms, set above a car port with carousel elevators, each one three tiers high and capped by roofs of weathered pine that were pitched at 20° angles so they almost appeared flat. The pods were interlinked by tubular glass and steel passageways leading from their second tiers. What made their uniformity somehow organic was the support structure each one had. Their skeletal frames of matt-burnished steel were legs which stood at different angles and heights depending on the lie of the land. They looked as if they were adjusting their weight and stance to embrace the earth on which they squatted. Here and there the architect had dotted a few expensive-looking cars, a number of tanned and suited men and women who even in their mannequin form seemed cheerfully at ease, powerful. And, positioned at car doors, in front of elevators, in the shrubbery there were other figures, more bowed and in attendance, a platoon or two of servants.

All around us was a murmur of approval. You could tell which particular man-and-womankind these spectators envisaged as themselves. Haf was giving wall maps and diagrams a scholarly look that told me she knew the topography by heart. I guessed that Maldwyn had sectioned this moonscape of iron and coal patches into a forensically planned mapping of further ownership and later availability that would have given the Domesday Book compilers a run for their money. Or his money. It wasn't a scam, of course. It was a strategy. A magnet. Be attractive if you want to attract. Silly me, as Ceri had told me. Haf had displaced any emotional revenge she might have wanted to feel at a personal level into what she took to be a more mature species of vengeance against those she headlined for me as these predatory exploiters, these fat cats, establishment bigwigs, land speculators, people movers, and here in this sanitised sanctum a whole ragbag of green and environmental and humane instincts flooded her cheeks, and made her blush with righteousness. Me, I couldn't see anything wrong with personal revenge, the quicker the better. Outside, Sir Ceri's black, chauffeur-driven Audi had pulled up. I saw Gwilym simultaneously emerge from a shoal of notables like an oil slick in search of a better beach. That would be Ceri, then. In the old days, between old friends, a nod of the head and the grip of a handshake would have sufficed. But, here, now, Gwil actually embraced Ceri, who, in turn, did not stiffen. They were almost kissing. Ceri turned, smile at the ready, and then the wince did come, in the shape of a frown directed my way. I had been standing so as to make sure that I would be in his eyeline. I positively beamed. My mouth cracked open so wide that it could have accommodated the San Andreas fault line. He looked hard at Haf. He would have read the letter. This was my counterstrategy. And I could tell it had disturbed him. Then things got even better.

Maldwyn's nose was squashed into a wrap-around bandage. His eyes were two small blood oranges, peeled, and the cuts and abrasions to his cheeks were a homage to the beating the Tonypandy heavyweight champ Tommy Farr took in the seventh round from Joe Louis in 1937, as told to me by the old man. I don't recall Tommy having a broken arm after his slugfest with Joe, but my Tommy had given Mal one, for sure, if that sling was anything more than a fashion accoutrement. The conspirators huddled together. Ceri had changed colour when he saw Mal up close and personal, from ruddy to off-white. Gwilym had coloured in the contrary fashion. And Mal just stood there, his facial tints way off the chromatic scale of any palette used since Matisse completed a painting of his wife in green and crimson. I wondered about his teeth since his full, oh-so-kissable lips were split and scabbed. He opened them, with some difficulty, to spit something out. I muttered an "Oh" out loud with a soft purr of appreciation since there were at least two teeth missing, and his smart-arse tongue was swollen into inarticulacy.

Sir Ceri could see that standing about was no good, that action was needed. He moved forward and onwards, the smile back in place, whilst Maldwyn hung back, consigned to his wake, with just Gwilym bobbing along beside him into the hall. Haf and I were swept along as the crowd moved in. We were close enough now to see Bran on Ceri's other side, where his bulk had protected her from view. Mal, flanked by Wheelie who had pushed open the double-doors for him, limped down the aisle to sit in the front row. There were about two hundred chairs in the inner auditorium, rows of gilt-framed red plushed seats for the expectant backsides of councillors, estate agents, businessmen, journalists, accountants, politicians, academics and developers. A panoply of the professionally purposeful. We sat near the back and watched as the stage party assembled. The backdrop was a screen displaying the words:

Canolfan Cymoedd y Dyfodol
Future Valleys Centre
And to the bottom right:
Tir y Werin : Bywyd y Werin
A People's Land : A People's Life

To the side and behind the stage party were ten-foot-high pop-ups with pictures of past, present and glorious future. There was a podium with a microphone to the left, and shiny metal boxes with pinprick blue lights. The local Mayor thanked everyone, introduced Dr Gwilym Jones, and quickly sat down. Gwilym puffed himself up like a pouter pigeon, made a few stirring remarks about historical oxygen levels, social adrenaline, and the valleys heritage – all just broken and breached ramparts apparently – before switching to a PowerPoint presentation that hailed the foresight of civic leaders, business entrepreneurs and academic creativity, all of which was set to propel us from this very base camp to the Himalayan heights we would need to reach, socially and culturally, from the foothills of entrepreneurial endeavour where we were now stranded by our past. He, himself, he modestly muttered was a mere sherpa for others in this final ascent. It was, all in all, to be a quick two-step into the future. Gwilym gushed a little more about the combination of architectural genius and locality which we had beheld in the model in the atrium, a sure-fire Gold Medal winner when built, in his opinion, and how it was making use of the sole real attribute that was left to "our people" – I liked that "our" – namely, the landscape, blighted or pristine, contaminated once, now cleared for use, an "Alpine Echo" which we, in our inane yodelling up and down the streets of a defunct past had failed to register as our true legacy. But here it was at last, caroming off the higher slopes of the foresight of our truly visionary leaders, to invigorate those below who could now look up, and hear the call. Gwilym's speechifying flourished, on and on, for ten minutes, with more and more exotic blooms pulled from behind his back, out of his sleeves and out of his mouth, as the screen behind him dispensed with its headlines, slogans and logos, to flash images, from black and white and grey miserabilism to the cool, sharp pictography of the architectural present, and on to the fully imagined and animated hub that was our "only hope", our very own patch of kryptonite, the super-messiah of a Future we must embrace, otherwise we perish. He ended with an introductory paean of over-the-top praise to Ceri which relished the great, self-made, articulator of the best we had been and the better we could be, in the person of the man who had, at this late stage in his distinguished career, agreed to head up the consortium that would deliver the *Canolfan* from concept to full reality in the next five years. Sir. To a ripple. Ceri. To a wave. Evans. To a crash. Applause. And Ceri diffidently rising, but at last on his feet. Alert, as ever, to the mood. Aware, instinctively that Gwilym had lost the audience, minutes ago, with his burbled boosterism and digital flash cards. Ceri walked slowly from his reserved seat in the front row to the podium. He paused. He began,

"Thank you. All. And thank you, Dr Gwilym Jones. Friends, I'm afraid I can't, this morning, match the informative flow of all that eloquence. And, as for pretty pictures, well, as you know, I don't do those. Technically incompetent, me. I fear I am, in my own person, my very own PowerPoint presentation! And with my voice, well you all know me, I won't need that microphone either, eh"."

Laughter. A self-deprecating smile. And he leaned forward into the audience. Somehow, no longer speaking at them or to them but being, at one, in speech, with them. A conversation in all senses except for the fact that it was only him doing the speaking. I felt that I had come only to learn that, sink or swim, Ceri would not drown. I just still wasn't absolutely sure which shore he would strike out to reach.

"Where flattery is so shameless, Mr Chairman, blushing thanks are always inadequate – I must remember to come back sooner and stay longer. Does wonders for my self-esteem: political Viagra never felt better. And all this vigour on my home patch. For here, of course, I really am at home. Amongst friends, some very old friends. With comrades, unfashionable word for what we thought ourselves to be once. In the justest of causes.

Home ground. As I said. Names and places I carry with me wherever I now go. And sometimes, nowadays, there *are* only names to remember for some places long gone. Names, my friends, which are, still, for some of us like a roll call of battle honours. Battles fought. Some won, and most lost. Always with honour.

I drove here, up the valley, to this green and hopeful place this morning on our new bypass roads. European funding, of course, won by our own government, for you, for us. And very welcome, too. But there is a less welcome truth, as well. By these roads I passed around or looked down on townships and villages and streets upon whose very formation more clichés have been bestowed than we might hear in a bishop's Easter sermon. The sentiment is put there, precisely, like the roads themselves to avoid the close-up look. In every sense, we have been by-passed.

Even perhaps betrayed. Yes, I think so. A betrayal. But, as ever, of what, by whom? Betrayed by successive governments – whatever their political hue – fobbed off with the empty promises of empty warehouses, empty factory spaces, empty industrial estates. Betrayed by local government, too, in my very own vineyard of endeavour, where too often a want of imagination has been in cahoots, too many times, with a lack of faith. And betrayed from within. Betrayed by the feral, the anti-social, the resentful, the feckless who betray themselves by betraying the generation to come, and the memory of those who have been! And, for the rest, we close our doors. We blank our minds. We are atoms without fission. The chain of reaction amongst us is a mere flicker of yesteryear. And betrayed too by me. By people like me. Maybe, most of all because we have ceased to be the advocates. We speak, too often now, like the dummy on the ventriloquist's knee.

Why? *Because* we still cling to a learnt mantra. One which declares that however much is changed, all around us, materially for the better I grant if spiritually for the worse perhaps, that, still, our values, our core sense of communities and cohesion remain as ones to cherish. Bollocks! It's all bollocks, and you know it, because the whole edifice, our culture, our society, our sense of ourselves was built on a concatenation of forces, an historical chain reaction if you like, which cannot be repeated, or even sustained. It is arrant nonsense to suggest we can regenerate all that has withered on the vine with buckets of social manure, vials of economic potassium and dollops of cultural bio-energy. If this was indeed once Labour Country, in a profound sense that went way beyond the merely political, as you and I know it was, then it can no longer be so except in name and, maybe, a lost, hopeless yearning, can it? We must find new ways to go down those new roads we have built. Otherwise we, and they, will go nowhere.

And that is why we are here today, is it not? Able at last to speak out truthfully because of the ark of this stunning project which we are able to float amidst the deluge, even in our wreckage. You have seen the plans. You have seen the scale models. You have noted how the architects of this spaceship of hope explain and illustrate their vision. Let me remind you of it. Only the landscape can be our salvation now, and only if it is returned from the depredation of industry and restored with care and expert attention. At the tops of all our valleys. Attention paid to that detail of waterfall, rock screes, copses with real trees, not the suffocating blanket of pine trees sown for profit. Only then will we truly attract new blood, new energy, new money, new owners. Friends, the fantasy of a cultural tourist trade, buoyed up by industrial museums and heritage trails, is the chimera of a 1980s dream that was always fantasy. A knee-jerk reaction to replace a History which had already vanished. a simulacrum of a vacuum. Since then, increasingly so and whoever is in power, we have learned to accept our fate, to embrace even the search for employment in the cities and towns spilling off the motorway, whilst we stay in dwindling and ageing numbers here. they tell us now, our expert carers, that at the mouths of our fabled gulches we can indeed gather and commute to work but that, *here*, we must see that landscape is all, our last best hope. Not mean streets. Not meaner people. But a beauty of natural shape or form that can entice others, provided we ensure that entry in and exit from the mothership, is pleasurable and painless. The Valleys, our valleys, have now to find their final destiny as ... a national park. The newest. The latest. The best.

The Vision, this new dream, by-passes the detritus of our past, by shutting it out. At last a future that is made afresh, clean and whole, not one regenerated piecemeal and messily. This future will open up, properly, at veritable gates – gates through whose portals we will funnel the work done for the spaceship – the cooks and chefs, the cleaners, the gardeners, the drivers, the bar staff and waitresses, the electricians and plumbers and carpenters, the brickies, security men and receptionists, to all who will ensure that the new, and perhaps, why not passing-through inhabitants? are protected to think, secured to relax and gated to be special. That army of workers will, naturally, come and go every day, their pockets clinking with the gold with which their labour has been bought. So, my friends, today we are asked to behold a new model for the future, one which can, from this beginning, spread and take root across all our hills and valleys. Who in their right mind would spurn this way out of the past to cross over into a new world?"

* * * * *

He paused to let a burst of clapping punctuate his speech. He had moved effortlessly to the shore I did not have in mind. As the applause faded I left Haf still sitting towards the front and walked to the back of the room, a physical escape from all this my only exit left. On the platform Ceri had continued Then he continued, his tone imperceptibly sharper, his blend of demotic speech and oratory mixed for the occasion as ever. It was a masterclass. Ceri had not lost it. I had underestimated him. Energy would gravitate to the darkness none of us could escape.

1997:TIME TOLD

So I must let it begin, this ending of mine. My eyelids are shut tight, pulled down like blinds over the cavities of my sunken eyesockets. All the better to see the only sights I wish to see. For me alone. Especially, they stay closed against them. Those who detain me for a while yet, for what little remains.. My carers. I do not resent them, as they only do what I had arranged to happen when it came to the last go-off, and the Home is aware that I have decided to leave them all, as a team, a substantial, unexpected sum. They will, I hope, be as pleased as they will be surprised. My solicitor will see that it happens, and that the Legacy Trust I have created, with its specified use, will reach the other recipient of my earthly goods after my death. This does give me comfort. Yet I am impatient by now for its trigger, and the delivery to come.

The carers are in the room. I hear them whispering whenever they hover near me, over me, circling around my raised hospital-style bed, its padded sides making it more like a child's cot than a geriatric's, ministering to me four times a day on their timetabled pattern. I hear them counting out my pills. They lift my top lip and push the pills into my mouth. I lie propped up by my Egyptian cotton pillows, stuffed with duck feathers, no expenses spared I had made clear, my pension pot ample until my death. All arrangements made before, a decade ago now, I went to live out my final days, and complete my work, in this top-of-the-range Nursing Home, formerly that mid-Victorian gentleman's residence. And Dai's boyhood home. South-facing. Very desirable once. They, the carers, cannot see my smile for it no longer exists on any plane of physical existence. I am fast leaving all that behind. So I am smiling. Somewhere.

The carers wipe my mouth, mopping up with tissues the water I have dribbled from the glass proffered to wash the pills down. They no longer bother with straws. I will not suck on them. First sign, they say. I wonder if they can smell my breath. I make small, guppy sounds as the water slips down. I exhale with little puffs of air, a quiet gasp of tastes

169

and fumes. I remember that I used to recoil from such old man's odours in others. A rancid mix of stomach acid and decaying teeth, seeping up out of me now, breathy past papery lips, mottled with purpled blood blisters and flecked with the foam of my spittle. I would have involuntarily drawn back whenever I had been forced by close contact with relatives to scent the left-over sourness of decay. Now, I am myself its source. Almost a hundred years of backed-up inner staleness.

I do not smell, however, from any bodily neglect. They wash me, with a flannel cloth and sponge and soap. They use a basin of lukewarm water to clean my hands and face and, when they frequently must, all orifices, from ears and nose to arse. I would, once, have been horrified by such an intimate intrusion. Not anymore. I submit. It is as if I am shut down. Running repairs only. A matter of time.

I hear them muttering. They are cheery today. They express surprise, yet again for they are nothing if not repetitive, as if any kind of familiar mantra banishes the need for thought, and wonder that I still have enough of my own teeth left to chomp and chew with my ochred stumps on the pap they spoon into my mouth in gobbets. It seems I will have them, gold inlays and all, as long as we both shall live. Made to last, eh.

And while I wait, I tune into their voices. A dialogue, of course, since there are always two of them. Doubled up, like the police on patrol. Are they afraid I will bite? Fat chance. Or is it insurance against the blame of a sudden lurch to death's exit on my part? They needn't worry. I won't sue. By his voice only, the male sounds to be in his early to mid-twenties. I have grown antennae in sensory and auditory matters. He chatters the most. The female carer is, I'd assume, in her forties. She is more methodical, more attentive to detail. I do not think they are indifferent towards me but, how else, they push and pull me for the inert thing I have become, how else to clean me, medicate me, feed me, leave me, finally, to just be. I think that if I could I would now stop them. I do not need to be any longer. I even credit them with some intuition of this beyond their drilled and dutiful ministration of their tasks.

The man says, "Poor Bugger, s'not like living like, s'not really, is it, know what I mean, just zisting, like, feel sorry for 'im like, poor old sod."

The woman says, "Yeah, I'd rather go if it was me."

He says, "I know, yeah, but not like there's a choice, though, not really, is it."

The woman says, "Lift him up a bit for me, Tony, under his armpits, that's right. There we are, OK darling, that comfier then. Good."

Tony says, "Bit of a whiff on him, Gloria. Should we change his pad now?"

Gloria says, "Nah. He's all right for a bit. Do it later. Bit of a rush on now. There's the one downstairs to see to, an' I gotta go shopping before I go home. Do him next time. Tuck him in on your side, Tone. Bit more, love, put his head on one side of the pillow. Towards the window. I'll lift the sides up. Click 'em tight and it's all done. Ta."

So it goes, these paid-for visits. In and out. Thirty minutes max each time. Fed and watered. Turned over. Propped up. Wiped clean. Tablets given. Tucked in. I know the routine as well as they do. Sometimes, though I'm sure they cannot tell, I fall fast asleep as they go about their business with me. Most of the time, the rest of the time, I sleep anyway. In my sleep I have time to see, ponder, feel, sense, even taste somehow what has gone as if it was fresh and new. As long as this still happens, I will not be ready to leave, not even from this husk which contains me, and everything that once made me.

* * * * *

In sleep I have no control over the order in which thoughts and sensations unwrapped from memory come to assail me. I delight in this. I am their plaything not their master. One surprise package arrives after another, and some flee on the instant they arrive, where others, for no apparent cause, choose to linger. No reason, from any direction of mine at least, appears to lie behind whatever surfaces for me to contemplate.

Yet I can tell, as they are paraded before me, the differences between the memories as they carom the one off the other. Here, what was once incidental, meaningless even, until it became other. There, what I thought to be life-changing, until that altered too. The speed with which it all floods in does not blur my vision of anything. Each memory retains its particular weightiness of effect at the time of its original happening, the particularity of each staying intact, however trivial, however momentary, however intense in the actual life. And I am not frightened anymore, by any of it, as I once was when the enormity of a near non-existence so closely touched me, and would not, for years on end, cease to trouble me. Awake or asleep.

The kaleidoscope of memory which turns and shifts its shapes within me is a slide show I can almost enjoy since I know how it ends, and begins, and runs over and over again. Here I am being hurtled again down the deck, practically vertical at this point, a sluice of unstoppable seawater throwing me bodily against unknown others, many women and children, nursemaids and babies, grown men and the ship's crew, all clutching and screaming and clinging to anything. A half-full lifeboat is tilted precariously over the side of the great ship, threatening to spill its human contents, until it somehow breaks loose from its divots and bumps the ship once, twice, before it smacks with a judder and a self-righting slap into the flat calm of the cold Irish Sea. Everything stops, or so it seems in memory, or was it just before that, the moment I caught his eye, clear and sure as always, and saw his hands clasped around her waist before he pushed her into the boat which fell. And so I jump. Into the sea, but amongst ropes and haulage gear and rivets, all torn or sheared away as the Lusitania rolls on its side, its four great funnels almost horizontal at the last, and I am swimming away from her. Gouts of muck and hot cinders rain down on us and hot cascading spouts of steam and water.

With the ship gone, the sea is a wretched habitation of debris and bodies, as if the last of the ship has become a foul midden of our past existence. *Monogrammed bed linen, table napkins, wine crates and chicken coops, upturned soup tureens and paper book-boats that were orderly libraries, flotillas of entangled deckchairs to which people cling as best they could in the backwash from the sinking. Amongst all this I float, and see men roll on and off wooden barrels and women grasping at passing spars and chests of drawers. Some push others away from them. They smack at each other with paddles. Those whose life jackets have been wrongly attached, back to front, drift helplessly, faces into the water. Dead babies, their sightless eyes turned to the sky, are sodden bundles bumped along in this swirling stream. I hear the cries of the living. I make no sound.*

And then, I am younger, walking home from school, a fee-paying prep for the sons of professional men, taking a short cut across the new city's municipal park. I am heading north, passing an empty bandstand, skirting the bushes alongside the red gravel path, when from the cover of the thick, glossy leaved shrubs I see the four of them, boys of my age, around eleven years old or a little more, who swarm around me and taunt me. I am smacked in the face by an open-palmed hand. They jeer at me. I am punched by a closed fist, its knuckles bony and hard onto my mouth. My lower lip is split. I try to pivot away from them. I try not to cry but I do as my satchel is torn from me and is opened, school books and pencils scattered onto the path. I feel no pain, then or in memory, only my shame at not being able to stop sobbing, my chest heaving uncontrollably so that I cannot take a breath, only gulping air, sobbing and helpless before them, laughing at me, pushing and shoving me to stumble into the bushes. Calling cripple, cripple, cripple. Running away to the south of the park where the river is its boundary. I do not remember what comfort I had at home. For sure there was some. For sure it has not helped. I slip back further.

I am five or six maybe. My hand is cradled in my Father's palm. We are coming out of our house. The four-storey stone built late Victorian villa, newly built to his own specifications, on the wide road where we live to the north of the park and the city's madcap mock castle and the grandiose department stores of its commercial centre. It is quite early, around eight thirty in the morning. The avenue is, as yet, only fringed with the encased saplings which will, soon enough, become broad leafed chestnut trees. We do this journey together, on foot, many times in the decade to follow. As the years pass I will let go of his hand and he will stop carrying me on his shoulders at the half-way point of our walk. He tells me that to walk as far as I can is good for me. That it will help with the recovery of my foot. That it will aid the recuperation of the regular adjustments it requires, my left foot, my club foot, encased in its clumpy boot with the corrective iron strapped up my lower leg to, somehow, but how, re-dress its deformity. It never does. I will carry it, as it and I grow together, and its hateful ugliness, throughout my life. I will learn to compensate for it by throwing my weight forward and to the side to propel me on, but it always hurts. I see my father wince if he hears any whimper from me, so I do not, unless I stumble and then he grips me to steady my clomping gait. Good boy, says my father. Good father, is what I will forever think of him, this builder of a city, this begetter and support of a cripple.

All around, as we walk by straight lines and right angles down the grid of the city to its great docks, it is the literal case that year by year, at times month by month, buildings of each and every kind are filling the space of streets and roads and squares. It is a rapid, unprecedented growth. My father, builder and architect, prospers. If it is 1904, I am seven and in a preparatory school set across from the park that has been laid out by the Council on land donated for the recreation and leisure of all citizens. At home my mother fusses over me, an only child, and our two live-in maidservants tut-tut over my handicap. In 1910, because in sleep the years shuffle to their own rhythm, I am thirteen and a reluctant boarder at an English Public School just across the channel. I am excused sports of all kinds. I do not mind. I do mind being removed from the fervent life of the coalport city. It breathes the air of a future *world, of destiny, not the somnolence of the gentlemanly training I am given. I yearned to be home.*

To be going with my father, looking up at him, as he strides out. I am determined to keep up. We hurry past the glitter of glass-roofed arcades of shops and the display windows of the cave-like department stores which dominate the city centre. They are both the frippery and the essence of the modern world we know we are blessed to inhabit. Our destination lies over the bridges, following the churning river which comes to us from the hills to empty itself as a whirlpool of turbulence, into the city's great Docks. Towering coal hoists filled, and tipping lump coal by day and night into the holds of waiting ships, all moored together as if a continuous set of decks. Coal trucks, mile upon sinuous mile of them backed up on rail tracks, all laden to the brim with best Welsh steam coal, crags of bituminous fuel to make the whole world turn, spun on its axis across all the ocean by this Welsh gold.

And I listen intently to him, Mostyn Arthur Lloyd, architect and speculative dreamer, tell me, Taliesin Arthur Lloyd, called Tal from the beginning by him, my father, who we now are and how we have been fashioned, and of all the world which thereby so knows us, and of what closer acquaintance with it will hold for me.

Not to be. Though he will never know it, or suspect it. Not to be. For I will, like this place, shrink away from acting in that greater world, and will settle instead for being the Secretary.

* * * * *

The ford was there long before the bridges that he built for its better crossing than by stepping stones in dry weather, which was infrequent. The first one, this was in 1746, though being of good seasoned timber, rough-hewn as well as some masonry, was swept away by flood after two years, and two more, both stone-built completely, were in their time pulled down in the central parts by the sheer force of the river in full spate, for which the bridges were too top heavy, and squat besides, to withstand the force, so that, after several more years of trial and disaster, and the near bankruptcy of himself, he did, William Edwards the stonemason who was, too, a minister of religion, a prayerful preacher to his small, upland congregation of shepherds and farmers, their wives and children, raise up a fourth bridge of hewn quarried stone, but this time as an arc with three cylindrical apertures on each side of its curving abutments. These were his genius mark, these openings which were of diminishing size from three to nine feet in their diameter, with the largest holes placed at the bottom end of each curvature of the stone arc so as to allow the onrushing water to flow through unhindered by any barrier to its torrent. In such manner, the central crown of the bridge stood firm, no longer pushed upwards to the destruction of all. This was finally completed by Edwards the stonemason in 1756, and its span at over one hundred and forty feet as a single bow was a wonder and a triumph. Faith and Reason thus signalled Power over Nature. And this bridge stood.

Before the Bridge, quickly so capitalised in its distinction and distinctiveness by visiting travellers and landscape artists, there had been nothing to distinguish this place other than as a sometimes fording spot where farmers, and occasional wayfarers, might manage to cross when the river abated, at its own infrequent will. All too often, impatience led to a loss of transported animals and goods and, at times, impelled by a need to reach markets to the western side, too distant if the ford was not to be risked, then, with peril ignored, lives were also lost. Edwards the stonemason, stubborn and God-guided, had spanned the river for these humble reasons of mercantile transport and of time saved in a world still dictated to by weather and seasons for its very existence.

Yet, though a European wonder and done in oils and as lithograph and its image transposed for the court of Catherine the Great onto the finest porcelain, on its own spot as itself it soon signified little more than its origins as its agrarian utility was bypassed. The swelling of industry, notably of iron making, tilted old balances from barter to commerce within two generations. The Old Bridge, Yr Hen Bont, thus became no more than a symbol, ignored for its former use. The iron puddled and hammered for ships and engines, and all the appurtenances of both peace and war, was dram-hauled by horse and man from the fearsome Merthyr works just twelve miles to the north, skirting the lower slopes of the precipitous and narrow valley of the river Taff until it widened below the Bridge, whence from the climacteric year of 1794 the metal was loaded onto barges, to be horse-drawn down the new canal a further twelve miles to the south to the as yet inconspicuous outlet of Caerdydd.

The energy required to fuel the voracious maw of Empire was here, inland, in these fabled Hills. Artisan shaping followed on the basic making of iron. Where the rivers from the sylvan tridentine gulches of Tâf, Cynon and Rhondda met and intermingled manufacture now began. Of chains principally, weighty engorged loops and thickly twisted iron for ships' anchors and for cables and bridges, made on that spot to await their turn by transportation down the canal to the sea. This latest was due to the ingenuity of two cousins, both christened Samuel, and one named Lennox and one Brown. They came to establish their own enterprise, with some one thousand souls set to work, and a vast fortune made as the

French wars against the Emperor Napoleon were fought, and won by 1815, the monies banked and invested to multiply by the cousins. Around their works through this time there was no real, human settlement established, not as yet, with all needs, basic and otherwise, supplied until the 1820s from a single storey brick building which held the dry goods and the provisions brought daily to the place by wagon, travelling down the new turnpike road. Any passengers coming from the east or south to the place arrived by a horse-drawn coach, which ran higher up on a cut made across the right-hand side of the hillside, whilst besides no coach would ever be able to cross the river by ascending the incline of the Bridge to its apex and then down as steeply off the Bridge, which had only been ever meant, in the intent of Edwards the stonemason, for those on foot or pulling laden sleds or for pack horses. And, therefore, other than the Bridge there remained in its vicinity little of the form of human endeavour, so that it was as if the Bridge, called familiarly Y Bont Gam in Welsh for its humpbacked crookedness, but Newbridge in English more correctly after Y Bont Newydd, stood and stood until, after almost a century had passed from its foundation, it really did become a Bridge redolent not of its by-passed era but one, rather, as emblematic entry point to a world even more unimaginable than that of iron had once been, a bridge geographically situated as signpost to the world which has made us Welsh most blessed of the ancient tribes made anew in an utterly changed world: the World of Coal.

To the north and north west of the Bridge, on its far side, were the wooded cwms and shadowed valleys, where formerly the picking and pocking for coal for the iron industry, and some domestic use, was done in patchwork fashion. This was notably so in the pastoral Rhondda until the rich lodes on offer in the lower reaches of the valley were mined at an accelerated rate and tramways of iron rail had to be laid and the so-called Doctor's canal, after the pioneering Doctor Griffiths, was gouged out of the loamy earth in this present century's first decade. Thereto, and thereafter, rail lines for steam trains were thrust down contiguous valleys and cross-hatched at their confluence at the now growing hamlet of Newbridge, from where after 1841 turnpike and canal and old tramroad, too, could be spurned for the railways which could take a heavier burden of iron and of coal, quicker and then even quicker and bulkier, to the gathering argosies being readied to send such compressed power out from the gargantuan docks created to send our mineral treasure across the oceans of the entire globe.

Which is to say, too, that in this sense the Bridge, as focal point, was also emblem of the entire town now enabled to spread and prosper at this junction of rivers, and so set to embrace the civic duties it has been our happy lot to foster. An unruly workforce, from pits and tinplate works, in increasing number merited, and required in truth, the concomitant arrival of law courts and petty sessions, itinerant judges and a resident magistracy, the clerks and officers of the law, all to ensure transition from the inchoate beginnings to the respectful coherence of established societies. For, make no mistake, intimidation and apprehension were the tools which had to be supplied to winnow out, and if need be to suppress, the unrighteous and the wilfully disruptive, whether that of rebellious Chartists set on the overthrow of the propertied and of social order itself, or of those of the criminal class too readily nurtured in the huddle of dwellings strewn hither and thither. We had, some of us of the professional classes and shopocracy, to lay out a grid of streets from this mess, to name them and see that their inhabitants could be serviced to good purpose, as well as held in check. There was much disquiet, many malcontents and slow progress. But we can look back and affirm that civilisation came, in short order, to these hitherto unexpected urban environs set around and about the Bridge which itself, as if fate had always meant it, brought one final gift, that of nomenclature to its place. It came about in this manner.

So much correspondence, a novel flood of written communications, for business and the development of its practice and profit, and all delivered by postal service, had streamed into this particular Newbridge at mid-century that confusion of a literal kind was threatened, one which could delay, if not halt, our progress. This was because new bridges had come to be built in numerous other places over this time, though none in strict reality like our Bridge, with the consequence of a lack of alacrity in sending orders and requests and other official business back and fro to their proper destination. Wheretofore our Postmaster, the fulcrum in his own persona to act for distant Authority and the near Masters, and wishing to ensure both security and speed, decided to particularise the specificity of the location by means of a unique place-name. To this end he took a local appellation of obscure origin, namely Pont-y-ty-pridd, meaning the Bridge-of-the-earthen house in a crumpled English and itself an allusion, possibly, to a once mud-and-turf house thrown up in the course of one night for shelter near one of the bridges whose construction had been undertaken by Edwards the Stonemason, and, with a ready wit, he, the Postmaster, corrupted this name, through elision of its literal Welsh components, to turn it into Pont-y-pridd, or Bridge-of-the-Earth, meaning nothing other than the thing itself becoming in this way more than itself, and none other such anywhere than in this our unconfinable place.

The begetter of this inspired orthographic falsity, nay more an inspired invention!, was Charles Basset, Postmaster, who, thereby, in 1856 ended the prior existence of the place long since to that time known as Newbridge on the banks of the Taff where, whilst strolling in that year of 1856 on the banks of the river Rhondda near where it swelled the Taff with its vigour, the weavers James

James and Evan James, father and son, composed the music and wrote the words of what has become such an anthemic hymn to the ancient lineaments of our Brythonic race, affirmed anew in this modern Cymru, our triumphant and ascendant Nation.

Hanes y Bobl y Bont, Myrddin, 1876. (Translated from the Welsh by Yr Athro G Ellis Pierce BA (Oxon), MA (Cantab), 1910) Taliesin Arthur Lloyd Papers. Miscellanea, Box 4. National Library of Wales. Aberystwyth.

The audible crackle of public synapses which, it is claimed in the history books, signalled the year of nineteen ten and the frenetic years which followed closely on, well, that one passed me by, and if I noticed it at all, it was as a kind of historical tickertape. What stays with me, what I can yet savour, was the intensity, the pulse of being alive, when I was with my father. There was nothing antique in his company, for all was new, and much of it he seemed to me to have created himself.

I felt it then, and sense it still, as a sort of kinetic energy of forms which jumped off the map of his mind and were touched out of their flattened origin into three- dimensional shape by his vision. Or perhaps it was the genius of that time which, in our place, had altered almost everything in the shuttering of a camera's eye. In my later contemplation of this, I am convinced that for his generation, not mine for whom it was just the way of things, the leap from blank canvas to this madly peopled life was almost incomprehensible. I mean that it could not all be taken in as if it was the only normality. He walked through the city with me, I think, to show me the world we lived in because he could not make its meaning comprehensible by telling me about it. He had, I'd argue, no choice in any case since we had no ownership, at that time, of what our recent history had been. That species of intellectual knowledge, necessarily dessicated for our later digestion, was a generational lag behind the beat of wonder which his experience of living through such a warp of space and time had given him. This, I am sure, he knew instinctively, and tried therefore to imbue me with such an insight by making me see and feel along with him.

The days of my father, Mostyn Arthur Lloyd, architect and sometime scribe, were partitioned by his set activities into segments, banked pieces of invested time, and well spent before the first Great War scorned the folly of hopefulness. But, for a while, time as such was given a physical meaning. Its motion was anchored by the palpable presence of organised growth, expanding from our own located centre of being as a magnet of attraction to the whole world. People were pulled in to us for more than the security of work and wages. The offer was bigger than that. It would be rightly said that we were, and I mean precisely where we were, American in deeds and dreams. In my early days there seemed to be people everywhere attesting to that, both individually and as if bound together by it.

As I walked across the city with him, perhaps when his morning's business at the Coal Exchange to consult with clients and friends was done, we would be buffeted by people hurrying, never strolling. Pulled and pushed by a wash of tides of people. In and out of side streets and back alleys and main roads, and up and down the wide thoroughfare of the Docks, incessantly traversed by carts and hansom cabs and an increasing number of motorised vehicles squishing their iron-rimmed tires through mounds of horse droppings and mud. The constancy of movement was entrancing and, at the same time, disturbing. For me it would only be found again in New York city in the century's second decade. Was it danger I smelled? Or just the shiver of the unexpected, a mass warning against all complacency? In our Docks neighbourhood the unknown and the familiar were uneasy companions.

My father, as we walked, would tip his grey homburg hat to any acquaintances, slight or otherwise, man or lady, but did not move a hand to flick its brim otherwise. There were, in those crowded streets, sweet and acrid clouds of scent and face powder and sweat, impossible to avoid, puffed into the common air. These people, not known to us of course, were the numerous ones we hurried past. For their part, seafarers and coal trimmers, dockers and costermongers, prostitutes and waitresses, white and yellow and black and half-caste, went by, all passing and re-passing, oblivious of order or decorum in their own, briefly uncontested corner of the earth.

The noise they made, nailed boots clattering on the stone-slabbed pavements and laughter shrieking out from the pubs amongst the melancholic sibilance of concertinas and the da-di-da beat of music hall ditties, was melded into the shunt of engines and the whooshing emptying of the coal hoists. Squealing and grinding machinery was the not too distant accompaniment to the throng of human presence in the tenements, lodging houses and shebeens which spilled away from the rectangular grid of avenues and squares intent on grander purpose and statement. Here were the banks and shipping offices, and the foreign embassies doubling up as coal merchants, buildings that were pillared and collonaded to several storeys high. Stamped into the grey stone and black marble were their insignia, the names and symbols of great company concerns and, often enough, of their founder-owners. In style they were imitative, copies of Venetian palazzos or French baroque edifices, imposing an assured assumption of the architectural grandeur to come. In substance, they were proclaiming the undeniable future which they felt was awaiting them. The promise had been made, and half-fulfilled already, by the massive crenellated frontage of the Coal Exchange which had preceded them two decades earlier.

To go into the Exchange with my father was to tingle with the buzz of being admitted to the heart of all which ultimately mattered. Buying and selling. Profit and even more profit. Coal for money and cheques, once a million pound one he told me, just for coal. The sprung wooden floor of the immensity of the main hall, the centre of the web which spun itself out from here across the globe, hummed with the voices of the traders and dealers who were crammed together from wall to wall. At one end of the hall, just below the promenade of the wrought-iron wrap- around balconies running its length, was an ornate, mounted wall clock, flanked by the carving of two rampant dragons, and bearing on its face the warning motto "Tempus Fugit". But it had not, as yet, run out. Rather, our time stood still for we had stolen it and transformed it into the solidity of space. Our space. Confident space. Male voices occupying the private rooms for coffee and dining. Male bodies glimpsed when heavy glass panelled doors swung silently open and shut on their oiled and gleaming brass fixtures. Power and Dominion. Trade and Empire. Capital and Labour. Wales in its new World.

Outside, if Welsh was spoken it would be by men of the class or profession of my father to one another. English was the common language in this city of Business and the lingua franca of those who worked for or served others. The world in miniature which had been assembled to mutual if unequal benefit echoed itself back in French or in Norwegian, in Somali tones and West Indian accents, in the clipped vowels of Finns and the abrupt consonants of Germans, and to this linguistic babel was added Italian and South American Spanish and, yes, Catalan and Russian. I make it sound like a chorus of intermeshed arias, background to our own prideful solos. Nonetheless, it is indeed the vocal music I once heard before we fell into the greater silence which replaced it.

* * * * *

The wind which comes persistently off the sea is salt-laden. The ozoned air it brings is quickly clogged with the rich, musky tang of tallow for ships' candles and the throaty aftertaste of tarred hemp for ropes. The endless columns of coal trucks clank into each other and then stall before they shudder into line again to undulate slowly down mile upon mile of rail track across the docklands to unload their burdens at the wharves. The ships, sails unfurled and banging into one another's sides, wait for their assigned cargoes, always the same cargo. Coal. Steamers hoot and bustle amongst the older vessels. My father throws dice for silver on a backgammon table with his friends, all seated at the back of a favourite coffee house, and elsewhere other men squat on their muscled haunches to bounce and spin their dice against a back wall, playing for copper coins, their eyes alert for the police, always burly and always in twos, for Power needs to be protected and order kept, especially here and particularly in 1910.

Memoir Fragment, c.1964. Unpublished. Taliesin Arthur Lloyd Papers. Box 1. National Library of Wales. Aberystwyth.

I gather, from their assumed indifference, that they are entitled to vote today. They do not seem inclined to do so, my carers. Not from what they say to each other anyway. I could be mistaken, though not from the talk they bat to-and-fro over my bed. Another vote, they say. The nobs again, they say. More jobs for them, they say. Another talking shop for politicians, they say. Money for them for sure, they say. Not for us, not representing our interests, are they, they say. They are, it seems, less disinterested than they claim, despite the chat to the contrary, more agitated, their lack of interest I surmise as being felt to be cut adrift from any purpose they can detect. All is abstract, sucked dry, hollowed out. And into the void has come the incubus of political taxidermy. No wonder they wrinkle their noses. Yes, I am clear that they are ignorant of issues in general even if the detail on offer palls. Their gabble reveals them as opinionated. Too opinionated to bother to vote at all. This is not, however, abstention as a principle. It is what they have been driven to, this sullen, brute refusal. Their right, as they claim inwardly, not to endorse any further, anymore. Not in their name, though it will be done in their name notwithstanding.

I, too, will not be voting. Not considered able to do so in my state, I suppose. Quite right, too. I would not, in any case, wish to do so, though not for their reasons. It is their future to endure, no longer mine. If I could engage with them, my only query would be concerned with what seems a lost desire to shape things. At all it seems, for I grant the aspiration was never a simple one except for the cheer-leaders of the world. The desire and the outcome have rarely been, in my experience, congruent. The gap may be widening. The roots of their resentment understandable. It is the exhaustion of things with which they have been confronted. I am turned over in bed by them, and none too gently. Perhaps they sense my resentment of them, an enemy of theirs, of a sort. Once, for those who came before them, to act was to commit to what was unbidden, unstoppable, as a future which might be theirs to alter not merely endure. They leave me to myself.

* * * * *

Before the Great War, there had suddenly appeared amongst us a defining physical presence which you encountered wherever you looked. Buildings that were chiselled, carved, embellished, to be a counter-presence to base reality. It was a kind of consciousness that was embodied in every small township and village settlement across the coalfield of the valleys and hills. Miners' Institutes, Welfare Halls, and their attached Libraries and Reading Rooms. These were a testament by virtue of being a focal point. A vision in both senses. I came to understand that they were suggesting an attainable, different future to what was brute and driven all around. If you could see or could have entered them in their time of pomp you would have caught your breath at their defiance, at their daring, at their being willing to stand comparison. My father, architect for these too, understood their challenge. He examined them, added to them, wondered at them.

I found them entrancing, for they were not cold in purpose but alive, organically so, in their endeavour. Each had a reading room with magazines and periodicals on long oak tables and with newspapers of every kind on sloping racks, the papers held open by long wooden poles, and to be read standing up. There were, behind glass cases or on open shelves, books bought by committee to be loaned out to individuals, books catalogued as they arrived and date-stamped as they left. On ground floors there were airy rooms for public meetings or lectures or talks. Upstairs there would be larger halls, with wrought iron balconies, often able to seat fifteen hundred or more for drama or oratorios or male voice choirs or a distinguished speaker from outside the district. There were games rooms, largely for the snooker which the colliers loved to play and excelled at, with four or five baize tables, their verdant nap immaculately tended as if they were indeed green lawns. Or maybe corners for table tennis or card playing, cribbage and whist, or dominoes and chess and draughts, whilst before the post-war municipal parks and recreation grounds were built to ease the grimness everywhere found outside such buildings, there might be basement swimming pools, tiled and water-rippled for twenty yards or more of their length. No bars. No alcohol. No bad language. No vandalism. Civic ships with their own horizons of desired destination to reach.

I read, many years later, in one of the new academic histories which tried, lamely I would say, to discover a lost time of aspiration through a snowstorm of reductionist statistics, and with a flurry of metaphors, that these Institutes were, somehow, "the brains of the coalfield." Not so. Not in any precise sense that is meaningful. Better to think of them as suppliers of sustenance for the brain. These buildings were a three-dimensional expression of human reason and human sensibility. They were then, in themselves, a statement of purpose, one of secular redemption against the unaccountable rights of Power. Their own implicit power was explicitly collective, and when that faded so their social grandiloquence became muted, made individual.

Most, in a finally diminished society, succumbed by the Sixties to the ruins of fire or neglect, and largely through self-destruction, too. I can only conjure them up in my mind's eye by recalling my father's architectural lexicon, a kind of poetics to remember their prosaic function of common purposefulness.

Once you would have entered into a palpable future, via the buildings, by walking up marbled steps through pedimented doorways flanked by glistening mullioned windows. There were some which soared above street level for four or even five storeys in height, classical in their composition with, first, dark ashlar at ground level, then with plaster pale Doric pilasters, or in red brick to carry a triglyph frieze across the façade. There were windows which were segment-headed below and long round-headed ones above for the piano nobile, or, perhaps, a bullseye window set apart in a pedimented gable. Central entrances were enriched with terracotta, glazed and unglazed, bright in reds and yellows and blues. Structures might be hewn out of grey Pennant stone or shaped out of the local, rock-faced sandstone with buff-stamped terracotta embedded. Everywhere there arose, for delight, ornamental balls, curvaceous gables, sky-lines etched with swan-like pediments, and against the otherwise stubborn monochrome of people's everyday lives a polychromatic riposte to actuality cued in by blue in sandstone or red in brick and white in that expensive Portland stone which elsewhere, graced the swelling city centres.

As a child, before the foundation of my known world fell in, I had no sense of ruins as any kind of destiny. We had no need, then, of shields against disaster, so flashingly brilliant were our swords of action. My father, Mostyn Arthur Lloyd, was a builder, and you did not build with the past in mind. What he made, or rather designed to have made, were as heraldry of a common, more widespread glory that was to come. Nor do I mean by this those gestures to Wall Street, the temples to money, trade and coal which swanked and preened themselves in the city on the coast. It is more what he caused to happen, to body forth, to the north of that city where the once alpine ravines had become coalfield valleys and where the mining townships were thrown up to house the inwards rush of people into settlements which were not, for a while yet, communities.

We often ventured in that direction. We would, my father and I, take a train, passengers and freight served on the parallel lines of track which were etched into the coalfield from east to west and north to south. In each township there was a client to visit, a site to inspect, a hand to shake. The getting of coal, the begetting of buildings. The townships, valley by valley, were practically continuous. Kinked rows of terraced housing swerved and bucked their way along and up and over improbably perpendicular hillside slopes and lunatic gradients. More people here, amongst the Hills as we were then inclined to say, than in all the ports and towns which sent out the coal. A density of people which rivalled the numbers per square mile anywhere in the world. Barbarism and gentility cheek by jowl. Rivers made black by small coal in suspension, fouled by dead dogs and cats and human refuse and human excrement, a stench in the unmade stone-strewn streets and a brawl on every corner when the pubs closed on Saturday nights. To counter that the building of Town Halls and Churches and Chapels and Public Libraries and Municipal Theatres and Police Stations and Fire Houses and Sanitation Works and Board Schools: the capitalised paraphernalia of civic purpose expressed as physical infrastructure.

Only my father, Mostyn Arthur Lloyd, progressive in his politics and booster by conviction, the godhead from whom by osmosis more than instruction I took on an unshakeable civic faith, was purse-lipped on all other consequences of the upheaval which had taken him, and thousands upon thousands more, from the land to a life no longer dependent on the land but only on its utter depredation. This I would learn later, after his time. To me he rarely spoke, except in measured tones, of colliery enterprises, first hacked out of and then sunk deeply into those clefted hills.

When he walked with me, hand in hand, through the gateway town to the hub of the coalfield in the first decade of this century his eyes and ears were attuned only to those marvels of progress and improvement to which he held fast. The sight of tramcars and electric lighting and public urinals and the appropriate statuary erected as tribute to the Founding Fathers, the marble busts of the Great Men he would single out for praise. None more so, though no statue yet for him, than his friend and acquaintance from town and school, a man whose lifespan from the 1880s had witnessed and paralleled such hitherto unimaginable changes, Frederick Hall

Thomas, the proper name of the public schoolboy who had made himself into the bridge between gentility and barbarism by becoming the idol of this raw working class world as the boxer, Freddie Welsh, a virtual collier and an emblematic patriot, one for whom, like my father, the Chronicle was only a diorama to their unassailable hubris.

Memoir Fragment, c1964. Unpublished. Taliesin Arthur Lloyd Papers, Box 1, National Library of Wales, Aberystwyth.

THE PROGRESS OF TIME

1742
First chapel in the Rhondda, built at Cymmer

1755
William Edwards's third one arch bridge erected over Taff at Pontypridd

1790
First colliery level opened at Gyfeillon, by Dr R Griffiths

1794
Glamorganshire Canal opened to Navigation

1798
Glamorganshire Canal made navigable to Cardiff

1801
Population of Cardiff, 1,018; houses 327

1806
Walter Coffin bought the farm at Dinas and started levels, connecting tramways with Pontypridd

1810
First Carmel Chapel opened

1812
First Penuel Chapel built

1818
Pontypridd branch of Brown-Lenox's Chain and Cable Works
opened

1826
Death of Dr R Griffiths

1840
Taff Vale Railway constructed to Navigation (Aberdare Junction)

1841
Taff Vale Railway opened to Merthyr, 24½ miles
First pit sunk, Gelliwion (Maritime)

1849
Great Western Pit opened

1850
Pontypridd Gas Company incorporated

1851
First Judge, Pontypridd Circuit appointed, December

1855
First Sessions held at Pontypridd

1856
Tune "Hen Wlad Fy Nhadau" composed in Mill Street, Pontypridd
by James James; words by his father, Evan James
Pontypridd County Court established

1857
Roman Catholic Church built at Treforest

1861
Tabernacle Welsh Baptist Chapel built

1864
Gyfeillon Pit sold to Great Western Coal Company

1869
St Catherine's Church, Anglican, erected at a cost of £7,000
Spire 162ft

1870
Welsh Congregational Chapel, Zion Street, built

1871
Glyntaff Burial Board formed

1873
Great strike in South Wales coal and iron trades commenced
Victory of South Wales Choral Union at Crystal Palace, under
the leadership of "Caradog", July 10th

1874
Pontypridd Local Government Board established

1875
Stipendiary Magistrate appointed

1876
Pontypridd Rugby Football Club formed.
Hanes y Bobl y Bont, written and published by the Bard and
Antiquarian, Myrddin

1877
Pontypridd Markets Company incorporated

1880
Llantrisant and Taff Vale Railway Bill passed

1883
Pontypridd and Caerphilly Railway Bill passed

1885
Old Town Hall built at a cost of £1,600, to seat 700
William Abraham, "Mabon", elected for Labour cause in
Rhondda, December

1889
Barry Dock Railway opened for passenger traffic, February 8th
Turnpike gates in South Wales abolished

1890
Great railway strike in South Wales, August 7th to 14th
Public Free Library, Gelliwastad Grove, built; cost £2,000
Pontypridd Fire Brigade established
New Town Hall erected at a cost of £5,000, to seat 1,700,
exclusive of stage

1891

Captain Lionel Lindsay appointed Chief Constable for
Glamorgan, January 5th

1893

Great Western Colliery disaster, 58 killed, April 11th
Disturbance in South Wales coalfield; Military called out,
August 14th
Welsh rugby XV win first Triple Crown

1894

Explosion at Albion Colliery, Cilfynydd; 276 killed, June 26th

1895

Pontypridd Urban District Council formed
Unveiling of the Fountain, Pontypridd by Sir Alfred Thomas
(the donor) October 3rd
Consecration of Pontypridd Synagogue, October

1896

Opening of the County School, Pontypridd, September

1898

Soldiers at Pontypridd, coal strike, July

1899

Gelliwastad Institute opened by Miss Clara Thomas (coalowner)
Llwynmadoc, September

1900

Mafeking rejoicings, May 18th, South African war

Pretoria Day rejoicings (bonfire on the Graig, June 12th

Murder of Pauline Lacy by her black husband, William Augustus
Lacy 24 Barry Terrace, Pwllgwaun, July 6th, executed August 21st

Taff Vale Railway men strike, August 20th – 31st

Keir Hardie elected MP for Merthyr Boroughs in General
Election as Independent Labour Party Candidate

1902

Philip Evans, ex-policeman, shot Mrs Saddler in the Holly Bush
Inn and then shot himself, March 27th

1904

Opening of new nurses' home at Tyfica Road by Miss Clara
Thomas, June 23rd

Presentation of bust to Sir Alfred Thomas MP, unveiled at the
Town Hall, by Lord Tredegar, September 29th

1905

Pontypridd electric tramcars started running, Marth 6th

Coal trade four years' agreement signed, December 2nd

Welsh XV beat New Zealand Fernlanders in Cardiff Arms Park,
15th December

1907

Mabon unveils monument in Llanfabon Cemetery to 11
unknown victims of the Albion Colliery disaster, July 1st

The Rt. Hon. David Lloyd George at the New Town Hall,
Pontypridd, July 20th

Boxing: Fred Welsh beats Joe White at Pontypridd, September 16th

1908

Miners' Eight Hours Act comes into operation, July 1st
Hunger Marches at Pontypridd, September

1909

The Rt. Hon. David Lloyd George visits district and descends
mine at Abercynon, June 3rd
Fred Welsh defeats Josephs at Mountain Ash, July 12th
Miners' demonstration at Pontypridd, August 16th
Fred Welsh defeats Johnny Summers in London, November 8th

1910

Earth tremor in the Rhondda, February 16th
Coal agreement signed, April 8th
Pontypridd Labour Exchange opened
Coal strike in Cambrian Collieries, Rhondda, November 1st
Riots in Tonypandy, Rhondda, November 7th and 8th
Metropolitan Police sent to Rhondda Valley
Military in Pontypridd and Rhondda
Great storm doing much damage
Fred Welsh defeats Driscoll: fight given to Welsh on a foul by
Driscoll (butting with head) in the tenth round, at Westgate
Street, Cardiff, December 20th

Some Events from Past to Present: A Town Chronicle
(Compiled by Mostyn Arthur Lloyd, RIBA, 1910)
Taliesin Arthur Lloyd Papers. Box 10. National Library of Wales

* * * * *

When I think of the size of our little country, and then think again how small that portion of it is that we call South Wales, I am lost in wonderment and filled with pride at the recollection of the things that have been done by the men of our race

South Wales has bred a fly-weight, in Jimmy Wilde, and a featherweight, in Jim Driscoll, as Champions of England. Wales had bred a middle-weight champion, too. Have we no-one ready to fill the late Tom Thomas' place? I believe we can find such a man. And not only a middle-weight, but a welter-weight and a heavy-weight.

Why not? A country where men can play rugby football as Welshmen play it – men who have beaten the best the world can send against us – can, I am sure, produce boxers with the same qualities of hardihood and skill and courage which have made her rugby footballers famous and feared the world over.

Boxing is the sport which fits in with the Welsh temperament. It calls for quick thinking, for ready hands, and nimble feet, hardy bodies and high courage. I know that Welshmen have all these things. I am looking forward to the time when we shall hold a straight flush from fly to heavy of British boxing championships. Even then the limits of ambition will not have been reached for there will be the world's titles to strive for.

(Freddie Welsh addressing crowds of well-wishers in Pontypridd a fortnight before the outbreak of the First World War. He had become World Lightweight Champion in London on 17th July 1914)

Miscellanea, (*South Wales Daily News* cutting, dated 22 July 1914) Taliesin Arthur Lloyd Papers. Box 16. National Library of Wales, Aberystwyth.

I was not taking any chances on not going. I had, whilst still in the house, put on my overcoat, the thick brown tweed one, and knotted a blue wool scarf around my neck. Knee high grey socks from school, knickerbockers fastened below the knee, a cableknit jumper as a final defence against the winter's cold. I was ready. They were still bickering. Mother, firmly saying not to take me. Father, uneasily, laughing at her. Scornful, but uncertain. Trying a different tack. Me, shuffling in the hallway, as near to the door as I dared to be, kicking the toe of my right foot against the stiff, heavy heel of the restraining boot on the other. Father, in the parlour, wheedling. He had put his hands on her shoulders. Saying, softly, Marged. Again, Marged. She was only Margaret outside the house. Needs to know how to take care of himself. Will never be able to do that. Voices intermingled. Old enough. Too rough. He's a boy. A man to be, though. Will be all right, with me. A night not to forget, Marged. A sigh. I would go. The night would be forever.

A late December night, five days before Christmas. After November's blasts of wind and rain it is dry and frosty cold. I am thirteen years old. Morfydd, my six- year old sister, is awake upstairs, trembling over the season's excitement. My father, Mostyn Arthur Lloyd, sport and enthusiast, plants a moustachioed kiss on my mother's brow, buttons up his ulster, adjusts the bowler hat he has grabbed from the table in the hall and hurries me through the front door out into the night before any second thoughts delay us.

He was right that I would not forget. Not the moments of our walking, him almost jerking me along, me willing my foot forward to keep pace with him, trying not to scrape it, confident of not falling, my hand enveloped in his firm grip, the scent of his eau-de-cologne sharp on the night air, the stained glass transoms of the baronial villas of our avenue, some now brightly outlined by electric lights from within, others fuzzier with the yellowed aura of earlier gas brackets, one after the other glinting before us until we reached the river bridge that drew us alongside the fantasy castle and onto the ancient boundary street which had once marked out the western limit of the former, old town where, suddenly, as if we had been swept in amongst them, there were crowds and clutches of men, seemingly whirling aimlessly forward, a vortex of working men in caps and mufflers amongst gabardine-coated and bowler-hatted men such as my father. My stomach was clenched, but whether in an anticipatory dread of the unknown or the fear of joy I did not know, and how could I when both were present.

Outside the bulbous façade of a grand hotel which commanded, with its wraparound bulk, the corner of two intersecting roads, my father was hailed by two friends. My head was patted in congratulatory expectation. There was to be a delay in proceedings. We went inside the expansive and plush lobby of the hotel, upward and outward sweeping stairs, deep red carpets and marble pillars, gilt-framed chairs positioned in alcoves, a gleaming mahogany reception desk, and men milling all around, in and out of the side bars. I was found a velvet cushioned window seat, and told they would not be long.

Lemonade was brought for me by a waiter, and drunk before they returned. A roiling wave of chatter and shouting, lurching bodies pirouetting around me, a rumbling wall of noise. My father and his friends materialised, ruddy faced now and holding cut-glass tumblers of whisky. They stood over me, protectively almost, and their talk was instantly, without pause of the Fight, the Bout, the Contest, the Mayhem which we had come to witness. They prided themselves on their appreciation of the finer points of boxing. They compared the contestants. Spoke their names with awed respect. The classic style of the incomparable Driscoll, the darling of the dress-suited gentlemen of London's National Sporting Club. His piston-like left leads, not a powder-puff puncher either, ghosting in and out of contact, wraith-like, impossible to pin down, so difficult to hit. Cardiff's very own, Irish-bred in Newtown, sensational on both sides of the Atlantic. A world-beater. But, said my father, six years older and will be lighter by, at least, six pounds between the weigh-in and the first bell. Their man, his friend, Fred Welsh. Never just 'Welsh' for them, any more than they would ever call the Roman Catholic devotee 'Jim', always just 'Driscoll'. If anyone could nail him, at last, it would surely be their, our, Fred. Two fisted and non-stop, Freddie Welsh, no pugilist more intelligent and aware, said my father. A proper lightweight at nine stone seven pounds to Driscoll's reality as a bare nine stone featherweight. Watch and see, said my father, for Freddie has art and power combined to conquer the dancing tactics of the slum bred papist. I shivered. Heads nodded. I listened. Sentiments were echoed. The tone and the terms were ones I had never heard before. There was, all too clearly, something at stake which had pricked them into this betrayal of their normal selves, drawn them into such uncaring and unhindered public indiscretions amongst themselves.

At home I had long heard my father tout the name of Freddie Welsh as that of an exceptional person. A man of breeding, at least of the kind that was acquainted with middle-class manners and respectability. That he had roots in the land before his home town, and that of my father, had begun its explosive rise to industrial glory. Then, as my father told it, there was the romance, the derring-do, the get-up-and-go which took a restless sixteen-year old, the former public school boy, out of an engineering apprenticeship and, through his own volition, made him, turn by turn, into a down-and-out American hobo, a Philadelphian shop assistant, an amateur boxer and, just four years before his encounter with the famed Driscoll, a self-taught professional fighter. Soon, an unbeaten one before all-comers, back home and in America, too. At twenty-four he was a future world champion his backers

believed, with my father vociferous amongst them. So what was at
stake in the American roller rink, the fight's makeshift venue across
the street from the hotel was, in the glitter of madness to be seen
in the eyes of my father and his friends, the future itself.

The bout had been re-scheduled for nine-thirty, an hour beyond
the previously fixed and agreed time. The weather had become
bone-chillingly damp. The roller park had been re-arranged to
place the canvas-floored ring in the middle of the space, with rows
of chairs in depth on all four sides. None of the rows had been
elevated for ease of sight, except for those on a small, erected
platform in one corner of the ring to seat the Lords and Gentlemen
– members of Jim Driscoll's patrons and supporters who had made
the rail journey from London to see the nonpareil of the Sweet
Science. At the outer limits of the tin-roofed hall there were ranks
of raised benches where Freddie Welsh's valued 'collier friends' had
travelled down from the valleys to the north to take advantage of
the specially targeted half-price tickets which their favourite had
urged upon the promoters. Many of these working men would have
been, at this precise time, out of work for the past few months, on
strike at the Cambrian Collieries, in a dispute which in November
had seen rioting, looting and mounted hussars on the streets.
Almost ten thousand spectators, altogether, were in the American
roller rink before the rival, half-naked, boxers entered the arena and
ducked under the ropes to step into the ring.

What I have remembered, over and over as the years went by, was
how strained, how fevered with tension everyone seemed, how fraught
with anxiety it all was. I was only, as yet, a boy but what I encountered
that night was, I can assert with the candour of time past, a rite of
passage which disfigured for good any romantic conception of sport
and heroic courage which a boy, or a man, say such as my father, might
have wanted and nourished. But, first, there was the fascination,
dreaded and not to be denied, with which I had to look.

The two principal figures, moving on the balls of their feet above us in the ring, were indeed an embodied contrast of personality and style. Jim Driscoll, the older man at nearly thirty years of age, seemed gaunt, with a troubled look about him. He had a sort of plaster or bandage around and under the back of one ear. At ringside there were mutterings about his having been unwell, that he suffered from boils, that his friends had advised against the fight, but that Jim Driscoll was never one to disappoint and that, in any case, a kind of friendship had soured into a sort of grudge. His chest was concave, almost sunken in at its top, and he looked, to me, to be too skinny to be a boxer. Unlike, of course, Freddie Welsh whose own black hair had no tell-tale flecks of grey and who, taller by an inch and heavier by half a stone or more, beamed the good health and demeanour of the clean-living and disciplined athlete he self-promoted at every turn. A sure winner, my father and his friends muttered to themselves.

Whether it was the late hour, the waiting, the cold air seeping from outside, the surly mood that drink could bring on or something less tangible as 1910 drew to a fractious close, I know not, but there was, from Driscoll's tight-lipped grimace to Fred Welsh's lifting of his gloves to the benched seats, nothing assured or reassuring about any of it.

To one side there was a small brass band which had been playing, hesitantly, enough, a few music hall tunes and, finally, a tremulous version of Hen Wlad Fy Nhadau which only a few voices took up to sing. Nothing like a rugby crowd, said one man near us. It was more observation than complaint. My father lit more than one cigarette taken from the silver monogrammed case my mother had given him in January of that year for his fortieth birthday. He puffed at them with some zeal but threw them, in short order, onto the wooden floor where they smouldered and glowed at our feet. The referee, from London, and a famous man, actually sat for the whole contest in the middle of the front row. My father pointed out his bulk in a black, sable coat, collar turned up against the draughts of coldness. Giving off more light than heat were electric arc lamps whose ghastly blueish white aura was concentrated on the square of the ring. From the low, raftered ceiling, small red-white-and-blue flags, strung together as an attempt at festive bunting, fluttered amongst the clouds of shag tobacco smoked from pipes on the benches. On the floor cigar smoke wreathed the faces of men nipping at whiskey from hip flasks passed from mouth to mouth. From the benches we could hear brown glass flagons of ale and porter being clinked and swigged. There were no ladies present, or women of any kind inside the arena. No cheers came as, at long last, the contestants touched gloves in the middle of the ring. Their seconds retreated with them to their respective corners, and then stepped outside the ring where they stood with towels and buckets. When the bell was struck the two great boxers bounced on their toes and Driscoll moved out to circle his more stolid prey. It apparently began as it had been expected to begin. The rest, as it went on and as I perceived it, was to be without shape or pattern. I knew, for me, that it was also ugly and meaningful.

All a surprise, they said afterwards. But how cunning, they all said. They said it was jab, feint, swerve, jab, all right, but that it was Fred, not Driscoll, who set out his stall that way. That he was, almost from the off, quicker, too, and Driscoll, minute by minute and round by round was wrong-footed in this fashion, growing so irritated at the loss of his accustomed rhythm that he made the mistake of trying to overwhelm Fred Welsh – of all people, they said! – with two-fisted all-out attacks. Maybe. It is what they said had happened. What I, in my first innocence, saw was Freddie Welsh, a fixed and infuriating grin deliberately set on his face, using his longer arms to tangle Driscoll up, then holding Driscoll's deadly left arm at the elbow with his own right, and pulling Driscoll downwards into the cave of his own body before turning him with force and, all to the blindside of the immobile referee outside the ring's square, thumping and thumping Driscoll with the heel of his gloves, more skin-covered than padded then, over and over into Driscoll's kidneys until he could be seen to wince and give out little cries of pain whilst elliptical, swollen, welts spread and visibly throbbed across his lower back, with Freddie Welsh smiling and whispering in his ear. We could hear Driscoll's seconds, his cornermen, swearing and shouting out protests to the unmoved referee. But this was not the National Sporting Club. This was not London.

Halfway through the fight, if that was what it was, Driscoll slipped on the canvas. Right in front of us he went down onto one knee. Just a slip on the damp canvas floor. Freddie Welsh stood over him, and he extended a gloved left hand to let Driscoll rise to his feet. And as he did so Fred Welsh abandoned any kind of upright stance. He crouched as Driscoll stood erect, he ducked under him and he rubbed his head upwards, as hard as he could, right into Driscoll's face and across his bandaged ear onto the wound of the boil on his neck. When Driscoll recoiled he raked his open-palmed glove over Driscoll's eyes and then stood off to clutch him once more, swivel his opponent's emaciated frame and alternately bore into and bang his fist into Driscoll's kidneys, again and again. They said, later, that Driscoll had pissed blood for a week.

What I saw was what punching at will does to a body: to swell the tissue around the eyes, cut across the prow of the nose with a slash to the bone, split and crack open the lips, decorate the air with spirals of blood in suspension, jerk back a head with a single uppercut, rock it to and fro with combinations of rights and lefts, make white flesh livid. With no interference at any stage from the portly, seated Mr Eugene Corri, the referee, the graceful Jim

Driscoll, after a few, hapless attempts to weave his own designs, had been caught, physically and then psychologically, in the fisherman's net which Freddie Welsh had cast for his prey.

In the tenth round, held tight once again by Freddie Welsh's grip and his disdain for rules which Welsh had long since learned to by-pass in America, Driscoll gave up on boxing's laws of engagement, the mastery of whose boundaries had burnished his own reputation as a maestro, and in this place for this time he left his acquired ringcraft behind him to become, again, the streetfighter who had once scrapped with fellow apprentices for entertainment and with fairground boxing booth punters for coins. Driscoll, his head the only weapon still available for him to use with his arms invariably pinned, thrust up bodily into Freddie Welsh's chin, knocked him backwards and drove into him with his whole head which he butted, hard and harder still, butting his opponent, who had discarded all rules, across the ring, Freddie Welsh flailing his arms to no effect to stop an enraged and overcoming Driscoll who had so ended the unlawful punishment, and the grin with which Welsh had demeaned him from the start.

Everyone was standing and shouting. The referee had finally got to his feet and was pushed into the ring where he used his size and authority to some purpose at last. He grabbed Jim Driscoll from behind, holding him by his arms. And, with that fighter weeping and, on his knees, he disqualified Driscoll and ostentatiously awarded Fred Welsh the victory by holding up the winner's right arm. The grin returned. Mayhem followed.

The principal seconds – Boyo for Fred, Badger for Driscoll, as was said with glee – were screaming at each other. You Welsh cunt! You Fenian bastard! You fucking, cheating Welsh scum! You dirty, fouling Irish pricks! Stools and buckets were hurled across the ring. Blows were given and taken. Beer bottles were being chucked from everywhere towards the ring. Police constables, around six of them, had rushed down the aisles but were being tripped, punched and kicked. My father was shielding me from a thrash of whirling men, shouting, "He's but a lad! He's a boy! Make way. Let us through!"

We both half-fell amongst the scattered chairs. I was on my feet before he was. The crowd was being charged into by more policemen. Through the gap made by this foray, we scrambled to the exit. Outside was not much better than the free-for-all inside the roller rink. Fights were breaking out at will and haphazardly. We crouched behind the corner of a low wall, waited for a lull nearby and hurried back home the way we had come nearly five hours earlier.

My father, Mostyn Arthur Lloyd, patriot and nonconformist, his shirt front spattered with the blood of others and his own spittle, his face aflame with whisky and triumph, dragging me along so fast that I was lifted from the ground, running and laughing alongside him as he yelled out to the world and to anyone who passed us or who opened a window onto the street:

"Cymru am Byth!

Cymru am Byth!

Freddie Welsh has won!

Champions of the world!"

And he held both his arms aloft. A Champion.

Memoir Fragment, c1964. Unpublished Taliesin Arthur Lloyd Papers. Box 1. National Library of Wales. Aberystwyth.

Gloria and Tony have a habit of addressing each other as Glore and Tone, in a manner almost wilfully designed to irritate my moribund generational sensibilities and my secretarial rectitude. I scratch at my own pomposity like an itch that connects me to life. Their lives more than mine. I listen in to them. They wonder how I am feeling. Inside. They appear to think that longevity is the same as having a long life. It is not. I could tell them. Life, as it passes, is always brief. Yes, in retrospect, there might be a lot to remember because things, people, occasions all pile up to be picked over. Such amassing, though, is only just that, a pile. Most of it can be discarded readily. Its bulk is not some kind of inert extension of life. That, life itself, remains momentary, evanescent, disappeared almost before or as soon as it has occurred. And it is as quick to pass, too, in the memory of it, because its being long drawn-out becomes necessarily compressed for the use of later consideration. Especially so when the momentary is also momentous.

I can testify directly to that. For an instant, the world is there to possess and win, and the next, no world at all, no life, no more moment by moment to live. For the people of my earlier days this became, alas, a common knowledge we shared, even if we too often kept silent about its meaning, telling each other that survival was all that truly mattered. That was wrong. Perhaps, if I am to be fair-minded to the lesser knowledge Glore and Tone have, I have to grant that they could not be affected by any such realisation. The past half-century, unlike that first fifty years of my time, has been more tick-tock than explosive. My dreams, for all that, circle and probe the memory of what was so abrupt, so abyss-like, so savage in finality.

The Great War more than anything. Though I did not go to it, what it was and did was destructive of more than the massed dead we mourned and could not quite comprehend in their disappearance. My father, Mostyn Arthur Lloyd, architect and infantry officer, too old in his mid-forties to have volunteered to go, though he went leaving us and was missing, presumed dead as the mantra went, before the first

Christmas of that war came. Nothing really to be presumed about his disappearance. Oh, he was dead all right. I was given the news, kindly enough, at school and told to go home for a while to comfort my mother and sister. I packed all I had. I knew I would not return.

I am dry-eyed through this wide-awake dream of sorrow. Whatever grief there was once felt for that ebullient man, my father, has atrophied. It was real and deep though, and would, as the war went on, send my mother and sister back to live in the comfortable family farm-house of her spinster sister and bachelor brother, my later and forcibly enlisted uncle, who did survive. As I have said, of a sudden survival seemed the only ticket worth having. My clubfoot would spare me the trenches and bullets and a young death for I would have been nineteen when the slaughter of the Somme came in 1916.

But I had already survived by then. By chance, of course. Indirectly, my father would have been the cause of my death if I had drowned in the waters of the Irish Sea. Of all the piled-up things I can pick over from those days on the Lusitania, to and from America, and there are many such and they have accumulated for me deeper and more terrible meaningfulness even to this day, I would guess that the assumption of others would be that the sinking, the disaster, the loss of life would haunt my mind and overwhelm all else. Not so. Or not exactly so. Not for me.

At the beginning of it I was asleep. Dead to the world in my First Class cabin. Early afternoon when the ship's alarm warning sounded. I had caroused all night into the dawn. Drinking. Not accustomed. My head splitting. My stomach a wretched ache. The Glee Party my sole companions. Avoided all others. Rowdy and affable Welsh choristers, the Gleemen of Gwent returning from their American tour. I buried myself amongst the joviality. Soused by daybreak. Blistered. Bladdered. Pissed, to me a word from a later time. Accurate enough for my eighteen-year old state of drunkenness. I had been sick. Slept on a bench on deck in the cold drifting in from the ocean. I was sick again. Stumbled away into the cabin, had it to myself, my companion not there. On the bed, fully clothed. Comatose. Even after the alarm went at ten past two in the afternoon. I had checked the pocket watch attached to my jacket through its lapel. Outside the cabin people running, pushing, some crying out for information. Most were clutching their lifesavers, the Boddy belts that some already wore. I turned back to fetch mine from the cabin but I only carried it away, with some papers. My Notebook, which I had kept for a diary, a few photographs of her, of us. All into an oilskin wallet I had bought in Manhattan to use against the sleet and snow. Tied up with waxed string and buttoned up in the inside pocket of the hacking jacket I was wearing. The inrushing sea water was swilling above the knee in the corridor, knocking some down by its force, the great ship listing already at an impossible angle. Details only. What mattered, and will always matter, is that I went looking for her.

These superb ocean greyhounds constitute the ultimate word in the way of passenger service. There are gymnasia where daily exercise in a great variety of beneficial forms can be enjoyed. There are verandah cafes, sun decks, smoking and drawing rooms, libraries and new 'lounges', so called, where light refreshments are served at any time of the day or night. The best cooks to be found in the world are on board, and the menu is unsurpassed. A doctor is at your disposal, chiefly for social purposes, as it seldom happens that anyone is sick, because everyone is happy. Sleeping accommodations of the Cunard steamships are most excellent. The passengers' quarters are located amidships. Perfect ventilation is the rule. Even the lowest staterooms are at least twenty feet above the level of the sea. Special Cabins de Luxe, marvellously appointed with the completest and most luxurious of everything that can contribute to the comfort and well-being of the occupants can be engaged in advance. The quadruple screw and the magnificent size of these floating palaces cause them to cleave the ocean waves with a barely perceptible motion, so that mal-de-mer is a thing that will interest you in an academic way only. Here is health, joy, information, education, growth, outlook, that will inspire you for the rest of your life, give you topics of conversation, things to write on and talk about, and put you in touch with the best that world has seen and said and done. Aboard ship you can depend upon it you will meet a charming and select company of ladies and gentlemen ... everything that can add to the pleasure, diversion and education of its guests has been provided, in ample measure, by the Cunard Steamship Company. These behemoths of the vasty deep ply between New York and Fishguard and Liverpool. This is the most expeditious route to and from the Old World.

Pamphlet. Autograph signature. Elbert Hubbard
(American philosopher and fabulist)
"Are you a Citizen of the World?" (1912) Taliesin Arthur Lloyd Papers.
Miscellanea Box 16. National Library of Wales, Aberystwyth.

Sunday, 21st March, 1915
Liverpool. Aboard RMS "Lusitania"

I have uncapped the mottled blue-and-brown Conway Stewart fountain pen which belonged to my late, dear Father and have begun to write for the record. I am sat on a well-upholstered wing-back chair with rounded arms and sturdy tapering legs which sink into the rose-pink carpet of this most splendid of all ocean-going liners, the Cunard Line's Royal Mail Ship "Lusitania". There! I have written it, so it must be, and it is!, the Absolute Truth. Though, let me add and pinch myself, that I can still scarcely believe it even as I sit at this splendid desk. Everything that is around me is indeed "splendid", and I cannot hold back the adjective! The desk is leather-topped, dark green and sumptuous to touch, with high walnut wood sides for privacy.

I paused there, a few minutes ago in this writing, taking a moment to contemplate my good fortune, and to fully take in my surroundings, but will here and now, with care and duty, resume my intended daily account of my great adventure.

All is calm around me. Only the thrum of the ship's turbines can be heard from somewhere in her bowels. A few globe lamps are glowing above the writing desks, of which only a few are occupied at this time of night, mostly by some ladies. Others of the fair sex, near mother's age I would venture, are sat on the chairs and sofas which richly adorn the room. They are turning the pages of the books they have selected from the glass-fronted bookcase which runs the entire length of one wall and almost up to the highly ornate white wood-and-plaster ceiling from which hang a number of small brass-rimmed chandeliers, all sufficiently a-glitter in the subdued light. I know father, master as he was of detail and effects, would have wished me to notice, as I duly do, as if it is all matter-of-fact for me.

It is nothing of the kind! Inside, I am not at all calm, but indeed struggling not to feel out-of-place and rather over-awed. Since, I have decided that this notebook will serve as a diary, I will endeavour, private and confidential from other eyes as it is, to be open and honest with myself as to thoughts and feelings both. And, equally, to be meticulous in my accuracy of outward descriptions. Taken together, as subject and object, it may seem that I am intruding on the life of another. In strict fact, I suppose, I have become such "another" by the turn my life has taken, and with such rapid speed. By my keen grief at the loss of my father, which I try, manfully I hope, to put aside for the sake of all; by my excitement, scarce containable, in taking up my new, and first salaried!, position as an assistant secretary; by the thrill of knowing, from the steady motion of the ship beneath my feet, that we are now fully at sea, racing across the Atlantic ocean to New York City; and flabbergasted above all else by the grandeur of the ship itself.

We came aboard late yesterday afternoon – it is now ten pm of this day – and my exploration of the "Lusitania" has scarce begun. Before embarking I had, as Father would have wished, boned up on the bare facts about the vessel, and from dockside at Liverpool, looking up at those four immense, tilted funnels in their orange-red livery, with dozens of seamen flitting about their business above us before the gangways were lowered, I could well believe that all of the incredible facts I had gleaned about here were the unvarnished truth. Only, now that I am a part of her as a passenger would I confess readily that they give one no idea, from the outside, what a paean to luxury and civilisation she is, the acme of our world surely, which the mechanics of description merely serve to frame. Even so, the statistical measures of her build and her performative powers, of her competitive success and her commercial supremacy, are magnificent tokens of the genius that has gone into her making, and I will put them down here as I have learned them off by heart, before I turn to convey what my own eyes have since beheld and what has made my heart to swell with such a pride in the glory of our British Empire.

She was launched nine years ago on the Clyde in Glasgow, the second city of our Empire, and began her in-service career in 1907 as the then world's largest ocean-going liner. She was soon to be the fastest, too, taking the Blue Riband for the quickest transatlantic voyage. Satisfactorily enough, regaining it from the Huns. Her length and width, at almost seven hundred and ninety feet and eighty-eight feet respectively, was not to be matched until the larger, and slightly faster, sister ship the Mauretania was launched in 1908. The sisters still vie for glory but "Lusitania," my first love, has won my heart hands down! She is powered, via twenty three coal burning boilers, by six huge steam turbines and four enormous screws. She can average over twenty six knots, can easily exceed that rate of speed at sea and completes the crossing to America in under five days. There are ten decks, for her height is seven hundred and sixty feet. There are some two hundred and sixty First Class staterooms to accommodate over five hundred passengers, with one hundred and forty five cabins in Second Class for four hundred and sixty souls, and three hundred and two cabins in Third Class for over one thousand people. That amounts to a total carrying capacity of well over three thousand transatlantic voyagers, along with a crew staffed at eight hundred in peacetime to steer us safely and serve as well. What a triumph for British engineering! And, as she cuts through the waters, her prow lofty and narrow, her mien imperious and impatient – this is a flight of fancy from me, I confess! – a Britisher knows who truly rules the waves!

Anyway, coming back to earth and all that, I intend to go all over her, above and below to see her inner workings, provided permission is accorded. My goodness, though, she is less a ship to the casual eye, notwithstanding the pulsating hum of her power, more a De Luxe hotel set afloat. She is a Temple to the achievements of that mercantile and pacific endeavour to which we, as a nation, aspire. She is gold and white with blood red splashes of colour for carpets and furnishings. She is an unstoppable edifice of momentum, a tribute to our race. And, assuredly, the perfect proof in her perfection that we are destined to conquer in this wicked war which the Hun has brought upon himself, and which we will, we must! end soon.

That last was the gist of the confident exchange of views amongst the half dozen or so gentlemen with whom we sat in the Smoking Room after our first night's light supper taken just after we had left the Mersey, a scatter of city lights to our stern and some ragged last cheers from the quayside before we were covered by the darkness over a placid Irish sea. That was the conversation, and also the placing of daily bets in what is called the Ship's Pool as to how speedily we will make progress each day on what is the Lusitania's one hundred and ninety ninth westward crossing. I, naturally, stayed quiet in the company, only replying directly to any kind enquiries made about myself. Otherwise, I deferred to the lead taken by Mr Rhys-Evans who has asked me to address him as Arnold in private. We share a First Class stateroom, so that is bully of him. Formal address, then, only for business matters, as is appropriate when others are present, since he is very much accorded respect as the principal secretary to Mr D. A. Thomas. I am to be his assistant, hurrah! set, over the next few days at sea, to learn the ropes. I will be expected to practice and be a typewriter when required, though to be a stenographer without any formal training would be a stretch too far. Also, to act as a general factotum in the way of retrieving and sending messages, managing other correspondence and copying. All necessary work since I am given to understand that "D A" as Rhys-Evans calls him will not cease to work at his business during the entire voyage. I have not as yet had the pleasure and privilege of meeting up with him on board ship, or yet thanking him again for the opportunity he has afforded me. That is to be for tomorrow after breakfast, a meal which I am told he will probably take alone in his single stateroom.

On this anticipatory note I can end my first entry.

Monday, 21st March, 1915
RMS "Lusitania"

It has been an eventful day. As it comes to a close I sit again at what I have already come to regard – somewhat proprietorially, I confess! – as "my" desk. Tonight I feel, rather oddly, both bound and liberated at the same time. (And certainly full-as-a-tick after dinner with Arnold!). I think it is because, with U-boat attacks a possibility in these waters, the ship's running lights have been doused from bow to stern but inside all is as it was and makes one feel the master of one's destiny, as if "At Home" in the middle of the ocean. All behind us is left, to be waiting there for our return. All that is before us awaits our coming. So here we are, as the deepening Atlantic trough causes "Lusitania" to pitch and roll ever so slightly, home for now.

Last night I slept poorly, unaccustomed perhaps to the ceaseless throb of the ship's engines and, at dawn, disturbed by the sounds of domestic preparations being made, as in any grand hotel I suppose. My companion, Arnold Rhys-Evans, however – soon to become a good friend and valued mentor, I'm sure! – slept like a log. That is if logs can be said to snore! He is, of course, a seasoned traveller and at ease with the tasks we will be set. I am neither, needless to say, and remained restless on both counts until I could bear it – my excitement and my anxiety – no longer. I got up as quietly as I could, washed and brushed and dressed myself, and left him to slumber on in our comfortable, indeed sumptuous, cabin.

A word on that first, and then more on him. There are so many impressions of place and people I want to jot down here when they are fresh in my mind, ready to be ordered into line. I will start, then, with B92 our First Class Stateroom. It was not easy to locate when first we embarked. There are endless winding corridors. There were people, visitors and passengers and stewards directing them, all milling about. Bulwarks and gates and bridges and appropriate notices prevented any haphazard mixing of the various class of passenger either on deck or in the distinctive public spaces. In our cabin, when I found it at last, I met up with Arnold Rhys-Evans who had come up separately from London with our employer. He had unpacked and was resting on the rose silk counterpane of a brass framed mahogany bed. Mine, identical in all respects, faced his berth. He had greeted me warmly, by standing up and saying, "You must be Arthur Lloyd, eh?" And, then, shaking my hand, he said, "Do call me Arnold, when we are not in company."

He is a delightful chap, I think, and has been most kind to me, making me feel at ease, so to speak, for he has considerable experience of business even though he is only some few years older than me. Twenty-three, or so, I believe, though I have not asked directly. He was engaged by Mr D. A. Thomas after completing his Law degree at Cambridge and seems intimate with all manner of detail, personal and professional, which it is his responsibility to keep ordered. I am to assist in that by ensuring all correspondence is dispatched forthwith and what is received is filed and answered. We have, hard by the Purser's office, two dedicated Marconi operators in their own equipped space. Arnold has pointed out the transmission wires attached to the funnels and tells me that we are in constant touch with one continent or the other, and instantly so, other than for a brief time in mid-ocean. This service is much in demand, for trivial as well as practical purposes, and he warns me that I may need to queue for it, but to be both persistent and insistent with them, since Mr D. A. Thomas brooks no delay in his business transactions.

Indeed, in our stateroom, shortly after I had returned from my walk on the deck this morning, the telephone, fixed to the wall and with which there is the ability to communicate with other cabins on board, rang so abruptly that I was startled into inaction before its jangling but, fortunately, Arnold was wide awake by now and, no slouch he, picked up the receiver and said, "Yes, sir?" without hesitation or further query. It was to say that Mr Thomas was somewhat indisposed and that we would not meet up with him that day since he was confining himself to his own rooms. We were free, Arnold said, to enjoy the day as we wished.

Which brings me to the issue of over indulgence. In food, I mean. Arnold has taught me the nature and meaning of the word "sybaritic". After breakfast, lunch and now dinner, over two days already, I am all too well acquainted with its consequences. I had worn evening dress, as is the custom in First Class after the first night of settling in, and can feel my stomach swell beneath jacket and shirt. Never had I eaten so well, or so much. At dinner today caviar, a first for me and in its salty fishiness not to my taste so that Arnold enjoyed a chuckle at my expense, and then a beef consommé, a clear soup in fact, a fillet of sea bass lightly browned in butter, roast partridge, cauliflower and asparagus in another buttery sauce, discs of golden potatoes, with apple charlotte, or countless other wonders! for dessert, then coffee with petit fours to end. Luncheon had been scarcely less demanding with hors d'oeuvres of sliced meats and crudités leading on to poached salmon, then sautéd veal or roast lamb with mint sauce, my favourite from home I confess and nicely English against all the French dressing-up as Arnold said. I could not resist, either, plum pudding and thick dollops of custard, far better than school! I swear, here and now, to be more restrained but the waiters are ever ready to cajole us, whilst at breakfast the chafing dishes are ever-topped up with succulent kidneys, rashers of back bacon, all manner of cooked eggs, fried, scrambled, poached, boiled and even raw, to be swallowed whole as a pick-me-up for excessive imbibing, says Arnold, who is wiser than I am in these matters. From experience, too, I have thought to myself. So far I have persuaded him that I do not, myself, relish strong drink. I fear he means to test me before we make landfall, and that, to please him as my shipboard companion, I may yet need to succumb.

In between times we have played whist in the smoking room with two American gentlemen and perambulated on deck since the weather has, so far, been kind to us. But I have saved for the end of this day's jotting my sense of wonder which the "Lusitania" induces in one. She is a ship only in function, for as ornament she is a declaration of Human Progress and Order in all things. For my part, and no doubt with my father's injunctions finding a path through my thoughts, it is the unity, or should I say the conjoining, of Technology, the unparalleled splendour of our future, with the Tradition of civilised living, which we are set on defending in Flanders and which whispers, nay shouts! all around us. Nowhere more so than in the First Class Dining Saloon, all done as I have been told by the steward, in the style of Louis XVI, its superb domed ceiling with its painted medallions of cherubs and nymphs surrounded by plaster work of fruits and vine and amiable deities, all above a balcony enclosed by golden iron scrollwork, supports held up by Corinthian pillars, their decorative tops a dark gilt with ivory white for their length and reaching down from the balcony to the richly carpeted floor below, where dark red horse-hair stuffed dining chairs are set around tables laid for two to five diners, or even more convivial companions. We are certainly highly spoiled, I must say.

Arnold tells me that second class passengers are scarcely less well catered for than first class as a Cunard policy, though there is no social intercourse for we have our own central, electrically operated gate-door lift to move between decks and the interlinked public spaces on our own deck, from smoking to music to drawing rooms, and my beloved library. You can, across a barred gate or over a pontoon bridge, glimpse some of that other type of traveller, bearing my own actual second-class status, if I am to be honest! as a Diary must.

But around and about the ship itself we see none from Third Class, a more basic and regimented, but still comfortable level of accommodation and sustenance Arnold thinks, unless that is you look down onto the small aft deck below as seen from the First Class Verandah café. Arnold and I did exactly that this afternoon, leaning on the rail and smoking his "gaspers," hand-rolled tobacco in paper not the more refined cigarettes which he proffers to others after dinner from a flat initialled silver case. Below us, thickly coated and muffled by head scarves tied over their hats were a group, say ten or so, of young women and girls, with a few men, less wrapped up but with their caps pulled firmly down against the sea breezes, and all decidedly foreign in appearance, dark-eyed and rather swarthy as to skin. Arnold wondered if they had passports for entry. He and I both carried ours as was compulsory since the British Nationality and Status Aliens Act was passed by Parliament late last year. Arnold is knowledgeable about such matters. He surmised that the ones we were looking at were Italian, or possible Jews from Poland or the Russian Pale, escaping pogroms and seeking the freedom of the New World via the British Empire. He was a bit sniffy about them and even flipped his gasper, its lighted end flickering out as it fell, down onto the deck. One of the girls, decidedly striking in her looks I thought, glanced up. She looked indifferently at us, and said nothing. We turned our backs on them and went inside.

Tuesday, 22 March
RMS "Lusitania"

The weather has worsened somewhat today. A westerly gale brought a heave swell, towering seas at times, through which the "Lusitania" seems to crash and rise to no ill effect, dividing the deeper blue water into sheets of luminescent green, leaving whirlpools of white foam in her wake. The positive side to this is that we go faster towards our destination. The ill effects of the weather were confined to the passengers! Mr Thomas has still been indisposed and Arnold has been lying down most of the day, just managing some toast and a cup of bouillon which our steward brought. I, on the other hand, have been busy. The summons came via the wall telephone from Mr D. A. Thomas. Arnold answered and conveyed my task to me. It was to meet with the maid servant, who is in attendance on Mr Thomas, at the Purser's office at twelve noon to receive from her the various communications which Mr Thomas wishes transmitted, some to London, others to New York. I was to collate the replies when we heard back and arrange with the maid (whose name I learned was Gwennie) for their later collection. There were also, to be had from her, loose sheaves of blue-lined foolscap paper with red margins, whose annotated columns of figures, names and dates, and various jottings in our employer's clear hand, I was to take away to copy in neat transcription (this latter was painstakingly tedious and consumed my afternoon), and then file away for safe-keeping. I believe all went satisfactorily in this, my first clerical duty, for I heard nothing untoward about it.

My head, however, had spun and spun all day since noon. It is a wonder I could concentrate on the minutiae of financial transactions and fill in the lined columns with their figures. And it is all because she, Gwennie, is a daisy. I am smitten and do my best to chase away such foolishness. I must put it down, for all that, if only for my eyes here, that she is uncommonly pretty. Eyes that are coal black orbs, thickly tressed brown hair with golden gleams, and which she wore pinned up in a most becoming fashion. She was simply dressed, not maid-like at all, though that is understandable when acting outside her cabin duties, in a full, pleated dark woollen skirt that fell onto neat, black button boots, whilst a grey cardigan wrapped her around, from throat to waist.

"You must be young Mr Lloyd", she'd said, quite boldly and in an accent that proclaimed her origins were in the Hills, and she had smiled as I blushed. I could not prevent it, and felt the warm flush rise from my neck. She is quite small, just beyond the five foot mark I'd guess in her stockinged feet, olive skinned and modest in demeanour. I had shuffled in front of her to join the queue at the Purser's, conscious suddenly and ridiculously so of my boot. She did not appear to notice my clumsy motion, nor did she hurry away as she extended a hand which held a thin, leather satchel with the papers. I managed to say, gruffly enough, since what a stupid, surly fellow I can be!, that I was not so young. She looked at me, coolly enough I must say, and said, well younger than she was anyway. Then she turned and walked away. I want to ask Arnold all about her, yet dare not, he will not find it appropriate at all, and I dread his funning me.

The day passed in this rather unexpected combination of tedium and reverie. At five o'clock, as arranged, Gwennie knocked on our stateroom door. I did not move from the chair at the desk. I could not stop trembling. Arnold had answered to her knock. The return answers were ready and put in order along with the original inked foolscap she had presented me with earlier. Arnold said, "There you are, my girl. I do hope Mr Thomas is as recovered as I am becoming. Take good care of him, Gwennie. Here are the papers. Good-day to you." He had looked over at me and smiled one of his quizzical smiles, but he cannot know. "Well, well," he said. "Some tea? I feel up to it again, Tal my lad." He rang for the steward and as he refreshed his toilet, I read, the words swimming before me, a romance by Mr Rafael Sabatini.

Over our tea things – hot buttered toast, some Gentleman's relish, a salty paste spread Arnold much enjoys, not so much myself – my mentor began to josh me and I did not overly care for it. It began with his idly examining our "passports", a single page folded into eight and kept within a cardboard cover, each with a personal photograph. I do feel as if I am somehow secured by mine, established in identity so to speak, my signature in blue ink across its bottom, the first thing I have ever officially signed. The photograph is a bit of a let-down so far as any personal vanity may be figured in, for I seem startled and rather less at ease in my confidence than the possession of a passport should necessarily entail for a British citizen, even for one, at eighteen, not yet able to cast his vote. It is none of this, however, that tickles Arnold's fancy. It is rather the brief "personal description" each holder must give of himself. Oh, look Tal, he said, under "Shape of Face", yours says, did you do this yourself he asks and pops a square of toast into his mouth, "Forehead: broad." He says he would think it more to be "narrow" and as for "Nose" more "thin" than "aquiline" and it is true I had long considered the word before committing it as a self-description – whilst for "Eyes" I had written "blue, wide spaced" and he snorted out more like "watery, agog". It was innocent fun I know but I had not liked it. His own was, indeed, more accurately honest as in "high" for forehead, "brown" for eyes and "large" for nose. But what really irked most, when he saw I was not amused, was his saying that I had not put down my most obvious physical distinction. "Your club foot, Tal, old chap" he said. "Your club foot. Can't hide that, old boy. Nothing to be ashamed of, by the way, just bad luck is all. And, by the way", he said, "Meant to ask before.

Does it hurt? Much, I mean?" I felt bewildered by this turn of events, and more so when he mused out loud, "I wonder what dear little Gwennie's personal description might be, though she won't have written it herself you may be sure."

The episode ended with his declaring the need for some air after being confined all day. Later he took me by the elbow and said that he was sorry for being such a confounded ass, and that it was, in a manner of speaking, a way of preventing my becoming an ass in the manner he had been. I have written this down as it happened since I remain confused by it and can only assume he was made ill-tempered by his mal-de-mer. Before we turned in after supper, where all was joviality again, I made sure to remove my boot out of his sight and be in bed before he could glimpse my affliction, which does indeed after any prolonged time spent upright on it hurt like the deuce, though I will not show that pain. To anyone.

Wednesday, 23 March 1915
RMS "Lusitania"

The sea has settled to a calmness again and today's Ship's Pool appears set for he who predicts a very fast time. The placid weather perked Arnold up, too, so that he began the day with the proverbial hearty breakfast. It feels as if we are being fattened for the slaughter! Even as I completed that last remark I though it ill-considered and in rotten bad taste with all that our boys are suffering in France. I plead myself as callow and immature and rejoice that nobody else is destined to read my foolishness. What else? Well, lots to say really. Not least my first official meeting, in Arnold's company, with Mr D. A. Thomas.

We were summoned to meet with him in the Smoking Room at eleven sharp. I spent the time after breakfast until then contemplating my father's hand in this good fortune of mine. Mr Thomas had remembered our family after father's death in battle. There was a letter of condolence to my mother, recalling his professional dealings with father, and with some delightful personal touches added. Not the least of which was a mutual admiration of the art of boxing! Father had been present, with thousands of our compatriots at the Harringay arena in London in July 1914, just a month before the outbreak of war, when Fred Welsh had finally become the Champion Lightweight of the entire world by beating the American Willie Ritchie. Mr Thomas had bumped into father in the jolly aftermath of that famous victory. He had wondered, in his letter, how he could be of assistance, in any manner, at such a sad and difficult time. My temporary appointment as an assistant secretary to sail with him on the "Lusitania," at a modest but welcome salary, was the outcome after the cursory interview he gave me at Llanwern, his country house in Monmouthshire.

As we waited for my benefactor, Arnold said that the meeting would be a Council of War, a strategic preparation for the deployment of his plans in America. So it proved to be, largely between the two of them, but it was for me rather more than that, just the thrill I mean to be in the close company of this Great Man. He is a veritable Titan, I am sure, but also, for me, such a warm and encouraging support, putting me at my ease (or almost so!) at once.

Anyway, as Arnold had said, he was punctual to the dot. We had made sure to be in place a quarter of an hour in advance. We stood as he entered the room. One or two gentlemen nodded in his direction. Arnold gave out a hearty, "How are you, sir? Much restored, I trust," and, as he thanked Arnold he also gestured for us to sit. There were no handshakes or preliminary remarks. He comes, I feel, to the point in all things, and all things first in the order with which he wishes to deal with them. That was to be me!

He looked directly at me, leaned forward slightly in his chair so that he was positioned nearer to myself than to Arnold, and, in a quiet, rather flat voice, he said, "I was, indeed, as I wrote to your mother, and subsequently told you, dear boy, deeply affected to hear of your gallant father's death on the field. A terrible loss for all who knew him as I did, and my personal condolences once again to the family entire and to yourself, Arthur. It will not be easy to bear for a while yet. You will have to muster the strength, as will so many in this ghastly conflict we are forced, for a while yet I fear, to endure. For my part, I am mightily pleased that you are able, prior to your going up to Oxford, to assist us, especially Mr Rhys-Evans here, in our little endeavours. I hope it will suit, for yourself, and then who knows, eh? as well as for ourselves. Dispatch and confidentiality will be crucial in all things, eh?"

My reply was doubtless mumbled. I think I stared at him as he spoke rapidly and inconsequentially, about the weather and arrival soon in the New World. As he did, I studied him. Everything about him was somehow as if arranged, not for effect though, almost for its opposite, the effacement of anything which might startle or affront. The overall impression his appearance gave one was that of greyness. A single breasted lightweight pale grey jacket worn over a similar waistcoat. Darker grey woollen trousers. His shoes, not boots, were black and gleaming, his stockings a thickly knitted battleship grey and the floppy bow tie which lay beneath the fly-away collars of his white shirt was of silk, pearly grey with darker blobs of grey for its spots. Mr Thomas was I had ascertained from Arnold not yet sixty years old, fifty seven if I am to be exact, but his pallor and gravitas seemed to accrete further years to his earthly existence. His lips were rather thin but seemingly as if poised to open, and they pucker, perceptibly so, before he speaks. A signal as to this is given by his eyes first, for they seem to switch suddenly from a cold bluey- grey to something more akin to the hot, blue inner flame of a Bunsen burner, before he chooses to pronounce. He has a habit, too, of pulling his hair down with his right hand on his parting, although not a hair on his head is out of place. There are grey flecks amongst the sleek brown. Withal, when he stands Mr Thomas is slender, well-proportioned for a man of his age, not quite the six foot attained by Arnold, but well erect beyond my own five foot five. My only demur, in what I am aware sounds to be rather an unabashed eulogy at this first acquaintance, is that his hand, when he shook mine on leaving, is surprisingly flabby in its grasp and clammy in its feel, quite unexpected given the rigour he shows in all else. And, disconcertingly, that he stares, from very closely, into your face as if his eyes, behind his gold rimmed pince-nez, are myopic. Worse still, but I am determined on the candour of a true Diarist, his breath comes from out of him as a foul miasma, an odour from some stagnant depth. Arnold had warned me of the halitosis, as he calls it, of which no-one will speak to Mr Thomas. But nothing could have prepared me for the sour contrast of that stink with his overall neatness and delicacy of being.

Now I will need to compensate here on these pages for my appalling, thankfully hidden, rudeness to him in recording my sensation. I will atone by rejoicing in the memory that for an hour or so I was given a lesson in the profundity of his insight into the world and its ways which he so abundantly possesses. I have been privileged, already then, to sit before him and be made to contemplate.

He had begun by putting me further at my ease, over the coffee and sweet digestive biscuits, by sharing my enthusiasm for the *Lusitania*, The Ship, and what did I think of her? We quickly moved from the vaporous clouds of praise to the precise in terms of measurements, and the engineering wonders as to her speed and potential. As Arnold's head drooped so did our employer's tilt upwards in interest. Of course, statistics are his thing. He was a Senior Wrangler at Caius, Cambridge, reading Mathematics for his degree and he has since led the way in describing, understanding or predicting the production and exports of coal from our vast geological basin in South Wales. He is in this field what one of our great rugby cracks is in our national game: a non-pareil. I believe I impressed him, in my small fashion, by my schoolboy cognisance of some of the facts as to dimension and power but, clearly he had one primary lesson to impart at this stage of my knowledge, and it can be summed up by the word, and the concept too!, of coal itself, that fuel of our age and, as he went on to stress, the essential prop of all our civilised being. I was enthralled.

First, he told me with some pride in his voice – which I must say is more impressive for its quiet, forceful delivery than for any colour to its tone, and rather without an identifiable accent of region or class, other than that of education and authority – that the *Lusitania* herself was ravenous for good Welsh steam coal which filled half of her cavernous stokeholds. At full speed she eats up one thousand tons of coal a day or, as he quickly calculated, one and a half thousand pounds of coal go into the furnaces each and every minute. The facts and figures pour out of him with the statistical wizardry of a latter-day Merlin. Total coal production from South Wales stood at over thirteen million tons in 1914, and from the mid-Rhondda alone, where his mighty Combine of collieries dominates, the figure was one third of that. He employs in these concerns some twelve thousand men and that does not account for all his other interests in shipping, railways and mineral exploration. He sees, no doubt, that my eyes widen, unable to comprehend the magnitude of his undertakings nor the wealth he must have accrued. He seems, is this his secret?, to intuit my thought process. He smiles. Money? That, he says and looks intently at me, is not it at all. He appears, though not really I sense, to swerve. Now he tells me that he chucked the House because the common run of politicians were pack animals with only their own self-preservation and, if possible, self-advancement in mind. They were a menagerie. He was a solitary. And here he winked at Arnold, as if for confirmation, and Business, as he emphatically pronounced it, was the only game to play. That there are rewards from it was not to be gainsaid, but I needed to understand if I was to work for him, in a private and confidential capacity he stressed, that monetary reward was only a means to power. He then actually said, "Take this to heart, Arthur, and commit it to your inner mind for future reference, for it tells you of my deepest beliefs and the future direction I intend to map out as this war, a war of inestimable opportunity, presents the hazard of fortune to those with energy, foresight and willpower to speculate, accumulate and gain." Then he waited for me to open my official notebook, not this one of course, and to scribble as fast as my fountain pen would allow. His dicta, thus: "In England we are only now beginning to realise the attraction of Business, its core social and economic function, as our

American cousins realised it long since. Think why it is that those Americans who have made vast sums of money still remain in business? Do they retire to the country? Do they adorn the gasbag chambers of political life? Not the Carnegies or Morgans, I can tell you. So why then? For more money? Not at all, not in the least. It is because, my boy, the greater their business grows, the greater they are enabled to employ all of their powers, of imagination and execution, the more, in short, they are enabled to do things. Business – write this down carefully, Arthur – business is the modern equivalence of war. War, then, is business by any other name. We must profit from both. Why, if Napoleon had been born fifty years ago in America he would have been a dangerous rival to Mr Rockefeller. Or …", and here he squeezed my elbow and snorted a chortle, "if in South Wales, then to me! Eh?" He seemed to have finished and sat back in his armchair. Arnold, who had perhaps taken down some such speechifying himself at some time, nodded to indicate I should not cap my pen as yet. Mr Thomas' concluding words on the subject were to the effect that in Business, today, risk was for the brave to take and only a conqueror born could surmount its difficulties, and reap its rewards. "For the many who need from the few who can," he added.

After this the conversation proved to be more focussed on the notations and communications he wished Arnold to prepare for his business arrangements to be met directly when we disembarked. I was, it seemed, to be kept busy sanding away the subsequent files, accumulated information and confidential documentation. There would also be a deal of cabling, queries and answers in both directions, to be sent and to be received. Their interpretation was for him alone. At the conclusion of these two hours he declared that he would retire to his cabin for luncheon but that before he did so he wished to make me personally a business proposition. I sat up rather bold upright at this and he had to pat my hand and tell me not to be alarmed. It was rather, he said, that if I proved to be an asset, as he was confident I would be, there might be a more permanent employment for me in what might prove to be more and more troublesome times. By which he meant, he said, and made a wry shape with his mouth, he anticipated that after the volunteering, in which his daughter Lady Mackworth was proving to be a first rate recruiting officer, diminished, the call for troops would increase to the point of conscription, from which, he said, and it was the reason I now saw for his slight hesitation, I would be excluded by dint of being a cripple. He hoped that I did not mind his being so blunt in using such a term, but that there it was and for me to see it as a silver lining amongst whichever clouds scudded across our horizon. Anyway, I was to see how it went. Naturally, for I am sure he means well and that all is in my best interests, I thanked him.

The rest of the day passed, aside from the lengthy sitting down for meals to which I have grown wearily accustomed, in a blur of activity. It is strange how normal all this now seems. And tomorrow to go quickly as our last full day at sea.

Thursday, 24 March 2015
RMS "Lusitania"

Today concluded with the traditional end of voyage concert party held in the Dining Saloon to which the Music Room's Grand Piano had been removed. It continues, in strict fact, as I sit down to write this. I have excused myself from what was a decorous enough affair, not at all rowdy, with the ship's orchestra in attendance, some dancing in which Arnold looked very much the part in his tails – a veritable Vernon Castle one lady remarked, very much to his liking as I could see – , and with a few rousing songs to cheer the heart. No-one says it aloud but there is an electric atmosphere that crackles rather with the thought that we have, almost, crossed without any incident. A little nostalgia, too, perhaps at the conclusion of the voyage. Just before I left, Ivor Novello's new song, "Keep the Home Fires Burning", was struck up and sung with gusto, drawing laughter when one voice, an acquaintance of Mr Thomas said Arnold, shouted out, "As long as it's with best Welsh steam coal from the Rhondda!" Mr Thomas, himself, did not make an appearance though we had been at his beck and call via the telephone and by hand-written communications all morning and well into the afternoon. The last call on us came around five o'clock, just after we had taken tea in the Verandah café, when the maid, Gwennie, crossed the floor to find us. The messages were given straight to Arnold who said he would act on them with dispatch and for her to return for the outcomes to our stateroom at six o'clock. She half-curtsied to him and, I am sure, though I was desperate not to let my gaze linger on her, she gave me the slightest hint of a smile as she turned on her heel. I cannot help but record that moment, and in despite of what I now seem to know, if Arnold can be trusted, and why should I doubt him yet wanting so to do, as to the circumstances to which I have been so foolishly blind.

This is the way it is then. I write it down to burn it onto this page and into my soul. It was, as I say, Arnold who sat me down before we went to dinner. He began by telling me that the look of calf-love (his hideous phrase!) in my eyes and through my whole being, was too self-evident as Gwennie had stood before us, demurely dressed in grey skirt and white blouse and patiently attentive, awaiting the answers to Mr Thomas' queries. This time, in such proximity, I stared at her without let as Arnold shuffled papers and placed them in order of the priority with which she was to hand them over. Occasionally she seemed to cast a look in my direction, from downward eyes to a quizzical look up. And it was this that made Arnold decide, he said, to put me in the picture. He took out his cigarette case and lit one for himself after I had declined.

What I was to understand, and what I am now coming to terms with here, is that so far as Mr Thomas is concerned the world, all of it and all that is in it, radiates out from his centre and is seen from no other perspective. Thus, it was not that yesterday he was flattering me with his unwarranted attention, it was more that he was projecting what he wanted me to believe, to see, to feel, to desire. In short, Arnold said, he is very good at telling whoppers in which he also implicitly believes. Arnold said that he was telling me this for my own good and that he himself, though long inured to the ways of our employer, had previously suffered from the fires of self-inflicted mis-perception whose torment he did not wish for me. My puzzlement was plain.

Arnold said to think of it in layers. Take politics, for instance. The declared verdict, by D. A. Thomas, Member of Parliament for first Merthyr Boroughs and then Cardiff, from the late 1880s to 1909, was that it was a second-rate profession for ditherers, dolts and conmen. The actual case was that his lack of a convivial presence, of a talent for speech-making in the House and on the hustings, as well as his general ambiguity of political principles, had led to his being consistently overlooked for any ministerial office despite the capacity for administrative and policy matters he undoubtedly possessed. Then again, there were his oft-quoted remarks that if he had been a working man or not a Liberal by inclination and profession, he would have thrown in with the infant Labour Party and even espoused Socialism as a creed. Bunkum, said Arnold, another trick to make himself stand out, seem distant from more dim-witted coalowners and also claim to be wiser than any miners' leaders who increasingly did support variations of that crackpot philosophy, by being, in the end, himself and publicly self-proclaimed, as philosophically against all politicians. Not philosophy, at all, said Arnold for Mr Thomas was born into wealth, privileged by wealth, and made wealthier yet, yea unto Croesus, by the happenstance of inheritance in the coal business and by his ruthlessness in capitalistic ventures. Indeed he was, first and last and always, a Capitalist, and one whose drive was to pile up his pounds and his pennies at the expense of all and sundry. What did I know of his first action when war broke out? Nothing? Well, I will be told then that he moved with alacrity to buy up all the German holdings or enterprises within the Empire upon which he could lay hands, and stressed to the world and his wife that it was his patriotic duty to seize these assets and control them. Privately, he had said it was a great dodge, a chicane of which he might feel justly proud. This great Britisher, too, was prone to be dismissive of both the little Englanders and even littler Cymros who snapped at his heels. And his own imperial pretensions were severely limited, behind the scenes of public life, by his contempt for colonials from the far-flung Dominions and their gabble of prairie reporters out to promote them. No, it was America, and the Idea of America alone for him, and Arnold was clear that for Mr Thomas loyalty was neither to place nor people but always to the economic interest that could be derived and sustained therefrom. Also to be included on the balance sheet were the gains from any personal prestige which might be garnered from his public profile and public services. I was to understand that this autocratic spirit was, in his own self-regard, a Superman whose will was not to be brooked or even curtailed by any illustrious tribunes of the people via their Labour organisation nor by their hobbledehoys in mob-like riotous assembly. He saw himself at this time, Arnold said, as a conduit, a lighting conductor if you will, between a territorial Empire that was passing, a moribund Europe that was cracking up and an economic Imperialism that was building afresh via a New World untrammelled by ties of sentiment and any fatuous inertness. His constant trips, back and fro, to America from, 1913 to the present moment of crisis, were all in aid of developing his interest in coal, shipping and railways, all on that continent, with a view to flooding and disrupting the export home market's global primacy with more cheaply dug, transported and bunkered coal. American production and his own world-wide assets in play together. Arnold said there was no sentiment in his dealings, that he foresaw the dwindling of the great coalfield at home, even the decline of coal itself as new energy superseded it. Hence, the wholesale buying and opening up for development of the huge fields of tar sands for oil production in the far north of Canada. The War was a graspable piece of good fortune and a fluke occurrence of good luck, in that his deepening relationships with American moguls, especially the great anglophile Banking House of J. P. Morgan, made DA the key figure in opening up lines of credit which could finance the Empire-at-war, so that it might tap into the capacity for endless munitions supply which was uniquely presented by American engineering and manufacturing. The voyage we were undertaking was an advance trip to lay out the ground face-to-face. It was at the root of all the coded and intricate messages and information upon which we had been working on his behalf. Arnold had then given me a cold look and almost sneered when he said it was all in the interests of bringing to an end the horrors of the Front, wasn't it, and Mum's the word.

Arnold had then carefully extinguished his cigarette. He poured himself a brandy and insisted, as he put it, that I take a snort, too. Arnold said he would come straight out with it, but he didn't, not right from the off. All that he had told me, and in the strictest confidence, was, he said, only to open my eyes to the Juggernaut beneath whose wheels we lived or died. And we should be proud to be in that position, as erstwhile, if junior, bosom companions of this Colossus. He said that others were not so fortunate, at least not at first sight. Others were enemies. Others were merely employed. Others were expendable. Some were just lesser. Playthings. Picaninnies. To be of use, to be cared for, to be kept. Then he said that he could see I was taken with Gwennie, and that she did indeed have a girlish charm and a lissom carriage, but that I should, and sharply, see in her the parlour-maid she had been, the maidservant she had become, and the exclusivity of her current presence, since she was the personal property, so he said, of Mr D. A. Thomas. When I said nothing, not a protest nor a quizzing, not anything, Arnold said that for God's sake, Tal, she lies in his bed, she fucks him as he wants, and she is no doubt better rewarded for such service than for any other she ostensibly renders, and I was to forget her. But I will not. I will despise her instead.

239

Friday evening, 25 March, 2015
The Waldorf-Astoria, 33rd and 34th Street
Fifth Avenue, New York City

I have decided to bring this Diary to an end, and with it the self-indulgence I now detect as its root, if unwitting, purpose. Whatever has withered in me as the result of my own stupidity or through the deceptive ease with which others have gulled me, unwittingly or not, its schoolboy awe now feels sickly and witless. Who cares what I felt at the sight of the "Lusitania" navigating the Narrows and being pushed and tugged into place at Cunard's Pier 54 before we could finally disembark? Or that the noise of this great metropolis came to us over the water long before we docked, and saw its crowds, its skyline, the serried ranks of horse drawn cabs and even row upon row of motor cars all framing the ship's arrival as if it was "Lusitania"'s due? I can only say to myself here, that I have answered mechanically in these last hours to all that was put to me. I avoided the near presence of the slut and her owner who took one cab whilst Arnold and I followed in another after clearing the Customs Shed and organising transport of our luggage.

The Hotel is a wondrous thing. Without parallel for size or luxury. Built as two entities. In the Renaissance style as my father had taught me. We, Arnold and I, have separate rooms on the 16th Floor. Mr D. A. Thomas and his body-servant have adjacent rooms, or so I suppose, on the 4th Floor. Night has settled over the city and its sights will be for tomorrow, along with the work routine into which I intend to throw myself as hard as I am able. Yet my mind races and races, love-sick with no good to come of it, I can tell myself it is idiocy, that it will pass, but I cannot make it stop. I can veil its loathsome effect by stopping this Diary, this foolish indulgence, its introspection along with its descriptions the sores I must not pick away at anymore.

Personal Diary, March 1915. Taliesin Arthur Lloyd Papers. Box 1.
National Library of Wales. Aberystwyth.

They have left me alone to lie still and quiet in my bed for a few hours. Carers have their own timetables and must arrange matters so that their charges fit into an allotted schedule. This is caring. Not loving. I am not complaining. I think they think I sleep. I do not. I finger the lesions of memory when they itch. On the reef of my old age they have accreted like barnacle clusters. They are the outcomes of spent time. I cannot change them, I must accept them, but since I live on so do they, affecting me if I consider them as they once were, for then they give me no rest. In this way they become again beginnings not endings, what ifs not full stops. And in this irksome sense they itch away, though the actual end of me is so near, demanding my futile attention, reminding me of how I so easily accepted, but did I really have a choice, what was to be concluded before it might, possibly, begin. These are not meant to be riddles. I am too weary to toy with puzzles. These are the life sentences meted out, to me and to others, by the happenstance of fall out. Time for remission, time to stop the compulsion to scratch. Not a selfish plea, a hope that for whoever is to come after all this there can be a release, a riddance. The dead, so far as the really old are concerned, are more alive, more crowded, more numerous than the living who are only, from this point on, the background murmur to our otherwise mute existence. Dates, too, the further back you take them as the actual markers of a life that has been lived become just variously numbered dominoes whose serial falling collapses decades which clatter down one by one as they are tapped. Years, months, days, minutes flit past, insignificant units amongst the sites of memory we are forced to inhabit. Advantages to this to be sure. Despite the common wisdom. Advantages in growing old, and older still. The faculty of memory. So long as it holds you tight you live. Until it goes, it is the gift which remains. It means that once you have stumbled piecemeal through the passing of life, once you have lived it, that you have it all served up to savour, for yourself, all at once. No longer the fretful business of turning over the cards of anticipation, of having to live on to find out what comes next. You know what's next. And what's coming. You. And then not you. Which means that the dipping in and out of the memory pot is neither inconsequential nor random. It is all that there is, a smorgasbord of experience. And, oh yes, you think that there was that and maybe it could have been other, but was not so and cannot be altered. And another thing, as I have long known, is that you can do whatever you like with it, according to need or inclination pile one part upon some other unrelated part or shuffle them about without sensibility or discrimination. I mean, who cares. Not you, and so no-one else unless a virtual obituarist who makes everything out from birth to death to be a linear procession. The dreams only you possess confound that lie, even if only you know that is the case. At the end of life the deeper issue of what linear implies has to be pushed to one side to refuse, so long as you may dream on, its logic. What I like, anyway I am trying to tell myself so, is that having it all come back in any order is a kind of freedom, a sort of control. They have left me to sleep until they come in the morning, unless I cry out or push the large, red plastic button on the side-table or tug at the thick white cord which hangs at the side of the bed. Unlikely, as they know, and I know I will do neither of those things. I will have one last dream before then, I think. They have dimmed the side lights and switched off the one overhead. I am cinched in tightly under a tuck of sheets. I am propped up and between pillows. Gloria was the last to leave me tonight. They had taken it in turns, or so I heard them, to go to vote before the polling station closed. It was she who had persuaded him. I approve in silence, whichever way it went. I want, repentant, to reach out to tell them, the Secretary in me guilty, that they have the means not to be reduced to lesser than they could be. That people like me, too readily, passed a lifetime of expertise in measuring them and making them standardised as statistics. That their messy humanness was too often too much with which to deal if they were to be helped, tidied up to be delivered from themselves and from the forces, uncontrollable ones, which periodically, for I had seen this, came to overwhelm them.

I do not claim that it was this kind of intervention alone – shoring *things up, making social defences against economic floods – which served to define betterment for them. Not at all. In the most important ways, outside my own being and abilities, control of a different kind was, for a time at least, exerted and exercised after struggle, and sacrifice. Yes, strikes, and, yes, political take-over, and, yes, organisational power and protest against what was an otherwise given norm and, to the delight of the historians who have thrilled to the fever-pitch spike, riots and bloodshed to dispute the flat-line of mundane existence. Only, in the end of it, and for sure the end of what was, here and then, particular and specific, has come and gone, that it did, all of it together, amount to a defence of hard-won things and to their shoring-up against inevitable loss. Small victories were, most of the time and amidst the social carnage of greater defeats, the only next steps to take. That there was no overwhelming, unalterable change for the better. That what had been painstakingly gained could be taken away, piece by piece. It is what I would tell Tony and Gloria if I could. That just the fact of their survival, generation by generation, is both the most vital story to tell, and the most difficult since it runs so against the tides of public history. It does not happen, this survival, to everyone everywhere. And it only happens when there is a chance to hold on and take things forward by re-invention. Nor do I mean by any of this, the satisfactions of just being fed and kept warm and almost made secure against poverty and wars. Miseries are visited upon all people everywhere. So, what I am reaching for is some revelation of the meaning of love and how to tell of it so that it remains central in focus even when it diminishes, becomes momentarily peripheral when the glare of brute necessity blinds us with its harsh illumination of our pettiness. But I cannot tell that story whole because I have scarcely lived it myself. I cannot tell that story because I would be required to show it. I cannot show it unless I make it up so as to pretend that telling about it, how it was all framed, is the secondary not the primary means of grasping what happened, so as to understand it. And I do not believe that, nor in the consolation of re-ordering life* which it might afford for others. I, too, once longed for the undeniable beat of the heart. But I was constrained, as we all were from our place in time, by the silted layers of confusion deposited in the mind. We lived caught between dream and deed. Half-light. Maybe we had to settle for it. I am still not sure. Sometimes, when they come in the morning to switch on the electricity and every corner of the room is lit up, I wish, again, for the softer shimmer that came from an oil lamp, with shapes and presences conjured up rather than cut out for viewing. Films, movies as they say, do that. Edit. Falsify. Much more than a still-life photograph. No pretence to reality there, not in the way moving, flickering images create the illusion of substance. Whenever that last twenty minutes on the Lusitania returns to me, it is the sounds of screaming and praying and cursing and singing and the noise of metal grinding and crashing into wood, and the clothes and faces about to go into the sea, all these damn my peace, and never any kind of stitched-together tissue of connectivity, the narrative of story or film. We betray ourselves by letting the con trick have its credibility of form. Awful, but the case, that when I sat in a picture house three years after the Lusitania's sinking to watch the silent movie which climaxed with its end, I was, along with the others, staring up at giant mouths-agape and giant eyes bella-donnaed open-wide to convey horror, whilst the sound was a piano tinkling and swooping, in awe not denial. Was it, I wonder, because the starring role of a French opera singer trapped by the travails of war was taken by a doe-eyed beauty, the stage and screen actress Rita Jolivet, who had been so much admired as she strolled on the Boat Deck of our liner, and survived? Or was it, propaganda after the event, more truly convincing than the jumbled, inchoate sequence of happenings which I had, improbably, survived? The film was <u>Lest We Forget</u>. I prefer to think of it as <u>Lest We Remember</u>. It is not pain or terror which seeps into my sleep when I go back to the Lusitania, it is the hopelessness of being a pawn in someone else's game. The lingering horror of the murder, the one thing we all put to one side in our public outrage and *sentiment, was that the moment opened the way for the acceptance that the century would be marked out from then on for all the murders to come, of the nameless as well as the famous, of the wholly innocent and the possibly guilty, of children killed in numbers with our faces averted, of citizens slaughtered by their counterparts as readily as soldiers in arms. No Front Lines and Home Fronts. No separate boundaries. Barbarism made naked to the sight. Denounced. Excused. So, yes, I remember the names and the faces and the voices and the gestures but the larger truth to tell is that we were all, from that one explosive moment, to be reduced to the anonymity of victimhood and to the blank registering of lives which were merely, in the end, numbered as saved or lost.*

It was reading Margaret Rhondda's rather perfunctory obituary in *The Times* which led me first to consider writing my own account of lives which had for a time intersected. Her death in the summer of 1958 came just before my official retirement that autumn. I would have time to reflect perhaps. It was not entirely the case that the inadequacy of that death-notice, as a summary summation, spurred me to write something other than the documented accounts to which I was professionally accustomed. I could certainly have done her more justice as a woman of principle who never wavered, whether as a militant suffragette or a businesswoman and advocate for women's rights, and, once she had found her role and her confidence in the post-war world, as her father's titular successor in industry and politics. I might had had some amusement, too, in describing the journalistic world of the opinionated and the sometimes louche circle which she so readily financed. Or, better still, the opportunities which came her way, and which her father had already half-grasped in the decade before he died, to turn away from the diminishing returns of the coal empire he had constructed at home to find other, superior reserves to exploit in distant lands. He had discerned his new landscapes to exploit for untold profit. Others, after him, followed his path. To this end, I had noticed the intense and rapid growth in the excavation, after 1945, of the tar oil sands of north western Alberta, heavy crude oil from bitumen deposits, nearly all at surface level, the largest deposits for such oil and gas in the world. Fortunes to be made with new means of getting at the oil now available from the 1950s. Her father had invested over half a million pounds between 1913 and 1916 in the Peace River Development Corporation to do precisely this in that then relatively unexplored region. After his death his daughter actually travelled there, a long and hazardous trek by rail and riverboat and horse-drawn vehicles in those days, and wrote amusingly enough about her adventures in the Far West Wilderness in a kind of Jerome K Jerome style, but she did not invest any further. On her death the vast fortune she had inherited was as nothing compared to what it had once been. Do I feel schadenfreude welling up inside me at this outcome? Straightforwardly, yes. The tentacles had been extended – a lavishly appointed steamboat for business and trade, the SS D A Thomas, had been manufactured and plied the Peace river in its eponymous owner's lifetime, and a lesser, sister craft, the Lady Mackworth, had tugged along to lay their imprimaturs on the future of the region – but the octopi had retracted its feelers. All this, and more about her personal aggrandisement of wider causes into her personal psyche, might have given some acid to my pen if I had wished to pursue a Stracheyean line. My interest, however, and my motivation, too, was both more waywardly tangential and sharply personalised. I had visited her, at her request, shortly before she had died. Margaret Rhondda, as she liked to be known, had given me a letter, one addressed to me in the summer of 1918 after her father's death, and, though opened by her, not read by me until forty years had uselessly vanished.

We had not greatly cared for each other from the start, she far too prickly and off-hand, me a subaltern, and, besides, anything that took her father's attention away from herself was barely tolerable to her. She had arrived in New York two weeks after we had settled into the plush grandeur of the Waldorf Astoria – that is, as Baedeker will tell you, the original two buildings, put up in the 1890s I should add, not the new one erected in 1931 after the old opulent hotel, on 5th Avenue at 33rd and 34th Streets, had been demolished to make way for the Empire State Building – and mostly working out of Mr Thomas' suite of rooms. On her arrival Arnold Rhys-Evans and I were relegated to a specially arranged "office" space, equipped with telephones and teletype. Our direct communication with her father became, once again, rather brusque. As for Gwennie, she was re-assigned, half of the time anyway, from the (as yet) untitled Mr Thomas to his titled daughter, Lady Mackworth, noted suffragette and, in wartime, the ardent recruiter

of men for the armed forces on behalf of the patriotic war effort. I
should not cavil at this for we were all ardent in that year before
the Somme bled away so much of life and ardour. In bright and
gay and cosmopolitan New York the wife of the huntsman and
country gentleman, the complacently bovine Sir Humphrey
Mackworth, some years older than his wife, enjoyed gallivanting
on the great avenues and dining out after sampling light-hearted
theatre. Her obituary reminded me of how profoundly different in
taste and interests the Mackworths were. She divorced him a few
years after the war ended on the somewhat spurious grounds of his
adultery, certainly rigged-up for the purposes of the courts. I cannot
have been aware at the time of any issues of difficulty within her
marriage and I cannot recall any untoward hints coming from that
inveterate gossip Rhys-Evans. It was easy, thereafter, as I read of
her later domestic arrangements with her intellectual woman
friends to speculate. None of it was, then or now, my concern.

When we met again, in her London flat in 1958, she was
courteous with me, if a little distant in tone, the which I could assign
to her obvious illness. It was not long from this time of our meeting
that she would die from cancer. She was somewhat drawn in her
looks, but still open-faced and with alert eyes. A stoutish, quite
handsome woman, almost seventy five I had calculated. She had
given me coffee and sweet biscuits. We had chit-chatted, reminisced,
inevitably about the Lusitania. I had talked of my long and
subsequent career in university administration after my Oxford
degree in Greats, first as a junior assistant and then all the slow way
up to the heady heights of a Deputy Registrar, and of my secretarial
role on the various and numerous governmental commissions I had
served over the years. The perpetual Condition of the People tut-
tutting. And, as small talk, of my plans for a little travel on retirement,
not far I thought, in Europe only. And no, I had not married and so
there was no family. At which she looked a trifle grave. I mistook it

for some sort of sympathy. A moue made in regret. And then she told me of someone else who had met with her recently. At his original request, she added, as opposed to my visit, which had come about at her request, and for a reason she added.

On a chased silver tray set on a low coffee table were three hand-addressed envelopes. She gave them to me in turn to read the letters they contained. The envelopes were ink-smudged, two with old postage stamps from 1915, one with a more recent 1953 stamp. That was the one I was asked to read first. It felt an odd thing to do, this silent reading, in front of her, and her already aware of the contents of the envelopes. She looked steadily at me, and with no visible emotion, as I read the note to Lady Rhondda, with the two other letters apparently included, from a Dai Thomas to request a meeting to discuss their contents. All to be at her convenience. When I'd scanned it she said that she had not replied then, and had not met him until a few weeks ago. The enclosed letters which had come into his possession were in their original 1915 stamped envelopes. She gave them to me. She said I would remember the principals. I recognised the handwriting of the first, the small, crabbed but legible script of D. A. Thomas, the Lord Rhondda-to-be. I read it twice, and lingered on her name at its opening. I had, of course, known that she had become pregnant with his child, the boy with whom I had played a little when I saw her last, on my second visit to Llanwern in the high summer of 1918. My first visit there had been made almost three years before when I attended him to see if I would be suitable to serve, at his suggestion before I went up to university, as an assistant secretary when he travelled to America on business. How excited, and gratified, I had been. Did I see her then, glimpse her perhaps – I don't think so – and I cling to the thought that I would have known it. It was only on the Lusitania, that first moment of encounter. I had pleaded with her once, in 1915, and again after his death, to leave his employment utterly. It was Arnold Rhys-Evans who had written to me at my college to tell me she was with child, and, later, of the boy's birth after her confinement. That she was well taken care of by the thoughtful acts of DA, and sent to live in Llanwern whilst his own role in wartime government deepened and increased. I was not to worry. Her duties, such as they were, were light and mostly consisted of looking after the child on which, when he infrequently arrived from London, he doted. When DA died, I was given to understand that things, naturally enough, had necessarily changed. Good old Arnold. What was to be understood was to be accepted. I had not tried to write to her, nor seen her at Lord Rhondda's funeral in London. It was, on impulse after that and my graduation, that I decided to act. To seek her out.

When I turned up at Llanwern, unexpected by her and unannounced by me to anyone, certainly not to his daughter who was to be the new, by royal decree, Viscountess Rhondda, Gwennie had been put to work in the scullery. I found her cleaning and preparing vegetables in a Belfast sink, the cold water from two brass taps splashing up her bare arms and soaking the front of her blue cotton pinafore dress. I said her name and she turned to see me. Oh, Tal, was all she'd said. No smile. Just that. The conversation between us seemed to tear at her even more than me. The child was lively, but in good spirits in his high chair, and the other servants, some amused and sniggering, let us alone in a corner of the kitchen. I remember the sunlight from a high window dappling her face, how blotchy and red her small hands were and the way strands of her black hair, more lank than glossy that day, fell loose and unattended from beneath her mob cap. I told her that with my degree finished, I would seek work as a schoolmaster, and adopt the child as my own. She had touched my cheek at that. Then, with decisiveness in her voice, she'd said that she had hopes that the boy, David of course, would be accepted into the family, as he had been before DA's death. That it would, wouldn't it, be best for him and otherwise in any case that she would not burden me. She said my declared love for her was a blessing to her but that I was to forget her, that my obsession would end, that a career and surely a family awaited me. And to go. And to forget her. Gwennie. His, not mine.

The second letter I read, from her to him, was a bruise I had thought I could no longer feel. It had happened that way. Choices had been made. She had accepted it, as Arnold would have advised. She had chosen and she had, clearly, not been rejected, so long as he lived.

I replaced all three letters in their envelopes and put them back onto her silver tray. I was scarcely surprised by any of this or perhaps only by its occasion, the reason she had for re-visiting such a disappeared time. Margaret had been sipping coffee as I read. She put her cup down on its saucer. She said she owed me an explanation now but that, first, there was one last letter for me to read. It had been in her lap. As she handed it to me I saw that it, too, had been opened. There was no stamp or franking on it. Just my name, rather scrawled, T A Lloyd, Esqre.

When I finished this letter I did not hand it back. It lay between my fingers, the notepaper slightly quivering as my hand trembled. What it meant was as clear as the moment was ugly with my grief, my anger, my love. Margaret, Lady Rhondda, was business-like. She said she would begin with an apology, but that there had been particular circumstances, and that, after she had opened and read the letter in the summer of its writing, she had considered how to act for the best. However, she said, that by way of a preface she had indeed met with the man who considered himself to be her half-brother and that she had both listened to him, an intelligent enough fellow, and acknowledged the contents, if not the veracity, of the letters he had sent to her five years previously. Her reasons for not replying to him at the time were bound up with the desire not to re-open issues which she considered better left as they had been left. Subsequently, with her own life ebbing away, and she shrugged and waved a hand to fend off the sympathy I had had no intention of giving her, it was time, she decided, to settle things more formally, and dismissively. To that end she had affirmed to her visitor that she did not believe her father had sired, her word, a child on the maidservant, Gwennie. Though she did grant, by an implicit route, that he might well have succumbed to the servant's wiles for closer attention, and needless to say, for reward. She had kept the letters, without his asking for their return or demurring in any way. He had seemed, she said, to be indifferent, once they had met, to the outcome of it all.

Lady Rhondda paused. I was also to know that Gwennie's son had come by the letters only after his mother had died in 1952. She assumed, she said, I might have so surmised, but did I actually know that was the case, and also that the son had not seen the mother since 1918. She tilted her head as if in query. I had no answers to give. I suppose I did somehow know, if only by dint of the working out of things, but it did not lessen the terror of what I was learning, being made to see, put up against what was an unwanted reversion to the truth, the unwanted story to be told about us, all of us, about me. About Gwennie. About the child. The letter addressed to me had already scared me with that knowing. Now, its first reader would, and did, make it worse.

Lady Rhondda, and how aching with contempt for the personal assumption of that place name I am now as I write her title down, gave out a little cough. Not quite a theatrical one, though not far off from one either. Gwennie had been forthright with her after Lord Rhondda's death. She expected nothing for herself, other than perhaps to be kept on at Llanwern, but she had hoped for succour, as was his due, for the child. Margaret, Lady Rhondda, as she had become all of a sudden, had dismissed the claim and shortly after that Gwennie had disappeared, for good, leaving the child behind and only two notes, one to her employer asking for the child to be cared for and, if not, for her married sister to be sent for to take him away. The other note was the letter Gwennie had asked to be forwarded to me, but only in the event of the boy having to go to live with his aunt. The cough came again. Now that I had read it, I would surely see that truth was nowhere to be had and that the girl who wrote such letters, and behaved in such a shameless manner, was capable of any trickery. Once read, deliberately so by her at the time, she said, in case further calumnies were being spread about her father, she concluded that her judgement was right. The boy would go where he best belonged. Amongst his only undeniable family, and that, out of charity, she would send an unsolicited allowance to assist with his care. As for myself, there had been no purpose in tormenting me with Gwennie's projected fantasies. I was young, of good family, sadly bereaved of my own father, and with a way to make in the world no matter whatever indiscretions I had been tempted into by the hussy she, herself, had mis-trusted, and with good reason I might agree, from the off. There, she had said, that is all. You may keep the letter, of course, and here is the address of the woman's son, as given to me by him, if you should wish to pursue anything further for yourself. After I am gone. Soon now, she said, and with a finality I took as my cue and excuse to leave.

I had not trusted myself to say anything to her about her deceit. Or her self-regarding arrogance. Of the harm she had caused. Of her assumption of authority. Of the hopeless legacy she had finally gifted me. I simply left, as I had been left, and a whole other life not to be lived shrivelled me up inside.

Fragment/Memoir, unpublished (dated1959,with ms.letter to TAL attached). Taliesin Arthur Lloyd Papers. Box 1. National Library of Wales. Aberystwyth.

Dearest Tal

I was so glad to see you again the other week when you called at Llanwern. What a fright I must have seemed, with no warning from you to make myself respectable, you rotter! I must say you looked quite the gent yourself and a bit filled out, nicely I mean. Anyway, we managed a talk didn't we and you could see, I hope, that I was right, and still am. I am sure though matters have gone a bit worse and I am writing this to explain with no thought to go back on what I said but only to let you know what might be for you now to decide. But only as you may wish. What is clear, dear Tal, is now that a little, very little, time has gone since he died that I will not be welcome to stay here, certainly not in the old way, with the child. She has made this plain to me even though I told her that the boy was his but she mocks me for that and worse things said too, so I have decided I will leave without further ado but suddenly so and that David will be found with a note to her asking for him to be cared for as his father's son. If not then she will have my sister's address to send to so that she can fetch him, and if that happens, as I pray it will not, then, and only then for this letter to be forwarded to you.

For me, I will find employment somewhere and send my sister what I can. She is a married woman, older than me, with three boys of her own. David will fit in there if he is not to stay, as I am praying he will, at Llanwern. Anyway, Tal, how fondly I think of you and you are not to worry about your Gwennie, only I will say, for I feel it to be true, although I cannot swear on it one way or the other that the baby, who came a bit before his time, not by much and was well, and how to say it, Tal, other than that he may be yours, yours and mine I mean of course not his. I do not forgive him, not really, though you know how I felt I had no choice and it would be for the best not to burden you so I have never said it until now and you are not to dwell on it if it spoils everything else. Only, if you read this you are to know that things might yet turn out different if you could bear to wish it. That is for you. If I hear nothing from you I will understand and respect what you have decided. Here I swear that, and with all my heart, I will remember you and cherish our short moments together through all the life, and all its twists and turns, which is to come, and I hope for happiness for you.

Your (very own) Gwennie

Whenever I re-read her only letter to me, and there were many unbidden times when I had to do that, it was always its hinterlands, of what had been and of what could not ever be, which shadowed my thoughts of her. Of Gwennie. Our brief time had been only a parenthesis between the sailings on the Lusitania, outward and then homeward bound in May 1915. The return voyage was tinged with uncertainties and anxieties even before our party went aboard. The Thomases, father and daughter, had been bullish. Warnings in the Press from the German Embassy that enemy shipping suspected of carrying munitions was fair game for their U-boats were pooh-poohed. The Lusitania was specifically named. To this day there is no direct evidence, other than for transportation of gun cotton, that she was carrying munitions for the Allies. Some said the double explosion heard after the torpedo hit her might be explained by arms exploding, others that it sounded like a spontaneous combustible explosion from the coal bunkers being flooded. The mystery, if such it is, was sustained by both wartime belligerents from their opposite viewpoints at the time, and remains such. We were certainly a ship of children as well as celebrities. The latter seeking a rapid and luxurious crossing, with no real fear for their safety on such a fast ship until jitters set in on the last night as we approached the Irish coast and U-boat waters; the former accompanying their parents, many from our Canadian dominion on their way to serve in the Great War. Ninety four little ones drowned, and thirty five babies. Other passengers, ill-fated indeed, had been transferred at the last moment in New York when a British ship in the harbour was commandeered for war service and its passengers transferred to the Lusitania. That meant we were delayed for a few hours and finally departed in thick fog as the Gleemen of Gwent gave out lustily with "Star Spangled Banner" and "It's a Long Way to Tipperary". The fog had lifted as we reached open sea but my spirits had not.

My role had been marginalised. Professionally, I was a discard. The ship itself had had a make-over. Its distinctive livery and even the name of Lusitania had disappeared. No messages were to be sent from the Marconi House in case their interception betrayed our position at sea. At a personal level, I was distraught. Not difficult, I would guess, for that to be understood by him. Perhaps he had detected a look, an attitude, a disinclination to be amiable on my part. Any business he did now was conducted privately, alone with Arnold and his daughter. I dined with them in the salon. If he remained in his stateroom the stewards, and Gwennie no doubt, attended him there. I scarcely saw him, and I met with Gwennie not at all now. Arnold said nothing, though he gave me hard looks from time to time. On the second day out I was told of my new duties. In the afternoons I was to turn Arnold's short-hand notes of his one-to-one conversations with Mr D. A. Thomas into copy for Arnold's later writing-up (and some years on he gave me a version for my interest, and kept in my Papers). For the rest I was to be another kind of eyes-and-ears and I realised more and more how we were all, those under his sway, adjunct collaborators in the great project with which he thought himself engaged. Nothing of this world, in interest and influence, was to escape him, or his acolytes acting on his behalf.

And so, as ordered, I scanned the *Cunard Daily Bulletins* which were issued on board – snippets of news, details of activities, of the menus set and served, and all replete with pen portraits of the celebrated and the famous who were sailing across the wartime ocean, trailing with them the fascination they held for all of us. Some were adept at celebrating themselves. I was instructed to seek out the greatest of these self-promoters and see if he could be persuaded to submit for an interview to be published later. It proved to be no difficulty. Elbert Hubbard was also travelling First Class. He was hard to miss as he sauntered, on a sun-lit afternoon, on the Promenade Deck.

Hubbard was one of those rare ones who insist on staying in the memory, year after year, in all his physical presence. The men I had encountered to that point in my short life did, if anything, dress down so as to be a part of the background. Their tastes were muted and sober as to clothes, the hues grey to brown to black and cut to a severe perfection of form. Elbert Hubbard broke all those rules. He seemed to be a cross between a cowboy come to town and an artist forsaking his attic garret for the adulation of a popular success. His coats were long and loose, reaching below the knees of his baggy corduroy trousers. His hats were invariably broad-brimmed Stetsons. His shirts were made of fine cottons, often coloured as blues or pinks, and the soft collars were cinched together by large, floppy bows of silk. Heeled boots enhanced his moderate height. His lank hair was cut like a page boy's and hung long in curtains below his ears. And in 1915 he was consulted by high and low for his views on everything and everyone.

This task of mine was all a part of D. A. Thomas' greater scheme to unite opinion forming journalism with profiles of the distinguished and the news-worthy. Arnold said he saw it as a way of by-passing the fumbling of politicians. Instead, decide on the line and go straight to those who, in all spheres, including politics, aspired to influence. Or let them, as he wished it, be influenced. I was to be a gatherer of tit-bits. With Elbert Hubbard I fell lucky. To my surprise he had cocked his head when he heard my voice exchanging pleasantries with a fellow passenger and said that by my accent I was not only a Britisher, I was a Welshman, too, like many he had met in the western coalfields of Pennsylvania. I readily assented and was then taken aback when he followed this up with a query. Did I know, I must do, of my incomparable fellow countryman, Freddie Welsh? I was quick, and delighted, to explain that not only had I seen Welsh box against Driscoll when I was but a boy, but that, in happy addition, Mr Welsh was a fellow-townsman and sometime acquaintance of my late father. All this in a gush from me before he had grabbed both my hands in his and practically shook me off my feet. I don't think he noticed my crippled state at all.

As I write this it is hard to conceive how instantly, resplendently, famous was Wales and its achievements then. To have a lightweight champion of the world was as natural as to have, soon, a Welsh Prime Minister of the British Empire. Hubbard's interest was, as it transpired, closer still. He whirled me around by the elbow into the path of his wife and introduced us by shouting aloud "Alice! Here's a young fellow who knows Fred Welsh." Into the Verandah café, decorative with palm trees and trellis screens and wicker-work chairs, and to sit down for coffee and for Hubbard's genial amusement at the coincidences in life which he treated as fate. One such, I discovered later, was his essay musing on the sinking of the Titanic in 1912 and, with friends lost amongst the drowned, he had wondered how he would have accepted that as his own destiny. Coincidence certainly spun for him into fate a few days later. The happier intertwining of the champion, himself and now me, was the spark for him and the conversation which took me, too briefly, out of my doldrums of spirit. Why!, he had exclaimed and slapped the table so hard that the coffee jumped out of the cups, did I know that Freddie Welsh had been slated to be on board the Lusitania for this very voyage and, what's more!, to be travelling in the company of the Hubbards? I did not. And did I know that Freddie was a frequent guest, and active participant, at the extensive farm and settlement they had created in East Aurora? Had I heard of it? I had not. Well, he said, changing groups of people from all walks of life came to lodge with them for varying time durations, and there they communed with each other, body and soul I was to understand, and listened to Elbert Hubbard express his views on an alternative way of being together as humans and his considered opinions on how to realise a new, alternative and better world. The secret was to find inner strength through meditation, physical perfection through yoga, intellectual mastery of the best in all religions and none, the discarding of the conventional and spurning of orthodoxy. So, pantheism, engagement with arts and crafts as William Morris had taught us about style, form and function, a strict vegetarian regime as carried out by Tolstoy, and, of course, the Motherhood of God in a feminising world. Freddie, he said, had become an ardent disciple-practitioner, and he, Hubbard, was an admirer of the perfection of body and mind which Freddie Welsh exemplified. An object lesson. A pathfinder. A symbol of what the ordinary man-in-the-street might achieve. In strict truth, he said, a saviour of the world has come amongst us. He, Hubbard, was intending to visit Wales to see for himself where Freddie Welsh had originated. He would talk to all and sundry. He was going to write a biography of that remarkable young man, athlete and autodidact, did I know he carried an extensive library with him wherever he went this aesthete and philosopher of the trained mind and disciplined body. He looked down at my clubfoot, sticking out at an angle for comfort, tapped my arm a few times and said that I, too, especially the afflicted like me, could benefit.

I took no umbrage from that, nor was I anything but captivated by this Great Showman. If he was a fraud, as many alleged then and subsequently, he was a captivating one. Perhaps because, chameleon-like, he managed to represent, from moment to moment, whatever it was he felt you might like to hear or to be. Ideas fizzed. Cordiality was exuded. And, in my turn, I was quizzed, and soon rumbled I am sure as to being not a complete innocent in our contrived encounter. Oh, he knew and understood the value and the power of publicity, and had no qualms about being used by it, but only in order to draw even more from it for himself. He had, more or less, invented his own past, though his obituaries would take him at his own face value. This imagined past of his, it seemed, licenced him to invent his own desired future. Stepping-stones were all he needed.

He knew of DA, of course, and would be delighted to meet with him. It was indeed arranged, directly through Arnold, or perhaps by Margaret whose views on the "Woman Question" Hubbard warmly endorsed. On this one occasion when I met him alone, he was, after the initial induction of me into his world – I was to visit with him, he insisted, at East Aurora in upper New York State on a future return voyage – madly obsessed, or so it seemed to me, with his madcap scheme to visit Berlin to confront the Kaiser, personally, about the horror of the war which the German Emperor had, personally, allowed to be unleashed. He was sure his own cachet in the world would smooth the path to a tête à tête. He spoke in paragraphs, lucid and structured as if he had written all the words out already, and he oscillated, for my callow benefit I think, between the twin poles of the fate which awaited all of us, our destiny he said, and the freedoms, in everything he said, which we must assert for our well-being, even within the bounds that were set. He was exhilarating in his enthusiasm for being open to experience and for his willingness to confront whatever might occur. He talked with no mealy-mouthed bravado, such as I was hearing elsewhere, about the danger we might be in on this crossing. Yet, he said, he was confident the Germans, when and if it came to it, would not send a passenger liner to the bottom, and yet why if they did, he said, embracing his wife at this point, and scattering our coffee cups across the table so that a steward rushed over to clean up, well, then, he said, it could even be a good thing for him since he would drown with the great ship and so succeed in his last remaining ambition, which was, as a regular hero who had gone straight to the bottom, to enter the Hall of Fame.

Which indeed, within a few days, he did, taking Alice Hubbard with him, both last seen calmly re-entering their stateroom as the Lusitania went down to her assigned fate. Poor Hubbard. His protean and polymathic embrace of life and its myriad possibilities would not have survived the rigid straitening of all our dreams. Yet he left a small fortune, the profits from his best-selling magazines and publications, enough to allow his colony of makers and doers to survive and outlast us all, the Lusitania's survivors as well as those lost with him.

I cannot think, if my early career as an interviewer had progressed further than that solitary week, that anyone else would have ever left me with such a sense of what was both mad and yet glorious in such human aspiration to hold all at the same time, everything together in hand and mind. As it was, my cack-handed attempt to similarly interview, Charles Frohman, the Broadway impresario and theatre owner, failed to elicit any response. Mr. D.A. Thomas was a great admirer, notably for his being the man who had brought *Peter Pan and his Lost Boys* from London to the Broadway stage in 1904. DA had seen and loved the play on both sides on both sides of the Atlantic. Frohman, however, remained a recluse in his deluxe Regal Suite except for the night, the last night at sea, when he threw a glittering party attended by the Thomases, and Rhys-Evans. Also present, paraded by their host as trophies, were the world's richest man Alfred Vanderbilt, and the Broadway actress, the alluring Rita Jolivet. With all of these I managed no interviews. Both men perished. She survived.

My employer, not yet made Lord Rhondda, survived too, of course, and a further transatlantic voyage he made in late June 1915, succeeded in finalising the lines of credit to see to the buying of armaments, already agreed, in principle in May with the Wall Street banking mogul, J. P. Morgan. I suppose with that, and with eventual American entry into the war after the loss of three hundred American lives upon the sinking of the Lusitania firmly put onto the balance sheet of justly motivated causes, and by his own unremitting efforts as war-time Food Controller, that his whole life might be deemed to be a success story, one for his daughter to laud and tell. His hubris did not, ever, for him bring on any nemesis. I would say nonetheless, that he failed. He did not know that at the time, or in what of life remained to him, or that all that vaunted future of ours would fall apart so quickly, as it did.

Memoir/Fragment (c.1964), Box 1. Taliesin Arthur Lloyd Papers. National Library of Wales. Aberystwyth.

At the early age of forty one, Fred Welsh, former lightweight champion boxer of the world has died on 28 July in New York City, USA, where he has been resident for a number of years. The New York Times has reported that his body was found, fully clothed, in a lower Manhattan hotel room which he had been renting by the week, and that his sole companion at the end was a book about the boxer's former friend and mentor, entitled *Elbert Hubbard of East Aurora*. It lay open at his bedside on a page with only one sentence from the sage on it: "Get your happiness out of your work, or you will never know what happiness is." It is believed that the deceased had been experiencing financial and other personal difficulties for the last few years after the collapse of his Health Farm in New Jersey.

He was born, Frederick Hall Thomas, in17 Morgan Street, Pontypridd in 1886, the son of the Hotelier Mrs.Elizabeth Thomas, nee Hall, and Mr.John Thomas, the well-known Auctioneer and Publican of this town. Freddie Welsh was world champion from 1914 to 1917,when America's Benny Leonard beat him on points over ten rounds. Latterly, he became an American citizen. The exact cause of death has not yet been ascertained. His brother, Captain Stanley Thomas, has refuted the claim that Freddie Welsh died penniless and insisted that there is property in California to support the independence of the wife and two daughters whom this great son of Pontypridd has left behind him when he failed to answer the final bell in his illustrious career.

Cutting. *Pontypridd Observer*, 31 July,1927. Miscellanea. Box 16.
Taliesin Arthur Lloyd Papers. National Library of Wales. Aberystwyth.

A Transcription of Some Notes of the Reflections and Conversations of Mr D. A. Thomas (later Viscount Rhondda), 1 to 6 May 1915, aboard the last voyage of RMS *Lusitania*, as compiled by his Secretary, Arnold Rhys-Evans

I had the great privilege of accompanying Mr D. A. Thomas, in his capacity as Chairman of the Cambrian Combine, on his trip to the United States of America from March to May 1915, a stay undertaken for reasons directly to do with his then business interests, past and future. Tragically, the voyage home ended with the vile and evil torpedoing of the *Lusitania* by a U-boat of the Imperial German Navy, causing the appalling loss of so many innocent lives, of men, women and children. A secondary result of this episode, as Mr Thomas' business abilities and connections were pressed into service by the government which Mr David Lloyd George from December 1916 led as its Prime Minister, was to be the laying aside for the duration of the war, of Mr Thomas' extensive plans for the exploitation of fossil fuels. Sadly, he did not see their fruition, dying as he did in the summer of 1918. I have thought that the jottings I made over those few days at his request as a kind of Table Talk of Confidences, might one day interest those who did not know him personally, and serve to remind the world, and indeed his native country, of his greatness and his foresight. I have written up these Notes, and added to them from my memory, by separating out some conversational asides and his interspersed reflections, so that they may be read as discrete, or thematic, entries. He was habitually to his intimates, and familiarly everywhere in the public domain which he so dominated and graced, known as "DA", and it is as such that I have presented him in these few pages.

DA on the Power of Coal

You know my love for the statistical. Nothing clearer or more graphic than figures. Think of Wales over the last one hundred years, from a population no more than six hundred thousand at the beginning of the nineteenth century to, as told by the recent census of 1911, a country of well over two million people, and the great bulk of the increase confined within the south eastern part, to populous Monmouthshire and, especially, to Glamorgan. Now, we may attribute this almost solely to the discovery and exploitation of coal, that mineral wealth which has spawned or sustained our ancillary industries, of iron and steel, and made metropolises of our coastal cities, our docks and our urban areas. From obscurity to prominence, a tiny speck of land is now an important factor in the whole of the civilised world. But there is more to say of the effects of the transformative power of coal, for the coal we dig out of our hills and send in our ships to every corner of the world has not only made a poor country rich and raised the living standards of all. No, it has also done for Wales what our poets, our preachers, our schoolmasters, our historians, our musicians, our politicians and our writers could never have done. It has, you see, and with all the conflict between Capital and Labour which we are currently enduring, produced a new order of things in every rank of Welsh society. It is why I say that coal, in itself, has long struck me as something which should, in all its transfigurative capacities, inspire a poetic soul not just a mathematical mind such as mine.

Seriously, consider this and then wonder, for coal is the source of all the significant and necessary physical power which enables civilisation. Coal is the means whereby modern existence moves at such a pace. Why, it is coal alone which enables mankind to dominate the conditions of his existence. I tell you directly, man without such power would have remained a slave to nature, a mere animal in his being. For my part I see Man's stubborn oppugnance to nature as his promethean spirit, exerted to prevent the stagnation of humanity. My socialist friends would not gainsay this lifting of all out of the mire of a laborious poverty. I would remind them that the outcome requires the organiser of industry which they too readily dismiss as the capitalist intent only on profit. Money has never interested me for its own sake but without its growth, nothing may be achieved. So the question remains "How?" not "Why."

DA on the Evolution of his Political Outlook

I would have to say that I lingered too long, perhaps, in the backwaters of political dabbling. I had certainly, and not to be coy about it, expected some manner of preferment after our electoral landslide in 1906. Not to be. Face did not fit, it seems, or perhaps my deemed lack of clubbability. Campbell-Bannerman, whom I had considered a friend, told me that as PM he only wanted first rate parliamentary debaters on his front Bench. Poppycock! Men with their brains on their tongues. Flatterers and Deceivers. Well, I entered parliament in 1888 as a solitary, and a solitary I remained. Not even asked to chair a committee. Ever! Lloyd George always had his knife into me after I smashed up his Cymru Fydd manoeuvres at Newport in 1896, though, hobbledehoy as that chancer was, he soon gave up on all that nonsense. And it became clear to me that if I could not serve as I wished then I would do better to chuck the House completely. As the world and his wife now knows, my increasingly full time dedication to business and my full hearted dedication to the growing concerns of the Cambrian Combine from 1906 led me to dispense with the whole pack of them after 1910. My true friends have often chided me for this, even accusing me of abandoning the national sentiments of my youth and the later imperial dimensions of the Liberal cause. Yet, granting myself the benefit of hindsight, not so I would argue. My politics was always an expression of intellect – mine own largely – and a calculator of need – that of my fellow humans. Early on my admiration for Mr Gladstone caused me to support his concept of Home Rule all round, but I did not, and do not, envision this as any kind of nationalist separation, either as an agenda or an arrangement beyond the administrative. Yet, that I am as Welsh as any cannot be gainsaid. Why, often have I addressed my supporters in Aberdare and in Merthyr in Welsh, the language I spoke habitually as a boy, and at home when my father was absent. Mother was easier with that, and with me, and I was known to my playfellows on the mountainside as Dai. The first ten years I believe should see no force-fed education. For my part I was sent away at just past ten years of age. Inevitably it changed the essence of me. Mind you, I never embraced any narrow Little Englander views of the world either, albeit one wrapped in the fancy dress of Britain and its Empire. My sense of the political is that of rights and of responsibility, not of privilege and overlordship. Autonomy of the individual and prosperity for the commonwealth. Again, the trick is the means to the outcome for such a desired combination. I take my wealth to be a responsibility. I see my Wales as a stepping stone into a better future.

DA on an America Future

You well know, since you have accompanied me on my trips across the pond since the year before this asinine war occurred, that I see America as both a haven and an opportunity. So much so that I have been inclined to raise the hackles of some by claiming that I wish I had been born an American. Perhaps I was, eh? I mean it to mean as one born to make use of opportunity at an opportune time. Or, put another way, mayhap I will be one yet when this war is ended. Wars generally bring opportunities to those who know how to grasp them. My own father was not slow to invest in American railway stock when the Civil War was concluded with the victory of the North. He talked to me about it at the time. How that country would now truly open itself up with the shackles of its agrarian South at last knocked away. I was an attentive nine-year old in 1865. He saw, you see, what was to come. And we all saw it happening, even if not with his acumen, as rails rapidly girdled that continent from east to west, and as all those fierce nomads who roamed the Great Plains to no purpose other than ill effect were, one redskin tribe after another, consigned to oblivion. Brought into a civilised state of being, by force and by treaty, the happy destiny of their wretched fate. Opportune wars have been America's means of advance from the beginning. We cannot divert such an unstoppable course, we can only follow its direction and seek to profit from it. You know how I have been examining the business possibilities inherent in the American coalfields in Pennsylvania and West Virginia this time over, in addition to the exploratory talks with the House of Morgan with which I was confidentially charged. I see no real barrier to the creation of an Anglo-American combine to extract coal at the low American cost and, with our own steamers built and owned, to ship it out for sale across the Mediterranean ports whose facilities we already control for docking and bunkering. Capital of five to six million will be required, the half to be raised by me in London and the rest from our wealthy and interested American Friend, who fortunately understands nothing of coal but who knows the value of a deal. We will need, for the nonce, to keep his name quiet. The advantages of such a consortium of his finance and our expertise are self-evident. As will be the claim I have secured on the as yet undeveloped tar sands, immense and oil rich, in the Peace River region of the north west of Canada. Vast deposits of bitumen for heavy, crude oil are practically on the surface, a storehouse of resources to exploit, for what is known is clear but what is, as yet, unseen can only be conjectured. We can make that remote wilderness a new power house for the energy the world, and Canada, will soon require. I have agents at all levels and in several ways looking into this closely, and furthering my interests. It may well be where my own energies will be expended for the next decade. There I will travel as soon as other duties and the turn of events will allow. I already have a steam ship fitted out for river travel and named after me, the SS *D A Thomas*, and a smaller vessel for Margaret. The coal of our great basin in South Wales will be harder and harder to get, and by no means inexhaustible, so imagination allied to intellect and divorced from sentiment dictates we look afar and elsewhere.

DA on the Press

Influence is all in a world shaped as much by opinions as by material things. So far I have dabbled only. Letters written for the Press, articles commissioned, editorials arranged. And, of course, the various provincial newspapers and journals I have acquired. I had the devil's own job to make the dinosaurs in the South Wales Coalowners' Association see the need for a publicity branch to be set up to direct opinion on industrial questions, especially disputatious ones. But they yielded. Parochial to the last, my fellow members however, rebut any open consideration of their obtuse standing on wider issues, or their attitudes towards trades unionism or reasonable wage settlements, say. They are oblivious to reactions, generally adverse ones, by the City or from those in Government.

More fools they, not to possess either insight or foresight. Now, in strict fact, a newspaper in London is a source of political power and I intend to have me one, and to spend money on it, even to establish such an organ from scratch, if needs must. Say an evening newspaper, one whose deep remit would be to allow for the publication of articles by chosen experts on special features, on industrial and economic subjects. It would require subsidising, of course, but I am millionaire enough by now to be able to afford such a hobby. The opinions to be influenced by such a venture would be not so much those of the man in the street as those of Parliament and Clubland. I will, in the end, lead those particular ninnies, one way or the other. Or someone else will, and to worse effect I would venture to say. And therein lies the future.

DA on Business Competition

Ideally, why should there be anything so cut-throat and competitive when co-operation and good sense might better prevail to maintain and equitably share profitability? You know that this was, in essence, the proposal I made in my paper of 1896 to the Associated Collieries, of which Cambrian was not yet one. That we would, on an apportioned basis, restrict output, not undercut each other, and keep profits and wages in a more or less steady state. The alternative was the curse of the Sliding Scale, tying wages to the pendulum swing in the price of coal. A set of affairs dependent on the demand for coal, or lack of it, on the open market, and so setting off inevitable conflict between workman and employer. QED in the lamentable, prolonged stoppage of 1898. And the consequential coming-in of a coalfield wide trades union, the Fed, which could be a force for moderation under a responsible leadership but which has, and still does, threaten to career out of control if the extreme faction, the so-called advance men now prevalent in its ranks, continue to hold sway. Thereby, mark my words, will lie the seeds of perpetual disaster in the post-war coal industry.

Of course what I had suggested was along the lines of the thoughts and actions then being undertaken in America where rampant competition in the commodity sector, oil and sugar and so on, and in construction and transport, railroads and steel and building works, had led to bankruptcies and crises and denunciation of all the excesses of free market capitalism. Setting a resolute face against all this ruinous competition were those who saw control and amalgamation, centralised and integrated, as the way forward by restricting and organising production so that prices could be kept high, and economic progress be assured. This was the lesson I derived from Standard Oil. This was the power a financier of genius such as J. P. Morgan could exert. Governments and politics were as froth to this.

I grant that there was subsequent railing by those outside the circle against so-called cartels and Trusts. But the principle of overall managerial control of the detail as well as the generality of an industry is key to success. It is why I have spun out from the Cambrian Combine, sales and marketing agencies, shipping interests, firms to buy and import timber for pit props, port facilities, coal by-product plants, insurance secured in-house, the exclusion of the middle man in everything. It is the future. It is the spirit of the age. And if you doubt me, or hold fast to a forlorn romantic nostalgia for the by-gone era of free-for-all trade, let me take you by the hand and escort you along Broadway whose dazzling electric Great White Way we have so recently walked. On this very ship we have an exemplum of my theory in action in the persona of Mr Charles Frohman. It was he, and a few like-minded theatrical impresarios and producers who met together over dinner in 1896 to put an end to the ruinous system of overbooking, undercutting, duplication and unreliability of dates and venues, which confused and lost both audiences and revenues. I wish I had been afforded the same attention in the coalfield in 1896 which these gentlemen secured in New York by establishing a Theatrical Syndicate. Suddenly, by co-operation and agreement, the leading lights of the theatrical world banded together to control actors, scripts, try-outs, publicity and all available, non-clashing dates. The subsequent product was offered as a complete package to all those who did not actually own the theatres, possession of which was largely in the Syndicate's hands, and if other independent theatrical venues tried to buck the system they were squeezed dry of product. Within a decade the result was order where there had been chaos and legitimate profit replaced ruinous rivalry.

Imitation, as is so often remarked, somewhat sententiously I grant you, is indeed the sincerest form of praise. And so it has proved as these theatrical moguls now jostle with like-minded groupings of rivals up and down the avenues of New York City. Frohman and his original associates had made their way the only way. Standardised production and a near monopoly of the particular product they brought to market. He told me over dinner aboard ship the other night that he fears the downgrading of the offerings made currently by our theatres – he owns five outright on Broadway and another in London – with the current rage for shop-girl plays and crook dramas and slangy Yankee farces, instead of the light comedy, romances and fantasies he conjures up so well. Every year he travels to London, as I do I suppose to New York, to seek out the new. I myself saw his *Peter Pan* production when it opened in London eleven or so years ago, and then again on Broadway where it had enjoyed similar acclaim. You see, piling detail upon detail, and control of them through imagination, is what gives the world the fare it requires, and not the dross it may haphazardly bring upon itself. Imagine a world without a Peter Pan. Unimaginable, or is it just unthinkable?

DA on his Philosophy of Life (and that of Mr Elbert Hubbard)

I was particularly intrigued to find that Elbert Hubbard is aboard and delighted to have met with him for, somewhat rum as he is, the cove fascinates me. He was born in 1856, as I was! Coincidence or Fate? Ask Peter Pan! He has something about him, undoubtedly so. Certainly in the somewhat extravagant way he carries himself, and, of course the manner of his dress. Why, I do not believe, whether in the dining room or on the promenade deck, or wherever else on board the ship for that matter, he has attracted any less attention than Miss Rita Jolivet and, my word, that young lady of the stage and silver screen, and one of Frohman's protégés, perhaps herself a future Peter Pan he says, is a real dazzler. But as for friend Hubbard, I found him as mysterious as he was fascinating, and I was as confused at the close of our hour-long conversation as I was at its commencement. And that after I let him do most of the talking, unusual for me you'll agree! Yet he has a way of reflecting on what is unsaid and saying what needs to be said if we are to remain socially connected but individually driven. Do you know his little book, *A Message to Garcia?* It is no more than two pages in length and, he tells me, he tossed it off in less than an hour as a filler for his magazine *The Philistine.* That was in 1899, in the wake of the warranted American invasion of Cuba. Yet it is not, per se, about the war between the United States and Spain. Nor any reflection on it, other than that an American officer was actually dispatched, with no real guidelines or directions, to take a letter from President McKinley to Garcia, a leader of the Cuban insurgents who was somewhere to be found in the mountain fortresses of the island. That is the excuse for Hubbard's meditation on get-up-and-go, on the spirit of dedicated service, on resolute action and on the willingness to perform a set task without demur. I had read it some time ago and found it relatively unremarkable for its style or its profundity. Yet, here is the thing, it has sold over the past decade, as a single-issue leaflet, over forty million copies and been translated – though not into Welsh I'd venture! – into all European languages, and Russian and Japanese, the which rival Empires actually distributed it to everyman in their rival armies and navies. Now that is what intrigues. He puts his finger on something, a factor which makes the world tick.

Naturally, I asked him for his views. He is not loath to give them, I'll tell you, and rather smug about it. But perhaps he should be when he has made a small fortune from such scribblings and can hold the attention of the practical world in his hand. He says of himself that he would be a socialist if such a desirable future world of mutual self-help and co-operation were possible. So would I be, I replied, but agreed with him that it is self-interest which makes the wheels of progress turn and no-one will do for others what he does not first do for himself. Then, too, he calls himself an anarchist, by which he means not one given to submit to the authority of dogma, religious or social, not beholden to past wisdom by rote, an ardent feminist – he admires Margaret greatly for her suffragette activity – and a vegetarian, and practitioner of yoga exercises in the interest of purity of blood, body and mind. Independence of spirit and mind Well, I agree with all of that, too, and told him I despair of the mushroom ministries springing up all over Whitehall, civil servants interfering in business and hindering our wartime efficiency, when success would more readily be achieved by letting the entrepreneurial spirit flourish without let or hinderance.

Look, he gave me a copy, which you can have to keep for yourself. I have marked a few passages. I will read a portion:

"I know one man of really brilliant parts who has not the ability to manage a business of his own, and yet who is absolutely worthless to anyone else, because he carries with him constantly the insane suspicion that his employer is oppressing, or intending to oppress, him. He cannot give orders, and he will not receive them. Should a message be given him to take to Garcia, his answer would probably be, "Take it yourself."

And I like this especially: "... one so morally deformed is no less to be pitied than a physical cripple; but in our pitying let us drop a tear, too, for the men who are striving to carry on a great enterprise, whose working hours are not limited by the whistle, and whose hair is fast turning white through the struggle to hold in line dowdy indifference, slipshod imbecility, and the heartless ingratitude which, but for their enterprise, would be both hungry and homeless."

Perhaps I should have copies made and sent to all the firebrands and their purblind supporters in the coalfield whenever they lay down their tools in a fruitless effort to conjure higher wages out of the ether. Hubbard sees both sides but also that the necessary connection between the two, owners and men shall we say, is the sole road to overall prosperity. That civilisation relies on the search for the compound force of individuals if it is to be assured.

Hubbard and I reflected together, also, on the art which stems from the science of boxing. I believe his interest in the endeavour relates to his understanding of the testing of a man's wit as well as his willpower. I took some pride in recording how at Cambridge I had been amateur light weight champion, and had once put my skills to good use on the mountain above Aberdare when some ruffians accosted me and a walking companion. Sad to say I even knew some of the fellows from our shared childhood days. And, of course, Hubbard and I, we discussed the incomparable Freddie Welsh, both of us wryly amused that this Frederick Hall Thomas who has so captivated the passion of our colliers at home is himself a public school man. It seems to fit the case all round, does it not? He had honed his body to box with the best but out-bested them by an application of American technique. His science is the foundation of his art. I see my industrial endeavours in much the same way.

I have asked Hubbard to call on me at Llanwern when he comes to South Wales so that we may discuss all this, and our boxing friend of course, at length and at our leisure. Many would find Hubbard an oddity, I find him more of a prism for the tensions of our age, and salute his own will as he strives through his art to express the power of the individual alone to create liberty for all.

DA on Home, his Family and Upbringing

I am not one given to dwelling on coincidences, as if fate pulled forth all of our existence, but I do think we are the creatures of the material. Take Hubbard and Welsh, for instance. It is not merely coincidental that their paths have crossed, and so mine with theirs. No, it is precisely the concatenation of lines of force in our respective progressive societies which draws such things together. I mean, of course, Wales, or our dynamic part of it, and America, or that ambition to succeed, which marks out this century as to be theirs more and more as our own British imperial pretensions shrivel. Wait and see, my boy.

And thus, the Atlantic is, for South Wales, our natural highway to the future, and on it we meet, and not by chance you see, as regularly as on our own lands. It is not just the seasoned traveller, the migrant, the man of affairs, such as myself, but the intermeshing of our popular cultural pursuits. Think. Who sang at the stern of this great liner as we left New York in fog and sang with gusto on until the sun broke through at the Narrows? Our very own choristers from Gwent – the Gleemen – with another barnstorming sweep of the cities of the eastern seaboard behind them. And remember the songs they gave us, vibrant voices at the pierhead with "Star Spangled Banner", then a yearning rendition of "It's a Long Way to Tipperary" and, once out at sea, to Frohman's immense delight he told me, that bouncy novelty tune, the very coon song of the moment, "Alexander's Ragtime Band." How we all laughed and cheered. We connect, do we not. No less than when that Wild West Circus of Buffalo Bill visited my birthplace of Aberdare in 1904, or as the two Lynton Brothers and Jimmy Michael from Aberaman, crossing and re-crossing the Atlantic, conquered all in the new mania for cycling races. Welsh is in the same mould, and Driscoll too I grant. It will tie us up together more and more. I know where my future horizons will be found. It might have been other if I had followed a conventional path, one that truly would never have been my own. Not for this Dai, anyway!

On my early travels, the year before I went up Cambridge, it was to France and Italy I went, and with my father's blessing, and so with ample funds, for he wanted me to be a gentleman in the mode that had been long established. The Grand Tour. Made worldly-wise before being properly educated. Rome for artistic splendour. Elsewhere for wild oats. Naples. A sprawl of filth. We indulged youthful fancies, as you might guess, no more said on that, and we dutifully made the horse-drawn trip to see the monastery at Monte Cassino. An impressive enough pile, though for me somehow redolent of stasis and the willingness to settle for past glory whilst the unsavoury denizens of the town below its hilltop wallowed in their poverty, tended their sheep and goats and took our pennies when they could. Not quite what my father, who never ventured abroad, even into England, had in mind. His own earthly work was all to stock up future wealth, and family fortune but his views, his beliefs, were all the issue of a rigid, almost doctrinaire Calvinism, with him definitely a sheep not a goat in that conspectus. In his behaviour, quite the opposite. Poor mother. And it was a gloomy household he led, with Sundays a shuttered misery. No joy from him. I wear my religion, ecumenical and elementary à la Anglican persuasion, very lightly. Rather like my marriage to the estimable Sybil. Elevated and arranged. Proper gentry, the Haigs. Douglas, her brother, now running the war at the Front, as Sybil, I'd venture, runs my country estate. I somewhat fancy Margaret is more of the Thomas stock, feisty and stubborn, and improper wherewithal thank God!

As to what finally turned me out as I became and am today, well, I'd have to confess, again, to thwarted ambition turned to good effect. I mean, to be sure, that I, and my siblings – the five of us who survived the seventeen children my mother bore my father – inherited more than moderate wealth, by dint of which I had set my own sights on political service. And I would not deny that the heroic aspects of that imagined life appealed to me as a young man, and I had soon tired of juggling figures to buy and sell in the City.

Though indeed my wife, Sybil, much preferred the social rounds of London and our house in the Home Counties to the provincial dreariness of Cardiff, as it was when we moved back, for me to work in the coal business first, then shortly to politicking. My parliamentary seats in Merthyr, then Cardiff, bore no fruit for me. So it was being, in a sense, impelled to use my ten talents during the past decade rather than sitting on them which made me as I am now in the world. Yet I have never gambled, risked all, in the manner of my forbears, though perhaps their restlessness imbued me with derring-do.

The night I was born, in late March 1856, in the upstairs front facing bedroom of that dreary house in Ysgurborwen, my father, Samuel was supervising work at the pithead of the colliery shaft which he had had recently sunk, and was, at the direct risk of all his borrowed capital, bent on extending his enterprises. I am told it was a night of great storm, rain and wind and window rattling gusts. He was fetched, for it was not sure I would live. My mother often recounted that he had stamped into the bedroom in his sodden work clothes, mud and slurry carried everywhere by his caked boots and dripping-wet coat, and when it was clear I would survive the troubled birth he announced that he saw no future for me other than the workhouse. He was then fifty six, at the end of his tether after all his small scale enterprises in coal-speculation in and around the town of Aberdare. Before that he had been a grocer, a wholesale dealer in tea and such commodities, in Merthyr. The mining bug had infected many of this middling sort, themselves the commercial spawn of the district's ironmasters. In my father's case, backed by in-laws and friends, the crucial step to greater fortune came when he bought into the opening up of coal seams in the adjacent Rhondda valley, and the rest you well know. He died in 1879, as old as the century itself. By then I had come to admire him for his determination and drive, though growing up under him was a doleful business.

He had been married before, you know, his first wife and child, for there was one I believe, early candidates for the grave. When he met my mother, Rachel, he was forty and she eighteen. Her family was of farming stock, copyholders on grazing, up-land farms for generations – part of my own desire to first rent, then own and now renovate the house at Llanwern, was that her grandfather had worked on that same estate as a lowly tenant – and my father's father had left similar work, as so many did around and about in Merthyr Tydfil, to haul timber and coals as a contractor to the Crawshays. It was a marital alliance of the middling sort, the ascendant sort I suppose, which they made. My mother, thirty four when I was born, was quite beautiful in my memory of her in that sole decade we spent together. It was widely said she had been a veritable Beauty in her youth. Dark, vivacious, gregarious. The dourness of my father eventually somewhat dampened her love of company and of gatherings, but his own ardour for her was obviously not diminished, as successive siblings of mine testify all too well,eh. She had to be spirited, in turn, in her own way. She learned how to temper his overweening control and his gloomy penny-pinching. A story for you. Once, in the first years of their marriage, she had gone to Swansea by carriage, and returned resplendent in a full-length fox-fur coat, one which had cost her a pretty penny. Enraged by her extravagance more than by her worldly vanity, I'd postulate, he seized the coat from her and threw it onto the coal fire which was kept ablaze in the parlour's hearth by day and night. Cool as a cucumber my mother said nothing. But when he was absent on business the following week she took herself post-haste to Swansea once more, and once more purchased a splendid fur coat, one even finer and more expensive than before. She made sure she sat at the hearth wearing it, despite the heat of the coals, when father returned. This time, she spoke, and it was to say she would buy yet another, and another, if he continued with his domestic arson, and that she, too, could and would withhold his accustomed credit.

My father had had a grammar school education and my mother no schooling at all beyond the rudimentary, so her intellectual horizons were limited. As to which of them was the more naturally intelligent, alive and shrewd in the human things of existence, I have no doubt. No, I admired but did not revere my father. My mother who died, aged seventy-five in 1897, surrounded in that lump of a house by the finest lace and china which money and her good taste could buy, was not admired by me, nor revered, only adored. And loved

To me in those first ten years, before I was spirited away to be moulded, she gave me nothing but love. We spoke together in her favourite tongue, a Welsh of the farm and the kitchen, salted by the Bible and sweetened by the songs she trilled in a lilting contralto voice, and I was, to her my mother, her own Dai, and nothing but Dai in those days. My time as David, my wife's and the wider world's David, had not then begun, and has not yet ended.

Arnold Rhys-Evans. Transcript of Notes from 1915. (Edited,1927) Taliesin Arthur Lloyd Papers. Miscellanea. Box 10. National Library of Wales. Aberystwyth.

Coal mining is by far the most important industry in South Wales. It accounted for 37.1 per cent of the insured workers in 1935; and even this represents a considerable reduction in relative importance, for in 1923 it accounted for 51.8 per cent.

Up to 1930 or 1931, when the situation was dominated by the depression [and] the future was extremely uncertain return to the 1929 level of output seemed a possibility. Since then, however, the history of the industry has been one of almost unrelieved gloom. Exports have dropped every year since 1929.

The profits of the industry have turned to a loss in the last three years.

The assumption (in 1931) of a return to the 1929 level of output and employment was too optimistic.

In South Wales as a whole the average percentage of unemployed men in the coal industry was 32.15 in 1931 and rose to 42.4 in 1932.

The Rhondda Valley, which is the most thickly populated and the largest of the ten areas of the coalfield contains the largest absolute number of unemployed coal miners. The percentage of unemployment for the whole valley, the highest figure was 52.0, was reached in 1932.

In Merthyr Vale the bulk of unemployment is concentrated in the returns of Merthyr and Dowlais which, expressed as a percentage of the numbers insured was more than 70 percent.

Expressed in whole numbers,the unemployed in the coal industry across the industrial region were 65,853 in 1931, 81,507 in 1932 and 62,155 in 1935.

The Second Industrial Survey of South Wales (for the National Industrial Development Council of Wales and Monmouthshire, 1937) Taliesin Arthur Lloyd Papers. Miscellanea. Box 16 National Library of Wales. Aberystwyth.

I was the Secretary. So I accumulated evidence. Documents, letters, sundry notes, personal and public. And so on. They lie in folders amongst my own collected papers, now deposited for future consultation and use. I had meant to make more sense of them, myself, in a memoir or a biography or a history of sorts. But all that ambition has turned out to be as fragmentary as my life itself. A pity, I think, because I have no great faith that anyone else can make of them anything other than a pattern book, one which can bear no connected resemblance to what was, how shall I say it, experienced, rather than expressed I mean. But that is not it either, and I wrestle once more with the displacement of experience into consciousness. Take Gloria and Tony, my remaining physical links with the humanity I am to leave. I actually do think they would understand me in all of this, if only I could, but exactly what, not teach perhaps, but enrage them. Yes, make them angry. Angry that they will always be seen as lesser. Less important. Less significant, Less worthy. Less everything. Even when they are scooped up for specimens to flounder in the nets of the new history-from-below. For what, indeed, if they do nothing, ever, than just live. If they are not seen, truly seen, as individuals in themselves they are, at best, allotted roles, at worst, dismissed. Those who assign to themselves higher functions also plot the lines of history of significance. Behind them, around them, all other faces are blurred. Hated or sentimentalised, caricatured or iconised, but always their reality blurred. This is not the self-serving distinction between individual vitality and social dependence which such as D. A. Thomas rendered into a cod philosophy. Everything I have seen and done tells me the opposite of that. When the divide is made in theory it is in order to justify the divisions made in practice. Always for a purpose. Not as people are, only as they are seen, transfigured through a perception not of their own making. It is why when I went to see Billy's exhibition, but not on the opening night in 1985, I had shuddered. Oh, it was sharp enough about what had been lost, what had been left, how lives had been dis-assembled into parts. I was moved, and I was dismayed. It was as if all had been given up in the wreckage. Why, I had wanted to ask him, though I had never then or later or before, of course, approached him or his father, or do I mean my son, why are there no faces here? Nothing that might join something up, make a connection. But then again, I had considered connections once myself, and had dismissed them back in 1958. Too late for me now. Too much time had passed. Too many other lives and faces also consigned to the oblivion on which superior knowledge insists. But Tony and Gloria should know that their Now is not maybe Later or back Then. They live in a present which is not, for them, a perpetual one, waiting for or anticipating being card-indexed in a file. It is a present which is vital because it is, framed by the landscape of their days and the emotions of their hearts, all in perpetual change. Billy's work had abandoned hope. I had seen such days before. After the War, the first one, the towns and streets were full of dazed and distracted men. They were an embarrassment. Blind, one-armed, legless, bandaged, openly weeping, shouting, mute, pitied, resented, marginalised. I did not have their excuse. It made no difference for all that, the war avoided by being a cripple even before it occurred. I was marginal to life, too, the greater part to come to be spent on the fringes of participation. Thoughts too clear to let me sleep, mercifully slip into sensations. Sounds and smells oddly enough, flitting amongst images. The eerie hush of parquet floored university corridors, miles on end over the years, the steam heat of clunky iron-ribbed radiators, the fuzzy texture of blotting paper and the smudge of ink blots, sharpened pencils ready to be worn down to their stumps, pink ribbons to tie up official documents, mimeographs and shorthand squiggles, a pervading smell of cologne and carbolic soap. All this was the cocoon for my life and a barrier against having to share or partake in what was threatening and dangerous, visible and audible, outside its protection. I would still not see or call this selfishness nor even a cynical removal as such. I was protecting myself against the further damage of hurt through involvement. It was not that I did not care personally but rather that I thought I knew only too clearly what to care could do to me, first in dollops and then in cascades of harm. What I had not calculated, as I lived on, was the greater loss which shadows such a turning away until the light goes finally. I had conceived of a life as a narrative which, in its wider reaches beyond the personal, does not have to be read. That those pages just turn. I suppose, if asked, I would have said it was just history moving along and to be accommodated, or not, as one chose or was able not to have to do so, either way. I was not wrong in that life can be endured in this way. I was wrong, though, to think this could or should ever be sufficient or, at its end, understood in that way, for if indeed everything must be read backwards nothing can be re-wound. Except in dreams.

In the 1890s and early 1900s forceful corrections of the deformity congenital talipes equinovarus (vulg. Club Foot) was commonly undertaken by means of the "Thomas wrench", a device invented by the Welsh surgeon Hugh Owen Thomas (1834 – 1891) to move the deformity through a plane by manipulation and bracing over a two months period. This condition, affecting at birth one or both feet, is caused by the foot being rotated internally at the ankle with the forefoot curved towards the big toe, causing an exaggerated arch of the foot with the heel turned inward and the ankle pointed downwards. If uncorrected the tendency is to walk on the ankle or side of the foot with concomitant stiffening of the joints, swelling of the foot, shooting pains and freezing of the foot, often requiring the application of a hot water bottle. Even after forcible correction by strict application of Thomas' brass wrench a leg brace would be required along with a specially constructed surgical boot. Not all treatments by this method were either successful or efficacious.

Handwritten Note (n.d.). Taliesin Arthur Lloyd, Papers. Box One. National Library of Wales. Aberystwyth.

It is time, then. Time for one last dream before I am cared for in the morning. It is the dream I will not let go. It is the dream which has never let me go. Erotic love is not sentimental. Nor is it compassionate. She did what no-one had ever done before. She kissed my foot, each and every one of its swollen toes, from big to little, and the turned over arch and the scarred heel and the brittle bone. She had not flinched when she saw it or even said some such inanity as "You poor thing". She just crossed the room to where I sat, my trouser leg rolled up to the knee, my foot on the towel besides the blue-and-white china washbowl in which I had soaked it in hot water and salts, and then smoothed it with oil of eucalyptus. I had been out on his errands, a long day carrying out his instructions, delivering his messages to banks and merchant companies across lower Manhattan. She I had neglected, despite his explicit orders to "keep her amused", or perhaps I had merely avoided all contact. Now, in the late afternoon as the fading light began to soften the city she had knocked on my room door and stepped inside before I could respond. Gwennie was dressed as if to go out, not as a maid. Framed in the doorway to the room she had smiled shyly as I said, rather stiffly, "Yes? May I be of assistance to you?" Her eyes, however, had taken me in all at once and she simply said, "No. Just stay there, Tal."

She patted my left crippled foot dry and cradled it in her hand. Without looking at me directly, she kissed it, slowly and carefully without even letting it leave her hand. I think I said you shouldn't or don't, but feebly, and to no avail. My foot tingled, but for this time with no hurt to it. I do not think anything more would have come to pass, not on my timid part anyway, if she had not stood from where she had been kneeling. I closed my eyes.

And closed as they are now, all the years between shed, I can see her when she whispered to me to open them. Slight and upright before me, her skirt unhooked, her blouse discarded, a pool of undergarments and stockings fallen on the carpet alongside her shoes and her hair released from its back-comb to fall to her slim shoulders. She was the first woman

I had so seen. With all that followed it is to these first moments which my memory has ever returned. She slipped my braces off my shoulders and undid the top button of my trousers to pull them down over my legs. She was quick with the buttons of my drawers and as quick to straddle me. It was all over in a tremble and no word had been said. There is nothing to tell to anyone about our loving, then or since, other than to feel it over and over again, not physically of course but as irreducible memory, whose whole form and shape can be revealed only to those to whom it was once shown. People may look at this inert body of mine, shrivelling and vanishing, but no one can see into my memory or know what I was, so fleetingly, shown of what is not ever fully captive. Except in the doing and the dreaming of life. And if the capacity for it ends, as it must, its compulsion never wavers so long as we live and feel. It is all I have truly learned. All else may flee from me, but not this that was, once, then. I gloried in her brown and pink tipped breasts, the dip between her belly and her thighs, the shudder she made as I shrivelled and fell out of her. Only it was not over. She helped me to my feet and kissed me again, this time on the lips, and she took me by the hand across the room to my bed. She undressed me completely and, though I thought she was leaving, it was only to retrieve her clothes, to lock the outer door and come back to lie next to me. I will not say we made love for I did not know what that was. What we did was neither slow nor tender nor concerned the one with the other. She had need of me and I was as if touched to life, a life of instinct and urge and appetite. What we did was just to fuck. And when we had fucked again, and later through all the days which had seen us left alone together in the city, then she showed me all the other things which others had shown her, and which I wanted too. We went together, on my allotted tasks, out into the city, entrancing enough in all its unsurpassable vitality but a backdrop now for what we were and did, its steamy energy and electric glitter as nothing to us other than a pause in our pleasure. We did not eat together in the hotel and only met in the lobby, circumspect and business-like, her to carry my satchels and papers on pretence of being an aid to the crippled secretary going about his tasks. It began to snow, wild and precipitate blizzards blown in from the north and east of the river to blanket the avenues and halt the traffic. We looked out at it from the windows of the new self-service restaurants where office workers gathered and lingered, in the warm, out of the unseasonable cold snap of that spring. The snow gave us time and delayed our employer and his party in West Virginia where they had gone, DA, Lady Mackworth and the faithful Arnold, to investigate his own ongoing interests in the coal trade, whilst we, faithless Tal and Gwennie, my saviour and his betrayer, followed the detailed orders which arrived at the hotel by telegram, and scurried out to fulfil them, and hurried back to close the door to my room and, both of us wet and snow cold to fumble with our clothes, standing upright together, half-dressed so that we could, without delay, fuck each other.

A mistake. But one I could not help but make. I asked about him. I knew it was so, that Arnold had not lied to me, but I wanted to hear her tell me, and the why of it. The mistake was not the foolishness caused by my being nothing much more than a love-sick adolescent wanting sole possession. It was in underestimating, or not comprehending in my ignorance of upbringing and intellect both, how strong she was, how resilient she had needed to be, how mature and balanced she had had to become so early in her life, and for so long. That strength is what I should have really wanted if only it had been possible for it to mean to me then what I saw it for later, what I can see it for now. Too late, because all too soon. What I lost was the glimpse of what love might mean; I proved incapable of it, of reaching out and letting go at the same time. It would have been impossible to hang on in any case because, as she told me over and over, I could not accomplish that, to keep her, and she must live on despite all else. What she did, with him, was a contract made and his was the possession of her, albeit of the lesser kind, the unimportant part. I urged on her, in the days and hours of the week when the others were still away, all manner of schemes and actions, and I drove us both at *times to despair and tears. She was, in this, almost as young and hopeful as I was; but it would pass, with nothing resolved.*

The afternoon they were expected back, all snow and storms gone as if they had never been, I sat alone in my hotel room. She waited to be of service in hers. She had insisted that we could not be together. She told me that all we could do was remember each other, and perhaps wait. I have waited a lifetime due to her insistence and my own folly. What might have been was never to become. So, let it be now at last.

EXTRA TIME

Nearing Merthyr the land became more barren. Soon it was grass and tips, then tips and grass and finally tips only. I meditated on the history of [the canal]. A hundred years ago it was the mode of transport from [the] valley. When there were plans for laying the steel rails on which a train would screech its way along the canal its owners, and many others, were terrified … it was stated most emphatically that the canal would easily convey all the coal ever mined in [the] area. Poor old barges, now just showing rotting sides through the canal mud; you would have had a busy time taking the five thousand or so tons a day down that narrow waterway.

The old wharfs are idle and rotting; the old mills can scarcely be found amongst the trees and fern. Copper works, iron works, brickworks; I see their ruins every day, and the tips from old and disused collieries. When are we going to make it compulsory that he who despoils a place must renew its beauty? Now it seems that anyone can come along, scatter horror and destruction until the chance of profit is gone, and then go away from the sight of his crime, leaving Nature to heal its grievous wounds … but it takes too long.

B.L. Coombes, Miners' Day (1945). Miscellanea. Box 16. Taliesin Arthur Lloyd Papers. National Library of Wales. Aberystwyth.

Billy paused at the double doors which his hand had stretched towards to open so that he could get out into the open air, away from the suffocation he was beginning to feel inside the Canolfan. From the platform he could hear the voice of Sir Ceri Evans, no microphone needed, reaching him with a deeper intensity in its tone. Billy stopped and turned back to listen.

"You're right to applaud! What else have we been trained now to do? How else can we think? What, after all, can be wrong with turning our people into peons? What's amiss with losing the haphazard hits of cultural tourism by replacing it with colonial settlements? We once made an art out of our very selves – in politics and in our common culture – why not become the artefacts necessary for the greater lives of others? I have, my friends, been giving this a great deal of thought. My conclusions are neither comfortable nor easy for me to state in front of the partners with whom I have worked on this enterprise, an enterprise that could, of course, work. But I have concluded, only at the cost of being an even greater betrayal than any we have yet experienced.

It would betray the one thing we still uniquely possess – our collective DNA, our sense of ourselves – and that is: our own history. We can never re-live it. We shouldn't want to, but we cannot be ourselves without it. It cradles the essence of what once gave us purpose. And you know what? That isn't heart and soul and sentiment. It isn't nostalgia. It's intellect. We thought once not just of what would improve some lives, but how to make it happen for all. In education, in and out of school, in the ambitions of our parents and the aspirations we had for each other at work and play. We created institutions that were indeed collective and voluntary, from trades unions to brass bands, from choirs to rugby teams, a committee not as a tired joke but as a director of purposefulness. Our people came together initially for the purpose of work and wages, but out of mere aggregations of people they created – one way or the other – communities of purpose. Are we to let all that achievement drift? Are we to spurn our potential to make our heritage a creative one again?

We must, even at this late stage, think with our imaginations not our slide rules. I propose in place of this gated commune for visitors, a new city on the hill for ourselves. On this land, in this place, let us create galleries to show our art, and wipe away the cataract of clichés that make us blind and others myopic. All landscape and no mindscape, my friends, makes Dai a dull boy. Let us create here space for studios and performance where our young musicians and film-makers and writers and dancers can come, on generous bursaries for residence, mentored by the best international talents we can muster. Let us remember that the miners' institutes and welfare halls were, with their book-crammed libraries and lecture halls, once the brains of the coalfield, and let us find space here for Institutes of Learning that can envision, not just administer or tinker with, a future. Let there be conferences, and debates, seminars and festivals, of music and theatre and science and sport and video and film, a sculpture park and a garden setting for the best of contemporary public art. Let it be open, let it be young, and let it be ours. A centre that both radiates out and connects inwards.

You know we have the tools and the means for it. But what we must have, here today, now in this place at this time, is the will. We must resist the cry that there is no alternative. You know who said that first, don't you? If we resist its lie we can create a future that comes from us and for us. Will you help me?

I am formally proposing this morning that we establish a new charitable trust, endowed by the funds hitherto received by Tir Werin who will, I know, freely give up prior claim to all the land they own, and the cash flow. The new trust – the Haf Trust, for this will be our summer of content – will elect members from communities across the Valleys to serve with elected and nominated members of the arts and sports community, backed by university expertise, even supplemented, perhaps, by a politician or two! I will be happy, if asked, to serve as an interim founding chair and drive this idea into a shape that makes it an international beacon of excellence. Have no fear that Europe will not support us on this. They will welcome the initiative. They will applaud a brave experiment. Will you? Will we? We must.

It is time, my friends, to become comrades once again, if only in an endeavour of this kind. The only gate to the present we ever need is that symbolised by Janus, who looks both backward and forwards in order to progress. I expect to be accused of idealism. I have been accused of worse. I expect to be pilloried for impracticality. I have learned little in a long life of anything that benefits us at all by following the narrow lines of rigid practice. I only wonder that we have not done this before. We have been atrophied, as I have been, by the shrivelling social veins of the culturally timid. If I seem, here today, to return to the political roots some claim I have spurned, think again! I am re-freshed not restrained by that past. Political life, we once understood, was what made us, together, free, because it made us, individually, engage with what we had in common. Our very humanity. Then, we did not hide away in the fearful corners of our spluttering, individual lives. We had so little we made the sacred flame of our values immense. We possessed nothing so we owned everything. And the chosen life of a man or woman in public life was the valued gift of a people which wished to make its voice heard wherever the silence of submission still held sway. Those voices were from the chorus, and it is time to hear that chorus sing out their music again, so that, together, we may drown out the siren calls of despair and helplessness.

I read academic papers that tell me that we have been cursed by the twinned poverty of deprivation and the poverty of aspiration.

But I know now that these were mere descriptions of the despond into which we sank, buoyed up by occasional sweetmeats and fair promises. I know now, with all the fibre of my being, that we have misplaced our proper weapons and must pick them up again if we are to end our poverty of intellect through fresh imagination, and replace our poverty of purpose with the dream of a city on the hill, one whose name and spreading presence will become legion."

* * * * *

When Sir Ceri Evans finally sat down, next to an ashen Maldwyn and a bewildered Gwilym, a polite ripple of applause near the platform quickly became an uneasy silence. The hacks, who had no handouts for this, could scarcely have kept up with the outpouring, and the rhetoric had been as unexpected as it was strictly retro. In the silence of the room, Billy Maddox put his hands together and clapped loudly. Then he just as abruptly stopped. Ceri looked down the aisle at him. Sir Ceri Evans winked at Billy. Billy stared back. He knew his prey was off the hook. They both knew it. If the thing Ceri had outlined lived, then all praise was his. If it stumbled and fell at any hurdle, then he was blameless for the failing of others. The money had passed hands, sure, but that would not be a story to reveal now. Gwilym would play the broker role that had always suited him. The business plan would be re-written, and Maldwyn would seek revenge. Sometime, somewhere. Bran would shrug and turn it into a PR triumph which, she'd claim, she'd been hatching all along. A committee would indeed form. But it would need Haf as well as Ceri to drive it. They would make, maybe, a suitable kind of father and daughter. Perhaps they were already. Billy saw Haf initiating some ragged applause, and smiling. Billy felt that it was all starting again. All wrong. Nothing had changed. Nothing would alter.

Sir Ceri Evans was being penned in by a few bewildered reporters in search of some enlightenment. Billy saw Haf moving across the space towards the huddle, to be nearer to Ceri, to listen more closely. Ceri looked across at her. He beckoned her on. She would need to be attentive now. They would have lots to do together, Billy thought, and much to learn about each other. He moved towards the exit and the world outside. Leavers were already milling about in the car park, readying their escape from the valley. Billy had his own planned, and none of those people figured in it. He spotted a brace of local taxis dawdling hopefully at the car park's far perimeter. He walked toward them. A ride back to the city to retrieve his bags and no goodbyes to say. Over his shoulder he heard a voice he knew too well ask if he was slinking off again with no fond farewells said to old friends. He turned to look at Bran.

"Same as before," she added.

"Not quite, is it?" he said, and knew there was more to come. There always was with Bran.

"I suppose you think you've settled something, don't you, Billy? Brought us all up short against the judgement of your smug rectitude. As ever."

"Not really, Bran. Just wanted a little reminder of why true things don't count for much, do they. But, you know, truth doesn't vanish either."

"Truth, Billy? Is that what you think this is all about? Truth? Is that what you really want?"

"It'll do. What I've got. Enough, and all that."

Bran stood closer to him. She said, "Your truth hurts people, Billy. It always did. You hurt your father before he died. You weren't even at the funeral. I went. Ceri went. You didn't even bother to come back afterwards. You hurt me. Do you like hurting people, Billy? Do you like to be hurt? What truth would do that for you?"

Billy felt that it should stop now, and that it would if he just turned again and kept walking away. Instead, he stood stock still, and waited.

"You asked me at the start of all this about Haf. About you and Haf. So, shall I tell you now?" Bran said.

Too many puzzles and ambiguities and games and questions had exhausted him. Get over it, he thought. Let it go. Let it be. Walk away. Now. But he spoke and knew that when he finished that he was inviting the response she had already decided to make.

"Look, Bran. I can see, really see, that Haf will manage. Her own life, I mean. To live it without any false supports or lies. But why not give her the chance for herself, to cut whichever ties she chooses to cut herself. Tell her. I'm presuming Mal is out of the picture, in all ways, and, as you've told me, and I believe you, so am I, and Tommy, a bit of rough distraction was it? He doesn't figure, which leaves Ceri, right? Because, big man in the strike and all that and good for exclusive interviews,eh? And certainly later on an item, so why not earlier? So, just tell her for God's sake."

"You poor bloody fool," she said. "Is that what you really think?"

"Yeah. Best guess. You always aimed high. So could be, couldn't it, and why not?"

"Could? Could have been? But what if it wasn't, genius? And, you know what, you'd be a better bet yourself. Only not. By a whisper, but not."

Billy stared at her. Transfixed. Bait taken.

"Then who? Tell me."

Bran stepped as close as she could without their touching,and said, "Your old man."

Billy flinched. But he knew when Bran lied. This was the truth, whatever that might mean for the future. She had not ended the telling of it. How after the exhibition, within a few weeks after he had left without a word said to anyone, she had gone to see his old man. On the basis of her reporting on the strike, the inside personal stories, she had secured a broadcast series commission for radio. New career opening up. The opportunity for one anyway. She wanted the old man's help, his advice, his related experience, his voice. She wanted his life, she said. Its history.

She laughed abruptly at that. Useless, he was. Couldn't even use the recorder she had left with him. Hopeless. That she thought when she retrieved the tape that he had been captured on it, but when she listened later on there had been nothing. Only silence. Before she said goodbye to him, the precious tape safe in her pocket, they had talked of Billy, of his mother, of all the things which had seemed for so long to have gone out of control. That he was tired. That she had held him in her arms when he cried.

Billy said he had never seen his old man cry. Bran said that she had cradled his head between her hands and kissed him. That it had seemed right and simple to comfort each other, and they had made love. Nothing felt wrong about it, she said. It only happened once, she said. That she did not see him again. Nobody had. He had died so suddenly before the Christmas. And that Billy was not contactable. Ceri had organised the funeral, and spoke at it. She said she was completely sure that Haf was the old man's child. And so your half-sister, she said.

Billy did not doubt her. The only doubts he had left were about himself. Bran walked back to the Canolfan. To pick up the pieces. To slot them back into the jigsaw they had all made from the life they had been given. Not my piece, was all Billy could see now, in whatever future could yet be imagined afresh. Not me, he thought. Not bloody me. Never. He headed away from all the false promises of Canolfan Cymoedd y Dyfodol.

The air, this high above the valley, was becoming fresher, with rain threatening to close in. Billy bummed a cigarette from one of the security guards. He cupped his hands around the proffered lighter held out of the way of the breeze. He walked across the car park to its edge, a low wall at its far end, and from the slopes beneath the wall a panoramic view of a gouged and torn landscape. Here, quarries sliced in slabs into the mountainside. There, the leach of iron ore on the rough grass tundras of a plateau. Further down, the reduced but still discernible black tumps, pricked with green patches and yellow gorse, which had once been conical tips of coal waste of a staggering size and dimension. Everywhere, glinting as the rain dropped through the sunlight, the rust of rails and the crumbled bricks of chimneys. All tidied up, but never gone away. In the far distance he could see yellow dumper trucks hauling their loads across the highways flattened for them between hillocks of small coal on the largest open-cast coal site in Europe.

Billy dragged on his cigarette until its flaking tip glowed. He flipped it up and over the wall with a flick of his fingers so that it fire-flied into a dying spiral. He turned back. He gestured at one of the local taxis. He told the driver the hotel's name in the city. The driver of the taxi opened a rear door for his passenger. As Billy bent forward to get inside he felt a light tap on his shoulder. He straightened up. He almost sighed. Haf.

"Are you going? Don't go. Stay," she said.

"It's done. For me," he said.

"You can do this, whatever it is you want to do, alone. You can turn it around," he said, not truly believing it, but hoping so for her sake.

"Use the Trust. Use the money. Use Ceri. You don't need me, Haf," he said. "And I'm going away, yes."

Haf grasped his left hand as he held the car door open. She did not let it go. She spoke softly to him, almost as if to a child.

"Do you think I really believe, Ceri?" she asked quietly. "That would be no good. Again. It would fizzle out, or worse. Die from the centre. No roots. None. It has to be done differently. Slowly.

With no let-up. Locally. Making it new. What was once like that, new and struggling for hope, has been hollowed out. Need to do it again, to get there again, but not in the same way. Has to be different If we don't believe, we will betray. Ourselves, I mean. You need to be here."

Billy looked, and said nothing. He did not want to believe. She let his hand go, and he swung into the backseat of the taxi. The driver had left the engine running. Over its purr, before it pulled away, Haf smiled at him.

"You need us, Billy," she said.

* * * * *

That he had no answer to that was answer enough. But he said nothing. He acknowledged her diffident wave as the taxi took him away, but he did not look back. Gestures had been too cheap all round. The dream through which they had been drifting had ended even if the tangled skeins of starts and shadows within it had not been unwound. He would have, soon he thought, to tell his half-sister who she was. That, he knew too, would finally define as well exactly what he was. He would tell her, as adjunct to all that, of the legacy he had been left in 1997. A considerable amount. An unknown benefactor. He could only surmise as to who and why. To be taken up and used by him for others if he went back home to stay. Perhaps for individuals to have support. Within a Foundation maybe. A different kind of Trust. Not for outward show. Ongoing, deeper. Haf would act on all this. There would be no ending. Why not, he thought, and maybe it might serve as another beginning for him, too.

He looked out of the window as the landscape fled away behind him as the taxi found faster roads. Back roads. Roads that could go two ways. A camera would still be hard to pick up and use to any purpose, as he had found, and untangling the threads of lives was, at best, a fraught, uncertain process. He knew the two acts, for him at least, would be connected to his belonging. And if that was so, really so, he knew that he would need to try again to look at and into faces, with and without a viewfinder, and with a perception made more direct than his technique and skills had once allowed him to be. Maybe tradition and imitation and the seduction of monochrome tints would no longer suffice. Framing images could be a cold boxing-in of life. Life was lived in colour even if it was garish, vulgar, fluid and sloppy. He would settle for less if it might mean more than just being an observer, a recorder, an exile. He leaned back in his seat.